"WELCOME TO THIS WEEK'S MEETING OF OUR BEREAVEMENT SUPPORT GROUP," I BEGIN.

"I want to start by reviewing the ground rules first, both as a refresher for those of you who have been here before and to inform our new visitor."

Predictably, most of those who have been coming for a while roll their eyes or shift impatiently in their seats. But reciting the ground rules is a must.

"First and foremost, remember that anything said in this room is confidential and is not to be discussed or relayed to anyone outside of the group. Remember that we are here to share experiences, not advice. Be respectful and sensitive to one another by silencing your cell phones, avoiding side conversations, and listening to others without passing judgment. And finally, try to refrain from using offensive language."

I pause and scan the faces in the group. "Any questions about the rules?"

I'm answered with a sea of shaking heads and murmured declinations.

"Okay then. Since we have someone new here tonight, let's start by going around the group and stating your name and who it is you've lost." I turn and smile at Sharon Cochran. "Sharon, would you like to start?"

I'm pleased when she nods, even though it's an almost spastic motion. My pleasure then dissipates as she completely derails the evening's agenda.

"My name is Sharon Cochran, and I'm here because the cops say my son committed suicide. But I know he was murdered and I'm hoping you can help me find his killer."

Books by Annelise Ryan

A Helping Hands Mystery
Needled to Death

A Mattie Winston Mystery
Working Stiff
Scared Stiff
Frozen Stiff
Lucky Stiff
Board Stiff
Stiff Penalty
Stiff Competition
Dead in the Water
Dead Calm
Dead of Winter

Coming in March 2020:
Dead Ringer

Books by Allyson K. Abbott
(who also writes as Annelise Ryan):
A Mack's Bar Mystery
Murder on the Rocks
Murder With a Twist
In the Drink
Shots in the Dark
A Toast to Murder
Last Call

Needled To Death

Annelise Ryan

KENSINGTON BOOKS
KENSINGTON PUBLISHING CORP.
www.kensingtonbooks.com

KENSINGTON BOOKS are published by

Kensington Publishing Corp.
119 West 40th Street
New York, NY 10018

All Kensington titles, imprints, and distributed lines are available at special quantity discounts for bulk purchases for sales promotion, premiums, fund-raising, educational, or institutional use.

Special book excerpts or customized printings can also be created to fit specific needs. For details, write or phone the office of the Kensington Sales Manager: Attn.: Sales Department. Kensington Publishing Corp., 119 West 40th Street, New York, NY 10018. Phone: 1-800-221-2647.

Kensington and the K logo Reg. U.S. Pat. & TM Off.

First Printing: August 2019
ISBN-13: 978-1-4967-1943-0
ISBN-10: 1-4967-1943-3

ISBN-13: 978-1-4967-1945-4 (eBook)
ISBN-10: 1-4967-1945-X (eBook)

10 9 8 7 6 5 4 3 2 1

Printed in the United States of America

For Larry

Chapter One

I can still see the shadows of death on some of their faces, evident in the droop of their eyes, the taut, thin line of their lips, and the pale, pasty coloring of their skin from spending too much time indoors hiding away from society and life. It's evident, too, in the tentative and wary way they walk, their shoulders hunched over defensively, as if they're expecting another grievous blow to descend upon them at any second.

Some people wear their cloak of grief for a long time. Others shrug it off in good time and good order, eager and able to get on with their lives, even if it's only a few small steps at a time. The people who are with me tonight tend more toward the former group, and it's my job to try to help them become members of the latter group.

I'm about to start the session when a new face enters the room—a woman who looks to be in her mid-to-late forties—and I'm tempted to clap my hands with delight. This would be both inappropriate and unprofessional, so I quickly rein in the impulse and focus on forming a smile that looks warm and welcoming, and hopefully doesn't show the excitement I feel. I hurry over to her, aware of the curious stares coming from the others in the room.

"Hello," I say. "Are you here for the bereavement group?"

The question is rhetorical, since this woman is wearing her mantle of grief like a heavy shawl. Her face is expressionless, her shoulders are slumped, and her movements are sluggish and zombielike. She looks down at me—nearly everyone I meet looks down at me in the strictly physical sense, since I'm barely five feet tall—and nods mechanically.

"Well, welcome," I tell her, touching her arm with my hand. "I'm Hildy Schneider. I'm a social worker here at the hospital, and I run this group."

She nods again but says nothing. I suspect her loss is a recent one, very recent. *Who was it?* I wonder. Based on her age, a parent is a good guess if one assumes the natural order of things. But I've learned that death doesn't care much for order.

"What's your name?" I ask, hoping to ease her out of the frozen, deer-in-the-headlights stance she currently has. She looks at me, but I get a strong sense that she doesn't see me. I've encountered this before and suspect she's mentally viewing some memory reel as it plays repeatedly. I tighten my touch on her arm slightly, hoping the physical connection will ground her. It does.

She blinks several times, flashes an awkward, pained attempt at a smile, and says, "Sorry. I'm Sharon Cochran." Her voice is mechanical, rote, with no lilt or feeling behind it.

"I'm glad you're here, Sharon," I say. "Can I get you something to drink? A water, or some coffee?"

She looks at me with brown eyes that are stone-cold and dull, and then shakes her head.

"There are some cookies, too," I say. "Can I get you one?"

Again, she shakes her head, her gaze drifting away from mine. The others in the room have lowered the tenor of their conversations to soft, whispered murmurs, no doubt so the newcomer won't hear them talking about her.

"Sharon?" I say firmly, wanting to bring her attention back to me. "Have you ever been to a support group before?"

"No."

"Okay. Let me give you a brief overview of how the group works. We meet every week on Thursday evenings unless there is a holiday that falls on that day. In that case, we often meet the evening before. Attendance is totally voluntary. Come as little or as often as you want and come as many times and for as long as you want. Typically, I pick a topic for us to focus on each week, and I talk a little about that topic before opening things up to the group." She is looking down at the purse she is clutching, fidgeting with its clasp, making it hard for me to tell if she's hearing me or not. I continue anyway.

"The members of the group have the option of discussing something relative to their individual grief issues and experiences, and if it happens to be related to the topic at hand, that's great. But it doesn't have to be. Anyone who wants to talk may do so, but there is also no obligation to do so. The others who are here tonight have all been coming for some time, and they do plenty of talking. You might feel like an outsider because of that, but I promise you that if you commit the time and effort to attending several sessions, that will dissipate. It's a very friendly and supportive group of people, and all of them share one thing in common with you. They've all lost someone close to them."

She looks at me then, and I see the first spark of life in those mud brown eyes. "How?" she asks.

I'm confused by the question. "How what?"

"How did the others die?"

"Oh. Well, there's a mix. And rather than my trying to give you any background on the others, I think it will work better if you let them tell you their stories." I again ponder who it is Sharon has lost. Maybe it was a spouse?

"Any suicides?" she asks. Her eyes are scanning the others in the room.

"Yes," I say. "Did you lose someone to suicide?"

She nods slowly, frowning and surveying the other attendees.

"There is someone here who lost her husband to suicide," I say. "She hasn't had anyone else who shares her situation up until now. I can introduce you to her, if you like."

"No." Flat, dead, robotic. "What about homicide?" she says, eyes still roving, though I get the sense that she isn't focusing on anything or anyone.

"What about it?" I reply, unsure where she's going.

"Has anyone here lost someone to murder?"

"No." Something in the back of my brain connects with something in my gut, and instinct makes me qualify my answer. "Well, none of the group members have lost anyone to murder," I clarify, "but I have. My mother was murdered when I was little."

I see a spark of interest soften her face, and she looks me in the eye for the first time. "Did they catch who did it?" she asks, which strikes me as an odd thing to ask before expressing some token condolence or inquiring about the circumstances. Though most people merely make an awkward attempt at changing the subject whenever I bring it up.

"No, they never did," I tell her, feeling a familiar ache at the thought. I glance at the clock on the wall and see that it reads two minutes past seven. "I need to get things started," I say. "But I'd like to talk with you some more after the group ends, if you can stay for a bit."

"Sure," she says, and she gifts me with a tentative smile.

I give her shoulder a reassuring squeeze and then address the room at large, speaking loudly. "Okay, everyone, let's get started."

This command is typically followed by one last dash to the snack table to get another cookie, or to top off a cup of coffee. Generally, I allow a minute or so for people to heed my request, and then I start regardless of what's going on or who might be still hovering over the cookies. Tonight, however, the presence of a newcomer has intrigued everyone enough that things get changed up. The music of the various conversations stops as if on cue and everyone quickly claims a seat as if we are playing a game of musical chairs. I suspect they are eager to rubberneck on someone else's misery for a change.

The dynamics always change when someone new joins a group. Most of the time it's a good thing, if knowing that someone is struggling with grief can ever be considered a good thing. I've been spearheading this group for nearly two years now, and its composition and size has ebbed and flowed, fluctuating with some regularity. This is good because when all the players stay the same, things can get stagnant. A little fresh blood always invigorates the group.

I've had people who came only once, some who came for a handful of sessions, and two regulars who have been here since the group's inception. The average stay is about ten to twelve weeks for most. Some come alone, others with friends or relatives. The size of the group varies, too, having reached twenty-two people at its peak, though for the past two months it's been a core group of nine. We are in Wisconsin, so in the winter months the weather sometimes forces cancellations or keeps the group smaller. Now that it's springtime, I've been hoping the group would see some new blood.

I always arrange the chairs in a circle, and while this configuration is designed to create a feeling of community and equality, people tend to form smaller niches within the larger circle, mini groups where they feel the most comfortable.

My two die-hard attendees (though I should probably try to come up with a less offensive descriptor, under the circumstances), the ones who have been coming since I started the group, are Charlie Matheson and Betty Cronk.

Charlie is in his fifties, a widower, with a full head of gray hair that typically stands like a rooster comb by the end of a session, thanks to his habit of running his hands through it. Charlie works here at the hospital in the maintenance department and fancies himself as some sort of soothsayer or prognosticator. He swears he can "read" people and predict their futures after chatting with them for a few minutes. While I don't deny that the man has accurately predicted the behaviors of some of the group members in the past, it has less to do with any special powers he has than it does his ability to recognize when he has annoyed someone to the point of action. It didn't take a wizard to figure out that Hailey Crane, a teenager who came to the group with her mother when her father died, would decide to leave the group after one session as Charlie predicted. The fact that, despite my attempts to rein him in, Charlie badgered the girl a couple of times to "open up" and "express yourself" when she clearly didn't want to be there helped with that prediction.

I had a stern talk with Charlie after that, and I've had to do so on other occasions as well, since his actions often necessitate a cease-and-desist warning. If I let him, Charlie would take over the group. I've come to realize that he sees himself as my assistant, a coleader or facilitator of sorts, a perception I try hard to extinguish every week. I should probably ban him from the group, but he has a reputation around the hospital of being something of a tattletale. Whenever someone does something he doesn't like he's quick to run to the human resources department and file a complaint. He knows how to play the system and isn't afraid to do so.

Since I can't steer clear of Charlie, I do my best to control him instead. I don't want to be on Charlie's bad side, so

I struggle to balance my occasional desire to kill or maim him with my best professional façade. I don't have the luxury of picking and choosing my clients or patients in this hospital setting, and it's a simple fact of my professional life that I won't like some of them, and some of them won't like me.

Betty, my other long-term attendee, is a widow in her fifties, a stern, hard woman with a sharp-edged face, a tall, lean body, and a no-nonsense attitude. She wears her hair in a tight bun and dresses in drab, sack-like dresses, holey cardigans, heavy stockings, and utilitarian shoes. Betty's husband, Ned, was a quintessential Caspar Milquetoast kind of guy who not only let his wife lead him around by the nose but seemed to like it. Theirs was a match made in heaven, but when heaven came calling for Ned, Betty found she didn't know what to do with her bossy personality. She and Ned never had any children—*Just as well,* I think, as I imagine little Bettys running around like creepy Addams Family Wednesdays—and not surprisingly, Betty doesn't have many friends. She came to the grief group because she felt befuddled and confused, a rudderless ship adrift on a foreign sea. And she found the perfect home for her acerbic style.

Unfortunately for me, her style is often at odds with what my group is about, and like Charlie, she can be a disruptive influence. The two of them keep me on my toes, I'll give them that. Tonight, with a newcomer in the mix, I know I will need to be extra vigilant and stay on top of them both lest things get out of control. They're like sharks smelling fresh blood in the water.

Charlie and Betty don't like each other, and they often seat themselves on either side of me—a subtle way, I suspect, of declaring their perceived leadership status. This works in my favor, however, because it's much easier to shut them up if they are within a hand's reach.

Charlie swears I once pinched him hard enough to leave a bruise on his thigh, a mark he offered to show me after everyone else had left for the night.

"Charlie, that would be completely inappropriate!" I chastised as he started to undo his pants.

He paused in undoing his belt and blinked at me several times. Then he smiled and refastened the belt. "Yes, I suppose it would be," he said with a shrug and a smile.

After that incident, I kept expecting a call from human resources, but it never came. Charlie was on his best behavior for a few weeks, though Betty stepped in to make sure my duties as group leader remained challenging. While she tends to ignore the women in the group, she has this seemingly uncontrollable need to harangue the men who come, muttering comments like "Man up, you big sissy" or "Warning, man cry ahead."

Betty would have made a great drill sergeant.

I steer Sharon to a chair and then settle in beside her, earning myself angry stares from both Betty and Charlie, who are seated in their usual places. I tend to sit in the same seat each week, and clearly neither of them anticipated me doing anything different tonight, since they are situated on either side of that chair. I resist the urge to smile, because I have to admit, I enjoy rattling them a bit. It's good not to let them get too complacent.

"Welcome to this week's meeting of our bereavement support group," I begin. "I want to start by reviewing the ground rules first, both as a refresher for those of you who have been here before and to inform our new visitor."

Predictably, most of those who have been coming for a while roll their eyes or shift impatiently in their seats. But reciting the ground rules is a must.

"First and foremost, remember that anything said in this room is confidential and is not to be discussed or relayed to anyone outside of the group. Remember that we are here to share experiences, not advice. Be respectful and sensitive to one another by silencing your cell phones, avoiding side conversations, and listening to others without passing judgment. And finally, try to refrain from using offensive language."

I pause and scan the faces in the group. "Any questions about the rules?"

I'm answered with a sea of shaking heads and murmured declinations.

"Okay then. Since we have someone new here tonight, let's start by going around the group and stating your name and who it is you've lost." I turn and smile at Sharon Cochran. "Sharon, would you like to start?"

I'm pleased when she nods, even though it's an almost spastic motion. My pleasure then dissipates as she completely derails the evening's agenda.

"My name is Sharon Cochran, and I'm here because the cops think my son took his own life two weeks ago. But I know he was murdered and I'm hoping you can help me find his killer."

Chapter Two

I often practice and rehearse my responses. It's an admission I don't make lightly, because I want people to view my words as spontaneous and sincere, not canned and practiced. But to avoid being caught off guard, I sometimes role-play with myself, trying to anticipate different comments or actions people may make or take, and then practicing my responses to them. I even watch myself in the mirror as I speak, trying to make sure my pale blond hair and narrow face don't resemble what one coworker once called "a talking Q-tip."

Unfortunately, Sharon Cochran's announcement is nowhere in my repertoire of anticipated comments. And judging from the stunned quiet in the room, no one else knows how to respond, either. Finally, Charlie breaks the silence.

"I knew it, you know," he says. "The minute you walked in here I knew there was something mysterious about you."

I frown at Charlie, and I'm about to say something to try to mitigate the awkwardness, when Sharon Cochran continues.

"You're all looking at me like I'm crazy," she says, fighting back tears. "That's how the cops looked at me, too. But I'm not. I know my son. They said he died of a heroin overdose, and technically that's true, but I don't believe he administered it himself. He didn't use drugs."

There are looks of skepticism, sympathy, and curiosity on the faces of the others.

"Okay, he used pot on occasion," Sharon says with a hint of impatient irritability in her voice. "But what college kid doesn't these days? And I'm telling you he didn't use anything else. He had no tracks on his arms, but the cops said that was because it was likely his first time shooting it up, that he'd probably been snorting it before. They think he either killed himself on purpose, or he was unlucky and got too large a dose on his first try. They said there was some really strong stuff out on the streets at the time, way more potent than the usual."

I'm momentarily at a loss for words, unsure what to make of Sharon's claims. Denial is a common phase of grief, and not just denial of the death itself. The loved ones of those who die from drug or alcohol abuse often claim someone else is to blame as they struggle to deal with their own guilt for not having done something to stop it. Was that the case with Sharon?

I also know that teenagers and young adults are quite adept at hiding secrets from their parents, and that only strengthens the denial later when things go terribly wrong. I know this not only from my training and experience working with people in that age group, but also because I was quite adept myself at hiding things from the adults in control of my life when I was that age.

In my case, those adults kept changing, which sometimes made the deceptions easier, and sometimes didn't. My own mother died—was murdered—when I was seven, and I never knew my father. I don't know if my mother knew who my father was, either, though I have reason to believe she might have had an idea on the matter. But things were complicated. She was what polite company refers to as a "lady of the night," forced into selling herself to support the two of us.

My mother got pregnant at sixteen, and her very religious, very strict Iowan farm parents disowned her. She ventured out into the world to try and make it on her own, and several months later, that first pregnancy ended up a stillborn. She tried to establish some sort of life on her own since her parents were still stubbornly refusing to let her come home, and two years, several low-paying jobs, and a lot of male customers later, she ended up pregnant with me.

She did her best by me, though heaven knows it wasn't much, and despite our situation I have some fond memories of her. Her death saddened me deeply and altered my life in ways I didn't always understand. It forced me into the foster system, beginning a long procession of parental influences, some good, most not so much.

I shake off thoughts of my own mother and refocus. I decide to give Sharon a gentle dose of reality. "What makes you think your son was murdered?" I ask. "What I mean is, why would someone want to kill him?"

"There was something going on at his school," Sharon says. "I don't know the details, but something happened that had Toby very upset. He ended up leaving his fraternity over it, and moving home. I tried to get him to talk to me about it, but he wouldn't."

"What year was he?" I ask.

"Freshman," Sharon says. Her eyes well up and she adds, "He had his whole life ahead of him."

The others in the group are riveted, clearly intrigued by Sharon's tale. The current mix of people in the group is a vociferous one, and one of my biggest challenges at each session is in getting them to talk one at a time. Yet now they are all silent.

"Sharon, I'm sorry this happened to your son," I say, hoping to get things back on track. "If you feel strongly that the police have it wrong, then maybe you should take your concerns to them and push the issue. But for here and now, with this group, our focus is on helping you to deal with your grief."

"Now, hold on," says Mary Martin, a sixty-two-year-old widow who has been coming to the group for the past four months, ever since her husband died of cancer. "We can't just dismiss her claims. What if she's right? What if her boy was murdered?"

"Yeah," pipes up Bill Nolan, a forty-something gay man who lost his partner to an automobile accident two months ago and has been attending the group since then. "Why can't we help her?"

He sounds as eager as Mary, and when I see the others in the circle nod in agreement—everyone except for Betty Cronk, who looks bored—I realize what's going on. The group has seized upon the mystery of Sharon's son's death as a distraction, something to take their minds off the typical grief therapy issues they normally focus on. While this isn't necessarily a bad thing—in fact, it could prove to be a therapeutic diversion if handled correctly—I don't want the focus of the group to shift away from its main purpose.

"I'll tell you what," I say to the group. "We'll let Sharon tell us what she knows, assuming there is anything more she has to share on the matter, and we'll focus on the details of that toward the end of the hour. But for now, I want us to stay focused on tonight's topic. Let's give the first half of the hour over to the topic at hand, and then we can shift later. Okay?"

Judging from the looks I'm getting, it's not okay. I understand their curiosity; I share it. A potential murder mystery is great fodder for keeping one's mind off other, more painful things, and it can give one a sense of purpose and direction. I've done some investigating into my mother's death, feeling the need to avenge her and bring her killer to justice. But her case is more than twenty-five years old—not just a cold case but a frigid one—and I've made only minimal progress.

As I read the facial and body language of my group—scowling expressions, arms folded over chests, bodies shifting anxiously in seats, heads turned dismissively away from me—I decide to go off the reservation, a term that Carla, one of my fellow foster sibs, used years ago whenever she was going to do something unexpected, which, as it turned out, was often. Carla was fun but a bad influence on me.

"How about we open it up to a vote with a show of hands?" I say. "Who wants to focus solely on Sharon's son's death and the circumstances surrounding it?"

Every hand in the circle goes up except Betty's. The others all turn to look at her and I debate whether or not the vote should be a unanimous one. If even one person doesn't want to stray from the program, am I doing that person a disservice by giving in to the whims and wishes of the others?

The dilemma resolves itself seconds later when Betty arches one eyebrow, mutters an irritated "Fine," and raises her hand. If it wasn't for the hint of a smile I see at the corners of her mouth, I'd be worried. But I suspect Betty is just as interested in this course of action as the others are. She just doesn't want to let on to the fact. It doesn't fit in with the reserved, in-control persona she's established here.

"Okay, then," I say, adding the caveat, "but only for this session."

The transformation on the faces in the group is startling and I worry that I've opened a dangerous can of worms here. "Sharon, do you feel comfortable giving us some more details about your son's death and the events that led up to it?" I say.

"Do I feel comfortable?" she says with a scoffing laugh. "I'm delighted about it. I've been trying to get someone, anyone, to listen to me ever since it happened. I know people think it's just some form of denial on my part, that I'm fixated on this as a way of avoiding the pain of it all. But that's not it."

"Then go ahead," I tell her. "But if at any point it begins to feel uncomfortable for you, feel free to stop. You are under no obligation to talk, okay?" Though I mean this, the hungry, eager expressions on the faces of the others make me think they'd try to force her to continue whether she wanted to or not.

"Okay," Sharon says in an oddly chipper tone.

"The usual ground rules still apply," I tell the others. "If this thing gets out of hand in any way, I'm going to call a halt to it, understood?"

Enthusiastic nods and murmured assents answer my question. While I still think Sharon's focus on this aspect of her son's death is, in all probability, a way to avoid, escape, and defer, I can't see the harm in letting the others shift their focus from their individual losses. At least for tonight.

It certainly isn't by the book, and I'm not sure other social workers or group managers would approve, but I'm willing to experiment a little. I've always liked thinking and doing things a little outside the box. Sometimes a lot outside the box. The fact that it's gotten me into trouble on more than one occasion in the past is a thought I gently push aside.

I just hope my boss is as open-minded on the subject as I am.

Chapter Three

It turns out Sharon Cochran is a born storyteller. She has a clear knack for organizing her thoughts and the necessary details, relaying them in an orderly and understandable fashion, and doing it all with just the right amount of inflection and emphasis on her words. As I listen with rapt attention to her story, I make a mental note to ask her later what she does for a living.

"Toby belonged to a fraternity on the UW-Madison campus," she says. "He pledged them and went through their hazing ritual, something he refused to tell me about. Everything seemed great for several months. Toby was getting good grades, and he sounded happy whenever I spoke to him. When he came home for Christmas break he was excited about switching his major. Originally, he planned on studying information technology and getting a teaching certificate, but suddenly, he had this big interest in computer programming and game development. He said several of his frat brothers were interested, too, and it really had him fired up."

I scan the faces in the group and see that Sharon has their rapt attention.

"Our Christmas was nice, but uneventful," Sharon continues. "It was just me and Toby. It's been like that all his life." She pauses, looks around the group, and adds almost as an afterthought, "Toby's father has never been in the picture." There are some nods and murmurs from the group, and after a moment, Sharon continues her tale.

"I didn't hear much from Toby when he went back to school after the holidays, and in March he called to tell me that he wanted to go to Florida with some of his friends for spring break." Sharon gives the group a squeamish look. "I've heard horror stories about what happens on those excursions, so I was none too happy about it, but I also knew that Toby could do whatever he wanted. He was nineteen and no longer living under my roof. I told him to be smart and careful, told him I loved him, and prayed it would go well."

"Did something happen during the spring break trip, then?" Bill asks.

Sharon shakes her head, her face pinched like she's trying not to cry. "He never went," she says after a moment. "Right before the break, he showed up on my doorstep. Said he'd dropped out of school and wanted to take some time, that he needed to think through some things." She pauses, inhaling deeply and letting the breath out in a prolonged sigh. "I knew something was wrong, but any attempts I made to get him to talk were met with stony silence. I figured he'd tell me what was wrong when he was ready, and I gave him some space."

"Did he go out during that time?" Mary Martin asks. Then, without waiting for an answer, she says, "One of my boys went through something similar when he was in college. Met some girl he was all crazy over and she was all he could think about, day and night. It turned out she ran with a rough crowd that was involved with drugs, and hanging with them nearly got my son arrested."

Sharon gives Mary a tolerant smile. "I know things like that can happen," she says. "But Toby didn't leave the house for nearly two weeks. He barely left his bedroom, though I did hear his phone ringing and dinging a lot, so I know he was in communication with someone and was getting a lot of calls and text messages."

"I assume the police checked out his phone?" Bill asks.

Sharon frowns at this. "They did, or at least they said they did. I worked mostly with an officer named Joiner, Brenda Joiner. I asked her to let me see the phone, but she said it was evidence. Even if Toby's death was accidental or by suicide, she said they could prosecute whoever supplied the drug to Toby, and that the phone might help them figure out who that was." Sharon frowns, staring down at her lap. "I don't think it helped, though, because according to Officer Joiner, almost all of Toby's calls and texts were from a girl he was seeing. She told me that the bulk of this girl's messages were appeals to Toby to get back together because he broke things off with her. Officer Joiner's theory was that this relationship snafu depressed him enough that he started using drugs. I asked her when it was she thought Toby was supposedly using these drugs, given that he never left the house, and she asked me if I was home all day and all night, every day, to watch him."

"And were you?" Mary asks a bit sharply.

Sharon's shoulders slump and she looks wounded. I know what her answer will be before she utters it. "No," she says so softly that I see some of the others lean toward her, straining to hear better. "I work eight-hour night shifts at the trailer factory in town. But I'd check on Toby every morning when I came home, and he'd be sound asleep in bed, wearing the same clothes he'd had on the day before, with either the TV on or a game console by his hand, some screenshot frozen on the TV."

"But he could have gone out during the night, right?" asks Stacey Tungsten, a twenty-eight-year-old girl whose brother died by suicide last year. Stacey has been attending my group for nearly nine months, not only to deal with her grief issues, but also because she fears suicide is a hereditary tendency in her family since an uncle and a grandfather also did the deed. As the mother of two young boys, Stacey is scared to death—forgive the terminology—that her kids may have inherited a suicide gene.

Sharon smiles meekly at Stacey. "Yes," she says. "And clearly he did go out on the night he died."

"Do you think his overdose might have been . . . could have been . . . self-inflicted?" Stacey asks, her own fear transparent on her face.

To her credit—and a little to my surprise—Sharon doesn't immediately dismiss this idea. "I considered it. I really did," she insists. "Clearly something was bothering Toby, and he was upset, maybe even depressed. But Toby not only had a great love of life, he was afraid of dying. And no matter how hard I try, I can't imagine him killing himself."

"That's a tough thing for any parent to contemplate," Stacey says pointedly.

Sharon nods. "I realize that I'm not the most objective person, given that I'm his mother," she admits. "But I'm also the person who knew him better than anyone else in the world." Her eyes well with tears and her voice is momentarily strangled with emotion. "I knew my son," she insists. "He didn't end his own life."

A collective silence fills the room as the group gives Sharon time to get herself together. After a minute or two, Bill Nolan says, "If it wasn't suicide, maybe it was an accident."

Sharon swallows hard and nods. I can tell she wants to deny Bill's suggestion outright, to once again state unequivocally that her son wasn't using drugs. She doesn't, though, and my respect for her increases. She wipes away the tears flooding her lower lids and straightens in her seat.

"Can you give us a timeline for the night he died?" Bill asks.

Sharon shakes her hands and rolls her shoulders, looking like an athlete about to start a marathon. I imagine whatever comes next *will* be a marathon of sorts for her, though an emotional one rather than a physical one.

"I work the graveyard shift," she begins, grimacing at the descriptive term. "On the night Toby died, he seemed more chipper than usual. He came out of his room and ate dinner with me for the first time in weeks, and we talked about current events—politics, the environment, the economy, that sort of stuff. He and I have always enjoyed discussing and debating. He ate well, too, and for the first time in a long time I began to think he was turning around, on his way back to normal. At one point he even said something about going back to school in the fall and taking some summer classes to help him catch up."

The smile on Sharon's face, with all its fleeting hope and happiness, breaks my heart, knowing as I do how it all fell apart. She lost her child, a disturbing anomaly in the expected cycle of life and death, and one of the hardest losses to get over. Not that any parent truly gets over such a loss.

"Anyway," Sharon goes on, "we had a nice evening together, like old times. And then, around nine o'clock, when I was heading up to take my shower and get ready for work, he got a text message on his phone. I don't know who it was, or what it said, but the change in his mood was palpable."

"Did you ask him about it?" I say.

"I did, but he dismissed it, saying it was just some stupid fraternity crap. He said they were trying to get him to come back, and some of the frat brothers were getting irritated with his constant refusal."

"Did he talk about the fraternity much?" I ask. "Either before or after he dropped out of school?"

Sharon's brows draw into a troubled V over her nose.

"Not much. He did say once that he thought pledging the fraternity was a mistake, that he had hoped it would give him a leg up when it came to finding a job later on because of the connections, but that the brotherhood was tighter than he thought, and people like him . . ." She trails off and gives the group an embarrassed look. "By that I think he meant poor people, or at least not rich people. I mean, we managed well enough, and I make enough money to get by most of the time. Toby is . . . was a smart kid, and he earned a scholarship that paid for his tuition, room, and board. If not for that . . ." She doesn't finish the statement, but she doesn't need to. She does a quick visual circuit of the group and, apparently satisfied with the expressions she sees, continues. "Anyway, Toby told me once that there was a tight klatch of wealthy boys in the frat who maintained an exclusive club. They looked down on some of the boys who weren't as well off."

"Those social classes are everywhere," Mary Martin says. "That hasn't changed in centuries of human history. But from what you've told us about Toby, he doesn't sound like the kind of guy who would be all that bothered by classist snobbery."

"I don't think that's what made him drop out, if that's what you mean," Sharon says.

"What about the girlfriend?" Charlie asks.

"Or a boyfriend?" Bill throws out in a suggestive tone. "Is it possible your son might have had some confusion with regard to his sexual orientation?"

Sharon shakes her head, smiling. "Toby wasn't gay, but if he was, he wouldn't have hesitated to tell me. I have a brother who's gay, and there's an aunt on my father's side who used to be my uncle. Our family is open and accepting about that sort of thing."

"The girlfriend, then?" Charlie asks, resurrecting his question. "Did it seem like a serious relationship?"

"This last one did," Sharon says. "He had a few girlfriends earlier in the year. I didn't know much about any of them, and there might have been some I didn't know about at all. Toby tended to be a private person in that regard. I remember him talking about someone back at the start of the school year, but they broke things off after a month or so. Toby was disappointed, but not heartbroken. I know he dated a couple of other girls after that, though none of them seemed to stick. Then he met this girl named Lori when he started his second semester, and they seemed to really hit it off. He didn't talk about her a lot, but when he did, I could tell there was something different, something special about this one. He said they met in an English lit class they were both taking, and that they had a lot in common. The last time I asked him about her, he said they were taking things slow." She hesitates, squeezes her eyes closed, and pinches the bridge of her nose.

"Let's go back to the timeline," Betty says with irritation. "What time did you leave the house to go to work?"

"At ten thirty. My shift starts at eleven and it's a fifteen-minute drive. I like to get there a little early, so I have time to make myself a cup of coffee and get into the groove of things, you know?"

There are a few nods in the group.

"And when did you find out about Toby?" I ask.

Her eyes darken, her gaze growing distant, and the muscles in her face start to twitch, making me certain she's reliving the horrific moment in her mind. "The police showed up at my work just before four in the morning," she says in a tightly controlled voice. "There were two guys in uniform and they said they needed to talk to me. They took me to the employee break room and told me to sit down. I didn't want to, but I knew that if I didn't it would only delay things. I knew something was terribly wrong. When they asked me if Toby Cochran was my son, my heart was pounding so hard I could see my shirt moving with each beat. I said he was and asked them if he was okay. But instead of answering me, they asked me when I'd last seen him."

She pauses, swallows hard, and squeezes her eyes closed, trying to block out an image I suspect will be branded in her mind till the day she dies. "I knew from their evasiveness that something bad had happened to Toby. I begged them to tell me, and they finally did, though they didn't provide any specifics right away. They told me he had had an accident and that he was . . . dead."

Her eyes snap open at this and she fixes her gaze on Mary Martin, her face an expression of disbelieving fury. "An accident," she says in a tone of disgust. "That would make one think of something like a car wreck or a house fire, right?" Mary nods, as do several others in the group. "I asked them what kind of accident it was. They didn't answer right away. They just kept exchanging looks back and forth. I finally got mad and yelled at them. I think I might have dropped an f-bomb or two," she admits, looking mildly regretful as she finally releases Mary from her eye-lock. "Anyway, it did the trick. They told me they got an anonymous phone call to check on someone who was in that abandoned warehouse down by the waterfront, the one that's slated for demolition later this year?" More nods, along with some impatient looks that say, *Yeah, yeah, get on with it.*

"The cops told me it's a popular spot for druggies and that they chase people away from there on a regular basis. My first thought was that the building had collapsed and Toby was inside when it happened. The idea of a drug overdose wasn't anywhere on my radar. When they told me they found him dead inside the building with an empty syringe hanging out of his arm, I actually felt relieved for a moment." She squeezes her eyes closed at this, lets out a humorless laugh, and sniffs. "I was relieved because I thought they'd made a mistake, that it couldn't have been Toby they'd found, because no way would he have been shooting up drugs. Right?"

The question is clearly rhetorical since we all know the outcome to this story, so no one says yea or nay to this. Until we know for sure if Sharon's denial is born of ignorance and blinders as opposed to some nefarious goings-on, no one seems inclined to speak or pass judgment of any sort.

Sharon swipes at her face again and then continues her tale. "It took them some time to convince me, and even then, I kept holding out hope. I wanted to go home, check the house, knowing I'd find him in his bedroom sound asleep. Instead, they took me to the medical examiner's office, where I . . ." Her voice chokes off, and she squeezes her eyes shut. Several people in the group squirm uncomfortably in their seats, even though this sort of emotional wringing is something they've all encountered here before.

"You identified his body," I say softly.

Sharon, taking small, gulping breaths, can only nod.

"Did they try to resuscitate him?" I ask. "The cops all carry Narcan now because overdoses are such a common thing these days."

Sharon gives me a sad look. "No," she manages in a shaky voice. "They said it was too late, that he was . . . he'd been . . ." She sucks in a deep, shuddering breath. "He was already cold and stiff."

With this she hangs her head and begins to sob quietly. The group immediately converts into consolation mode, with murmurs of "Sorry for your loss" and "We're here for you" and "It's okay, let it out."

I let this go on for a minute or two, knowing Sharon needs to vent and that the rest of the group needs to succor her. Then Mary Martin hands Sharon a fresh wad of tissues and the moment has passed.

"I assume the police talked with you about Toby," I say, hoping to steer us back on course. "Who he hung out with? Who his friends were? What his activities were leading up to the time of his death?"

Sharon swabs at her nose, nodding. "They did," she says nasally. "Though I don't think their hearts were in it. To them it was just another junkie death, one less drug addict to worry about." She sneers angrily. "I told them about the school thing, and how Toby reacted and behaved. I asked them to look into it, but they just kept telling me that that kind of behavior is typical among drug users."

Unfortunately, the cops were telling Sharon the truth; that sort of behavior *is* typical among that group. But something about Sharon's conviction regarding her son rings true to me. There is more to this story, I'm sure of it.

Now I just have to figure out how to get to the bottom of it.

Chapter Four

The rest of the group is as intrigued by Sharon Cochran's story as I am, and several of them leap at the chance to become amateur investigators. It takes some convincing on my part to get them to see that this would be a bad idea, and it's only after I promise to follow up with some of my "connections" that they back down, with the caveat that I must keep them informed and updated.

There is a small problem, however. I may have oversold my connections. They consist of two people I recently had dealings with on another case. One of those is a Sorenson detective by the name of Bob Richmond, and the other is Mattie Winston, a woman who works as a medico-legal death investigator for the ME's office. I didn't spend a lot of time with either of them, though I spent enough time with Detective Richmond to know that I'd like to get to know him better. He's tall, handsome in a rugged, etched sort of way, and has an intensity about him that I found instantly appealing when I met him.

Of course, I haven't seen him since, but Sharon Cochran's son's death is the perfect excuse to do so. For a brief second or two I question my motives in wanting to help Sharon, but I shove my qualms aside. I want to help her even if it doesn't involve Detective Richmond. As someone who has experienced the loss of a loved one to murder, a murder that was never solved, I feel a kind of kinship for people in Sharon's position. I've always been an avid reader of mysteries, and I suspect it's my personal history that has given me this predilection.

Any initial reservations I had about letting the group take this detour from the planned agenda are assuaged when I see how the members swarm around Sharon when we're done, taking her into their midst, offering her their support, and letting her know she isn't alone. I can tell from the look on Sharon's face that this support means a great deal to her, and as typically is the case, the injection of new blood into the group has invigorated the others.

The goodbyes linger longer than usual, but eventually it's only me and Sharon left in the room, and I ask her to stay so we can talk some more.

"Sharon, I meant it when I said I want to help you figure out what happened to your son," I tell her. "I'd like to begin by talking with you some more about the days leading up to his death, and if you wouldn't object, I'd like to visit your home and take a look at his room."

She hesitates, frowning.

"I know it must seem like an intrusion, but I honestly think it will help. And after you and I have talked some more, I'm going to have a chat with someone I know at the police department, a Detective Richmond, to see if he would be willing to look into the case. I also know someone I can talk to at the medical examiner's office. Maybe there was something in Toby's autopsy that was missed."

"I already suggested that to Officer Joiner," Sharon says, looking frustrated. "She didn't take it well."

"You know, they hear that sort of stuff from surviving family members all the time. Maybe if it comes from some-one else, an objective outsider, they'll be more willing to take another look." I see hesitation lingering on her face and try one last entreaty. "What can it hurt?"

She shrugs grudgingly at this. "I suppose you're right," she says with a sigh. She glances at her watch, sees that it's nearly nine already, and adds, "But it will have to wait until morning. I need to be at work soon."

"I won't need long," I say. "You said you don't leave for work until ten thirty. How far is it to your house?"

"Not far," she says, resignation creeping into her voice. "I suppose we can do it now."

"Good. I'll follow you."

I make a brief stop in my office to get my jacket, purse, and keys, and then we head out to the parking lot. Sharon's car is an older-model Toyota I'm willing to bet she bought used. And judging from the blue smoke it belches as I follow her to her house, I'm also betting that it's on its last legs.

Her house—a rental, she tells me as we traverse the sidewalk leading to the front porch—is on a side street near a park, and only five blocks from the warehouse building where Toby was found. Most of the houses on the street are Victorians, and while the neighborhood may have been populated with middle- and upper-class families back in the 1920s when the houses were built, many of the homes have now been split up into duplexes, their innards gutted and reorganized like those of a Thanksgiving turkey. The tenants are mostly younger couples and singles, people who can't yet afford to buy their piece of the American dream.

Sharon's house is an exception, a Colonial style box with two stories that is still a single-family home. It's smaller than the other homes, but I note that the grounds are in better shape than most of the others, the front yard well kept, the house bordered with flower beds that are currently sporting a vibrant garden of daffodils and multi-colored tulips typical for this mid-April time of year. The porch, a concrete stoop with wrought iron railings, has a small bench to one side with flowerpots on either side of it. In one of the pots there is a healthy-looking rosemary plant, and in the other is a collection of what looks and smells like basil and oregano. The combined fragrances of the herbs and the early spring flowers make for a heady, welcoming air.

The inside of the house smells just as good, the air redolent with the scents of cinnamon and apple. I wonder if Sharon recently baked something to create these smells, or if they're the result of some artificial air freshener. Standing at the base of a steep set of stairs that split the house in two, I see a living or family room to the right and a dining room off to the left. The furnishings I can see appear gently used, unmatched, but comfortable. The hardwood floors are in desperate need of a good sanding and refinishing, but they are clean.

I shuck my jacket and Sharon takes it and hangs it in the small coat closet, doing the same with her own. Then she points up the stairs. "Toby's room is the one on the right," she says. "Mine is to the left. There is a small third bedroom at the top of the stairs that I've been using for storage. This house doesn't have any closets in the bedrooms."

"That's typical of some of these older homes," I say. "Back when they were built a lot of people used wardrobes and dressers for all of their clothes."

"My mother had something she called a chifforobe," Sharon says with a fond smile. It's fleeting, and the smile fades as she looks about worriedly, as if she's assessing what I'm seeing and trying to see it through the eyes of a stranger. I sense she's concerned I'm going to judge her, and I understand why. As the single parent of a child who has been labeled a junkie, and who apparently overdosed, I'm sure she has experienced people passing judgment on her parenting skills, some of them undoubtedly doing so with more than just sidelong looks and supposition.

"Your house is warm and welcoming," I say to reassure her. "There are so many wonderful smells, and everything is very clean and tidy. It feels very inviting. I should get some interior design ideas from you. My house is a hot mess of junk, and I'm afraid my cleaning skills aren't what they should be." This isn't true, but I doubt Sharon will ever see the inside of my house, and even if she does, I doubt she'll remember me making this claim.

She smiles and blushes at the compliment, looking away. I see her shoulders relax, but one hand strokes at her hairline behind her ear in a nervous gesture that tells me she isn't used to, or comfortable with, flattery.

"Is it okay if we go upstairs to Toby's room?"

She glances up the stairs, and a cacophony of emotions plays over her face: fear, sadness, reluctance, doubt. "Why don't you go on up there and I'll join you in a bit. I want to go pack my lunch for work."

"Okay, if you're sure you don't mind?"

"I don't. You go ahead." With that, she turns and enters the dining room, presumably on her way to the kitchen.

I head up the stairs, carefully navigating the narrow steps and keeping a grip on the wooden banister, its surface worn smooth from the touch of hundreds of hands like mine. At the top there is a small landing, and Sharon's homey touch is apparent here, too. Off to one side is a rocking chair with wide, flat arms, its seat and back padded in material that boasts a rustic cabin-in-the-woods type design. Behind it is a standing lamp, and to one side of it is a small square table with a paperback resting open and facedown. A glance at the cover tells me it's a romance novel, and it makes me wonder about Sharon's love life, if she has one. I make a mental note to broach this topic at some point.

There is a small bookcase against the wall at the top of the stairs. On its top shelf are three framed photographs: one with Sharon and what must be a younger Toby, around age seven or eight, and two pictures of a handsome teenager with a thick mop of dark hair, large brown eyes, and a charming smile. The resemblance to Sharon is notable. The lack of any sort of father figure is also notable.

The door to Sharon's room is open and the interior is lit with the soft glow of a couple of lamps. The décor is the same collection of used, mismatched furniture I've seen elsewhere, though it's all tied together with scattered touches of maroon, dark green, and gold present in the lamp shades, a throw on the chair, pillows, a comforter, and an area rug that covers the floor at the foot of the queen-sized bed. Like the rest of the house, the room looks inviting, comfortable, and cozy.

Feeling a smidge guilty at this intrusion, I turn away and move toward Toby's room. The door is closed, as is the door to the spare room. I consider peeking into the third room, but decide not to do so, at least not now. Time is limited, and I want to spend as much time in Toby's room as I can.

The door, a four-panel affair like the others, is plain and painted white. As I reach for the doorknob, I wonder if Sharon keeps the door closed all the time, and how often she's ventured inside since her son's death. Am I about to enter a shrine to Toby? Has she changed anything in there since he died? I'm inclined to think not. His death is too recent.

When I open the door, the hinges squeak slightly, making a shiver race down my spine. The room is dark, and I fumble along the wall in search of a light switch. I find it and flip it, and as light floods the room, I suppress a gasp.

Chapter Five

Toby's bedroom is the antithesis of the rest of the house. It looks like someone set off a bomb in the middle of it. There is stuff everywhere: clothing, papers, gaming equipment, books, shoes, plates—some dirty but empty, two with remnants of food still on them—and an assortment of soda cans, water bottles, and coffee mugs. I can barely see the surface of the floor, or the tops of the desk and dresser.

There is a twin bed pushed up against the wall, the sheets and blankets a crumpled heap that is half at the foot of the bed, half on the floor, the pillow resting in a chair by the desk. The top of the desk is covered with miscellany that forms a moat around a laptop computer: pens, papers, mugs, cups, some silverware, two dirty saucers, a pocket-knife, books, an assortment of charcoal and mechanical pencils in a plastic pencil holder, a box of colored pencils, and a nearly empty tape dispenser. I'm surprised to see the laptop, because I thought the police would have confiscated it when they investigated Toby's death. Then again, maybe there wasn't much of an investigation. If Sharon's version of events can be believed, the police determined the cause and nature of Toby's death based on where and how they found him. I make a mental note to ask Sharon if she'll let me look at the contents of the computer.

I turn my attention to the walls, which are covered with taped-up drawings that explain the nearly empty roll in the tape dispenser on the desk. After studying the display for a minute or so, I realize that some of the drawings have been done on what looks like basic copy paper, others on more official art papers. The colored pencil drawings are on the heavier art paper and feature anatomical parts such as hands, feet, torsos, eyes, and a couple of vague facial profiles. The copy paper drawings are done in basic gray or black pencil and feature sketches of structures: buildings, castles, and some bridges. Neatly printed in the right lower corner of each drawing are two initials: TC.

The artwork is impressive—clearly Toby was talented—and I wonder if he switched his focus from human subjects to inanimate structures, or if it was the other way around. Or perhaps he traded off now and then, moving back and forth between the two. But something about the paper choice makes me think he was focusing solely on one subject matter before deciding to change. What triggered that change, I wonder?

Even though the artwork is fascinating and something I could study for hours, I know my time is limited, so I pick my way across the debris-covered floor to Toby's desk. Behind the laptop I discover some game cassettes for use in the machine beside the TV on his dresser. Beneath the games is a notebook of lined paper, and when I slide it out and look at the contents, I see that the first few pages are filled with gaming codes and clues. There is one drawer on the right side of the desk, and when I open it I discover more drawings rendered on plain copy paper. I take the stack out and flip through it. Like the other drawings done on plain paper, these are pictures of a structure, but unlike the others, every one of these is of the same structure and done in color. It's a footbridge built from wood, arching over a small brook. Some of the drawings contain the bridge only, others the bridge and the underlying water, while still others contain surrounding features: trees, bushes, riverbanks. Some of them appear to be a fall setting, while others show a winter scape. I slide one of the more elaborate pictures out of the stack and set it on the chair seat, then I return the others to the drawer.

I open the laptop and hit a key to see if it is asleep or off. The screen comes to life almost at once, prompting me for a password. Just for grins I type in the word *password*, but it doesn't work. I make a mental note to ask Sharon if she knows the password and move on to the dresser.

The top surface is layered in dust, letting me know that Sharon hasn't ventured into her son's room much, if at all. The rest of the house is too neat and orderly, and I now understand Sharon's reluctance—or at least part of it—to let me into her son's bedroom. I would think the state of his room is an offense to her neat, homey sensibilities and possibly something of an embarrassment.

The dresser drawers don't reveal anything of interest other than the expected clothing. I even squeeze all the rolled-up socks to check for hidden contraband, and bend down and examine the undersides of the drawers to make sure nothing has been taped under there.

I look under the mattress next, where I find a dog-eared copy of a girlie magazine, but nothing else. Then I move on to the closet. There is a shoebox on the shelf, but all it contains is a collection of baseball cards. I check the hanging clothes for pockets and examine every one, but they yield no results. I'm in the process of looking inside the shoes on the floor when Sharon's voice sounds behind me, startling me.

"Why are you looking at his shoes?"

I glance at her over my shoulder and smile. "It's a common hiding place kids use. Believe me, I know them all. I spent a lot of time in the foster system, and I learned early on that hiding things was often the only way of hanging on to them."

"Are you looking for drugs?" she asks. I think I detect a hint of resentment and disappointment in her voice.

"Yes and no," I say. "I'm looking for anything that Toby might have hidden, anything that he might have wanted to keep secret."

"My son had no secrets from me," she says in a hurt tone.

I give her a sympathetic look. "Sharon, every child has secrets they keep from their parents. It's a normal part of growing up and separating themselves in preparation for making their own way in the world. It's nothing to be ashamed or embarrassed about."

She folds her arms over her chest and looks away from me, her face pinched with pain, the fingers of one hand tapping out an impatient beat on her arm.

"If it helps, I haven't found anything in here that indicates Toby was using drugs. No paraphernalia, no literature, nothing. Though there might be something on his computer."

I toss this possibility out there like bait on a line, the fish I'm hoping to snag being her interest—or, at the least, her cooperation with letting me examine the device. Silence bobs in the air between us for a few seconds, and then disappears beneath the surface of her resistance.

"I looked at it after . . . when he . . . after the police came," she says. "It's password protected." She pauses, shooting me a pained look. "That's new, both the computer and the password. He never used to hide his computer activity from me, but he got that new laptop when he went off to college. Bought it with some of the scholarship money he received."

"Do you know the password?" I ask, even though I'm pretty sure what the answer will be.

She shakes her head. "I tried all the obvious things, and after several attempts I got a prompt asking for a fingerprint."

"Fingerprint protection?" I say, perking up.

Sharon shoots me a curious look. "Why do you sound happy about that? It's not like we have his fingers." Her face pales then, and her lips clamp together in a thin white line. After a few seconds, she says, "You aren't . . . you wouldn't . . . he's already buried." There is a look of horror on her face, tears welling in her eyes.

"No, no, nothing like that," I say. "We don't need his actual finger. If the ME's office had possession of his body, they have a set of fingerprints on file. There might be a way to use those to gain access."

She stares at me as she considers this possibility and I know that now is the time to seize the moment.

"Will you let me take the computer with me?" I ask her. "I'll give it to Detective Richmond and explain what I want. He may be willing to help me. And who knows what we might find?"

Sharon doesn't answer right away, and I suspect she's weighing the possibilities. We might find something on the computer to support her theory that her son was murdered, but it's also possible we might find something that supports the current theory regarding his death, that he was a drug user. Apparently, she finds the courage of her own conviction, because she nods. "Sure, okay. But I want it back when you're done."

"Of course."

"Do you really think this detective will listen to you?"

I bite my lip. "I don't know," I tell her, feeling compelled to be honest. "But I'm going to try my best." I pause and look around the room. "It would help if there was anything else I could take to him, anything else that seems wrong about your son's death."

"The whole thing is wrong," Sharon says, squeezing her

eyes closed and pinching the bridge of her nose as she fights back tears.

"What I mean is, was there anything else odd that happened in Toby's life, or anything here in this room that seems out of place, or not right, or just way off plumb?"

Sharon blinks hard and looks around the room, scanning the bed, the desk, the dresser, and finally, the drawings on the wall. Her eyes move lovingly over each one, and I see her tears start to well again. Then suddenly her expression changes, her eyes riveted on the drawing I placed on the chair seat.

"That bridge," she says. "There was something about it that bothered him. He drew it repeatedly, claiming he couldn't get it quite right. That's all he ever drew after quitting school."

Sharon's comments about the picture trigger a thought and I look around the room. I finally spy what I'm seeking in the knee well of the desk and give myself a mental slap for overlooking it in my initial search. After moving the chair away, I reach beneath the desk and pull out a plastic garbage pail. In it are a dozen or so wadded-up clumps of paper.

I grab one from the top, unravel it, and see that it is another picture of the footbridge, also drawn in color. I compare it to the one I kept from the drawer. Both include a thicket of trees, the leaves rendered in the colors of autumn, and a small path leading from the far side of the bridge into the trees. There are some minor differences in the two pictures, in the width of the path, the size of tree thicket, and the colors of the leaves.

I take out the other wadded paper balls in the trash one at a time, opening them and smoothing them as best I can. All of them are pictures of the bridge and its setting. There are subtle differences in each, sometimes in the layout and locations of certain features, sometimes in the colors, sometimes in both.

Like the ones in the drawer, there is a mix of seasonal backgrounds. The winter scenes show bare tree branches dark against a pale gray sky and the bright white of snow. I note how Toby let the white of the paper portray the snow, cleverly adding in subtle lines and perspectives that made the snowy areas stand out from the rest of the white paper background. The kid had some serious talent, and it saddens me to think that it's now gone.

"Toby did all of these drawings after he quit school?" I ask. I'm almost certain Sharon said that a moment ago, but I want to verify it because of the seasonal variances in the drawings.

"Yep," Sharon says. "That's the only thing he drew. He even doodled it on magazines or paper napkins."

I'm intrigued by this. What was it about that bridge that had Toby so fixated? And why were the drawings in the trash discarded and the others kept in the drawer? My years of surviving in the foster system imbued me with a strong gut sense, something I've come to refer to as my Spidey sense. And my Spidey sense is telling me these pictures of the bridge are important. I don't know how or why, but I know it's something I'm going to pursue.

Sharon glances at her watch and says, "I need to go to work."

"Of course." I unplug the laptop, close it, and tuck it and its cord under one arm. Then I pick up the drawing on the chair and add it to the pile of pictures I removed from the trash. "Is it okay if I take these, too?" I ask Sharon.

I see a play of emotion on her face and for a moment her expression is so sad and pathetic that I know I won't be able to bring myself to push the issue if she says no. "Tell you what," I say. "How about if I just take this one?" I show her the picture that had been on the seat.

The look of immense relief I see on Sharon's face tells me I've made the right choice. No doubt, her son's drawings are dear to her, some small piece of him that she still has.

I start to leave the room, but Sharon stops me with a hand on my arm. "You do believe me, don't you?" she says, her eyes pleading. "You're not just humoring me as some way of counseling me, are you?"

I look her in the eye the best I can, though it's difficult since she's a tall woman. "I believe that you believe," I tell her. "And I'm open to the idea that your belief may be right. I can't promise you the outcome of all this will be what you're hoping, but I will do my best to get you the truth. I think that's all any of us really want or need. The truth."

Her expression relaxes, and she flashes me a tentative smile. "I sense there is some personal truth that you're seeking as well," she says.

"There is," I admit, impressed with her sense of empathy. "But mine will likely be harder to find."

Chapter Six

I've lived alone my entire adult life, so I'm used to coming home to an empty house. For the past three years, however, I've had Roscoe there to greet me. Roscoe is my dog, a dark red golden retriever with soulful brown eyes, a loving, mild temperament, and a healthy dose of smarts. He came to me by chance when a patient who was brought to the ER following a car accident died from her injuries and the EMTs brought the twelve-week-old puppy that was in her car—fortunately in a crate, which saved him from incurring any accident-related trauma—to the ER with her. Her sole relative in the area was a niece named Deborah, who had no interest in some "dirty, smelly dog that probably isn't even housebroken." Deborah announced her intention to drop the pup off at a shelter, but after one look at those huge brown eyes and one lick of my hand by that tiny pink tongue, I knew that plan was a no-go. I asked Deborah if she would mind if I took the dog, and she was more than happy to agree.

I should have known the niece was going to be a problem when she insisted on correcting everyone who called her Deb-ra, or Deb, or Debbie, stating irritably that her name was Dee-bor-ah, enunciated with three distinct syllables and an emphasis on the middle one. Two weeks later

Deborah showed up at the hospital with the paperwork associated with the pup, which she had found while going through her aunt's things. Since she hadn't bothered to remember my name or title from her initial visit, she had to do some asking to figure out who I was. It didn't take long, since the ER staff knew the story of me and the pup. When I met Deborah in the ER waiting room and she showed me the AKC paperwork for the dog, my first thought was how kind it was of her to bring it to me. Silly me. It turned out her motives were far less benevolent. Once she discovered that her aunt had paid a thousand bucks for the dog two weeks before her death, a thousand bucks Deborah now thought she should have by selling the pup to someone rather than just giving it away, she demanded that I either pay her or give the pup back.

Giving him back wasn't an option. During that two-week interval we'd had together, I had bonded big-time with Roscoe, a name I found imprinted on a tag on his collar, a name I think his owner gave him because he came from Roscoe, Illinois. His sweet personality and obvious intelligence won me over easily, and the thought of giving him up literally made my heart ache. Roscoe was an orphan, just like I had been, and abandoning him at this point was something I simply couldn't do. After a bit of haggling in the ER waiting room, during which Deborah had refused to go anywhere else without either the money or the dog and had also made it clear that she had no qualms about creating a loud and upsetting scene, I agreed to pay her the money. I offered to write her a check, but she insisted on cash. Given that I didn't have that kind of money on me, I told her I was going to have to go to the bank.

I ended up taking my lunch break at a little after ten that morning, using it to visit my bank with Deborah on my heels. She even accompanied me inside the bank, making it clear that trust wasn't something she came by easily. I briefly wondered about her life and history, curious as to what had shaped her into such a cold, untrusting, and self-ish person, but then decided I didn't care. I did, however, take the precaution of giving her the money in a cashier's check rather than cash, and made her sign over the paper-work to me there in the bank with the teller as a witness, Deborah huffing her impatience the entire time. Once that was done, she turned and left without so much as a *thank you*, *screw you*, or *good riddance*.

I hollered after her retreating form with "It was a plea-sure doing business with you, Deb-ra," making sure she heard my mispronunciation of her name. I couldn't tell if it fazed her at all, but it wasn't important. It made me feel better, and that was all that mattered. That, and the fact that I still had Roscoe.

Roscoe's sweet demeanor and high level of intelligence not only made him a perfect pet but also an ideal candidate for work as a therapy dog. When he was eight months old, I enrolled him in a training program, and for the past two years we have been a team, visiting patients in the hospital, in the local nursing homes, and even at my grief therapy group at times. His calming influence and loving nature make him a big hit during these visits. Sometimes all some-one needs is to bury a hand in that soft fur. Sometimes it's Roscoe's head laid gently in a lap. And on one occasion, while visiting an eight-year-old boy in the hospital, Roscoe gently climbed onto the bed and settled down next to the delighted child, who draped an arm over his furry neck and hugged him tightly.

Roscoe provides temporary therapy to the people we visit on our rounds, but he's my full-time therapist—that is, if you don't count the psychiatrist I see on a regular basis. His smiling face and wagging tail are always there to greet me when I come home, and it gives me an instant mental and emotional boost.

Tonight is no exception, and I squat down to give him a hug as soon as I'm through the door. "Did you miss me?" I ask him, and he responds with a more vigorous wag of his tail. I set my purse on the table beside the door and put my briefcase below it on the floor. Then I grab Roscoe's leash from the coat tree, hook him up, and head out.

It's dark outside, but my neighborhood is well lit with the warm glow of lamps and the cooler blue light of TVs emanating from the windows of the houses we pass. I sneak peeks as we walk, playing voyeur to the lives of those around me who aren't hiding behind curtains or blinds. I see a couple cuddled together on a couch watching a Hallmark movie I recognize, a family of four playing what appears to be a charades type of game, a group of six adults—three couples, I think—gathered together around a dining room table drinking beers and playing some kind of card game, and a family room filled with teenage girls laughing and chatting with one another as their nimble fingers constantly work their cell phones.

These glimpses of family life both warm and depress me. It's a life I've never had or experienced, and I feel the lack of it at times. I try not to dwell in the land of self-pity too much, though, and if I do linger there overly long, Roscoe seems to sense it, and he'll nudge me out of my depression.

With all that happened at the grief support group meeting, the time I spent with Sharon, and my walk around the neighborhood, it's not a huge surprise that I dream of my mother during the night. My dreams of her these days are rare, and even though I'm left with a feeling of empty sadness when they do come, I welcome them. My memories of her are dim at best, her image fading from my mind more with each passing year. I have a photograph of her, but only one, and it's cracked and faded with age. It was taken when she was young, just before or around the time she found out she was pregnant with me.

Though I loved my mother and we had some good moments together, many of my memories of life with her aren't good ones. I recall a parade of skeevy, possessive, and often abusive men traipsing through whatever hovel we were living in at the time. Day or night, it didn't seem to matter. I worried a lot because sometimes I would find my mother bruised and beaten, or curled up in a corner crying, or stoned out of her mind. I didn't always understand what I saw, but I knew it was bad.

There were some pleasant times, typically occasions when my mother was more flush than usual with cash and hadn't yet had a chance to blow that money on drugs or booze. She would load me into our ramshackle car and we'd be off on some adventure together: a picnic at the park by the lake, or shopping at the mall, or a treat at the ice cream parlor. During those times when it was just her and me, I would often fantasize about a different life, one with nice clothes, an abundance of food on the table, and a home that didn't have a revolving door of male customers. But a fantasy was all it would ever be.

I awaken with a sense of loss. I want desperately to solve my mother's murder, to find justice for her, but I know that after so many years, the likelihood of that happening is slim at best. Yet every time I dream about her, I am imbued with a renewed sense of determination despite the long odds, and I can't seem to give up my quest. I suspect that my personal failure in this regard is behind my desire to help Sharon Cochran unravel the mystery around her son's death. Some part of me wonders idly if my new fixation is a healthy one, but this fleeting moment of illuminating self-awareness doesn't deter me in the least.

I let Roscoe out into the backyard to tend to his potty needs, and then I pour myself a cup of coffee from the small pot I set up every night to be ready when I get up the next morning. Once I let Roscoe back in, I get myself showered, dressed, and ready for work. I'm about to head out when there is a knock at my front door. Given that it's quarter to seven in the morning, I have little doubt about who it is. The only person who would show up at my door at this hour is P.J., the eleven-year-old, freckle-faced, redheaded bundle of energy who lives next door. And if it wasn't for the hour, she likely would have walked into the house without knocking. I gave her a key two years ago so she can come and go as she pleases, but I also told her that mornings are my quiet, private time, so she needs to knock when she comes by for that first visit of the day.

"Good morning, P.J.," I say after unlocking and opening the front door.

"Good morning." She squats down as Roscoe rushes over to greet her. "Good morning, you handsome boy, you," she murmurs to Roscoe, who wags his tail in appreciation and then licks her face.

P.J. showed up on my doorstep mere days after I moved into the house three years ago, asking me if she could play with my puppy. I said of course, and that was the beginning of a great love affair and a handy arrangement for me. P.J. comes to my house several times a day to walk Roscoe, and in exchange for this service I pay her twenty dollars a week. All of this evolved after her parents met and vetted me. They are nice people, but they are both devoted to and embroiled in their careers. Her father is the manager of the town's largest grocery store, and her mother is a highly successful real estate agent who opened her own brokerage right around the time she found out she was pregnant with P.J. Given that P.J. has a brother who is fifteen years older than she is, and has been out on his own for several years, I think P.J. was something of a surprise for her parents. I also think P.J. might have Asperger's, a high-functioning disorder on the autism spectrum. She is whip smart, but socially awkward, and doesn't seem to have any friends her own age. And when it comes to expressing emotion, she doesn't, except with Roscoe.

Our relationship developed over time, and after three years P.J. is comfortable with me, more so than with her parents, I think. A good part of that progress is due to Roscoe.

After giving Roscoe a scratch behind his ears, P.J. stands, takes the leash from the coat tree, and hooks him up. "Back in a bit," she says. She looks at me with my purse slung over my shoulder and my briefcase in hand. "You are going to work?"

"I am."

"Should I lock up when I'm done?"

"Yes, please."

"I'll be by after school and walk him again."

"That's great. Thanks."

Our conversations often go like this. Blunt and to the point.

I arrive at the hospital a few minutes before seven, my briefcase stuffed with Toby's laptop. I leave the briefcase in my office and head down to the ER to see if anything is going on that might require my help. The department is completely empty, so I hit up the cafeteria for more coffee and an egg and bacon biscuit, which I take back to my office.

I barely have time to get settled in behind my desk and log onto my computer when my boss comes in. Crystal Hoffheimer is a forty-two-year-old woman who never married, though she'll tell the story of Tom, The One Who Got Away, to any poor soul willing to listen. Crystal has been carrying a torch for her high school boyfriend, Tom

Reese, for twenty-five years, a torch that burns so hot and bright that it blinds her to the fact that she's throwing her life away over some guy who has not only moved on with his life, but moved out of the country. After serving in the military and being stationed in Germany, Tom met the true love of his life, married, and stayed there.

Crystal, who saw Tom off to the military thinking that the two of them would get engaged and married within the year, didn't take it well when Tom broke things off. Crystal's fixation with Tom and her savviness in mining social media tidbits borders on stalker status. She knows everything about the man: where he lives, where he works, the name of his wife, the names of his three kids, the names of most of his in-laws, and who some of his best friends are. Crystal is convinced that she and Tom are meant to be together, and that it's only a matter of time before he comes to his senses, ditches the "frumpy Frau," and returns home to her.

Aside from this admittedly unhealthy obsession, Crystal is a relatively well-rounded person with good sense in all other matters. She is fun to socialize with, great at her job, and successful in her own right, since she owns a home, a fancy hybrid car, and two rare Napoleon cats, tiny little fur balls with stubby legs and adorable faces. The cats are Crystal's children, at least for now.

"Good morning, Hildy," Crystal says from my office door. "How did your group go last night?"

I'm not fooled by her seeming ignorance of how things went. I know that Charlie feeds Crystal information on a regular basis, and since I saw him enter the cafeteria when I was leaving it, and Crystal is now holding a food container from there, I'm betting she's already gotten an earful. "It went well," I say. "We had a newcomer who changed the dynamic some, but for the better I think."

"I talked to Charlie Matheson this morning," she says,

confirming my suspicion. "He mentioned that the group did something different last night."

I smile benignly at her while silently cursing Charlie and his need to blab. "Yes, I decided to let things take a different tack, to see how it would go. The group has been feeling a little stuck and stagnant lately, so I thought something different might be good."

Crystal arches an eyebrow at me. "Be careful, Hildy," she cautions. "Remember that you're the facilitator for these people. Don't get overly involved."

I can't be sure exactly how much or what Charlie said to Crystal, but since he doesn't know about my trip to Sharon's last night, I assume he told her about Sharon's story and her plea for help in looking into her son's death.

"I think it's healthy to think outside the box from time to time," I say. "But no need to worry. I'm a professional."

"I hope so. I'm headed up to the floor to handle the discharges, though there aren't many patients today. You have the ER. Call me if you need help with anything."

"Would it be okay if I took off early today? I have some personal business to attend to, and I have plenty of comp hours built up from my group time."

As a salaried employee, I make the same amount of money every pay period regardless of how many hours I work. I'm supposed to work forty hours a week, but most weeks it ends up being more like forty-five because of the time I spend running the grief group and other groups I've offered from time to time, as well as situations that come up in the ER that require me to stay beyond my normal end time for the day. Those extra hours get banked as comp time, and I'm allowed to use them to leave early, make midday appointments with my doctor or dentist, or even take a day off without tapping into my vacation time. I currently have enough comp time built up to take an entire week off with pay.

"What time are you planning on leaving?" Crystal asks.

"Would it be okay if I took off after noon?" Since my shift normally runs from seven in the morning to three thirty in the afternoon, with half an hour of that time dedicated to lunch, this will mean three hours of comp time. I hope it will be enough to do what I want, and not so much that it annoys Crystal. Fortunately, Crystal is reasonably flexible with stuff like this most of the time.

"Sure," she says. "The floor isn't busy right now. The census is really low, so it shouldn't be any problem for me to cover." With that, she disappears from my doorway.

I have follow-up phone calls to make to patients and family members I've had contact with recently, and I do those right away. Once they're done, I take Toby's laptop out of my briefcase and set it on the desk. I try several passwords, getting rejected each time, but wanting to ensure that the fingerprint ID will come up. Sure enough, after four attempts, I get a prompt for the fingerprint. Just for grins, I try applying my own finger, and it is quickly rejected.

I lean back in my chair and stare at the computer screen, thinking about how best to approach Detective Richmond. My preference would be to see him in person, though calling is also an option. But then I decide a phone call is too easy to escape from, too easy to ignore. I want to make my appeal face-to-face, so he can see my sincerity and eagerness to pursue this case. Of course, I also want him to see me, to gauge if he might have any interest in a more involved relationship. I make a mental note to tread carefully, however. I don't want to mix my personal life with my professional one too much.

Even though I've decided Detective Richmond requires a face-to-face meeting, a phone call to arrange that meeting is necessary. I'm not sure how much I should tell him about the reason behind my request, fearful he might dismiss me right away. But I also don't want to anger him by being cagey and vague.

Then I remember that Bob Richmond isn't my only connection. Maybe I'd have better luck starting with Mattie Winston at the medical examiner's office. She was very kind and approachable when I dealt with her before, and she seemed receptive to new ideas.

After a moment of indecision, I make up my mind and call.

Chapter Seven

"Medical examiner's office. This is Cass. How may I help you?"

"Hi, Cass," I say in my best chipper voice. "This is Hildy Schneider. We met once before, a few weeks ago."

"Yes, of course. I remember," Cass says. "You're a social worker over at the hospital, correct?"

"Wow, you have an excellent memory," I say, figuring a little flattery to grease the wheels can't hurt. "I need to speak with Mattie Winston, but I don't have a direct number for her. Any chance she's in the office today?"

"She is, but she's on another call. Would you like me to have her call you back, or would you prefer to hold?"

"I'll hold. Thanks."

The sound of tinny music emanates from the phone, and I start mentally rehearsing my next words, wanting to sound as convincing as possible without coming across as crazy.

My first encounter with Ms. Winston was an awkward one, in that I had to admit to copping something that turned out to be a key bit of evidence in a case she was investigating. The victim had come into, and eventually died in, the ER, so I'd been involved in the case. When leaving the patient's room at one point, I spied a candy bar, the edge of which was sticking out of the pocket of the coat that had been taken off her and flung onto a chair. A little while later I found that candy bar in my own pocket. I didn't recall taking it, but I remembered seeing it, and envying it, and knew I had copped it. I knew it because I've done something similar many times before.

This odd quirk stems from my childhood in the foster system. Treats like candy bars were far and few between, and often as not, if you did get one, someone would take it from you, usually one of the "real" kids in the home. In most, though not all, of the foster homes I spent time in— and I got bounced around homes a lot—the biological kids received privileges that the foster kids didn't: food treats, special outings, new clothing . . . that sort of thing. Only twice did I live in a home where a kindhearted biological sibling was aware of and embarrassed by this class division and unfair treatment. Those two kids did their best to try and share with me and the other foster kids, to even things out, but their parents and blood siblings didn't share their empathy. They did their utmost to see to it that we foster kids got little or nothing. They would steal whatever we did get or sabotage an outing if given half a chance. The treatment I and other foster kids suffered at the hands of some of these families easily qualified as emotional and mental abuse, and on a few occasions, there was even some physical abuse.

I suppose part of it was my own fault. I wasn't a very agreeable child when I first entered the system. I was angry, frustrated, afraid, and lonely . . . emotions that often had me lashing out or acting in reprehensible ways. This got me bounced from one foster home to another as each placement proved to be a "poor match"—foster speak for "this kid's more of a pain in the ass than we want to deal with and not worth the money you pay us." Troublemakers like me and a few other fosters I came to know got labeled quickly, and the households willing to take us in were limited. Most of them were people who did it for the extra money it brought in, not because they had any altruistic interest or investment in any of the kids.

It was always hardest when I was sent to a home where I was the only foster kid. Clearly outnumbered, there was little I could do other than hunker down and try to survive. If the situation became bad enough, I would act out as much as possible in hopes of having the family send me back to be placed elsewhere. It was always better and less lonely if I landed in one of the homes that took in multiple kids.

The other fosters were my true and only siblings. Occasionally I'd run into one who exercised bullying rights, but overall there seemed to be an unspoken code of conduct we lived by. We supported one another as much and as often as we could. In fact, when one of us managed to obtain a treat or a privilege of some sort, we'd often try to find a way to share it with the other fosters. I'm still in touch with several of my foster siblings, and even though we've all gone our separate ways, we share a connection much the way regular siblings do.

My foster sibs understand my quirk. They know how important it was to hide treats, to take things when given the chance, and to get good at lying and charming one's way out of a confrontation. These were basic survival skills. I became so adept at grabbing and slipping items into a pocket, or up my sleeve, or in my shoe, or down my pants—wherever I could drum up a hiding spot—that I started taking things without realizing I was doing it. Not until later, when I undressed for the night, would I discover my hidden stash.

Despite my best efforts, I haven't been able to shake off this habit. It was this instinct, this impulse that led to me taking the candy bar from the coat pocket of the girl who died in the ER. When I realized what I'd done, I knew I'd have to come clean and turn the candy bar over, but I feared the repercussions that might come out of it. After much thought about how to deal with the situation, I finally decided to approach Mattie Winston, my gut telling me she would be the lesser of all possible evils in that regard. I'll never know if that was true, but Mattie was very kind and understanding. She even handled it in a way that kept anyone else from knowing what I'd done. For that, I am eternally grateful to her. Hopefully, she will be as helpful and understanding today as she was on that occasion.

I'm released from Hold Hell with the sound of Mattie Winston's cheery voice. "Hildy?"

"Hi, Mattie. How are you?"

"I'm good. How are you?"

"Hanging in there. I haven't copped anything I shouldn't have recently."

"Glad to hear it," she says with a chuckle. "And I'm glad you called. I've been wanting to thank you for taking on Kit Johnson. I hear she's doing well."

Kit Johnson, one of the twins who works at a local funeral home, got herself into a bad relationship with an abusive boyfriend. At Mattie's request, I stepped in to try to help Kit deal with the aftermath of that situation, which got quite violent and intense. Fortunately, things turned out okay in the end, and I still see and counsel Kit to this day.

"She is," I say. "And I was happy to help."

This is true for two reasons. Not only did I want to try to get this girl the help she needed, feeling a kinship as I do for anyone in an abusive situation, but I owed Mattie for the way she handled the candy bar incident.

"And we are happy you did," Mattie says. "What can I do for you today?"

"Well, I don't know if you remember me telling you this, but I run a grief support group here at the hospital."

"I remember."

"Last night I had a new member show up for the group, a woman named Sharon Cochran."

"Oh, yes," Mattie says. "Very sad. She lost her son recently."

"Yes, from a drug overdose, she said."

Mattie hesitates, and I gather she's gauging how much information she can share with me. Given that Toby's death and the cause of it were reported in the local paper, I don't think I've hit on anything confidential. Yet.

"That's correct," Mattie says, apparently coming to the same conclusion I did, though I hear a note of hesitancy in her voice.

"Sharon Cochran seems convinced that her son's death was no accident," I say. "She thinks he was murdered."

"I know. She's called here a lot, and to the police department, too. Unfortunately, there's no evidence to support her claim."

"Did she tell you about his recent problems at school, and that he dropped out suddenly?"

"She did. It sounded like the boy had a severe case of depression."

There it was again, that tone of . . . hesitancy? No, more like doubt. "You're bothered by his death, too, aren't you?" I say, taking a stab in the dark.

Mattie doesn't answer right away, and I push on, eager to continue with the momentum I've built. "There was no evidence of prior drug use, was there? And no known connections to any other drug users?"

"Hildy," Mattie says finally. There is a tone of frustration in her voice and I fear I've pushed too hard. "I'm sorry, but I can't discuss the details of the case with you."

I say nothing, letting the silence between us build and do my work for me.

"But," Mattie says with a sigh, "you might want to talk

to Detective Bob Richmond. He was the detective assigned to the case, if I recall, though I don't think he got involved much. It was a clear-cut scenario." She sighs. "But if it helps, I can put in a word for you."

Bingo! "I'll take any help I can get, Mattie. Thank you. And at the risk of pushing my luck, can I ask you one more thing?"

"If it's about that file you gave me regarding your mother's case, I haven't had time to look it over. Sorry."

"No, it isn't that," I say, though in the back of my mind I had been wondering if she'd done anything with it. "I have Toby Cochran's laptop. His mother said I could take it. It's password protected, but after a few attempts at a password, it prompts for a fingerprint identification on a scanner built into the laptop. Would it be possible to fake Toby's finger using any fingerprints you have on file, so his mother and I can gain access?"

"Interesting question," Mattie says, and I'm heartened by the fact that she doesn't simply dismiss me right away. "I'm not sure what the answer is, but I'll check into it. Though I imagine it would have to be his mother making the request. I'll have to get back to you, if that's okay."

"That would be great! Thanks, Mattie. I really appreciate it."

"Just a thought, Hildy," Mattie says in a cautionary tone. "If you want Detective Richmond to reopen this case, it might be better if you don't mess with anything that could be considered evidence."

"I know," I say. "But I'm trying to find something that might be considered a smoking gun. I suspect the detective won't be inclined to reopen the case without it."

"True enough," Mattie says with a tone of resignation that lets me know I have my work cut out for me. "Keep in mind that the answers you get aren't always the ones you want."

"I've told his mother that, but I don't think she's willing to let it go. Not yet, anyway."

"Fair enough," Mattie says, and this time I hear a smile in her voice.

I give her my cell number so she can get back to me on the fingerprint issue, then I thank her again and hang up.

For the next couple of hours, I cruise the ER and help with some patient issues: a psych patient in need of placement, a homeless patient in need of pretty much anything I can offer her, and a family whose patriarch has just received a devastating diagnosis. While I'm helping with this last situation, my cell phone buzzes to let me know I have a call. I'm not able to take it, and when I check the phone later, I see that it was Mattie Winston calling back and that she has left me a voice mail message.

It is now one in the afternoon, a full hour past my intended leaving time, so I grab a ham and cheese sandwich from the cafeteria and eat it while I report off to Crystal at her desk. Before vacating my office, I listen to the voice mail Mattie left, my heart beating hard with anticipation. But all her message says is that she has spoken to Detective Richmond and I should call him. She has left a contact number, and I'm about to call it when I pause to think through the situation and what I'm going to say.

The fact that Mattie didn't address the fingerprint question in her message suggests to me that I'm not likely to get the answer I'm hoping for. And though I'm assuming she wants me to call Detective Richmond because he's willing to listen to me and reopen the Cochran case, when I think about the likelihood of that happening this easily, I realize it's unlikely. The more probable scenario is that Detective

Richmond will tell me to mind my own business, in polite, politically correct terms, of course.

I think again about how easy it is to dismiss someone over the phone as opposed to face-to-face and decide that a call isn't my best approach. It's time to put some of my conniving foster skills to work. I gather up the laptop, clock out, and head for my car—after a stop in the restroom to fix my hair and makeup.

Chapter Eight

Ten minutes later I'm standing in the lobby of the Sorenson police station, listening as a dispatcher named Heidi calls back to Detective Richmond to inform him that he has a visitor who wants to discuss a case. I see the dispatcher shoot me surreptitious looks a couple of times and answer some unheard questions from the other end with vague "uh-huhs" and "unh-unhs." I'm prepared to be turned away when she disconnects the call and says, "Detective Richmond will be out in just a minute."

"Thank you." I consider taking a seat, knowing that "just a minute" might mean anything from thirty seconds to half an hour or more, but decide to stand for now. Fortunately, I don't have to wait long, and I add a mental mark for punctuality in the pro column under Detective Richmond's name.

He greets me with a formal, "Ms. Schneider?" His hands are stuffed into his pants pockets as he crosses the room toward me, and they stay there.

It's been a few weeks since I last saw him, but he looks just as I remember him. He is tall, a little over six feet, and has hazel-colored eyes and an etched, well-lived face. "Hello, Detective Richmond. I don't know if you remember me, but we talked a few times briefly about that human trafficking case a few weeks ago?"

"I remember," he says, though I can't tell if he really does or if he's just saying so to be polite.

"Did Mattie Winston talk to you about me? About the case I'm working on?" I see the corners of his mouth twitch up slightly and know that something I've said or done has amused him for some reason, though I don't know what or why.

"She did," he says. "Let's go somewhere where we can talk."

Heidi buzzes us through the door, which Detective Richmond holds open for me. I pause in the hallway on the other side, since I'm unsure of where to go, and wait for him to take the lead. He does so, and his long-legged stride forces me into a half run to keep up as we move down a long hallway marked with doors. I see one with a name plate for Chief Hanson, but none of the other doors bear any form of identification. Some of them are open, and a quick peek inside reveals various crowded office arrangements, most with at least two desks. I'm a little out of breath by the time Detective Richmond turns down a short hall and opens another door, waving me through it.

I'm momentarily taken aback. I was expecting to be taken to an office like the ones we passed, but instead I find myself in a conference room. There is a large table occupying the middle of the room, and there are several cushioned chairs positioned around it. The décor is a hideous mix of colors and design, but the chair I opt to sit in—at the head of the table, since that's where Richmond indicates I should sit—is reasonably comfortable.

He takes a seat near the door, laces his hands together, and leans forward, arms on the table. "I understand you have some questions about Toby Cochran," he says. "His mother attends a support group that you run?"

"She does, yes," I say, answering the last question first. "It's a grief support group. And yes, I have some questions about Toby's death, as does his mother."

"I know his mother is having some difficulty accepting her son's death," Richmond says. I like his voice; it's calm, deep, and rich. "But the circumstances surrounding it seem straightforward."

I scrutinize his face, trying to see some hint of what I think I just heard in his voice. It was subtle, a slight inflection, but I feel certain I heard it. And then there is his word choice. His expression, however, is implacable; not surprising, given his occupation. Cops are taught to keep their masks firmly in place, to not show emotion, and to not react. I decide to take a leap of faith.

"The circumstances *seem* straightforward?" I pause long enough to see if I get a reaction. There is the tiniest muscle tic in one eyelid. Not much, but I'll take it. "You don't believe his death was straightforward at all, do you?" He opens his mouth to answer, but before he can utter a syllable, I add, "Neither does Mattie. There's something about this case that bothers the both of you, isn't there?"

I watch his eyes narrow and see that subtle twitch at the corners of his mouth again. "Ms. Schneider," he says in a tone of patient tolerance.

"Please call me Hildy," I say. "I'm a pretty laid-back person, not formal at all. And 'Ms. Schneider' makes me feel like some lonely old spinster."

Sadly, I'm getting close enough in age and relationship status—or rather the lack thereof—to qualify for this label, and as a result I'm a little sensitive about it.

This time it's not just a twitch. Richmond breaks into a full smile, and it lights up his face. "Fair enough," he says. "You can call me Bob, and I'll call you Hildy. Deal?"

"Deal."

"And yes, you are correct in your assumption that there

is something about the Cochran case that bothers Mattie. Unfortunately, it's nothing more than a feeling at this point. The evidence we have *is* straightforward."

I notice he didn't include himself in the bothered category, but I feel certain he's on the list. "You reviewed the case, then?" I say. "Because Mattie told me she didn't think you were very involved in it since the circumstances . . . um . . . seemed straightforward." I put a bit of skeptical emphasis on those last two words.

"That's true," he admits. "If foul play isn't suspected, the case doesn't require the investigative efforts of a homicide detective. The ME's office and any police officers on the scene can make that determination."

"And they did so in this case?"

Bob nods, but quickly adds, "Even so, I did look into the case, because Mattie was bothered by it. She couldn't say why, though, and I didn't find anything irregular, so I haven't delved any deeper."

I give him what I hope is a coy look, though a foster sib from years ago once told me the expression made me look demented. I've practiced it in a mirror since then, and I think I have it down now, but if someone comes into the room bearing a straitjacket, I'll know I still have work to do.

"So, tell me," I say in what I hope is a slightly flirtatious tone, "what do I have to do to get you to delve deeper?"

Richmond . . . *Bob*, I correct myself, blushes, coughs, and looks away from me, reacting to my efforts like a teenage boy. "I . . . um . . . there isn't . . ." he stammers.

Mattie Winston picked up on my interest in the detective right away when we worked together a few weeks ago. Apparently, subtlety isn't my strong suit. I recall her telling me at the time that he didn't have a lot of experience in the romance department, so I chalk up his current stammering and awkwardness to that. I realize that if I'm going to have any hope of making progress on that level with him, I'll probably have to take the lead.

Then again, maybe I haven't honed my coy look after all, and he's stammering and glancing away because I look idiotic and crazy.

I reach down into my briefcase and pull out Toby's drawing of the footbridge. "Does this look like any place you know?" I ask, sliding the paper over to him.

He picks it up, studies it, and shakes his head. "Why?"

I tell him about the other drawings in Toby's room, and his mother's comments about his recent fixation with this bridge scene. "Something happened to the boy at school, and his mother was never able to get him to talk about it. But it had to have been something big, something significant. He obsessed over this drawing during that time, which makes me think it might be relevant. The kid had a full-ride scholarship that included his housing, and he belonged to a fraternity on campus. He had his whole education mapped out and paid for, and yet he suddenly got up and walked away from it all. Why?"

"Drugs?" Bob offers. It's the obvious answer, and one I knew would be coming.

"Except he didn't have any marks on his arms, from what I understand. And there was no evidence he was using IV drugs prior to the night of his death."

"These kids use other routes," Bob says. "IV drugs are one step in a long line of progression. Unfortunately for this kid, it was the last step."

"I take it he tested positive for other drugs?"

Bob starts to shake his head before he remembers who he's talking to. "I'm not at liberty to share that information," he says, sounding genuinely apologetic.

"His mother can request the autopsy report, can she not?"

Bob gives me a grudging shrug. "Yes, she can."

"Then I'll have her ask for one immediately. She'll share

the information with me, so you don't have to tell me now. But if you don't, I'll just come back and bug you some more."

Bob's lips twitch again. "You are a very persistent woman," he says.

"That's just one of my many redeeming qualities," I say, and before Bob can respond, I bombard him with questions. "I'm curious to know if you were able to lift fingerprints from the syringe you found in Toby's arm. I'd also like to know if you were able to analyze the heroin, to trace its origin, and with that, the seller. Also, were there any signs of a struggle? Did you find anyone who witnessed Toby's final moments, or who might've been with him prior to those final moments?"

Bob leans back in his chair, fingers laced together, hands behind his head. He narrows his eyes at me, and it's all I can do not to look away. But I'm determined to hold my ground with him.

After a good thirty seconds or more of the stare-down, he says, "You're not going to let this go, are you?"

I don't give him an answer. I just smile.

"Fine," he says with a sigh of resignation. He brings his arms down, resting them on the table, fingers still laced together. "I'll take another look at things."

"There's one more thing," I say, and Bob rolls his eyes at this. "Actually, two more things," I add with a grin. "I have the boy's laptop. Did you guys look at it at all?"

"No," Bob says, looking abashed. "There didn't seem to be any need to do that. Why? Did you find something on it?"

"It's password protected. His mother and I made a few attempts, but we weren't successful. And after several failed attempts, the computer prompts us for a fingerprint identification. I was wondering if it would be possible to create Toby's fingerprints from what you have on file?"

Bob arches one brow, looking intrigued. "That's an interesting idea," he says. "Give me the laptop and I'll see what I can do."

I shake my head and smile at him. "No way," I say. "The only way I'm handing over his laptop is if you let me be in on the examination of it and the investigation of this case."

"I can't do that," Richmond says with mild exasperation.

"Too bad, so sad," I say in a singsong voice.

"But I *can* arrest you for obstruction or some such," he grumbles.

"Go ahead," I say with a shrug.

During my childhood years I spent enough time getting hauled into police stations and threatened with juvie that I'm not fazed by his threat. I reach over and retrieve the drawing, sliding it back inside my briefcase. Then I stand, preparing to leave the room, wondering if Bob will make good on his threat.

"Hold on," he says. "You said you had two things. The laptop is one; what's the other?"

It's the perfect opening. *It's now or never,* I tell myself. And I take the plunge.

"It has nothing to do with the case. I was wondering if you would have dinner with me sometime?" My heart is pounding so hard I fear it will beat its way out of my chest.

Judging from the stunned look on Bob's face, this isn't what he was expecting. "I . . . um . . . it isn't . . ." He is blushing to the roots of his hair, and his stammering attempts at an answer jangle my nerves.

"For Pete's sake," I say, mildly irritated and a lot nervous. "Here's the deal. I'm a single woman who's approaching the downhill slide to forty, and I've never been married. I don't date much, and I've learned to be happy on my own.

But I find you attractive. There's something about you that intrigues me, and I'd like to explore it some more. Maybe it will go somewhere, maybe it won't. But life is too short not to try. All I'm asking for is a dinner. I'll treat, so worst-case scenario you get a free meal out of the deal."

Bob cocks his head to one side, arches his brows, and smiles. "I haven't dated much, either," he says. "And I admit, I find your straightforward approach to this refreshing. I'm not very good at the games people play."

"I'm very good at them," I say with a wink and a smile. "But I promise not to play any games with you. What do you say? Can we go somewhere for dinner?"

"Sure."

"Tonight?" I wouldn't blame Bob if he's surprised by my brazenness, because I'm rather stunned myself.

"I can do that," Bob says without hesitation.

"Do you have a favorite restaurant here in town?"

"I do. Pesto Change-o."

"Excellent choice. Should we meet there, or do you want me to pick you up?"

"We can meet there. I'm on call tonight, so I need to have my own wheels."

"Fair enough. How does six o'clock sound?"

"I will see you then."

I give him a nod and a smile, and then I leave the room. I walk down the hall and out to the lobby area with my shoulders straight and my head held high. With a little finger wave to Heidi, I exit the building, walk over to where my car is parked, and step onto the grassy area in front of it. Then I bend over and promptly puke up my lunch.

Chapter Nine

I pray there aren't any cameras focused on the parking lot, even though I know the odds of that being the case are woefully small. I can only hope that Detective Richmond won't ever view the footage and see me barfing in front of my car. After wiping my mouth with a tissue I find in my jacket pocket, I climb into my car and head for home, detouring long enough to hit the drive-through at the local Mickey D's to get a soda so I can wash the taste of barf from my mouth.

It's only two thirty in the afternoon, so I have plenty of time to prepare for my dinner date. As I'm queueing my way through the drive-through line, I reach up to adjust my rearview mirror and leave a smudge on the glass. This gives me a brainstorm of an idea.

As soon as I'm home, I let Roscoe out into the backyard. He meanders around, sniffing various areas, and finally lifts his leg. Once he's back inside, I log on to my personal laptop and do some research. Then I rummage around my house and gather supplies: a compact containing facial powder, another containing four shades of eye shadow, two makeup brushes—one large and one small—a desktop tape dispenser, and a roll of packing tape. I also grab an ordinary lead pencil, a small paring knife, and a box of gloves and a scalpel I lifted from the hospital sometime in the past. One never knows when one might need latex gloves and a scalpel, right? Once I have everything gathered, I place a call to Sharon Cochran, hoping I won't wake her.

She answers on the second ring and sounds chipper enough to ease my mind. When I say that I want to come by again, she hesitates, clearly reluctant. Once I explain why, she relents.

It is now after three thirty, and I hurry over there. Sharon must have been watching for me, because she opens the front door before I have a chance to knock. She is dressed in a robe, and her hair is messy from sleep.

"Hello again," she says.

"Hi. I hope I didn't wake you."

"No, you timed it perfectly, in fact. I'd just gotten out of bed when you called."

I breathe a sigh of relief. "Thanks for letting me do this."

"Do you really think it will work?"

I shrug. "I'm not sure, but I figure we have nothing to lose by trying." She waves a hand toward the stairs, and I head up them with her on my heels. Inside Toby's bedroom, I look around and eye the gaming console. I point to it. "That's a good place to start, I think."

Sharon watches me as I walk over to the dresser and start removing items from my bag. I put on some gloves, open the facial powder compact, and run the larger makeup brush over its surface. Then I pick up one of the game cassettes. Holding the brush just above the dark colored label on the game cassette, I twirl it between my fingers.

Small bits of the powder drop onto the surface of the cassette, heavier than I want. I blow gently across the surface and then examine it, hoping to find a fingerprint. But there is nothing.

I scan the other game cassettes and dismiss them for now. They all have dark, colorful labels on them, and I realize I'm likely to get the same results. I move on and examine the controller next. It, like the console, is light beige in color. I survey the eye shadows, the darkest of which is a sable brown shade, and dismiss them. Instead, I take out the pencil and the paring knife.

Sharon is standing off to one side, watching me, and when I take the knife out, she takes an involuntary step back, looking wary. I smile at her in what I hope is a reassuring manner and then walk over to Toby's desk. I grab a blank piece of copy paper, lay it out flat on the desktop, and then put the paring knife to the lead in the pencil. It takes me a few tries to figure out the right angle and amount of pressure, but eventually I create a tiny pile of fine lead scrapings on the paper. I go back to the dresser, disconnect the controller from the console, and carry it over to the desk using as little contact as I can. Then I take out the smaller makeup brush, which has soft sable bristles on it. I splay the bristles by pushing the brush against my gloved hand and then dip them into the lead shavings. Holding the brush over the controller, I use the same twirling motion I used with the compact brush. Once I've managed to get a fine layer of the dark dust on the surface, I gently brush it off.

To my delight, I see four distinct areas where the lead dust has stuck to the surface in patterns resembling fingerprints: two on the left and two on the right. There is enough detail visible that I can discern a line running through both of the prints on the right.

"Did Toby have a scar of some sort on one of his thumbs?" I ask Sharon.

"Yes, he did," she says, a hint of excitement in her voice. "His right thumb. He sliced it quite badly once trying to remove the partially opened top on a tin can. Had to have four stitches in it."

I feel an empathetic twinge in my own thumb for a

second, having done something similar once myself when I was younger, though my injury hadn't been as bad as Toby's. My hands are shaking with nervous excitement as I set the brush down and take out my roll of packing tape. I pull out a short length of it and try to rip it on the serrated edge of the dispenser, but it's too short a piece. Seeing a pair of scissors in the pencil holder on Toby's desk, I use them to cut my piece, taking care not to touch the center of the rectangle I end up with. Then I place the cut piece of tape over the smallest of the prints on the right side of the controller, trying hard to get the tape down without wrinkling it or smearing the lead dust. I'm only partially successful, and I curse silently to myself. I lift it anyway, and then stick it down on a piece of plain copy paper.

"Wow," Sharon says from over my shoulder, seeing what I've done. "That's amazing."

"I'm afraid it might not be clear enough," I say, rolling my shoulders. "I'll try to do better with the second one."

My second attempt does go better, and when I have placed my tape on the piece of paper, there are clearly visible arches and whorls visible in the print. I suspect Toby used a finger on his right hand to supply a print for his computer, most likely the index finger. The scanner is located on the right side just below the keyboard, and given the angle that would be required to use it, it would have been awkward to use his thumb. Despite this assumption, I go ahead and retrieve the left-hand prints as well, figuring the practice can't hurt. Judging from the size of the prints, and considering the way a gamer holds a controller, I feel certain they are thumbprints. Hoping to get an index or middle finger, I turn the controller over and repeat the whole process on the bottom side.

Once again, I'm able to obtain prints, though only the right one looks clear enough and full enough to be of use.

Based on its position on the controller, I surmise that it's the index finger. On a whim, I decide to back the tape lift of this print with another piece of tape, creating a clear, see-through print. This takes some finagling on my part and some assistance from Sharon with the tape roll and cutting, but eventually we manage.

With that done, I look around the room and see a water bottle on the bedside table. I'm not sure if the plastic surface will work well for harboring a print, so I'm pleasantly surprised when I see one emerge. Unfortunately, my attempts to transfer it to the tape make it come out smeared and unclear.

Next, I try the remote control for the TV. The back of it, which is where his fingers would have touched, assuming he used his thumb to push the buttons, is black. The dark lead dust won't show up, and the face powder and eye shadows reveal only smears.

I stand in the middle of the room, looking around, searching for other options. My eyes settle on the closet door, which is painted white. Carefully, I fold the paper with the lead dust on it and carry it over to the door. After setting the paper on the floor, I dip my brush in and start dusting the edge of the door. To my delight, I see four clear prints emerge close to one another in a spot where Toby must have grabbed the edge of the door. Since the closet door handle is on the left side and the door opens swinging to the right, I determine these must be prints from his right hand. I lift all of them at once with the tape, using a long piece, and then place it on a new piece of copy paper.

Satisfied, I turn to Sharon. "I think I've got what I came for. If these don't work, I don't know what will."

"You didn't bring the laptop with you?" Sharon asks.

"No, sorry. I left it at home." I don't tell her that I left it behind because I was afraid she might ask for it back.

Sharon looks crestfallen.

"I'll let you know if it works," I tell her. "I'll try it out as soon as I get back to the house."

"Okay." Her expression is both hopeful and fearful. I imagine she's excited over the possibility of accessing the contents of the laptop, but also nervous about what we'll find on it.

I thank her profusely and take my leave, anxious to get back to the house. By the time I get there, it's already close to five o'clock, and I don't have much time before my dinner date with Bob. My logical brain is telling me to put the fingerprints aside and get ready for dinner, but I'm far too excited to be logical. Roscoe watches me with patient curiosity, no doubt wondering when I will shift my attention to him.

I take Toby's laptop out of my briefcase and set it on the kitchen island. I open it and try a fingerprint at the first password prompt, pressing one of the paper-backed tape prints over the sensor, thinking that perhaps there is no actual password, just the fingerprint. It doesn't work, and I'm not sure if it's because my logic is faulty or my fingerprint is. I go ahead and type in passwords until the computer tells me to use a fingerprint, and then I try the same print again. It still doesn't work. I try again, repositioning it slightly, but no luck. Next, I try prints of other fingers, having started with the right index as the most logical choice. When those don't work, I try a right thumbprint, even turning it sideways when I realize that position would be the most comfortable. Nothing.

Frustrated, I think about the scanner and what it might be looking for. Is it heat sensitive? Does it require more of a 3-D image? Is the coloring off?

I'm about to give up when I see the one clear print I made with tape on both sides. I look at it a moment, envisioning it as a finger, and even wrap it around my own index finger. But when I do that I realize that the ridges of my finger are likely to be mixed in with those of Toby's. I grab a glove from my copped supply and pull it on. Then I wrap the clear print around the end of my index finger, positioning it as close as possible to where my own print would be. Holding the edges of it with my left hand, I place my finger with the tape on it over the scanner and press down. I keep it there a second, and when nothing happens, I roll my finger slightly from one side to the other.

The computer desktop springs to life, making me gasp. I stare at it for a moment, and then clap my hands together and yell, "Yippee!" like a three-year-old who's just been offered a cookie. For a moment I can't think of what to do next, but then realize I don't want to have to go through the fingerprint debacle again. I was lucky to get it to work this time, but there is no guarantee it will work again. I spend the next few minutes figuring out how to change the password to something of my choosing and disabling the fingerprint scanner.

When that's done, I scan the task bar icons and spy one for an email program. I launch it and watch as the program opens, but then I hear my front door open, so I shut the program down and close the computer.

"Hi, Hildy." It's P.J., and Roscoe immediately abandons his spot at my feet and hurries over to her, tail wagging with enthusiasm. P.J. bends down and kisses him on top of his head, her dark red hair blending perfectly with Roscoe's fur.

"Hello, P.J."

"Sorry I didn't come walk Roscoe right after school. My stupid mom made me go shopping with her." She rolls her eyes and Roscoe closes his in heavenly bliss as P.J. absent-mindedly scratches him beneath his chin.

"No problem."

I see her attention is riveted on the laptop sitting in front of me. "Did you get a new computer?" she asks.

"No, it belongs to someone else. I'm just borrowing it."

P.J. eyes me with suspicion. "Why?"

"Something I'm working on." I glance at my watch and before she has time to ask another question, I say, "Listen, if you want to walk Roscoe now, I'm sure he wouldn't mind. I need to be somewhere in half an hour and I'll probably be gone for a couple of hours."

"Where are you going?" P.J. has very little understanding of the social niceties most people ascribe to. That, along with her high intelligence and insatiable curiosity, makes for some awkward moments at times.

"I'm meeting someone for dinner," I say, not wanting to elaborate. "And I need to hurry so I'm not late."

"Where are you going to eat?"

"At Pesto Change-o."

"Yummy." She smiles, looking beatific for a second, and then her eyes narrow. "That's only five minutes away. You have plenty of time."

"I need to change," I tell her. With anyone else I'd simply leave the room and escape this interrogation, but I don't want to leave P.J. alone with Toby's laptop. I wouldn't put it past her to try to look at it. Nor would I put it past her to figure out the password I used: Roscoe. But if I pick it up and carry it with me into the bedroom, that will arouse her curiosity even more.

P.J. eyes me from head to toe—an admittedly brief scan—and narrows those eyes even more. "You look fine," she says, taking in my work clothes: basic slacks, a blouse, and a blazer. "Unless . . ." Her eyes widen and she gives me a sly smile. "Do you have a date?"

"What? No. Well . . . maybe. But not really." Damn the girl. She has me flustered.

"It's about time," P.J. says with a hint of disgust in her voice. "You've been alone way too long."

"Some people like being alone," I tell her. This rings

false even to my own ear, and judging from the look P.J. gives me, she isn't buying it, either.

"Come on," she says, heading into my bedroom with Roscoe trailing along behind her. I follow them, relieved the issue of the laptop has been momentarily resolved. P.J. walks over to my closet, flings open the double folding doors, and then stands there a moment, staring at the things inside. I have my eye set on a pair of black slacks and a dark, burgundy blouse, thinking that the darker colors are slimming, but P.J. reaches into the closet and pulls out a navy blue, knee-length, A-line skirt and a blouse that's slightly tailored and made out of a soft, shiny fabric in a lighter shade of blue.

"Blue is a good color for you," she says, tossing the items on my bed. "It sets off your eyes." She bends down, grabs a pair of beige heels from the floor, and sets them in front of me. "These will add an inch or two to your height," she says. She stares at my face for a few seconds, and then adds, "You should refresh your makeup. You look kind of tired."

I'd be stunned by her presumptuousness and bluntness if not for the fact that I've experienced it before. And I've learned from those past experiences that P.J. has a good eye for these kinds of things. She looks at Roscoe, says, "Come on big guy. Let's go for a walk," and leaves my room.

I watch the two of them long enough to make sure P.J. heads for the front door and doesn't give the laptop a second look before I start dressing.

The clothing change only takes a few minutes, and as I look at myself in the mirror I realize that P.J. is right about the color. I remember when I bought the skirt, which was more of a midi length on me at the time. Few items of clothing fit me off the rack, because I'm too short for most adult styles and too round to shop in the kids' sections. Thanks to my physical shortcomings—in the most literal sense of that word—I have to have most of my clothes tailored. Fortunately, I have Tamela, a talented seamstress and one of the kids I spent several years with in a group home. Tamela lives in a town about an hour away, and she alters my outfits for me for a nominal fee. She also serves as one of the few people in my life who I can call a friend. Because of our shared history, we understand each other in a way other people can't. Tamela gets me. She understands why I occasionally filch items that aren't mine and have no memory of it later, and why I hide some of the food I have in my house, even though I'm the only one who lives here. It's hard for me to make friends with people who haven't been in the system, though I do a grand job of faking it much of the time, if I do say so myself. My social work training taught me that.

What it didn't teach me was how to fix my hair into something that doesn't look like a flyaway rat's nest, which is what it resembles now. I give it a quick spray and try to tame it into submission, but my cowlicks—the closest thing to body my hair has naturally—refuse to stay down. After a few minutes of frustration, I give up and adopt an if-you-can't-beat-them attitude about things and use my fingers to make the rest of my hair stand up in a borderline punk style. It doesn't work as well on a thirty-something woman as it would on a younger woman, but for now it's the best do I can do. I touch up my makeup, pack up Toby's laptop in my briefcase, and hurry out before P.J. has returned, relieved she won't be casting her critical eye on me one last time. I don't lock my door. Sorenson is a reasonably safe town, and the people who live in this neighborhood do a good job of watching out for one another.

I make it to the restaurant with two minutes to spare, feeling excited about the evening ahead for a couple of reasons. One, Pesto Change-o has amazingly good food. I could do without the magic show its owner, Giorgio, likes to put on, but I'm willing to put up with it if it means getting a delicious Italian meal. The second reason I'm ramped up is that the dinner is a date of sorts. I mean, it is a date, right? I asked a man out to dinner and he accepted. Doesn't that make it a date? I realize there is another perspective.

I've intrigued Bob with the Cochran case, and I have the boy's computer. Did Bob agree to the dinner simply to work on me some more about handing over the laptop? Or is he honestly interested in me on a more personal level?

Time will tell, I suppose, and I try to convince myself that it isn't that important, however it turns out. Nothing ventured, nothing gained, right?

I try hard to assume an air of relaxed indifference, but as I park and get out of my car to head inside the restaurant, my legs feel frighteningly wobbly.

Chapter Ten

The aromas of basil, oregano, garlic, and tomatoes make my mouth water the moment I enter the restaurant. It's a busy Friday night and there's a good crowd here already. I'm not sure if Bob has arrived, since I don't know what kind of car he drives, so I scan the existing diners. I don't see him, though it's only a minute past the hour.

Giorgio comes up to me, smiling broadly and producing a paper bouquet of flowers from his sleeve.

"I'm here to meet someone," I tell him. "Mr. Bob Richmond?"

"Here I am," says a voice behind me. "Sorry I'm a little late. I hope you haven't been waiting long."

I turn around and smile at him, craning my neck so much it lets out a loud crack. "I just got here myself," I tell him.

"Let me show you to a special table," Giorgio says. This makes it sound as if we are getting special treatment, but I know from past experience that Giorgio says this to everyone he seats, regardless of where their table is. Ours is one of the nicer ones, however, a square table for two next to one of the windows, covered with one of Giorgio's clichéd red and white checked tablecloths.

Bob is gentleman enough to pull out a chair for me, but

I suspect part of this gesture stems from his desire to be in the seat that gives him a view of the entrance. As a cop, this would likely be second nature to him. It's an impulse I not only understand but share. I like having a broad view of my surroundings for a different reason than Bob, most likely, but the underlying principles are the same.

"May I bring you some wine, and perhaps an appetizer?" Giorgio asks. "I have a special tonight on stuffed mushrooms."

"I would love the stuffed mushrooms," I say. "And I'll have a glass of your house red."

Bob's brow furrows and he says, "Just water for me, I'm afraid. I'm on call tonight. But the mushrooms sound great."

"Back in a flash," Giorgio says, producing a literal flash in his hand before he scurries off.

"I see you brought your briefcase," Bob says, arching one eyebrow in question.

"Yes, I did. I have Toby's laptop in it."

"It's a bit risky to be carrying it around, isn't it?"

I shrug. "I don't want to let it out of my sight."

Bob gives me a curious look. "Your interest in this case seems a little . . ." He trails off, not finishing the sentence.

"Over the top?" I say with a smile. Bob shrugs. "I don't like things that are left hanging. And I have a personal interest in cases like this."

"You mean because of your support group?"

I straighten the napkin-wrapped silverware so that it is perpendicular to the table's edge. "It's not just that," I say, glancing out the window. "I have an unsolved case of my own."

I look at him and he tilts his head, giving me a curious look. He says nothing. I figure he's willing to see if I want to offer more information rather than him ask for it, and I appreciate this consideration.

"It's my mother," I say, looking away again. "She was murdered, and her killer was never found."

"Damn," Bob says, sounding sincere. "When?"

"A long time ago." I attempt a smile that I know falls short. "Like almost thirty ago. It's so cold, it's frostbitten."

"How old were you when it happened?"

"Seven."

"And your father?"

"I don't know who he is," I tell him with another of those forced smiles. "My mother . . . um . . . well, there's no easy way to say this. She was a hooker."

Bob's eyes grow big at this and he leans back in his seat, staring at me like he just saw me appear out of thin air. Granted, this is Pesto Change-o, but not even Giorgio is that good.

"I suppose I've just changed your opinion of me," I say, feeling myself blush.

"I hadn't really formed one. Well, not much of one," he equivocates. "Just that you're stubborn and determined." He pauses, and I see the barest hint of a smile at the corners of his mouth. "And a bit of a manipulator," he adds finally. "But beyond that . . ." He shrugs.

I'm tempted to object to his impression of me, but I don't. He has me pegged well so far.

Giorgio arrives with our drinks, a basket of warm Italian bread, and a dish of whipped garlic butter. He informs us the mushrooms will be out in a few minutes and then asks if we are ready to order. Neither of us has looked at the menus, but we both say yes at the same time. Clearly Bob has his favorites here, the same as I do. He orders cheese ravioli with a side of sausage, and I go with the lasagna, though it's always a toss-up for me between that and the fettucine Alfredo. We both opt for ranch dressing on our salads, though the raspberry vinaigrette does give me pause.

As soon as Giorgio's gone, I take a big gulp of my wine. Bob has hardly taken his eyes off me since we sat down, and I'm not sure if I should be worried or flattered. "Tell me a little about yourself," I say, slipping into my social worker role. "Are you a native Sorensonian?"

Bob shakes his head. "I grew up in Racine but came here for a police job. I figured a small town like this would be a good place to get my feet wet before I moved up to the big, bad city." He huffs a small laugh. "Never made it to the big city, though. Worked my way through the ranks here and became a homicide detective. And then I tried to retire four years ago."

"I take it you didn't like retirement?" I say, snagging a piece of bread and buttering it.

"Oh, I liked it well enough, though it was more of a semiretirement, actually. I picked up shifts from time to time, and it was one of those times when I met Mattie Winston. It wasn't long after that when I got shot, and that changed my entire life."

"Mattie mentioned something about you getting shot," I say. "When did it happen? I've been at the hospital here for a little over three years now, and I don't remember you coming in through the ER."

"It's been three and a half years, give or take," he says. He helps himself to some bread, slathering it with a thick coat of the garlic butter. "Did you move here three years ago?"

I realize that as a cop, Bob Richmond is as well trained—maybe better—as I am in getting people to talk about themselves, making conversation, and diverting the subject away from himself and back to me. It's going to make for an interesting give-and-take, I think.

"Yes," I say. "I moved here from the Milwaukee area. I have no family attachments anywhere, so . . ." I let the rest of the thought hang out there, allowing Bob to either fill in the blanks with whatever he wants or ask more questions.

"Milwaukee to here?" he says. "That seems an odd move. Sorenson isn't what you'd call a big attraction. Why leave a city the size of Milwaukee for a small town? And why Sorenson?"

"Are you interrogating me, Detective?" I ask in a teasing tone.

He blushes and says, "Sorry," in a way that makes me think he truly was just curious. Though I'm betting he did a bit of research on me before meeting me here. What detective worthy of his badge wouldn't? I'm also betting he didn't find much. Outside of my juvie record, which is supposed to be sealed, I've lived a relatively low-profile life.

"I'm teasing you," I say with a smile. "Go ahead and ask what you want, and I'll answer anything I'm comfortable with. As for why I left Milwaukee, it had too many bad memories for me. I spent most of my time there in the foster system, and I ended up in some rather dicey living situations. It got better once I was out on my own, and I was happy enough while going to school. After that I worked for the county for a while, and then switched to a health care setting. I found I liked that better, so I stuck with it." I pause and take a sip of my wine. Bob, in good-listening fashion, takes a drink of water, prolonging the silence between us.

"But Milwaukee never really felt like home to me," I go on, letting him win this clash of silence. "And when I was looking into my mother's murder, which I suppose is one of the reasons I stayed in Milwaukee as long as I did, I discovered that she had a client, someone who she saw regularly, who was from here."

"Really?" Bob says. I can tell his detective antennae are twitching. "Who?"

"I don't have a name," I tell him with a regretful look. "All I know is that inside a box of my mother's things that I went through a few years ago, I found some old letters from this person. He mentioned Sorenson often, and the envelopes had a Sorenson postmark; that's how I know he's from here. Unfortunately, they didn't have a return address."

"He didn't sign the letters?" Bob asks.

"Oh, he did, but not with his full name. Every letter was signed the same way: 'Can't wait to see you again, R.'"

"Just the letter?" Bob says. I nod. "Hmm, kind of intriguing." I smile. He smiles, too, but after a few seconds, his fades. His eyes narrow and his head cocks to one side. "Wait a minute," he says slowly. "How old are you?"

I feign surprise and a hint of appalled indignation. "I'm thirty-six. Why?"

"How old was your mother when she gave birth to you?"

"Eighteen. I was her second pregnancy. Her first was when she was sixteen and still living with her parents. They wrote her off when it happened, banished her from their home. They were strict Iowan farm people, and very religious. Can you imagine? Being thrust out into the world on your own at the age of sixteen? And pregnant, to boot?" I shake my head in disgust, overcome with the feelings of anger and indignity I feel whenever I tell anyone this story.

"Have you ever met your grandparents?" Bob asks.

"No, and I have no desire to do so. Not that they'd be willing to see me. Though no one ever said anything about it, I know enough now about how the foster system works to know that someone has to have approached them back when my mother died to see if they would take me. And it's obvious what their answer was. If they were able to toss their daughter out the way they did, I'm sure they felt no love for me, her bastard child."

Bob flinches slightly, an almost imperceptible reaction that I doubt he knows he showed.

"Sorry if I come across as crude," I say, hoping to soften the blow. "But I get so angry every time I talk about what my mother's parents did, the way they treated her. It's their fault that she lived the life she did. It's their fault she died. And it's their fault I ended up in the system."

"Do you know what happened to your mother's first baby?"

"Stillborn. Or at least that's what my mother told me. She often said I had a big sister who was up in heaven looking out for me."

"And the only potential family connection you have left is the man who is your father?" Bob says. Something in his tone alerts me to a change in his demeanor. He doesn't sound as sympathetic as he did a few moments ago.

I shrug. "I know it's a long shot, and the odds are that if I did find him he'd want nothing to do with me."

"You think this man who wrote the letters and signed them with an R might be the guy?"

"It's possible. He seemed to know my mother well. And if he isn't the guy, he might know who is."

"But if she was seeing multiple men, she might not have known who your father was."

"She wasn't always hooking," I say, feeling oddly defensive. "There were periods of time when she tried to make things work with a regular job, and that was the case when she got pregnant with me. Or so she told me. She said she was seeing only one guy at the time. She called him her special guy, and she always told me they were in love. But I think he was a sugar daddy, and the sugar stopped when she got pregnant. Maybe he was married. Who knows?"

Bob scrutinizes me. "If your mother was alive today, she'd be, what . . . fifty-four or so?"

I nod.

"Which happens to be close to my age," Bob says. "I'm fifty-two."

"Really?" I'm genuinely surprised. I figured he was older than me by several years, given his talk of retirement, but I know cops who retired after twenty-five years and were in their early twenties when they started. I pegged Bob as one of those and thought he was in his late forties.

"And my name, my legal name, is Robert Richmond," he says, folding his arms over his chest and eyeing me with suspicion. "Two Rs for you to pick from."

It takes me a moment to understand what he's getting at. When I do, I'm quick to disabuse him of the idea. "No, no, no," I say. "I don't think you might be the mystery man."

"You don't?" he says. "I wondered at the age difference when you asked me to dinner. Thought it a bit odd."

"To be honest, I thought you were five years or so younger than you are," I tell him. "And age is not an issue for me anyway."

"Right," Bob says, clearly not convinced.

A waitress shows up with our mushrooms and our salads, and I can tell she senses the awkwardness at our table. Her attempts to be light and cheerful fall as flat as a punctured balloon. She hurries off, appearing eager to escape the miasma of tension surrounding us.

"I know you can't be R," I tell Bob, leaning across the table toward him. I grab the large fork in the dish of sizzling mushrooms and spear one of them, moving it onto my plate. Then I spear a second one and put it on his.

"Is that so?"

"It is." I smile and wink at him. Then I dole out two more mushrooms, one to him and one to me. "I saw him once, you see," I go on. "Not up close and not very clearly, but I saw him well enough to know that he wasn't nearly as tall as you. And his feet were a lot smaller."

Bob is still staring at me with that suspicious look on his face, but as I fork out the last four mushrooms, divvying them up between us, I see his gaze briefly divert as the luscious aroma wafts up toward his face.

When I'm done, I lean back in my seat and smile. "I invited you out to dinner for one reason only," I say. "Because I find you attractive and want to get to know you better. That's it."

"What about the Cochran thing?" he says. "You didn't invite me to dinner hoping it would give you another chance to try to convince me to look into the case?"

I start to say no reflexively, but I catch myself. "Okay, so two reasons," I admit with a sheepish smile. "But the Cochran thing is totally secondary. I asked Mattie Winston about you several weeks ago, when I first met you during the Paulsen case."

Bob winces briefly when I mention this earlier case— not surprising, since it involved the death of a young girl. He then stares at me, seeming to weigh my testimony like the experienced cop he is. Apparently, he finds my story truthful enough. Either that, or he can't bear to ignore the delicious smells emanating from the mushrooms a second longer. His arms unfold, his face relaxes, and he reaches for his fork.

"Okay, fair enough," he says, slicing into one of the mushrooms with the side of his fork.

I put a bite of one into my mouth and close my eyes for a moment, savoring the flavors. "Oh my, these are good," I say after I've swallowed.

Bob is staring at me again, but his expression is one of amusement now. He takes a bite himself, letting it roll around in his mouth.

"You know," I say, deciding to take advantage of his momentary gustatory ecstasy, "I don't really need you to look into the Cochran case." I stab another bite. He is chewing, so he questions my statement with an arch of his brows rather than with words. I comply. "I got into Toby Cochran's laptop all by myself."

With that, he spits out his mushroom.

Chapter Eleven

"You did what?" Bob says, glaring at me. He picks up his napkin and dabs at his mouth, scowling over the top of it.

"I got into Toby's computer. I made some copies of his fingerprints at his house and used one to bypass the password."

"You made copies of the fingerprints," Bob says in a tone of disbelief.

"I did." I smile at him. "They were quite good, if I do say so myself."

"How?"

"Some lead pencil shavings, some face powder, some clear packing tape, plain copy paper, and some makeup brushes I had lying around." I shrug. "It wasn't all that hard. I'm sure they aren't good enough to hold up as evidence in court, but one of them was good enough to get me into that laptop."

Bob drops his napkin, leans back in his chair, and stares at me. His expression is an odd mixture of admiration, appalled amazement, and irritation, like the look one of my foster parents gave me when she saw how many candy bars I'd been able to lift at the grocery store without getting caught.

"Okay," Bob says. He looks away, off across the room, screwing his mouth up as his tongue works to loosen something stuck in his teeth. Nice teeth, I note. "Clearly you are both resourceful and highly motivated," he says in a tone of voice that suggests "resourceful" and "highly motivated" are code for "a pain in my ass" or something equally unflattering. "Did you find anything interesting on the laptop?"

"I haven't had a chance to look at it yet," I admit. "I got into it right before I had to leave to meet you. All I had time to do was change the password and disable the fingerprint ID."

"You need to hand that laptop over to me." Bob says this in a firm voice, though I detect a distinct lack of conviction. I think he knows I'm not going to do what he wants.

"I'll give it to you when I'm done with it," I say. "But I want to look at it first. I promised his mother I would. And you haven't officially reopened this case, have you?"

"It's not that simple," Bob says. I can see his exasperation growing, and just when I think he's about to truly lose his temper with me, our food arrives.

The waitress sets our dishes down with a flourish and a running commentary of what I suspect are rehearsed lines she uses all the time—how nice we look, how good the food smells, how much she likes my hairdo, how smart our menu choices are, how handsome Bob is—that sort of thing. Once again there is a palpable cloud of tension hovering over our table, however, and it makes her lines sound more forced than what I imagine they typically do. She departs quickly, looking relieved to escape.

Bob says, "I could have you arrested, you know."

"Could you?" I say in my best sarcastic voice. "For what?"

"Withholding evidence," he grumbles.

"Well, you haven't reopened the case, so there's no evidence to be had officially, and I think you need a warrant to access something like a computer, don't you? Or at the very least permission from Toby's mother. And I'm not withholding the evidence, if it even is evidence. I told you I'd give it to you once I get a look at it. Or . . ."

I let this final option hang in the air between us, like a ticking time bomb. Bob narrows his eyes, trying his best to be angry with me, or at the very least, annoyed, but he isn't pulling either one off. My years in the foster system and my training as a social worker have made me very good at reading people, and I can tell Bob is intrigued, amused, and entertained by my efforts, even though he wants to be angry. His professional persona is warring with his personal one, and in a matter of seconds the personal one wins out.

"Okay, I'll bite," he says to my unstated option. And to punctuate this comment in the most literal sense, he stabs a piece of sausage from his plate and pops it into his mouth. I watch him a moment, the way he savors the first bite, chewing slowly, relishing the flavors in his mouth. But the way he saws off another bite of sausage, attacking the link with his knife and fork in a savage, vicious manner, makes me back off on my smugness a little.

"I thought that you and I could look through the laptop together, tonight after dinner," I tell him. "I'm willing to share it with you, under one condition."

He chews, eyeing me with amused irritation, waiting.

"I want to help with the investigation. I will accept whatever outcome we arrive at, and I promise not to get in the way, or compromise evidence if it turns out there is something more to Toby's death."

"You're already in the way and have potentially compromised evidence," Bob says. It's a challenge, but judging from the twinkle in his eye, I suspect it's not a serious one. I say a silent prayer that I'm reading him right.

"I do have the laptop in my possession," I counter,

taking a bite of my lasagna and letting the taste explode in my mouth.

"Yes, you do. A foolish move on your part. Look at your size and look at me," Bob says with a hint of menace in his smile. "Who do you think will win if we wrestle over it?" He awaits my answer by shoving a whole ravioli in his mouth.

"You could take it from me, true enough," I say, feigning a worried look for a few seconds. Then I smile and deliver my coup de grâce. "But you're forgetting one thing. I gained access to the laptop long enough to change the password. I also disabled the fingerprint ID. So right now, the only person who knows how to get into that computer is me." Following his style, I eat another mouthful of lasagna.

Bob stabs a ravioli and holds it aloft on his fork. "Well played, Ms. Schneider," he says. He pops the ravioli in his mouth, chews, and swallows. I wait, feeling smug but trying not to look it. "So where are we going to examine this laptop—your place or mine?" he asks once he swallows.

"We could pick someplace neutral." As soon as these words leave my mouth I want to take them back. Unless my neutral location is a motel room, I've just blown any hope I might have had of building a little romantic tension. Then again, this is a first date, and despite some people's belief that one can hop into bed with someone they find attractive for any reason and at any time, I'm a bit more old-school than that. And I suspect Bob is, too, since Mattie told me he hasn't had a lot of relationship experience. I've had several relationships over the years, but they've all failed, so I'm no paradigm for success in the romance department, either.

"How about Dairy Airs?" Bob says. "We could go there for some coffee and dessert after we're done here."

"That could work," I say, deciding dessert helps make up for any lack of romantic headway.

"Okay, then, we have a deal," Bob says. He stabs a piece of sausage and puts it in his mouth. After chewing for a few seconds, he swallows and sighs. "I'm going to have to do a bunch of extra reps tomorrow morning to make up for all of this," he says, waving his fork over his plate.

"Reps?" I say. "Do you belong to a gym?"

"I do," he says with some pride. "I've been a dedicated customer for the past two and a half years, ever since getting shot. I used to be, well, a lot bigger than I am now. Getting shot gave me a new lease on life, and I'm a workout fanatic now. You should try it."

"Getting shot?" I say, nearly choking on my bite of lasagna.

"No," Bob says with a snort of laughter. "That came out wrong. I meant you should try working out at the gym." His expression sobers and he stares at me, horrified. "I didn't mean to imply . . . I mean, you're not . . ."

"Don't get yourself in a tizzy," I say, holding up a hand to stop his bumbling attempt at an apology. "I'm self-aware when it comes to my body. I know I need to lose some weight, and I also know I should exercise more." I put down my fork and lace my hands together, elbows on the table. "I accept your invitation," I tell him. He looks momentarily confused, no doubt wondering what the hell he invited me to. Technically, he didn't invite me to anything, though the implication was there. "What time do you normally go to the gym?"

His face relaxes then as he gleans my meaning. "I usually get there at five in the morning, work out for an hour and a half, and then I shower and head to work so I can be there by seven."

I consider this. "Well, I have to be to work at seven, too, but I'm afraid that my after-shower preparations are a bit more involved than yours." I cup the ends of my hair with my palm. "It takes some work to look this good, you know."

Bob smiles and takes another bite of pasta.

"And I don't think I could or should try to work out for an hour and a half," I tell him. "The most exercise I get these days is walking my dog, Roscoe."

"Walking is good."

"Yes, well, it would be better if I was the one walking him most of the time. But my neighbor's eleven-year-old daughter, P.J., walks him way more than I do. Those two have a love affair going on."

"What kind of dog is he?"

"A golden retriever. Sweet, smart, and affectionate. Kind of like me."

This segue effectively alters our conversation for the rest of the meal. We chat about our jobs, past cases—always in general terms that don't include the names of those involved—and mundane things like the weather, the economy, and local politics. When our meal is done, we pass on dessert, exchanging a look between us that says our prior plans are still on. I pay the bill per our earlier arrangement, and then the two of us head outside to our respective cars.

Chapter Twelve

Minutes later Bob and I arrive at Dairy Airs, a restaurant owned by a local farm family. They raise dairy cattle, so the place specializes in dairy-related foods: cheese sandwiches, cheesecakes, ice creams, milkshakes, and some specialty custards and puddings. Bob and I each park in an empty spot, his three spaces down from mine. His car, I note, is a nondescript, older-model dark blue sedan that to me screams undercover cop. We meet at the door to go inside.

"This one is my treat," he says, holding the door for me.

"Okay. You choose the seat." I walk beneath his outstretched arm without having to duck or stoop.

He picks a two-person table at the far end of the place. It's in a corner nook by a window, but thanks to variations in the land outside, we are elevated too high for anyone to see directly in. Bob grabs a chair that is positioned with its back to the front of the restaurant, moves it perpendicular so that it's facing toward the window, and motions for me to sit in it. I do so, realizing that while this gives me a better window view, it puts my back to the main part of the restaurant. Bob takes the remaining seat, which backs against a wall, giving him a view of the entire restaurant. It seems we will be rubbing elbows as well as knees, though I'm not foolish enough to think his arrangement has any romantic inclinations behind it. He simply wants to be in a good position to see the laptop screen along with me, but also to monitor any nosy people who may be near us.

A waitress arrives seconds after Bob is seated, and though she gives him a quizzical look over his altered seating arrangement, she doesn't comment. She does, however, greet him by name. "Bob Richmond! How are you?"

"I'm good, Tabby. How are you?"

"Can't complain. I could, but who'd listen?" She laughs at her own joke while Bob and I both chuckle politely. "Can I get you some water for now, or do you know what you want? You haven't been here in a while."

"I know what I want," Bob says, "but I'm not sure if Hildy here does." He shoots me a questioning look.

"Would you like to see a menu?" Tabby asks.

I shake my head. "What flavors of cheesecake do you have tonight?"

Tabby rattles off a mouthwatering list of culinary delights, and I settle for a slice of Baileys and Kahlúa cheesecake with a cup of coffee.

"I'll have the same," Bob says.

Tabby hustles off and I, eager to get to the task at hand, take out Toby's laptop. I set it on the table, open it, and turn it away from Bob's watchful eye. He sighs, but doesn't protest, and as soon as I have typed in the password, I turn the computer so he can see the screen as well. He's barely had time to study the desktop icons when Tabby brings our desserts and coffee, forcing me to turn the computer away again. As soon as she is gone, Bob and I look at the laptop's desktop with eager curiosity.

"He has an email program," I say, pointing to the icon I'd clicked on earlier. "How about we start there?"

Bob nods and I launch the program. As it opens, Bob reaches over and places a hand atop mine. "The Wi-Fi here may not be secure," he says in a low voice.

"I think we're okay. When I was on here earlier I saw that Toby has top-notch virus software. It popped up with a window that showed me it had identified, isolated, and removed some malware, and had done a virus scan in the last twenty-four hours. Besides, I don't think we're looking for any government secrets here."

"Who knows?" Bob says, surprising me. Then I decide he's just kidding me.

I see that we have our work cut out for us as the mail program downloads a little over two weeks' worth of emails, filling the inbox with new items. We eliminate twenty or so as spam, and another twelve that are news feeds from several online sources. The remainder appear to be from three individuals; a conversational thread with a subject line of "No More."

Tracing backward on the chain of emails, we find it originated with Toby, who sent it to each of the three respondents two days before he died. It reads:

I'm sorry, I thought I could let it go but I can't. Physical distance hasn't given me the necessary psychological or emotional distance I need. I hope you all understand.

The first reply is from someone named Mitchell Sawyer, who simply says that he agrees and understands. The second response is from a Liam Michaelson, and it says:

Don't overreact, Toby. You're getting in over your head. Walk away.

Toby replies to Liam's email with a reiteration of his determination to see it brought to a halt, though he doesn't clarify or mention what "it" is. At this point, someone named Alex Parnell enters the fray with:

> Toby, let it go. It's not worth what it will cost you in the
> end. Don't try to be a hero. Heroes often end up dead.

"Well, there's our first hint of a death threat," I say to Bob.

He makes a dismissive face. "Not much of one. A warning perhaps, but generic enough that I don't give it much credence. Let's read the other ones."

In between bites of cheesecake and sips of coffee, we wade through the rest of the thread. The next email is another reply from Liam.

> Alex is right, Toby. Get on with your life and quit trying to
> ruin ours.

Toby fires off a reply that he is not trying to ruin anyone's life but is, in fact, trying to save others from suffering in the future. This prompts another response from Mitchell.

> Leave Toby be. He'll do what he needs to do and I'm sure
> he knows he'll have to accept the consequences of his
> actions. Right, Toby?

Liam answers this with an angry plea to Toby:

> Please consider the impact your actions will have on
> others, Toby. You are playing with fire and you're not the
> only one who's going to get burned. Stop being a selfish
> prick and think about what you're doing to other people!

Toby's terse reply:

> What the hell do you think I'm doing? I'm not the enemy
> here. Silence is. I can't change what's already happened
> but maybe I can change the future. It has to STOP!

Bob and I both take bites of cheesecake—my last one, his penultimate bite—and savor the flavors while we digest the contents of the emails. I break the silence first.

"What do you suppose they're talking about?"

Bob licks his lips and then dabs at them with his napkin. "Not sure. Maybe some kind of drug thing? Any idea who these people in the emails are?"

I shake my head. "His mother might know, though." I take out my phone and dial Sharon Cochran's number. She answers on the second ring, her voice full of hope. I feel a twinge of guilt, knowing she is expecting answers when all I have for her are more questions. At least for now.

"Did you find something?" she asks, forgoing any type of formal greeting and verifying my suspicion.

"Maybe," I tell her, "but it isn't anything concrete, at least not yet. I need your help in identifying some people."

"Who?"

"Friends, or at least acquaintances, of Toby's."

"Oh." She sounds disappointed. "I'll try, but I really don't know many of Toby's friends, at least not the recent ones."

"How about the names Mitchell Sawyer, or Liam Michaelson?"

Sharon doesn't answer right away. "Well, he did mention someone named Mitch at one time, but I don't know his last name. I'm sure I never heard of anyone named Liam. I'd remember that name."

"In what context did Toby talk about Mitch?" I ask.

"I think he was in Toby's fraternity."

"Okay, how about the name Alex Parnell?"

Sharon hesitates again before answering, and then precedes her answer with a sigh. "No, sorry."

"It's okay."

"Where are you getting these names?" she asks.

"From emails on his computer."

"You got in!" she says, now sounding excited.

"Yes, but I'm only just starting to sort through the contents."

"I hope you can find something that will help convince the police to take another look at his case."

"I think I already have," I say, smiling at Bob. "I'm with Detective Bob Richmond right now and he's looking at the computer with me."

"Only because you wouldn't let me have it," Bob grumbles sotto voce.

I widen my smile at him. "Let me get back to it, Sharon, and if I find anything else, I'll let you know."

"Thank you, Hildy."

"Don't thank me yet," I tell her. "Let's wait and see what develops." I disconnect the call and take another look at the contents of Toby's inbox, focusing on the email headers.

"These are all email addresses with '.edu' at the end, meaning they're university addresses. Sharon Cochran thinks Mitch is someone from Toby's frat house. Maybe the others are, too."

Bob is busy scribbling the names and email addresses in a small notebook he pulled from his jacket pocket. When he's done, I say, "Now what?"

He frowns, studying my face for a few seconds. I'm not sure what he's searching for, but apparently, he doesn't find it, because he lets out a frustrated sigh. But then he surprises me by saying, "I don't suppose you'd invite me over to your place?"

I give him a sly smile. "Why, Bob, I thought you'd never ask."

Chapter Thirteen

Bob Richmond follows me to my house, and as we approach the front door I hear barking from inside. Roscoe sounds fierce and ferocious, but as soon as I have the door unlocked he greets me with his usual tail-wagging, butt-wiggling excitement. If only I could get a man to greet me that way.

After devoting a few seconds to me, Roscoe shifts his attention to Bob and sniffs him, planting his nose firmly in Bob's crotch.

"Roscoe!" I say. "Be good." I give Bob an apologetic look. "He's normally very well behaved, but he does get excited when I have visitors."

I take Bob's jacket, hang it in the hall closet, and then give him a mini-tour of the ground floor, which consists of the living room, kitchen, a tiny guest bath that I think was once a closet, my master suite, and a dining area that is currently doing double duty as my home office space. I don't throw dinner parties much—in fact, I've never thrown one—so this setup works well for me. Off the dining room/office area, behind a pair of French doors, is a screened porch.

"I have three bedrooms and a full bath upstairs, and a partially finished basement," I tell him. "It's a lot of space for just me, but it's an old house, built in the nineteen twenties, and it needed a lot of work when I bought it. Still does, for that matter. I figured it would make a good investment because I like doing home improvement projects. I'm pretty handy with a tool belt, believe it or not."

"I believe it," Bob says, looking around. "Did you redo the kitchen?"

"I did, though not by myself, of course. I also created the master bedroom and bath on this floor. That space was originally a butler pantry, a laundry room, and an enclosed porch. I hired people to do the major stuff, like the electrical, plumbing, framing, and drywall, but I love doing woodwork, and I trimmed out all the windows, doors, and walls. And I installed the hardwood floor in the bedroom and the tile floor in the bathroom."

"Impressive," Bob says, eyeing some of my woodwork.

"One of my foster fathers owned a construction company," I explain. "He would take his two sons with him to his work sites on weekends and through the summer. When I complained that he should take me along, too, he did, and he worked my butt off. I think he figured I'd get tired of it and ask to be left home, but when he saw that I liked the work, he took me under his wing and taught me how to do a lot of stuff." I pause, smiling with the memories.

Sounding embarrassed, Bob says, "I haven't done much with my house, and it shows."

"It's never too late to start."

He shrugs and then changes the subject. "It sounds like not all of your foster family situations were horrible."

"No, just most of them. I had two that were nice. One was with the Davidsons, Kyle and Jenny. Kyle is the one who taught me the construction stuff. I spent three years with them, but when I was a sophomore in high school, they were killed in a car accident."

"That must have been hard for you."

"It was," I admit. "Their sons went to live with an aunt

in New York, and I got placed in a group home. I stayed in the group home until I graduated."

"And the other good home?"

"That was with the Muellers, Olga and Dietrich. They were an older, childless couple I was placed with when I was nine. They had two other foster girls besides me, one who was five and one who was seven. We got along well, and the Muellers were sweet. But six months into my stay there, Dietrich had a stroke and ended up paralyzed on one side. He could barely do anything for himself, and the doctors told Olga she should place him in a nursing home. She wouldn't hear of it and brought him home. But she couldn't care for all of us kids and Dietrich, so we all went elsewhere."

"Did you stay in touch with them?"

I shake my head, feeling a familiar guilt wash over me. "I was too busy feeling sorry for myself and trying to survive to worry about the Muellers. I tried to get in touch with them when I was in college but found out they had both died the year before. Olga had had a heart attack, and without her to care for him, Dietrich went to a nursing home. He died two months later, probably from a broken heart."

Bob is looking at me with a pitying expression I don't much care for, so I quickly change the subject. "Why don't you have a seat in the living room and I'll get you something to drink. What's your poison? I have some white wine, some red wine, some vodka, some sodas, some whisky, and coffee. Oh, and a six-pack of beer. I don't remember the brand because I don't drink beer. It was a gift from a neighbor."

"How about some ice water?" Bob says. "I'm on call."

"Right, I forgot," I say, and I head into the kitchen. I pour myself a glass of white wine, get Bob a tall glass of ice water, and go back to the living room. I expect to find him seated in one of the chairs, or on the couch, but instead I find him standing in front of my fireplace, looking at the three pictures I have on the mantel.

"Family?" he says, nodding toward the photos, all of which feature me and one other person.

"Sort of. That's Sarah," I say, pointing to the first one. "She was a foster sibling of mine. We were in the same group home for two years, and we've stayed close. And this is Tamela, also a foster sib from the group home and my very talented seamstress. This one," I pick up the only picture of a child, "is my neighbor's daughter, P.J., the one Roscoe is in love with." Roscoe, who is lying on the floor, pricks his ears and thumps his tail a few times at hearing mention of his name.

Bob looks at the pictures, then at me. "You don't have any blood relatives?"

"Nah," I say with a dismissive wave of my hand. "Just my grandparents, assuming they're still alive."

Bob gives me another of those pained, sympathetic looks.

"Hey, don't be feeling sorry for me," I say, thrusting his glass of water at him, feeling a little irritated. "I managed well enough, and I have foster siblings that I call family. Let's get back to the laptop, shall we?"

I grab the computer from my briefcase and settle in on the couch with it on my lap. I take a big gulp of wine before setting my glass aside and then opening the computer to wake it up. Bob sits next to me and I turn the computer away from his curious eyes while I type in my password.

"Where should we go next?" I ask him once the desktop is in view.

"Let's take a look at Toby's Internet history."

I tap the appropriate icon and launch the web browser.

Fortunately for us, either Toby wasn't worried about maintaining a history of his net surfing, or he was neglectful in limiting and erasing it. We follow his trail of web-based breadcrumbs to several sites. Most of them are of little interest, but there is one that gives me pause, and it's a site he bookmarked. It shows a satellite photo of a section of wooded acreage with a creek running through the middle of it.

"I wonder why he was so interested in this aerial map?" Bob says.

"I'm not sure why, but I bet it has something to do with this," I say, zooming in on an area. "Does that look familiar?"

We are looking down on a wooden footbridge that crosses the creek. There is a path, though not a well-worn one, leading to the bridge on either side. Following the trail, I see that it leads to a wider, more established trail on one end, and into the woods on the other end. Something about the place looks vaguely familiar to me, but after a moment of trying to figure out what it is I chalk it up to my familiarity with Toby's renderings of the area.

"That's the bridge in Toby's picture," Bob says.

I dig the drawing out of my briefcase and show it to him. "Looks like it to me. Clearly it meant something to Toby. Otherwise, why did he draw that bridge so many times?"

"His mother doesn't have any ideas about it?"

I shake my head.

"Maybe the bridge was some kind of rendezvous spot for drug deals," Bob surmises.

I don't really think this, nor am I convinced Toby was doing any drug deals. But I want to ease Bob into my line of thinking rather than get into an argument this early, so I shift the topic slightly. "I read in the paper a while back that labs can trace the source for a lot of these drugs by analyzing the contents and their specific ratios. Sometimes they can determine who provided it and where it came from. Did you guys try to trace the heroin that killed Toby?"

Bob frowns. "Not yet, but we did turn the syringe in to

the crime lab here. I don't know if Arnie—he's the local lab rat in the ME's office—has done any in-depth analysis on the trace we found. He might have sent it on to Madison."

"You haven't been putting much effort into figuring out anything about this boy's death, have you?" No sooner do the words leave my mouth than I want to take them back.

Bob leans away from me, looking irritated. "There hasn't been a reason to," he says defensively. "The kid's cause of death was obvious. He was found in an area known to be a hangout for druggies. And he had some recent changes in his life that pointed toward him being depressed."

I'm in it now, so I go ahead full steam. "Even though he had no tracks, no evidence of prior IV drug use, no evidence of *any* drug use, for that matter, you didn't think it was suspicious that the kid OD'd that way?"

"He's not the only person to overdose on the first time shooting up," Bob says, clearly riled. "You'd be surprised how many people die after their first shoot-up. Sometimes it's because they OD, but sometimes it's because the crap they've cooked is so toxic and mixed with so much other junk that it basically poisons them. Lately we've been seeing a lot of fentanyl mixed in with the heroin, and it's fifty times more potent. Is it common to have something like this happen on the first use? Not common, perhaps, but not rare or unusual, either. And there were no signs of a struggle at the scene. If the kid was injected by someone else against his will, don't you think there'd be evidence of a scuffle?" Apparently, this is a rhetorical question, because he doesn't give me so much as a second to answer. "Before you go judging me or anyone else on this case, keep that in mind, okay?"

"Okay," I say with an apologetic smile, hoping to damper the flames a bit. "Sorry. I wasn't trying to rile you. I just want to get to the truth."

Bob studies my face, scowling at me as I struggle to keep my expression appropriately and believably contrite. An awkward silence builds between us, and as I'm scrambling to come up with a way to break it and regain some of the camaraderie we had earlier, my front door opens and P.J. walks in. Roscoe hops up and hurries over to greet her, tail wagging.

P.J. stops short when she sees Bob seated on the couch. She buries her hands in the fur around Roscoe's neck and stares at Bob as if he's some alien creature she's never seen before.

I hand the laptop to Bob—a conciliatory gesture I hope will restore the peace—and make the introductions.

"P.J., this is Bob Richmond. He's a friend of mine. Bob, this is my neighbor P.J., the one I told you about."

P.J. glances at me for the briefest of seconds, then she releases her grip on Roscoe's ruff and closes the distance between herself and Bob. Stopping a foot or so in front of him, she extends her right hand. "Hi, I'm P.J., which stands for Priscilla Jean, but I hate that name, so please don't use it." She rolls her eyes dramatically with the word *hate*.

Bob smiles and shakes her hand. "It's nice to meet you, P.J."

P.J. withdraws her hand and asks Bob, "How was your dinner?"

"Very nice, thank you."

P.J. turns to look at me. "How fun."

"Roscoe is more than ready for a walk," I say pointedly.

P.J. walks back to the door, grabbing Roscoe's leash and hooking it up. Seconds later, they're both gone.

"Cute kid," Richmond says.

"Sometimes I think she's only pretending to be a kid. She's very intelligent, very perceptive, and full of energy. She doesn't seem to have a lot of friends her own age, which is worrisome, but she also doesn't seem depressed or lonely. I think she's just an old soul in a young body."

Richmond sets the laptop on the coffee table and leans back into the couch. "You're an interesting woman, Hildy Schneider."

"I hope you mean that in a good way," I say, biting my lower lip.

"Mostly," Bob says with a wink, one corner of his mouth twitching into a half smile. "I'll tell you what. Seeing as how you aren't going to let this case go, and you might be right that we dismissed it a bit too soon, I'm willing to make a deal with you."

"I like deals," I say. "What have you got to offer?"

"You turn this laptop over to me so I can get some professionals to look it over."

I give him a skeptical look. "Why would I do that?"

"Because it's the right thing to do, for one thing."

Playing to my sense of wrong and right is a smart move on his part, and I wonder if it's intentional. "And what do I get out of this so-called deal?"

"You can come with me to the police station and I will show you everything we have in the file on this case."

"Really?" I say, both suspicious and excited. "Isn't that against some rule you cops have?"

"It's a bit of a gray area," he admits. "But it's considered a closed case and there's no arrest record, so technically it's a public record, including the coroner's report. Of course, you'd have to fill out a bunch of forms and wait an eternity to get those reports, but I think there's a way around that. Have you ever done a police ride-along?"

"You mean when a civilian rides in a squad car with a cop to see what they do, that sort of thing?" Bob nods. "I've heard of it but haven't done it. I thought it was usually done with a beat cop, someone on the street."

"It can be, but detectives do them, too. You'll have to sign a release and submit to a background check."

"No problem," I tell him. "My record as an adult is clean." He arches his eyebrows questioningly at me, and I give him a sheepish smile. "I might have acted out a little when I was younger, but those are juvie records, and they're sealed. Besides, I didn't kill anyone or anything awful like that. Although in the interest of full disclosure, I should tell you there were times when I was tempted."

Bob clears his throat and says, "I'm going to pretend I didn't hear you say that."

I get up, walk over to my briefcase, and take out a pen. "Where do I sign?" I say with a smile, waggling the pen in my hand.

"The forms are at the police station. But don't get ahead of me here. I have one more request."

I give him an exasperated look. "You seem mighty determined to make an omelet for someone who isn't holding any eggs. I could take that laptop and walk away."

"You could," Bob concedes, nodding. "But you won't." He grins at me, and there's a smugness to it, telling me he knows he's got me hooked.

I should be annoyed, maybe even outraged. But I'm not, at least not yet. "Okay, what's your final demand?" I say in an exaggeratedly overwrought tone.

"You meet me at the gym every morning but Sundays for two weeks."

Whoa. Didn't see that one coming.

"After the two weeks, I won't hold you to it," Bob goes on. "I've been looking for a workout partner for a long time. Mattie did it with me back when I first joined, but she quit a long time ago. Something about the demands of motherhood and her youngest kid trying to destroy the universe, or some such." He waves away the objection with his hand. "Anyway, the gym lets members bring a guest for free for two weeks. After that if you want to come you have to pay for a membership. But it's not a lot of money, just twenty bucks a month. And the place is open twenty-four hours a day, so you shouldn't have any trouble fitting it into your schedule. I don't, and my schedule is often crazy."

I consider his offer. He's basically blackmailing me into working out with him, and that rubs me the wrong way, but I want to work on Toby Cochran's case, and I know this is going to be a prerequisite for him letting me do that. And all he's asked me to do is meet him there, not do any kind of workout or exercise. It's a potential out for me, and I tuck it into a back pocket in my brain. On the positive side, I do like Bob and wouldn't mind a chance to get to know him better, and a little exercise would probably do me some good.

"Okay, Bob, you have yourself a deal."

We shake on it, and I smile even though a tiny niggle of fear nags at my brain.

My exercise regimen for the past several years has consisted of the occasional dog walk, some mall shopping, and basic housecleaning. The rational side of my brain warns me that this gym thing sounds like a big mouthful to be biting off, and then the less rational, cliché-ridden side chants, *Nothing ventured, nothing gained*.

And then I figure, what the heck. If it kills me, at least I know there will be someone close by to investigate my death.

Chapter Fourteen

P.J. returns with Roscoe as Bob and I are packing up the laptop and preparing to head for the police station. I realize I'm so excited about my new arrangement with Bob that I momentarily forgot about P.J. and my dog.

"Are you going out again?" P.J. asks as I slip on my jacket. She wiggles her eyebrows and tilts her head toward Bob, who fortunately is facing the opposite way and doesn't see any of this.

"I have some work to do," I tell P.J. "Bob is going to help me with it."

"What kind of work?" In addition to being cute, energetic, and friendly, P.J. is also nosy.

"It's confidential stuff," I say with authority, hoping to deter any further inquiries.

P.J. shrugs this off with apparent indifference, though I suspect she is feigning it. "Okay, see you later." With that, she shows herself out.

"Two cars again?" I ask Bob. "Or can we start the ride-along?"

"Let's do two cars for now, at least until we get the paperwork done," he says. "Follow me and I'll badge you into the private parking lot behind the station."

I do as I'm told, parking in what amounts to a giant cage behind the police station. The lot is surrounded by a high chain-link fence with a rolling electronic gate that allows people with the proper badges to get in. I park a few spaces away from Bob, the closest opening there is, and follow him wordlessly to a door at the back of the big brick building. Here he punches in a code on a panel and I hear a faint buzz. He grabs the knob, opens the door, and waves me in.

I haven't been in this part of the station before, but I can tell right away that we're in a break room. In some regards, it looks like break rooms everywhere. There is a large table at the center of the room surrounded by a motley collection of mismatched chairs, a refrigerator against one wall, and two areas of countertops with overhead cabinetry. One of the countertops sports a sink and a coffeepot; the other a microwave oven. The general setup is nearly identical to a staff break room at the hospital that I frequently use, but that's where the similarities end. This break room has crumbs scattered on every surface, dried spills on the counters, coffee mug and glass rings on the tabletop, and several ripped cartons or food wrappers scattered about on the counters and floor. The sole trash can in the room is overflowing. The door to the microwave is hanging open, and the inside of the appliance looks like someone detonated a nuclear food bomb in it.

My fingers are literally itching as I survey the room, my mind urging me to jump in and clean before I do anything else. I recognize the urge for what it is—my fun brand of insanity—and try to quell it. There are much more urgent needs to tend to first, but the compulsion to start cleaning is so strong that I'm not sure I can resist it.

"What's wrong?" Bob asks, eyeing me with concern. "You look like you're about to throw up or something. Are you okay?"

"I'm fine, but this room looks like it threw up," I tell him, surveying it all in disgust. "Doesn't anyone around here clean up after themselves?"

Bob looks around the room in puzzlement, as if he's seeing it for the first time. This tells me he's used to the clutter and filth, and I can't help but wonder what his house looks like. I can't get serious about a man who's a slob.

Bob says, "I guess it is kind of a mess, isn't it?"

"You think?" I ask rhetorically, dripping sarcasm.

He looks at me and shrugs. "I don't spend any time in here," he says. "I walk through it a lot, but I don't stop or sit here. When I eat, I do it either at my desk or out somewhere. I guess I never paid much attention to it."

Obviously, he doesn't give it much stock now, either, because he exits the room without further comment, assuming I'll follow. With one last, longing itch of a look at the mess, I do just that.

We end up in a long hallway that I recognize from my previous trip, but instead of entering the conference room I was in before, Bob leads me into an office that contains three desks. I'm relieved to see that all three desks are relatively neat and organized. Bob points to the closest desk and says, "That's Steve Hurley's. The one in the corner over there is Junior Feller's. He's a detective who does mostly vice stuff, though he helps out with death investigations at times."

He pulls out the chair at what I discern by process of elimination is his desk and drops into it. I look around for a free chair nearby to sit in, but there isn't one. I consider stealing the one at Junior Feller's desk, but decide to stand instead, at least for now. Bob starts tapping away on his keyboard while I stand there awkwardly staring at the bare walls and shifting my briefcase, which contains Toby's laptop, from one hand to the other.

After a moment, a printer on top of a small side table

starts spewing out paper. "That's the ride-along agreement," Bob says with a nod toward the printer. "Read it over and sign it. As for your background check, it looks like we have a recent one from a few months ago and everything came back okay, so I think we're good to go. Unless you've robbed a bank or killed someone recently."

I know he's attempting to make a joke, but I'm too stymied by the fact that he found a background check on me. "Why would the police have run a background check on me before today?"

"We do them for the hospital."

That calms me. The hospital requires criminal background checks on their employees every few years, and I remember that I had to sign a release a few months ago so they could run one.

"You can sit in the break room if you want to read that," Bob says. "I need to take care of something else, but it shouldn't take long. Give me ten minutes, okay?"

"Okay."

I retrieve the papers from the printer and head back to the break room. I find a roll of paper towels and some spray cleaning solution beneath the sink and use them to clean the tabletop. I wipe down a chair, too, which is covered with crumbs and blotches of sticky residue. Once it's all dry, I set my briefcase on the table and settle in with the papers to read.

It's a standard release form except for the fact that it lists more than the usual sorts of casualties one might expect to encounter on your average day—things like gunshots, explosions, high-speed chases, and, oddly enough, nuclear radiation. It seems like overkill to me, and I'm surprised they didn't include a zombie or space alien invasion in the document. The last part of the form is essentially a confidentiality agreement, swearing me to silence and/or ignorance of anyone or anything I observe or encounter during my ride-along. This is no big deal, since confidentiality is a normal obligation and assumption for my day-to-day job.

I sign the form, push it aside, and then survey the rest of the room. Where to start?

I make the mistake of walking over to the refrigerator and opening it. Inside I find a biohazard lab of bacterial specimens growing in a variety of containers. Another quick search under the sink reveals a box of trash bags, and after removing one, I start emptying the refrigerator.

Bob finds me some twenty minutes later up to my elbows in the fridge with a sponge, paper towels, and cleaning spray. He stares at me for a moment, blinking, and then says, "What are you doing?"

"Trying to prevent any deaths in your department," I say, scowling. "Have you looked inside this thing recently? It should be included as a risk on that ride-along waiver I just signed."

Bob shakes his head, looking both bemused and amused.

"It was disgusting. I'm surprised the CDC hasn't been here to shut you down." I nod toward the trash bag I've filled, which is near the back door, neatly tied off. Two others are beside it, a culmination of the overflowing bag that was in the trash receptacle and the loose items strewn around the room. "Those need to go outside to wherever the nearest trash bin is."

Bob looks at the bags, then back at me, scratching his head. I've finished my cleaning of the fridge, and as I step back to admire my handiwork, he walks over to the table and tosses a manila folder onto its surface. "Are we going to research the case or clean the break room?" he asks, checking to see if I've signed my life and all liability away on the form he gave me earlier. Apparently satisfied, he rolls it up and tucks it in his pocket.

I shut the refrigerator door and look around the rest of the room, hands on my hips. "Can you at least take those bags out to a dumpster or something?" I ask, nodding toward the collection. "Some of the stuff that came out of here looked aggressive enough to take over the city."

"Yeah, okay." He isn't facing me when he says this, but I'm certain he's rolling his eyes. I can hear it in his voice.

As soon as he moves toward the door, I head for one of the countertops with my paper towels and cleaning spray. By the time Bob returns from his garbage expedition, I've cleaned off both counters and sprayed the inside of the microwave. The debris in the microwave will need to soak awhile so the stuff will loosen up. I walk over to the table and take a seat. Bob settles into the chair on my right, still eyeing me with that combination of confused, amused curiosity.

I reach for the file folder and pull it to me. Bob leans back in his chair, hands folded in his lap, watching me. Glued or taped to the inside of the folder cover is a picture of Toby, one of the ones I saw on the bookcase at the top of the stairs at Sharon's house. The first document inside the folder is the medical examiner's report. It's several pages long and includes some narrative, some diagrams, a few photos, and some test results. Some of the anatomical terminology is a bit above my pay grade, but I understand enough of it to parse out the general meanings.

The gist of it all is that, after an anonymous call to 911, Toby Cochran was found in an abandoned building in town that is known to be a hangout for druggies. When police responded to the scene, they found Toby already cold and with early signs of lividity—otherwise known as livor mortis or the settling of blood after death, a term I've heard used before in the ER—indicating he'd been dead for some time. As a result, no resuscitation attempts were made. There was some drug paraphernalia nearby, and a syringe with a needle attached was found in Toby's arm, the needle tip embedded in the cephalic vein in the left antecubital fossa. Fortunately, an accompanying picture translates this for me, showing the needle puncturing the inside portion of Toby's left elbow.

The door to the break room opens then, and a woman officer walks in. She is short for a police officer, I think—maybe five four—but is also muscularly built. She has curly, shoulder-length, dark hair and lively hazel-colored eyes.

"Hey, Brenda," Bob says.

"Hi," she counters, giving me a questioning look.

I'm about to introduce myself when Bob beats me to it. "This is Hildy Schneider. She's a social worker up at the hospital and she's going to be doing a ride-along with me. Hildy, this is Officer Brenda Joiner."

I recognize the name as that of the officer Sharon said she had dealt with.

"Pleasure to meet you," Brenda says, extending a hand. After our grips part, she looks around the room. "Someone finally cleaned up in here," she says with an appreciative tone. "I was going to try to get to it today if I had time."

"That would be courtesy of our guest here," Bob says, nodding toward me.

"Very considerate of you," Brenda says, walking toward the refrigerator and opening the door. "Holy crap!" She stares at the inside of the fridge for a few seconds and then turns that stare toward me. "Did you do this, too?"

I nod.

Brenda gives Bob a pointed look. "She's a keeper. Put her in cuffs if you have to, but don't let her get away."

I know she's joking, but I find the look Bob gives me afterward a bit unsettling. And titillating.

Brenda removes a canned energy drink from the fridge and pops it open while letting the fridge door close. She takes a long swallow, lets out a satisfied "aah" when she's done, and says, "See ya. Gotta go tame the wild ones." She extends her drink hand to me in a cheers gesture, and I acknowledge it with a nod and a smile. With that, she exits out the back door.

"I like her," I say.

"I think it's a safe bet that she likes you, too, after what you did to our break room," Bob says with a smile.

I turn my attention back to the autopsy report, skipping to the back pages and the summary conclusion. The findings are consistent with an overdose that resulted in respiratory arrest followed by cardiac arrest. Toby had no injuries or other health issues, and there was only the one puncture mark found on his body. An addendum tells me that Toby tested positive for both heroin and fentanyl, the drug Bob had said is often used to extend both the dosing of heroin and the sellers' pockets. I already knew this, in part because of news reports, but also because of the spate of overdoses many communities, including Sorenson, are now seeing. The number of overdoses that have rolled into our ER has doubled during the past year or so.

"I can see why Mattie Winston was bothered by this boy's death," I say to Bob. "His first time shooting up and he ODs and dies?" It's a point I've made before, but I can't help making it again.

Bob shrugs, looking mildly perturbed. "Tragic, but it happens, particularly with this fentanyl-laced stuff." He says this with the tired, rote tone of someone explaining something to a child for the umpteenth time. What he doesn't realize is that this fact is an annoying nuisance in my brain, something I can't ignore. My mind clings to it with the same tenacity Roscoe shows when I play tug-of-war with him using his favorite tug rope.

I flip back and look at some of the photos in the ME's file. The one of Toby's arm stops me, something about it niggling at my brain. "I assume you guys fingerprinted Toby, and the paraphernalia found in and around him?"

Bob nods. "There was a partial from Toby's thumb on

the end of the syringe plunger, and partials from two of his other fingers on the syringe barrel. None of the other paraphernalia had any clear, usable prints."

I study the other junk found around Toby's body in the pictures: a candy wrapper, a bottle cap, a small piece of foil, several beer and soda cans, and what looks like part of a blanket. "Not even partial prints?" I ask. Bob shakes his head. "That seems odd, doesn't it?"

"Maybe, but 'odd' doesn't prove anything."

"It also seems odd that Toby's prints would be clear rather than smudged if this was his first time shooting up, don't you think?"

I half expect Bob to get irritated with my questions, but he just shrugs again.

I close my eyes for a moment and imagine myself doing what Toby did. I see myself picking up the syringe in my right hand, jabbing it into a vein in my left arm, and then pushing the plunger that sent that deadly liquid . . . Then it hits me.

"You said you found his thumbprint on the end of the syringe, on the end of the plunger?"

Bob nods, and his eyes narrow. He shifts in his seat, as if he's uncomfortable.

"But no thumbprint on the barrel of the syringe?"

This time Bob shakes his head.

"That doesn't make a lot of sense. It would have been awkward to use his thumb to push the plunger, and there should be a thumbprint on the barrel." I reach over and remove a pen from Bob's shirt pocket, handing it to him. "Mimic what he did with your own hand, using the pen as the syringe."

Bob, frowning slightly, extends his left arm straight out and holds the pen in his right hand like it's a syringe, the writing end of it serving as the needle. His thumb is clearly on the barrel of the pen and when he realizes it, he shifts his hold until he has the pen in a fist-like grip. He hovers over the inside of his left elbow and pretends to plunge the pen into his arm, coming down at a ninety-degree angle. His thumb hits on the clicker of the pen, and when he touches the nib to his arm, he clicks the pen with his thumb. "Seems doable to me," he says.

"Doable but not logical," I say. "I'm not a doctor or a nurse, but I work in the ER a lot and I've watched enough of them insert needles and IVs into veins to know that you don't enter the arm at a ninety-degree angle like that. It's more like a thirty-degree angle with the barrel of the syringe almost flush with the forearm, like this." I take his pen and show him, using his arm. Then I hand the pen back to him. "Now you do it."

He does so, using the angle I demonstrated, and the fist hold he used before. When he attempts to push the plunger with his thumb he succeeds, though it's clearly awkward. Only the edge of his thumb pad meets the clicker, and the writing end of the pen moves erratically with his efforts. He looks at me, frowning, his mouth skewed in dismay. "The kid was inexperienced," he says. "Maybe he didn't know how to do it the *logical* way." He emphasizes the word "logical" in a manner that suggests he finds my idea preposterous.

I flip to a section of the autopsy report I saw earlier and tap it with my finger. "According to this, Toby's initial puncture of the vein was successful. There was no evidence of hesitation marks or multiple puncture sites, and he managed to access his vein without going through the other side of the vein wall at all. That means his technique was perfect. Odd for a first-timer, don't you think?"

"'Odd' isn't evidence," Bob grumbles. I don't say a thing. I just stare at him, eyebrows raised. After a second or two, he sighs. "You think someone else did it for him?"

"I think someone else did it *to* him," I counter.

Bob smiles tiredly. "But there's no evidence of a struggle. If someone was shooting him up with drugs against his will, there would have been evidence of that."

"Unless he was drugged ahead of time."

"What do you mean?" he says irritably.

I don't answer him right away. Instead I flip through the autopsy report again, searching for something. When I find it, I set the report down open to that page and point to the appropriate section with my finger. "They tested Toby for the presence of certain drugs. Here are the results. But there's a drug they didn't test for."

"There are a lot of drugs they didn't test for," Bob says, his impatience growing. "They can't test for every drug known to man. They test for the ones that are most likely to be present or most likely to cause the findings. Unless they have a reason to suspect the presence of other drugs, they won't test for them."

"Well, let's think for a moment," I say. "According to Toby's mother, something happened while he was attending the university. He not only quit school, he left his fraternity. What drug do frat houses have a reputation for using?"

Bob looks at me like he's considering a 51-15, the Wisconsin statute for the emergency detention of someone who's out of their mind. But then his expression changes, and he squeezes his eyes closed. "Oh, hell," he says.

Chapter Fifteen

"You're thinking GHB, the date rape drug, aren't you?" Bob says.

"I am."

"And they didn't test for it."

"They didn't. Not sure they could, to be honest. I dealt with a lot of date rape victims when I was in Milwaukee, and my understanding of the drug is that it gets metabolized very quickly and is hard to find with testing. Maybe we should run it by the ME's office to see what they think?"

Bob gives me a grudging smile. "Okay. Hold on." He takes out his cell phone, punches the face of it a couple of times, and then sets it on the table. I can see from the screen that he is calling someone named Arnie Toffer and that he has it on speaker.

"Arnie here," says a male voice after the second ring. "What can I do for you, Richmond?"

"I've got a question about a case you guys worked not long ago, a kid named Toby Cochran. Do you remember it?"

"Heroin overdose, right?" Arnie says.

"That's right. I'm wondering if there's any way you could do one more test on the kid for me."

"Depends," Arnie says. "The body has been released,

but we have samples of most of the fluids and tissues. What exactly are you looking for?"

"GHB."

"The date rape drug?" Arnie says. "Are you thinking he was trying to chase the dragon and injected it with the heroin? Because I can tell you . . ."

"No," Bob says, cutting him off. "I'm wondering if he might have ingested the drug before he shot up."

"Well, if he did, odds are it would have made it more or less impossible for him to shoot himself up, so . . ."

Several seconds of silence follow, and then Arnie says, "You're thinking it was a murder, aren't you?" There is a newfound level of excitement in his voice.

"I'm looking into some things," Bob says vaguely. "Would you be able to test for GHB at this point?"

"Well, it clears out of the system pretty quickly," Arnie says. "After two hours, more than ninety-five percent of the drug will have been excreted already. It depends on when he took it, how long before he died. Or if he peed afterward. It's excreted in the urine, and whatever urine is found in the bladder is generally collected on autopsy. Hold on a sec."

We hear the clatter of his phone being set down, and then the clicking of a keyboard. After several seconds Arnie says, "Yep, there is a urine sample for him in my lab. Want me to test it?"

"Yes, please," Bob says. "Can you do it tonight and call me back?"

"I can. But understand that if the test comes back negative, it doesn't necessarily rule out that the drug was used. We may be too far beyond the testing window. And if it comes back positive, it may not be usable as evidence. There are some studies out there that show the spontaneous production of GHB in refrigerated urine. As a result, the concentration of GHB in any urine that's been refrigerated for a length of time can increase dramatically."

"Got it," Bob says. "Test it anyway and let me know what you find."

"Okay. Give me half an hour and I'll let you know."

"Thanks," Bob says, and then he jabs at the screen and disconnects the call.

"He sounds excited," I say.

Bob rolls his eyes. "Arnie loves a good conspiracy. The chance to turn a routine, tragic drug overdose into a murder is what he lives for."

"What does 'chasing the dragon' mean?" I ask, recalling Arnie's comment.

"I think it originally referred to a means of inhaling vapor from heated heroin, opium, or morphine that's placed on a piece of foil. But in this case Arnie is referring to the addict's search for a better high, a stronger reaction to whatever their drug of choice is, wanting to repeat the thrill of that first high. But the more often they use a drug, the more it takes to get the same effect. When they can't reproduce the original high, they try to achieve it by combining drugs. That's how fentanyl ended up getting mixed in with heroin. Users want a bigger bang for their buck, but half the time they end up buying a death sentence instead."

"What a horrible way to live."

"Mere existence rather than living," Bob says. "These drugs are a scourge."

I nod and turn my attention back to the police file. Over the next half hour, I read through more of the ME's report, study the pictures of the scene, and then read the initial officers' report, including subsequent notes that Brenda Joiner added after she talked to Sharon. The objective, sterile nature of this portion of the report is a stark contrast to what I'm sure was a highly emotional conversation.

While I'm doing this, Bob excuses himself for several

minutes. When he returns, he is busy texting away on his phone.

"Did you guys trace where the nine-one-one call came from?" I ask.

"We did," Bob says, setting his phone down. "It came from a burner cell bought in Ohio. A dead end." He looks a little embarrassed and then adds, "Excuse the pun."

"I'm okay with it," I tell him, smiling. "Humor is a coping mechanism often used by people who work in high-stress jobs. I bet death humor goes back as far as the Neanderthals."

He gives me that 51-15 look again and I turn my attention back to the file. I flip through some pictures and then stop on a digital copy of Toby's fingerprints. The right thumbprint has a clear line running through it, and I remember finding that same line in the prints I recovered from his room. Then I realize what it means.

"Toby's death was definitely staged," I say, tapping the fingerprint page. "And whoever did it didn't do a very good job. Toby's mother told me how he sliced his thumb on the lid of a can, creating this scar you see here." I point to the fingerprint image. "That scar is on his right thumb. And yet the print you took from the end of the syringe plunger doesn't have that line in it." I show him the page of partial prints that were found on the syringe. "While the thumbprint is only a portion of the whole, it's plain to see from the whorl pattern that the part of it on the syringe includes the pad of the thumb where that scar was. And yet, there is no line on the print taken from the plunger."

Bob runs a hand through his hair and scowls, though not at me. He's staring at the pages. And then his phone rings. It's still sitting on the table and I can see from the display that it's Arnie calling back.

"That was fast," I say. "Arnie really is eager."

For a second, I'm convinced Bob is going to pick that

phone up and put it to his ear, not letting me listen in. He's angry, not at me directly, but I am the messenger and therefore a logical target. His hand hovers over the phone, his brows drawn down into a near V. Two rings, then three, then he lets out a sigh of perturbed resignation, jabs a finger at the screen to answer the call, and hits the speaker icon.

"Whatcha got, Arnie?" he says, forgoing any formal greeting.

"Your suspicions were spot on," he says, and I can hear the excitement in his voice. "Toby Cochran was likely given GHB. I can't tell you for sure how much or even when, but I'd wager it was given less than two hours before he died."

Bob's right hand goes up to his face and starts massaging the area between his brows. "Thanks, Arnie," he says.

"No problem. Just doing my job. Anything else you want me to look for?" Arnie asks, his voice peppered with panting excitement, like a hound dog on scent.

"What about trace on the body?" I say, the first time I've spoken during either call. I figure the answer is likely buried in the file in front of me, but if Arnie knows the answer it might save me some time. However, my question is met with silence on Arnie's end.

Bob stares at the phone for a few seconds as if also waiting for an answer, and then his brows arch with dawning. "Oh, sorry, Arnie. I forgot to mention I have someone else listening in on our calls. She's a ride-along I'm taking for a bit. Her name is Hildy Schneider and she's a social worker up at the hospital." Bob gives me a grudging look of admiration. "The GHB was her idea."

"Well, it's a good one," Arnie says. "As for trace, there wasn't much. Some coconut oil on the soles of his shoes, traces of which were also found on the floor of the building where his body was found. It was likely tracked in by someone, but there's no way to know when or who. It looked like the victim tracked some of it in, but there were other tread marks that didn't match his shoes that had coconut oil in them. There was also dirt on the victim's shoes, the sort of stuff you find in and around town here, but buried beneath that in his treads was a flower petal and some other soil, a dark clay with a lot of rotted vegetation in it, probably from a river or streambed. It contained CCA, or chromated copper arsenate. It's what they used to use to treat lumber until it was stopped back in two thousand three. At some point there was a wood structure in whatever area that soil came from. It might still be there. Wood treated with CCA lasts a long time."

"And the flower petal?" I ask.

"It was from a plum tree. From what I understand, there aren't any around the kid's house or by the building where his body was found. Of course, those things can get blown great distances, so who knows how relevant that is."

"Thanks, Arnie," Bob says. He's scribbling madly in his notebook. "Can you send me an official report on that trace evidence? I don't remember seeing it in the autopsy report."

"It probably didn't get included, because it was older soil stuck high up in the treads. There were other layers on top of it and there's no way to tell when the kid walked in the clay stuff. Izzy might not have thought it was relevant."

I reach into my briefcase and take out the laptop, setting it on the table. And then I remove something else and set it next to the laptop. It's the picture of the footbridge from Toby's room. I tap my finger on it and give Bob a pointed look.

Bob nods back at me—rather begrudgingly, I think—and then thanks Arnie again before disconnecting the call.

"Soil by a streambed, preserved wood, and a plum tree," I say, pointing to the water, the footbridge, and the trees in

Toby's drawing. "A coincidence? I don't think so. We need to find this bridge."

"Easy enough," Bob says. "That aerial view we found on his laptop had the latitude and longitude of the location." His mouth skews sideways as he chews the inside of one cheek, staring at the drawing. Finally, he tosses his pen down and leans back in his chair, looking at me. "Okay, Hildy," he says. "You've proven your point. The kid's case is officially open again and being investigated as a homicide. Happy?"

"Well, I kind of am, though I have to admit it doesn't feel quite right to be happy about such a thing, does it?"

Bob huffs out a laugh, shakes his head, and rakes his fingers through his hair. "You're an interesting piece of work, Hildy Schneider."

Chapter Sixteen

"We need to start with the bridge location, but I think we also need to pay a visit to the fraternity Toby belonged to," I say to Bob, eager to keep our momentum going. "I have a feeling it has something to do with why he quit school, and even if it doesn't, it's likely some of his frat brothers will know something about what was going on with the kid back when all this happened. It might give us some leads."

"Hold on," Bob says, putting up a hand as if to stop my flow of words and ideas. "You've done good so far coming up with thoughts about this case, but you need to remember you're not a cop."

"But I'm doing a ride-along, right? You'll take me with you to see the bridge and when you go talk to the frat boys?"

"I haven't agreed to any of that yet," Bob says irritably. "And anyway, I'm not going to do it tonight. I suggest you go home and we start fresh in the morning."

"Tomorrow is good," I say. "It's a Saturday, and that means the frat boys might be around during the day, since most of them won't have classes. What time should we meet?"

"Are you forgetting our other arrangement?" Bob says.

For a moment I think perhaps he's hinting at some sort of sexual rendezvous, the cues for which I obviously missed. Then I remember. "Oh, right. The gym."

"Yes. Try to sound a little more enthusiastic about it. It's fun. You'll see. It's easier when you have a partner to work out with. Let's plan to meet at the gym at five in the morning, okay?"

I don't want to. I really, really don't want to. Exercise simply for the sake of exercise is a form of torture, in my opinion. And getting up that early on a Saturday seems like cruel and unusual punishment. But if I renege on the gym deal, I'm pretty sure Bob will blow off my ride-along.

"Fine. See you at five." I start to pack up the laptop, but he stops me with a hand on my arm.

"Listen, Hildy, I know you figured out how to get into the computer and it's your find. Kudos to you for that. Seriously." He beams a smile at me that is obviously forced. "But now that the case has been reopened officially, that laptop is evidence. And if you muck around with it and find something else that could be useful, or better yet, incriminating somehow, it won't be admissible as evidence. Would you want to be responsible for letting a killer go free on a technicality because you let your pride get in the way?"

I narrow my eyes at him, cocking my head to one side. "What are you suggesting?" I ask, though I know perfectly well what he's suggesting. And I have a strong suspicion it isn't a suggestion at all. He's just being kind for now, letting me save face before he wrestles the thing away from me and throws me in jail on an obstruction charge. Suddenly, I feel very vulnerable, and I start to wonder if this whole evening has been a sham, a show to get me to play along just enough for him to shove me out of the way.

Perhaps sensing my suspicions, Bob makes another appeal. "I want to turn in the laptop to my evidence tech, Laura. She can look through it tonight while we're sleeping. That will not only speed things up; it will better ensure the evidence chain if she finds anything useful."

"You're not going to ditch me tomorrow, are you?" I ask.

I hate being so paranoid, someone who always suspects the motives of others as nefarious, but my experience, both in the foster system and as a social worker, bears it out. I've been lied to, ripped off, and manipulated by some of the best.

"I won't bail," Bob says. "I work out every morning."

"I'm not talking about the gym, and you know it," I say in my best chastising tone. It's the one that gets Roscoe to look guilty even when he hasn't done anything wrong.

"I'm committed to having you along for the ride on this case," Bob says with a reassuring smile. "You've earned it. But like I said before, don't let your pride get in the way and ruin it for Toby, or his mother. Please?"

That last bit is pure manipulation and I shoot him a look to let him know I know it. But he finishes it off with a pleading expression that melts me a little. "Fine," I tell him. "But you have to tell me if you find anything on it, okay?"

"Deal," he says. I shove the laptop over to him. "What's the password?" he asks, opening it and poising his fingers over the keyboard.

Clearly, we still have some trust issues, because he isn't going to just take my word for it. I tell him, and after chuffing a laugh he types it in. This is followed by a satisfied grin as he closes the thing and tucks it under one arm.

"Do you have the cord for it?"

I fish it out of my briefcase and hand it over. Bob gets up and heads toward his office. I'm not sure if I'm welcome to follow him, and when I catch sight of the open door on the microwave oven I remember that I sprayed the inside of it.

"Mind if I clean out your microwave?" I call out after him, figuring this will at least keep me in the station for now.

"Knock yourself out," he says over his shoulder.

I grab a sponge and the spray bottle of cleaner and go to town on the microwave's interior until I have the entire thing sparkling clean. Satisfied, I shut the door and wipe down the outside. After straightening a few items on the countertops—a basket of condiment packets and jellies, a toaster, and a coffee maker—I feel comfortable enough to leave the break room. I head for Bob's office hoping I'm still welcome there and find him chatting with a young woman with long black hair pulled into a ponytail. She is wearing glasses that make her brown eyes look buggy big.

"Ah, Hildy, I'd like you to meet Laura Kingston, one of our evidence techs," Bob says. "She works a lot of night shifts, and we share her with the ME's office, so some of her hours are spent over there and some are here." Laura offers a hand and a big smile. "Laura, this is Hildy Schneider," Bob continues as Laura gives my entire arm a vigorous shake. "She's a social worker over at the hospital."

"You're the one who figured out how to crack into this computer," Laura says. Though it isn't technically a question, I start to answer anyway. But the woman doesn't give me a chance. "That's quite resourceful of you. Very clever. Detective Richmond tells me he's reopening the case because of you and some things you uncovered. You might be a detective in the making, Ms. Schneider. It is 'Ms.,' isn't it?" A lightning-quick glance at my left hand. "Or can I just call you Hildy? Is that short for something else? It's a very pretty name, and not all that common, though I knew a girl once who had a grandmother named Brunhilde and she had people call her Hildy. Who wouldn't with a name like that, right?"

As she emits a titter of a laugh, I open my mouth to answer any one of the questions she's tossed at me.

"I mean, what kind of person would name a kid Brunhilde?" Laura goes on before I can utter so much as a syllable. "Although these days it seems like anything goes, doesn't it? Oh no! I hope your name isn't Brunhilde. If it is, I'm sorry. I didn't mean anything by it, just that it seems cruelly old-fashioned, you know? It's Teutonic in origin and means 'armored battle maiden,' which is quite fierce, don't you think? Still, if I ever have a kid, I'll give it a simple, ordinary name. None of these weirdo names. Do you have kids? It's a full-time job being a parent, isn't it? Not sure I'm cut out for it, but who knows what the future holds? If I do have kids, I'd like to—"

"Laura!" Bob says in a loud voice.

The woman stops talking and claps a hand over her mouth. "Oops, sorry," she says with another titter. "I have a tendency to ramble a bit."

A bit?

"Laura has specialized some of her studies in the areas of forensic botany and toxicology," Bob informs me. "She also has an MBA." Laura nods, her hand again clamped over her mouth. I can tell from her eyes that she's smiling beneath it. Verbosity aside, I like her. She's bubbly, happy, and exuberant. It's hard not to like someone like that. "Tell Hildy what you were just telling me about the soil and the plum tree petal we found on Toby Cochran's shoe," Bob says.

Laura drops her hand to her side and I see I was right about the smile. "Plum trees bloom in early to mid-spring, typically around late March or early April," she begins, talking a little slower than before. "Their flowers are very fragile and tend to fall easily. The bloom rarely lasts more than a week, and if a good stiff wind comes along in that time, it will be an even shorter bloom. Given the time frame this spring, it's a good guess that our victim was near this plum tree between the twenty-fifth of March and the fourth of April. Also, if the tree is to produce fruit at all, there must be another plum tree somewhere close by to fertilize it. Otherwise the flowers won't produce any fruit. And it would appear from the soil sample that the tree in question does produce fruit, because there is evidence of old, decayed plums in the soil. That means there is likely more than one plum tree in the area where Toby's petal came from."

"Any idea where that might be?" I ask.

"Sorry, no," Laura says with an apologetic smile. "At this point it's more a case of knowing it's the spot once you find it rather than being able to find it from what we have."

I look at Bob. "Have you shown her the bridge picture on the computer?"

He shakes his head and turns his attention to Toby's laptop, which is sitting on the desk next to Bob's computer monitor. He taps the touch pad a few times and then turns the laptop so Laura can see the image.

"Are any of those trees plum trees?" I ask.

She bends down and stares bug-eyed at the picture. "Can you zoom in some more?"

Bob shakes his head. "That's as tight as it will go."

Laura sighs. "Hard to say at this distance. I'd need to see the leaves closer. But there are definitely some plum-sized trees." She points to some spots on the screen along the border of the heavily wooded area.

Bob is writing in his notebook again and I see that he is recording the coordinates noted in the lower left corner of the image. He then prints out a copy before handing the computer over to Laura.

"Dig around and see if you can find anything."

Laura, apparently still cued in to her need to be quiet, whips off a snappy salute before taking possession of the laptop. She then turns to me and says, "It was nice to meet you, Hildy. You never did tell me if that's your full name or a nickname."

"It's short for Clothilde," I toss out quickly, hoping to keep her from going off on another rambling speech. "It means 'famous in battle.'"

"And you are in this battle," Laura says with a smile.

"It was nice meeting you, as well," I say, hoping she'll

take the hint. She does, and with one last smile at the two
of us, she hurries from the office.

"I think that means it's time for us to call it a night,"
Bob says.

"Yes, I suppose it is."

"Thank you for dinner."

"And thank you for dessert. And for this." I wave a hand
in the air.

"You earned it." He is standing by the printer, his hands
smoothing down the front of his shirt and slacks. He looks
nervous, as if he thinks I might be expecting something
more from him, but he makes no move toward me. Given
that we're going to be spending time together cooped up
in a car, I decide it might be better to keep things platonic
for now.

To ease the tension I say, "I guess I'll see you in the
morning. Five o'clock sharp."

He nods but says nothing, and after we stand there
smiling awkwardly at each other for a few seconds, I turn
and leave, heading out through the break room and the
back door.

When I get home, I let Roscoe out into the yard and
pour myself one last glass of wine. As I reflect on my day,
I decide it was both full and a good one. My spirits take a
bit of a hit, however, when I undress for bed and discover
several jelly packets in my pants pocket and realize I have
no memory of putting them there.

Chapter Seventeen

My alarm chimes, disrupting a dream about dancing syringes in a disco nightclub. Not my strangest dream ever, not by a long shot, and it's not too hard to figure out where it came from, given the events of the evening before.

I roll over and slap the alarm into silence, then flop onto my back, staring at the ceiling and debating whether to keep my gym date with Bob Richmond. The bed feels cozy and comfortable, the blankets soft and warm, and Roscoe is curled up by my feet. I feel my eyelids grow heavy and let them close for a few seconds.

I startle awake some time later and fling myself out of bed, convinced I have just slept through most of the morning, not to mention the gym appointment. My actions startle Roscoe, who barks and leaps from the bed, alert and at attention. I see from the clock that only five minutes have passed and murmur some calming words to Roscoe. He lets out one last *woof* for good measure and then flops down onto the floor. I'd be tempted to flop down again, too, but thanks to my little surge of adrenaline I'm now wide awake. I stumble into the bathroom and begin my preparations, nearly tripping over Roscoe in the process.

It doesn't take long to realize I haven't thought things through very well. I don't have any appropriate gym wear, not that I'd know what that is. My last association with any type of gym was PE class in high school. The best I can come up with is a T-shirt, some sweatpants that, like most of the pants I buy, are too long, and my walking shoes, a pair of beat-up tennies that have Velcro straps instead of laces. I roll the waistband of the sweatpants several times, which gets them close to a normal length but also gives me an extra roll around my middle. I settle for a combination of rolling and cuffing instead.

Roscoe watches me with a look on his face that says it all. I suspect he's embarrassed for me, because when I grab his leash to give him a quick outing before I leave, he turns his head away and refuses to move.

"Fine, have it your way," I tell him, tossing the leash back onto the coat tree. "Just remember that it's Saturday. Don't come whining to me when P.J. doesn't show up at her usual time."

Despite my warning, I'm not too worried. Roscoe has proven to have an incredible bladder capacity, going twelve or more hours at a time without so much as a leg cross. P.J. comes by before school every morning to walk him, rain, snow, or shine, and typically shows up by eight on the weekends.

I arrive at the gym two minutes before five, find the main entrance unlocked, and stop just inside the front door. I'm surprised to see several people already inside working out. Clearly there are more insane people in Sorenson than I realized. Given the hour, I figured Bob and I would be the only ones here, though I don't see Bob yet. I'm halfway through a mental curse when I hear his voice behind me.

"Wasn't sure you'd make it."

I turn and smile at him. I didn't hear him enter and realize he's surprisingly light on his feet for a man his size.

"Neither was I, but I did," I say, looking around at the various contraptions before us. "I've never been to a gym before and I have no idea what to do with most of this equipment. Can you help me?"

"I've got someone much better to help you," Bob says. He looks over my shoulder and does a *come on* motion with his hand. I look and see a cute young girl with huge green eyes and dark red hair come jogging toward us, her ponytail swinging gaily. She stops in front of Bob and smiles, not the least bit out of breath, and I see then that her face is dotted with freckles.

"Sherri, this is Hildy," Bob says. "She's my guest today and new here, so I was hoping you could show her the ropes."

"Happy to," Sherri says, beaming that thousand-watt smile at me.

"I'm going to go work my circuit," Bob says, and then he heads for a contraption rigged with a bunch of weights, wires, and pulleys. I'm disappointed to see him go—I admit I had a vision of him being the one to "show me the ropes"—but I'm also kind of glad because I have a bad feeling about what's to come and how much I'm going to humiliate myself.

Sherri gives me a quick once-over and says, "I take it you don't follow any type of formal exercise program?"

"Is it that obvious?" I say, embarrassed.

"No worries," she says. "We all start somewhere. Let's begin with a tour."

I'm relieved; a tour I can handle. Fifteen minutes later, she has shown me the entire place, from the women's locker room and showers, which I vow to never use, to the office area. She breezes over most of the exercise machines, telling me she'll go into more detail as needed later. Then we do a health questionnaire, which I'm able to pass without any red flags popping up, other than the fact that my BMI is nearly the same as my age. I'm a little shocked when I get on the scale, since I've been avoiding mine at home.

I tell Sherri that I'm not overweight, I'm just under-tall. She smiles at that, so I go for another one.

"It's hard to stay thin when you're what I like to refer to as fun size."

"We'll see about that," she says ominously, and I decide to quit with the jokes for now.

Sherri puts together a program for me, a series of exercises clearly geared toward helping me lose weight, build strength, and kill myself. She demonstrates each one for me, doing it with all the ease and charm of a late-night infomercial queen. It encourages me at first, making me think the machines can't be all that hard, but when my turn to try each one comes about, I realize Sherri is in great shape and I'm not. I try not to look embarrassed as she lightens the weights on the machines for me, and then lightens them some more when I still can't perform the demonstrated exercise. I'm sweating like a pig by the time we're done, and my legs are shaking so badly I'm not sure I'll be able to drive myself home. That's when Sherri informs me that this hasn't been my actual routine, but rather an orientation and warm-up. She then sits me down and fills out a form that details my actual exercise routine, the various machines I'm to use, how much weight to apply to each, and how many reps I should do. The mere thought of it makes me nearly blow a circuit.

During all this, Bob glances over and smiles at me several times, and once even gives me a thumbs-up as I'm struggling red-faced to try and keep the machine I'm on from ripping my arms out of their sockets. His encouragement bolsters me to the point that I think I can at least make it to my car before dying, though that is before I have time to sit with Sherri and go over my circuit. Getting out of my seat when I'm done with her proves to be an exercise in agony, the only form of exercise I expect I'll be experiencing the rest of the day.

Bob is still working his circuit when Sherri finishes with me, and I tell him I'm going home to shower and will meet him at the station in an hour if I'm still alive. Then, clutching the membership information Sherri has given me, I hobble out to my car. As I drop into my front seat with a groan, I decide the gym's marketing plan needs a redo. They need to seal up the membership stuff *before* they cripple their potential customers.

P.J. is bringing Roscoe back to the house from his walk when I pull into my driveway. "Where have you been?" she says, eyeing my tomato-red face and sweat-streaked clothes.

"I went to a gym," I say as I try to pry my screaming body out of my car.

"Really?" She gives me a coy smile. "Does this have anything to do with that detective? Do I smell a romance in bloom?"

"All you smell right now is a lady who nearly sweated herself to death." My pride kicks in, and even though I'm screaming in pain in my head, I force a smile onto my face as I head for the front door. I hope P.J. will drop Roscoe off and leave once we're inside, but no such luck. She unhooks him, hangs his leash on the coat tree, and follows me into the kitchen, where I go about fixing myself a couple of toaster waffles with a side of ibuprofen. Shades of some drivel Sherri muttered about healthy eating echo in the back of my mind as I wait for the waffles to pop up, but I mentally gag her, tie her limbs to one of the exercise machines, and then add lots of weights to it.

"I love those," P.J. says, eyeing my waffles when they pop up.

I roll my eyes at her. "Very subtle . . . not." I put the two warm waffles on a plate and hand it to her. Then I remove two more waffles from the freezer and drop them into the toaster.

P.J. knows her way around my house, and it doesn't take

her long to get out the butter, the maple syrup, and a couple of forks and knives. She settles in at the table in my kitchen and starts buttering her waffles. "Are you dating this detective guy?" she asks.

"I don't know," I say honestly. "I'm interested in him. But for right now our relationship is on more of a professional basis."

"You should totally date him," P.J. says, pouring syrup onto her waffles. "You need to get out more."

"Easier said than done," I grumble. "Dating is hard when you live in a small town and work all the time. You don't meet a lot of guys."

"What about online dating?" P.J. suggests, shoveling in her first bite of waffle. Mine pop up in the toaster, and I transfer them to my plate and then join her at the island counter.

"I tried that," I tell her. "I had this one guy who seemed interesting. He wasn't bad-looking, and his profile said he was a metalworker who lived in a gated community."

"Did you meet him?"

I shake my head. "Turns out the gated community he lived in was actually a prison and the metalwork he did was making license plates."

P.J.'s eyes grow huge, and she bites back a laugh. After swallowing, she says, "When are you going to see the detective again?"

"In about an hour. I need to shower and then I'm heading down to the police station."

"Are you stalking him?"

"No, I'm not stalking him," I say, giving her a look of exasperation. "I'm looking into a suspicious death for one of the people in my grief support group, and Detective Richmond is helping me. He's going to let me ride along with him for a while."

"Sounds like fun. Can I come?"

"Sorry, kiddo. Not this time." P.J. pouts but accepts her fate with good humor. She's a great kid: smart, funny, kind, and quick on her feet. I enjoy her company and I'm grateful to Roscoe for bringing her to me. I'm also glad her father is allergic to dogs, or so he says. I'm suspicious of his claim, however, given that I've seen P.J. go home with fur balls on her clothing and her father never seems bothered by the hair and dander. I suspect P.J.'s parents don't want the work, dirt, and expense of having a dog, so they use this allergy story to give them an out.

We finish our respective waffles and I excuse myself to go shower. By the time I come back downstairs I feel a little better, my tight, angry muscles loosened some by the hot water and ibuprofen. P.J. has left, but she has cleaned up our breakfast residue. After telling Roscoe to be a good boy, I leave for the police station.

When I arrive, the dispatcher on duty tells me Bob isn't there, and for a moment I'm afraid he's gone on without me, ditching me the first chance he got. But then the dispatcher informs me she is expecting him any minute and has me wait in the front area. Eager but nervous, I pace for the duration of my five-minute wait, partly to calm my nerves, but also because I'm afraid that if I stop moving, I won't be able to get started again. The effects of the shower have worn off and the ibuprofen hasn't fully kicked in yet. When the dispatcher finally buzzes me in, I hurry through the door and down the hall toward Bob's office, noting all the quiet, empty offices I pass along the way.

Bob is seated at his desk, the folder I looked at last night in front of him. He is on his phone, listening or holding—I'm not sure which—and not talking. His small notebook is in front of him on the desk, and he has a pen in his right hand. While he isn't writing anything, I see that he has scribbled down several things. He waves me into the room and gestures toward a chair that he must have dragged into the room. As I settle in, I try to read what he has written. I can't make it out without being obvious, and for a second, I debate going for it and being blatantly nosy. But my relationship with Bob, both personally and professionally, is still too new. I decide I need to give it more time before I start pushing boundaries, so I sit and wait.

I listen as Bob mutters some "uh-huhs" and "I sees." When he finally says, "Thanks," and disconnects the call, I lean forward, eager to hear what news there might be. But all he does is get up and crook a finger at me, indicating that I should follow him. He leads me back down the main hall toward the front of the building and in behind the dispatcher's desk. She acknowledges him with a nod but says nothing, and I follow Bob to a door at the far end of her desk. He takes a key ring from his front pocket and holds a fob up to a scanning panel mounted beside the door. There is a buzz and a click, and then he opens the door. This leads us into another short hallway, more of a large foyer area.

Bob nods to the left, where I see another door, this one with a mesh-lined window and another scanner on the wall beside it. "Our two holding cells are down there," he says. "We don't typically keep anyone here overnight. If that's necessary, we have to drive them to Madison or Portage."

"Wow, that's a long way."

"Kind of a pain, all right," he agrees. "But we don't have the staff to watch inmates overnight here. There have been some short-term, temporary exceptions, but as a rule, it doesn't happen."

There is a second door to our right, and this is the one Bob goes through, once again using his fob. This time we end up at the top of a stairwell. I mentally groan at the sight of the stairs, hoping my legs will have enough strength left in them to carry me down and then, presumably and more concerningly, back up again. As we descend, I realize that this lower level is bigger than most. The stairs go down at least twenty feet, maybe more. The reason for this becomes apparent quickly. After we fob through another door, we enter a large open area with a high ceiling.

"This is our garage," Bob explains, nodding toward the empty room, which I guess to be about two stalls wide.

"Really?" I say. "Who gets to park in here instead of the lot?"

"It's not for parking, at least not long-term. It's for unloading and processing evidence."

"Ah, I see."

Bob walks over to yet another door but doesn't have to use his fob this time. We enter another large room, this one filled with counters, cabinets, tables, a desk, and a lot of expensive-looking machinery. Standing in front of a counter against the wall to my left is a man who looks to be in his early to mid-thirties. He's a bit on the roly-poly side—not fat so much as well padded—and he looks to be only a few inches taller than me. His eyes are big and dark brown, and he has dirty-blond hair cut short on the sides with bangs in front. He's attractive in a boyish sort of way, looking like a cross between Michael J. Fox and Davy Jones from the Monkees' heyday.

"Hey, Jonas," Bob says.

"Good morning," Jonas counters with a smile, his gaze settling on me. "I see you've brought me a visitor."

"I have. This is Hildy Schneider. She's a social worker, currently employed at the hospital." Jonas arches his brows at this, and the two men exchange a look. "She's doing a ride-along with me," Bob explains.

Jonas approaches me and extends a hand. "I'm Jonas Kriedeman," he says, wrapping my hand in a grip that's warm and firm. "I'm an evidence technician for the police department."

"Nice to meet you," I say, returning his smile. Our gazes linger for a few seconds and Jonas looks away first, though

I note that he sneaks a peek at my left hand before turning his attention back to Bob.

"I take it you've reopened the Toby Cochran case?" Jonas says.

"Looks that way," Bob says with a glance in my direction.

"Well, Laura made some progress with that laptop last night." Jonas looks at me again, his head cocked slightly to one side. "Are you the gal who figured out how to bypass the fingerprint scanner?"

"Afraid so," I admit with a mixture of sheepishness and pride.

"Clever," he says with a wink. "I take it you launched his email program once you got into the computer?"

I shoot a guilty look toward Bob before answering. "I did, but I immediately closed it again without reading anything."

"Well, our victim had an email composed and ready to send sitting in his outbox, but it didn't get sent before the program was shut down. There was a big thunderstorm the night Toby drafted the email and the power went out in several places around town, so that might be why it didn't get sent originally. Toby had the laptop set up so that as soon as he booted it up it would search for a nearby open Wi-Fi system and automatically sign onto it. So when you opened the email program, the email got sent."

"Oh," I say with a grimace. "Who did it go to?" I say a silent prayer that it wasn't Toby's mother. Getting an email from her dead son weeks after the fact would be disconcerting, to say the least.

"It went to several people," Jonas explains. "And it seems to have stirred things up." He walks over to a counter and picks up several pieces of paper. Then he spreads them out on a table and motions for us to come look at them. They are printouts of emails.

"This is what got sent," Jonas says, tapping the first sheet of paper. The email is brief. All it says is: Sorry, I can't stay silent about it any longer. I need to tell someone.

I look at the recipients and see that it went to three people, the same three boys who were involved in the email exchange Bob and I read last night.

"And these are the replies," Jonas says, waving a hand over the other sheets. "They are succinct and to the point. Mitchell Sawyer's response is to Toby only and it's a demand to know who sent the email and how they know about 'it,' though he doesn't say what 'it' is."

"Liam Michaelson's reply also goes to Toby only, and he wants to know if a ghost has sent the email, or if Toby's death was faked. I imagine the first half of that query was somewhat tongue-in-cheek," Jonas says, "though it can be hard to discern context from emails."

"Alex Parnell's reply went to all three of the others and is the most laconic of them all, two simple words: 'Shut up!'"

"Do you know anything about these three fellows?" Bob asks.

Jonas nods. "Laura did some digging. They all live at Alpha Theta Pi, a frat house on campus." He walks over to a computer on a counter against the wall and starts typing. "I just sent the info Laura dug up to your cell phone."

Bob's cell phone chimes a second later to acknowledge the receipt. "Thanks," he says.

"That's the same frat house Toby lived in," I say, feeling a little ignored and left out. Plus, I think I deserve some of the credit since I had earlier recognized the fact that the boys all had university email addresses and had suggested they might be members of Toby's fraternity.

Jonas smiles. "Yes, it is."

"We're planning on visiting there," I say. Bob frowns at this while Jonas looks at me with an amused expression.

"Any luck on those coordinates I gave Laura?" Bob asks Jonas.

"Some," he says, his smile fading. "It's on private property." He walks over to the desk and picks up a piece of paper. "Here's the contact info for the owner."

Jonas hands the sheet to Bob, who glances at it and says, "Oh," in a disappointed tone. He then folds it up, and stuffs it in his shirt pocket.

"Yeah," Jonas says, sounding equally disillusioned.

My curiosity is thoroughly piqued but I'll be darned if I'll beg this boys' club to let me in on the deal. For now, I'm willing to bide my time and figure it out on my own. I have my ways. My years in the foster system may not have been the most nurturing, but they taught me some handy spy skills.

"Thanks," Bob says to Jonas. "Let me know if you come up with anything else." He turns to leave, and I dutifully fall into step behind him. We don't get far, however, before Jonas calls my name.

"Hildy?"

"Yes?"

"Pardon me if I'm being too forward, but I wonder if you might be willing to have dinner with me sometime? Maybe take in a movie?"

I'm stunned. And flattered. I think I see a frown flit across Bob's face, but it's there and gone so fast I can't be sure. I debate my answer for a moment. Jonas is an attractive and apparently eligible fellow, which is reason enough to accept. But the fact that he also has insider access to police business pushes me over into *hell, yeah* territory. My good angel tells me this is not a fair or legitimate reason to want to date the man, but my bad angel shoves her off my shoulder and points out that I find Jonas genuinely attractive, and if his job happens to come in handy for investigating my mother's death, that's just a happy coincidence. And besides, Bad Angel reminds me, it's not like I have an exclusive relationship with Bob. We've only had the one dinner together, and it was a mix of personal and business agendas.

"Sure," I say to Jonas. "That sounds like fun."

"How about tomorrow night?" Jonas says, surprising me even more. The man certainly knows how to get to the point, and I find this oddly attractive. I like decisive men, even if I do bristle if they ever try to decide for me. I never said I was a rational woman.

"Okay," I say after a nanosecond of thought. "Do you want to meet somewhere?"

"Would it be okay if I pick you up?" He smiles nervously. "Of course, if you're not comfortable with that for a first date, I understand. Though I think Richmond here can vouch for me."

Bob frowns, mutters something unintelligible, and looks at his feet.

"You can pick me up," I decide. "But I have to warn you, I have a vicious guard dog."

Bob snorts amusement at this, and the fleeting look of concern on Jonas's face fades quickly when he realizes I'm joking.

"How does six o'clock sound?" Jonas asks.

"That sounds fine. I'm looking forward to it."

I give Jonas my address and we exchange phone numbers, entering them into our respective cells.

We leave then, Bob scowling as he leads the way back upstairs. My leg muscles, as feared, complain loudly, but I find that the pain is easier to ignore due to my good mood. I hope the muscles will be better by tomorrow evening. It won't be much of a first date if I'm in a state of rigor mortis.

Once we reach the main hallway, Bob says, "Looks like we're taking a trip to a fraternity house. Ready to go rushing?"

"Ready and able. I hope the hazing isn't too rough, though. My childhood was basically one big hazing, and I've had enough of that, thank you very much."

Bob cocks his head slightly and looks at me, a curious expression forming on his face. "You are an interesting woman, Hildy Schneider," he says.

Chapter Eighteen

"Your childhood couldn't have been that bad," Bob says as we head out to his car. "You passed the background check without any problems."

"Good to know my juvie record is still sealed," I say, settling in the front seat and shutting the door. "I haven't always been a goody two-shoes."

He shoots me a curious look. "What did you do?"

I click my seat belt into place and tuck the shoulder strap under my arm, wincing as I feel the painful protest of muscles I never knew I had. He eyes me with a dubious expression, so I explain my actions before answering his question. "When you're my height these shoulder straps hit you in the face instead of the shoulder. Cars aren't made for short people."

He stares at my chest for a moment and then gives me a conciliatory shrug.

"As for my corrupt childhood, don't worry. Like I said before, I didn't kill anyone, at least not that I know of. But I did shoplift a few times." Bob narrows his eyes at me. It might have been the bright sunlight that made him do it, but I cave anyway. "Okay, a lot of times, but I only got caught a few times." He keeps staring at me and I fess up to more. "And there may have been a battery charge."

"Battery?" Bob says, eyeing me with amused skepticism. "Who did you beat up, a dwarf?"

I shoot him a wounded look. "Very funny," I say without humor. Then I square my shoulders and straighten up as tall as I can, though it's difficult since my feet barely touch the floor. "Actually, it was two kids," I say with some pride. "Both of them boys and both of them quite a bit bigger than me."

Bob eyes me again, this time warily.

"I was . . . shall we say . . . pushed over the edge," I tell him.

"The edge of what?" He starts the engine and shifts into gear.

"Sanity, I think." This earns me an arch of his brows as the gate rolls open and we get underway. "Let me explain. I was walking to a store a few blocks away, and I had to go past this alley that ran between the houses on the block. Down that alley I saw these two boys holding a squirming, whining dog. One of the boys was pouring liquid from a gas can onto the dog. That by itself was enough to light my fire, if you'll excuse the expression, but when I saw the other boy take out a lighter, I guess I went a little berserk. To be honest, I don't remember much of it, only that I was so filled with rage and anger at those boys that I could have killed them."

"But you didn't," Bob says.

"No, someone pulled me off them at some point. Otherwise, who knows? The cops showed up about the same time."

"And the dog? The boy didn't . . ." He lets the unspeakable act remain unspoken.

"No, thank goodness. It ran off somewhere. I went back the next day and looked for it. In fact, I went back for the next two weeks to look for that dog, but I never could find it."

"What exactly did you do to the boys?" Bob's voice is

warier than before, as if he only now realizes he's locked himself inside a small coupe with a raving lunatic.

"As I said before, I don't really remember it. It was as if my brain just exploded or something. But according to the record I bloodied both boys' noses and knocked one of them to the ground, and he hit his head hard enough to knock him unconscious. That was the boy who had the lighter. The second boy I kicked, and it broke the smaller of the two bones in his lower leg. They told me I also broke three of his fingers. Oh, and he had a black eye, as well."

I glance over at Bob, who is staring straight ahead as he drives, his face oddly expressionless.

"It was my word against theirs, and the dog couldn't be found, but the boys had the gas can and the lighter, and one of them had been bitten." I pause and shake my head. "I hope the little bastard had to undergo rabies shots."

This earns me a sidelong glance from Bob.

"Anyway, the parents of the boys were going to press charges, but when the police told them what the boys had been doing, they decided to let it go in exchange for the boys not getting charged. Plus, there was the whole pride thing associated with a tiny girl beating the crap out of not one, but two boys single-handedly. I was slapped with a battery charge and spent some time in juvie as a result, but it was worth it."

"I gather the moral of that story is to not piss you off."

I smile. "I suppose so, yes."

"Did you beat up anyone else during your misspent youth?"

"No, nothing beyond the typical self-defense, sibling rivalry kind of stuff, though that got intense at times. It wasn't easy being a foster kid. Couple that with my size and you get what looks like an easy target. I had to learn to defend myself at a young age. I wasn't always successful, and even then, I'd often be punished by my foster parents.

Didn't matter what the truth was most of the time. If it came down to my word against that of one of the bio kids in the household, I always came out the loser."

"How old did you say you were when you went into the system?"

"Seven."

"And your mom . . ." Whatever he'd been about to say, he apparently changed his mind.

"She wasn't all bad," I tell him, once again indulging my lifelong need to come to her defense. It's something my shrink has talked with me about a lot, though I don't think the talking has changed anything.

"I know my mother tried to make an honest go of things at times, because I remember her taking me with her to a restaurant and telling me to sit in a booth for hours while she waitressed. And she had a newspaper delivery route at one point, because I have memories of her handing me papers and me climbing out of the car to run them up onto the porches. But then the car gave up the ghost and she couldn't do it anymore." I pause and sigh. "The money was never enough even with those jobs, and the men were always there as a backup, I suppose, though at the end it seemed like it was a revolving door of them."

I pause, looking out the window at the passing scenery. Spring, with all its promise, is evident everywhere: in the brilliant, verdant leaves on the trees; the bright yellows, pinks, and purples of the wildflowers springing up alongside the road; and the rich, velvety brown of just-tilled fields made ready for planting. It provides a stark contrast to the darkness surrounding the memories I'm resurrecting. Bob remains quiet, the only sound in the car the slight hiss of an air leak in a window somewhere and the hum of the tires on pavement.

"One of those men killed her," I say finally. "He did it

while I slept in the next room. I found her the following morning."

From the corner of my eye I see Bob shoot a glance my way. I can't see his expression, but I can guess what it is. It's the same expression everyone gets when I tell this story: pity.

"She didn't die easily," I go on eventually, feeling my throat tighten. Even now, all these years later, that image, that fact, hollows out a spot in my chest, releasing a flood of locked-up emotion that threatens to choke my throat and flood my eyes. My head starts to throb with the effort of holding back tears. "She was strangled and stabbed, ironically with her own knife, one she kept under the mattress as a means of protection in case . . ." I can't finish but know I don't need to. Bob will understand.

"Did you see the man who did it?" Bob asks.

His question surprises me. Most people are compelled to offer stuttering condolences and then escape as quickly as they can when I describe what happened. Apparently, the detective in Bob has won out over his empathy. Or maybe . . . An idea buds in my mind, and I ponder it for a few seconds, weighing its potential. Then I tuck it away for later perusal.

"I didn't see his face," I tell him. "My mother always made sure I was in my room with the door shut before the men arrived. But sometimes I peeked out through the key-hole. I caught glimpses of the men, their backs, their legs, their shoes. And I heard their voices and . . . um, other things. But I almost never saw their faces. The house we lived in when she died was very small—it had been a carriage house at one point before someone threw up some interior walls and decided to rent it. The front door was only about ten feet away from my bedroom door, and it was off at an angle, so I couldn't see the men until they were walking past my room to go to my mother's bedroom."

"But you saw something of the man who killed your mother?"

"I did. The phone rang during the night, and it woke me. I heard my mother talking and telling someone to come over. I think I drifted off after that, but I woke again a little while later when someone knocked on the door. I climbed out of bed thinking I'd see who it was, but I realized my bedroom door was closed, and my mother had made it clear to me that when my bedroom door was closed I was supposed to stay in my room. I did, but I put my eye to the keyhole."

I glance over at Bob to gauge his reaction to my story. His expression is one of thoughtful curiosity now rather than pity, and his eyes are focused on the road ahead.

"I heard a man's voice," I continue, "and it was one I'd heard before. It stood out because he had an accent, a Southern drawl. My mother had several repeat customers, and I knew I'd heard this one before. All I could see of him was his pants, his shoes, and his right hand. He was wearing a ring with a big red stone with what looked like numbers around it on his fourth finger, and his pinky finger was a stub, cut off just above the knuckle. Later I figured out it was probably a class ring, but at that age I didn't know what a class ring was. I remember his pants were cuffed and creased, and dark blue in color. His shoes were black, and they had little tassels on them. Loafers, I would later learn, but again, at the age I was then, I didn't know one kind of shoe from another. And his feet and legs were wet because it was raining outside."

"Did you stay awake the whole time the man was there?"

"No," I say with a sigh. "It was standard stuff, and I was tired. I went back to bed and woke sometime later. My door was open, and I could see that it was daylight outside.

Morning time was always my mother's off time, and since my bedroom door was open, I figured she was up already." I pause, caught up in a memory of her. I can see her in my mind's eye, her fine, delicate features beneath a messy pixie cut of hair that inevitably stood up near her crown thanks to a persistent cowlick, her hands wrapped around a steaming mug of coffee, her blue eyes tired but full of love as she looked at me across the table.

"Mornings were our time," I say, fighting back tears. "If she wasn't up already, I could wake her once the sun was up. I looked in the kitchen first, but she wasn't there. I went to her bedroom and found her in bed. I tried to wake her, but I couldn't." I turn and stare out the side window, losing my battle with my tears and not wanting Bob to see it.

Silence marks the next few miles, and it's a surprisingly comfortable quiet.

"So you don't know for sure that the man you saw was the one who killed her?" Bob says after a time. "If you slept all night, someone else could have come into the house without you knowing it."

"Oh, but I do know. I know because a partial impression of that ring the man was wearing was found on her neck. The coroner's report has both a written description of it and a photo of the mark. It's so clear you could make out the number nineteen on her neck, presumably part of a date. And there were only three finger impressions on the left side of her neck, which is where the hand would have been if he was choking from the front. Then there's the timing. The man arrived right at ten. I know that because my mother loved the show *The X-Files* and she was watching it when the man called. I heard the closing music playing when the man arrived."

I pause, sucking in a shuddering breath. Even all these years later the memories are hard on me. "The thing that sometimes haunts me in my dreams?" I say, staring out the windshield but seeing into the past. "He had to have come in my room, or at least looked in on me. Because my door was open, and my mother didn't open it. Her time of death was not long after that man arrived. He killed her and then came to check on me."

Bob glances over at me but quickly faces forward again.

"He could have killed me, too," I say just above a whisper. "Probably would have if I'd been awake." I swallow hard. "How long did he stand there watching me? Did he stay in the doorway or walk over to my bed? What thoughts went through his mind?" I take in a bracing breath and blow it out. "In my dreams I sometimes see him, a faceless man standing next to me, that four-fingered hand reaching for me."

"Maybe he left and came back to kill your mother later," Bob suggests. "Maybe it was her who opened your bedroom door."

I shake my head. I know he's trying to ease my nightmares, but I've thought this whole thing through six ways from Sunday and I know what has to have happened. "It rained that night up until eleven," I tell him, "and the yard and driveway of our house were mostly mud. According to the police file, there was only one set of tire tracks and one set of shoe prints out there."

Bob shoots me a dubious look. "You have the police file?"

"I have a copy. It had been a cold case for two decades when I finally asked for it. I had to wait until I was eighteen and on my own, out of the foster system. And for the first six years or so, I was focused on getting an education. It wasn't until I graduated and got my first job that I really started to think about my mother's death and the fact that her killer was never caught."

"Where did it happen?" Bob asks. "I mean, where were you living when your mother died?"

"In Milwaukee. A detective who was working my mother's case got in touch with me from time to time when I was a teenager. He was the one who gave me a copy of the file. He was getting ready to retire and I guess he felt guilty or something."

"Are you still in touch with him?"

I shake my head and give Bob a wan smile. "He's dead. Died four years ago of a heart attack. He was a heavy smoker and very overweight."

Bob nods knowingly. "I was on that fast track myself. Fortunately, getting shot turned my life around."

I give him an amused look.

"I know, it sounds silly," he says with a chuckle. "But it's true. I was two hundred pounds heavier than I am now, retired because of my weight, and well on my way to an early grave. I was filling in on a case because Detective Hurley was sick, except he wasn't really sick." He blows out a breath and his lips vibrate. "That part of the story doesn't matter."

"It must have been scary for you."

"Scary and an eye-opener. I was in the hospital for a long time and almost died due to complications. When the doctors told me how close I still was to dying because of my weight, it struck home with me. I was in rehab for months, and by the time I got out I'd already lost close to fifty pounds." He gives me a sardonic look and adds, "Not a diet plan I would recommend, however."

"And not one I want to try," I assure him.

"Anyway, once I had that much of a start, I got determined. I joined the gym and kept at it. Changed my diet and my lifestyle. And here I am, two hundred–plus pounds lighter, feeling good. I'm even back to working full-time."

"That's quite a story. You should do motivational talks."

Bob's hands tighten on the wheel and his face flushes. "No, I'm not much for public speaking. I'm not much for talking at all outside of what I need to do for work. I've shared more non-work-related stuff with you on this ride than I do with most people when I'm with them all day."

"I'm good that way," I say, smiling. "People always open up to me. I think it's my size. Clearly, I'm no threat. And I like to think my social work training has helped make me approachable."

Bob makes a sound—a guttural grunt of sorts. I'm not sure if it's a commentary or a digestive issue. "You picked a good career considering your upbringing," he says. "I can't imagine a childhood like that. And you seem relatively normal despite it all."

"Define 'normal,'" I say with a laugh. "I have a good case of obsessive-compulsive disorder that my shrink thinks is due to my need to bring order into my life. And I keep finding random items in my pockets, things I've picked up and taken without any knowledge of doing so. I do it with food, mostly, but sometimes it's other things."

"You have a shrink?" Bob says, and I curse silently, wondering if I've crossed over into TMI territory and jinxed any hope of a relationship with him down the road, not to mention my continued ability to do this ride-along thing.

"I do," I confess. "It was part of the intake process into the foster system in the beginning, and when it was determined I had some behavioral issues, it continued. At one point it was court ordered. That was when I was twelve and got into a bit of trouble. A little matter of a boy I liked and a car he stole." I shrug. "I wasn't found guilty of anything, but the foster parents I had at the time told the judge that I was difficult to handle and had no respect for authority." I chuckle. "They were right that I had no respect for their type of authority, which was to function as their household slave while their own kid lounged around and did whatever she wanted."

I pause, shaking my head with the memory as if I can

somehow shake it away. "I went through a litany of shrinks in the beginning because most of them were a waste of time. The first one was a guy who had developed a theory he was testing out, something to do with scare tactics. His idea of therapy was to frighten the daylights out of me any-time I said or did anything he thought was disrespectful. The idiot had one of those blast horns he would fire, and a scream machine, and this chair that delivered mild shocks when he pushed a button. He was a real whack-a-doodle."

Bob laughs.

"I didn't stay with him very long, thank goodness. But some of the ones that followed weren't much better. Once I turned eighteen, I wasn't required to go to therapy any-more, but I've kept with it for the most part. It seems to help me."

"What made you pick social work for a career?"

"Two things. One noble, one not so much. The noble reason was that there were social workers I dealt with during my years in the foster system who really helped me and looked out for me the best they could. I thought I could do the same thing for other kids in the system, particularly since I had an insider's perspective."

"And the other reason?" he prompts.

"It was a boy—a boy I had a crazy mad crush on who was also studying to be a social worker."

"And did you get the boy?"

"Not exactly. He's a good friend and someone I still see from time to time, but his interests led him elsewhere."

Bob looks at me with sympathy. "He liked another girl?"

"Actually, he liked another boy." I shrug. "I tried for a while to convert him, but to no avail."

Bob chuckles and we fall into another comfortable silence. I'm thinking about the frat boys we're hoping to talk to, and I start planning in my head, playing out different approaches and the potential responses. After a few minutes of this, I look over at Bob and say, "Can I have your phone for a moment?"

Bob gives me a sidelong look of suspicion. "Why?"

"I want to review the info on the frat boys that Jonas emailed to you."

"Why?" Bob asks again.

"If I'm going to be talking to them and asking them questions, I need to be able to keep their details straight, don't I?"

The comfortable atmosphere between us vanishes as Bob pulls the car over to the side of the road, shifts into park, and turns to stare at me in disbelief. "You've gone mad, woman," he says.

Chapter Nineteen

"You can't seriously think I'm going to let you talk to these boys," Bob says in a tone of disbelief.

"Why not?"

He sighs and combs his fingers through his hair. "Look, Hildy, I said you could come along, and I might even let you listen in when I question these boys, but this is an official investigation, and you're not an official member of the team."

I anticipated this objection and have an answer ready for him. "Just how much information do you think you're going to get out of anyone strutting into this fraternity with your air of officious authority and your flashy badge? Who do you think these guys might be more willing to talk to, you or a harmless-looking lady like myself?" I flash him my best friendly, nonthreatening, lady smile, one I've used often in my job. I learned the value of seeming innocuous, sometimes even vacuous, long ago.

"We need official authority if we're going to use what they say later in any sort of legal proceeding," Bob argues.

"If someone divulges something you think is evidentiary, then you can always question them again later. But I promise you, if you go blustering your way into that fraternity this morning questioning people like the cop you are, they're going to clam up, lawyer up, and not give you anything useful. These Greek houses are a tight-knit, secretive, protective bunch as it is." I pause and give him my best pleading look. "Let me have first crack at them. We can do it with an open phone line if you want. That way you can hear everything I say and everything they say. Or I can record my conversations on my phone if you like."

Bob gapes at me, and then laughs. "You actually think I'd let you go talk to them *alone*?" Apparently, this is a rhetorical question, because he doesn't give me a chance to answer, which is just as well, since I'm certain he wouldn't like what I have to say. "You really are a madwoman! I never should have agreed to let you do this ride-along."

"Come on, Bob," I cajole. "Let me do it. I'll get more out of them than you will. And I'm trained for this sort of thing."

"Not a chance. For one thing, you're *not* trained for this sort of thing, because you aren't a cop. And for another thing, it's too dangerous. What if it turns out that whoever killed Toby is someone in that fraternity? You could be chatting with a cold-blooded killer."

"In a fraternity full of people," I remind him. "Hard to get away with murder when there are dozens of witnesses around."

"What if it's a conspiracy of some sort?" Bob poses, clearly unwilling to give in. "It could be more than one person is involved." He gives me a quick once-over. "It wouldn't be that hard to make someone like you disappear. I could do it easily."

The way he says this, combined with the look he gives me, is both titillating and frightening. I sigh. I can tell it's time to compromise. I have him upset enough with plan A that he'll hopefully be open to plan B, which was my goal all along. Bob Richmond doesn't have a clue that I've just played him.

"Okay, how about this?" I suggest, trying to sound contrite. "We go in together, but you don't say anything to anyone about being a cop. It's far enough outside your jurisdiction that no one should know you. We'll tell them we're a couple, the boy's aunt and uncle, say, and we're trying to find out more about his death because his poor mother—we can say she's your sister—is struggling with guilt."

Bob doesn't answer me. His face screws up in thought, his eyes narrowing, his lips contorting as he chews the inside of one cheek. His fingers play some imaginary keyboard on the steering wheel. I think maybe he suspects what I've just done, but he isn't sure enough to say anything.

"You'll have to be careful not to sound like a cop," I go on, taking advantage of what I assume is at least consideration on his part, if not outright capitulation. Then I lean forward and give him a once-over like the one he gave me moments ago. "We should probably change your clothing and hair, though. The way you look right now, you might as well have a lighted banner running across your forehead that says *cop*."

Bob appears mildly offended by this comment, and he looks down at himself as if trying to see what I'm seeing. Phase two of my plan is in place: get him focused on something else and make my accompaniment and participation an assumed thing, a done deal.

"We should try to pass you off as having some other occupation," I say. "What did you want to be when you were a little boy?"

"A cop."

I roll my eyes at him. "There has to have been something else."

"I did want to be a pirate for a time."

"Yeah, that's not going to work." It's all I can do not to smile, because I can tell he's fully engaged now. "It will help

if you lose the overcoat and the tie. And untuck your shirt."
I stare down at the floor and frown. "Your shoes are kind
of a giveaway, too, but I imagine we're stuck with them."

"Not necessarily. I have an overnight bag in the trunk,"
Bob says, acquiescing to my attempts at a makeover. "There's
a pair of jeans in there, and a sweater. I also have a gym bag
in there, but the clothes in it are kind of stinky."

"The overnight bag might do it," I say, nodding thought-
fully. "Let's find a place to stop before we get to the frat
house so you can change."

Ten minutes and the purchase of two cups of coffee
later, Bob emerges from the men's room in the convenience
store we've stopped at. He is wearing the jeans and sweater.
It helps, but he still looks too much like a cop. I frown,
studying him, and then tell him to bend over.

"What?" he grumbles, clearly not willing to oblige.

"I want to do something with your hair, but I can't reach
it," I tell him. "Bend over."

Bob looks around at the other customers, and at a mirror
hanging from the ceiling at the end of the aisle. "It's going
to look like I'm bowing down to you," he grumbles. "My
hair is fine."

"Okay," I say, pretending to give in. "I think you should
put on those boots you had in the trunk."

"Those are for snow or mud," he says.

"Today they're part of your new role. Please, just for a
little while. Those shiny black shoes of yours are standard
cop issue. You need to ditch them. And your sneakers don't
work with the rest of this."

With an irritated sigh, he takes his coffee cup from
me—I had obligingly offered to hold it for him while he
changed—and strides toward the exit. I follow, pleased to
see him head for the trunk of the car when we reach it.

There is some muttering involved, the words of which I can't make out, but when Bob once again slips in behind the wheel, he is wearing the boots. He sets his coffee into the cup holder slot on the console beside mine. And as he does so, I institute the rest of my plan.

"Hold still a second," I say, and then I take both of my hands and apply them to his hair, digging my fingers into the plastered strands and mussing things up as much as I can.

Not surprisingly, he pulls away from me, rearing back with an offended, "Hey!" He tries, unsuccessfully, to return his hair to its prior state of gelled and sculpted immobility, but I take hold of his arms and pull them toward me, ignoring the knife of pain that the movement triggers in the muscles of my upper arms and across my back.

"Stop," I say in a soft voice. "Trust me, okay?"

He scowls but lets me continue. I use my fingers and a tiny bit of spit to organize his hair into a disorganized coif that makes him look both younger and rakish. "There," I say, tilting my head to one side. "Now you look the part."

"The part of an idiot," he grumbles, giving me a sour look. He does a quick glance in the rearview mirror, sighs, and starts the car.

Fifteen minutes later we are both jazzed up on caffeine as Bob pulls up and parks in the street a block and a half from where the fraternity house is located. There are several fraternities in the area, a section of Madison's isthmus nestled between Lakes Mendota and Monona with an impressive view of the capitol building. The fraternity Toby and our quarry belonged to, Alpha Theta Pi, is located two blocks from the shores of Lake Mendota, though there are buildings around the frat house that block the water view at street level. Alpha Theta Pi is in an old three-story brick building featuring Colonial architecture mixed in with some modern updates, including handicapped access, parking areas, and bicycle racks.

We walk up to the front door, me at a half run as I try to keep up. My muscles are protesting strongly, but the pain eases a little the farther we go. By the time we step up onto the porch, I'm feeling looser, and my pain level has dropped from a-thousand-knives-stabbing-me-all-at-once to I've-been-punched-here-and-there.

Bob pushes the doorbell. We hear it chime inside, and it doesn't take long before a young man dressed in sweatpants and a T-shirt opens the door. His blond hair is tousled and messy, as if he has just gotten out of bed.

"May I help you?" he asks with a smile that looks only half-genuine. I expect he's surprised, curious, and perhaps a bit annoyed to find two middle-aged people on the doorstep, as opposed to some fellow students.

"We're Bob and Hildy," I say, putting on my best Midwestern smile. People in this area are generally inherently polite, but college students are a different breed, and I'm not sure we can count on them to respond in the typical manner. "My husband is the brother of Sharon Cochran, who is the mother of Toby Cochran, who used to live here."

The young man at the door appears to be having some difficulty following me until I get to Toby's name. Then his stricken expression tells me he's oriented all too well. Behind him in the shadows I see a couple of other curious faces peer around a corner, looking and listening. The young man before us starts to stammer, looking more uncomfortable with each syllable. "He's . . . Toby is . . . why . . ." He finally gives up and sighs heavily, briefly looking skyward as if he's hoping for some sort of divine intervention. Finally, he looks at us, his smile completely artificial and forced at this point. "All of his stuff was picked up long ago."

"We know that," I say. "That's not why we're here. Toby's mother is having a difficult time dealing with his death, as I'm sure you can imagine. We've been trying to help her as much as we can, and a counselor suggested that talking with some of the people who were around Toby right before he died might lend some insight." I pause, looking sad. "You see, Sharon feels as if . . . well . . . like she didn't know her son before he died. We're hoping to fill in some of the blanks for her, to help her understand better and come to grips with some of the harsher truths if need be."

Our young man licks his lips, shifting from one foot to the other. My request is one he'll have a hard time saying no to without looking like a total ass, and to augment the persuasiveness of my request, I add, "Sharon, Toby's mother, is an emotional wreck right now, so we thought it might be best if we talked to people, rather than having Toby's mother come here herself."

The floating heads behind our greeter have increased to four now. I sense Bob growing impatient beside me, and I'm afraid he's going to get frustrated and resort to cop mode any second and then barge his way in. I step in front of him and make one last appeal to our young man.

"May we please come in? It's chilly out here." I shiver to prove my point, and that default Midwestern politeness kicks in.

"Of course," the young man says, stepping to one side.

As we step over the threshold, a different kind of shiver shakes me.

Chapter Twenty

As we enter the building, the heads I saw a moment ago all disappear. We stop inside a small foyer and wait for our host to shut the door. When he turns to us again, I say, "There are some names we have, people we think Toby knew well. We'd like to start by talking to them, if they're here."

"Let me get Mrs. Barlow," our host says. "She's our housemother and she can probably help you." With that, he quickly disappears around a corner, leaving us standing there. I get a sense he is relieved to have escaped.

"You're quite the actress," Bob says in a whisper, leaning down close enough to my ear that his breath moves my hair.

"It's all about understanding how people think, what makes them tick," I whisper back with a shrug.

"And does that sort of manipulation work most of the time?" he counters.

I look up at him and smile warmly. "It worked on you."

I expect Bob to react with denial, or anger, or at the very least some mild irritation, but instead all he does is smile complacently at me. It's a bit disconcerting.

By some silent, mutual understanding the two of us take several steps forward, moving deeper into the house. After a few feet, the wall on our left gives way to a wide opening, revealing a large living room area. Straight ahead is a gallery hall that runs left and right, its walls lined with portraits. Beyond that is a suspended landing that splits a flight of stairs going up to the second floor into two more that come down either side of it into the gallery hall. To the right of the landing I see a short length of hallway and part of a large dining area with cafeteria-type seating. It is from here that our door answerer reappears toting a pleasant-looking, fifty-something, cherub-cheeked woman. She boasts a full head of blond hair streaked with white that is doing its best to escape the clip she has on the back of her head. She is a large woman, not fat or portly, but tall and sturdily built. The young man points us out to her and then promptly heads for the stairs, taking them two at a time.

The woman puts on that ubiquitous Midwestern smile and comes toward us. "Hello, I'm Carol Barlow. Welcome to Alpha Theta Pi." She extends a hand to first me, then Bob. Her warbling voice borders on shrill, though it still manages somehow to come across as pleasant and warm. It, and she, reminds me of Julia Child. After we exchange smiles and handshakes, she says, "What can I do for you fine folks?"

I repeat my spiel about Sharon and Toby, and our desire to speak to some of the boys who knew him.

"Such a sad thing," Carol says, looking truly troubled. "Why don't we have a seat and we can talk." She steers us toward the living room, which is furnished with several couches and chairs arranged in small groupings to create cozy conversational areas. There is a large fireplace along the wall bordering the gallery hall, and a grand piano in a far corner. A group of young men are seated on two couches that face each other in front of the fireplace, a coffee table between them. They are having a heated debate about the pros and cons of various styles and forms of government. Carol leads us past them to a small sitting area in the far corner near the piano that consists of a couch and two chairs around a small table.

"Please, have a seat," Carol says, gesturing toward the couch.

Bob and I dutifully settle in and Carol takes the chair to our left, closest to me. She leans forward, her smile still in place, though it is currently tempered with subtle hints of pity and sadness now that she knows the reason for our visit.

"I was so sorry to hear about Toby," she says, the smile fading. "He seemed like such a bright boy, not at all the type to get into that drug scene."

This piques my interest, and I lean forward. But before I can say anything, Carol adds, "Though I suppose these days it can happen to anyone. Lord knows there has been plenty of substance abuse here on campus lately."

"Do tell," Bob says, and I see him reach for the shirt pocket—and presumably the small notebook he typically carries in it—that isn't there. I place a placating hand on his arm in a gesture I hope Carol will see as supportive and loving as opposed to restraining.

"You knew Toby personally?" I ask.

"Of course," Carol says. Then with a proud maternal tone she adds, "I know all of the boys here very well. They aren't involved in any of that . . ." She pauses, looking like she wants to spit out something she just ate that tastes rancid.

"Any of what?" Bob urges.

Looking upset and, I think, the teeniest bit judgmental, Carol says, "Well, I'm sure you've heard about all the issues with the Greek houses here on campus over the past year or so. A dozen or more of them have been punished with probations or suspensions for drinking violations and hazing abuses."

"But not this house?" I say.

"Oh, my, no," Carol says, as if such an idea is anathema. "Not Alpha Theta Pi. Our boys know better."

"I'm surprised this place has a housemother," Bob says. "I thought those went the way of the dinosaur."

"They did," Carol says, her smile returning. "But a few have hung in there, and now we're making a comeback, in large part because of all the abuses that have gone on. They find that having a supervisory influence in the house has a calming and restraining effect on the residents. The fact that this house has avoided the sorts of scandals the other houses have experienced is often attributed to my presence." She looks pleased with her accomplishments.

"How long have you been here?" I ask.

"Five years. My son used to live here, but he died six years ago."

"Sorry for your loss," Bob and I both say at the same time.

"Thank you." Her eyes momentarily take on a faraway look. "I certainly can understand your reason for coming here and wanting to talk to the boys who knew Toby," she says, looking wistful. "Coming here and offering my services as a housemother was a way for me to be close to those who knew my son."

"What was your son's name?" I ask in my best bereavement counselor voice.

"Russell," she says, giving me a quick, brittle smile.

"How did he die?"

Bob shoots me a look, but I ignore him. If Carol wants to tell us she will. If she isn't ready, she'll find a way around it.

"Suicide," Carol says, and she does so without reservation, without lowering her voice, without any of the shame so many survivors in her situation display. She has come to grips with the situation better than most. "He shot himself. We're still not sure how he got the gun. According to the police it was stolen several years before and had been missing ever since. They figured Russell bought it on the street."

"How awful for you," I say, sensing Bob getting impatient beside me. "Did it happen here?"

Carol shakes her head. "No, they found him in James Madison Park. It's not far from here. The cops think he must have walked there in the middle of the night."

She looks at us, scanning our faces, searching for pity, I think. I don't dare look at Bob, though I suspect his expression is more likely to be one of irritation or impatience than anything. I reach over and take one of Carol's hands, forcing her to look at me rather than Bob. I pin her with my eyes.

"Suicide is always difficult," I say. "It seems to come as such a surprise for many. Was it like that for you?"

I see tears well in her eyes, and she nods. But she regains control quickly with a sniffle and a straightening of her spine. "That's how I came to be here. I wanted to talk to the other boys about it, not just about Russell and what he might have been going through at the end, but about suicide in general, how destructive it can be to the survivors, and how alcohol contributes to it. I was trying to create a legacy for my son, something to prevent other mothers from having to go through what I did." She shrugs. "I didn't intend to take a job here, but once I started coming I just sort of stuck. I've always loved to cook, and since I no longer had anyone to cook for at home, I started bringing food here and fixing it for the boys. They liked what I made and eventually asked me to start doing it full-time. I was able to convince the school to pay me a small stipend—I'm comfortable enough already financially—and started spending the bulk of my days here." Her gaze leaves my face and she stares off into space, smiling dreamily. "It didn't take long for the idea of living here to set in, and when the authorities saw how the boys seemed to be avoiding the trappings the other houses were experiencing, they started looking at bringing back the housemother concept."

"Good for you!" I say, giving her hand a squeeze and then letting it go. "What a wonderful way to honor your son's memory."

She smiles, looking abashed.

"No father in the picture?" I say.

She shakes her head. "No, he died when Russell was three. Car accident." Her gaze slides away at this and I know there's more to the story that she's not sharing with us.

"You were a single mother, then? That couldn't have been easy emotionally or financially."

Carol dismisses this with a wave of a hand. "I was lucky. My parents were quite well off, so it really wasn't too hard for me. Russell and I moved in with them. And Harlan, that was my husband's name, was well insured."

"Still," I say, looking at her sympathetically, "it couldn't have been easy for you emotionally. And given that, I'm sure you can relate to what Toby's mother is going through. She has so many questions. What can you tell us about him?"

Carol's smile fades and her face takes on a surprisingly stern and judgmental look. "I can tell you that she should be the one here talking to me and the boys. The fact that she isn't explains a lot. No wonder Toby turned to drugs."

Chapter Twenty-One

I'm stunned by Carol's response. "What do you mean by that?"

"I mean, if Toby's mother really cared all that much about him, she would have been here by now, or would be here today, looking for answers. And yet you're here instead. I think bad parenting is behind so many of the troubles young people have these days. I suspect Toby's mother wasn't involved enough in his life, and that's why he turned to drugs and the kinds of people who do drugs."

"That's a bit harsh," Bob says.

Carol shrugs. "Perhaps, but it's often true."

"I take it you weren't a very good parent either," Bob says, his mouth tight. "Otherwise your son wouldn't have killed himself."

I shoot Bob a *what the hell?* look. If he is hoping to shock or offend Carol, he is quickly disappointed.

"That is correct," Carol says unemotionally. "I wasn't there for Russell the way I should have been. That's why I'm here now, to make up for what I didn't do right the first time."

I intervene quickly, hoping to keep this conversation from deteriorating into something that won't help any of us. "Carol, how close were you to Toby?"

"Not as close as I am with some of the other boys," she says, shifting her gaze to me. "He was quiet, kind of a loner, very focused on his academics and gaming. There's a game room up on the second floor, and often that's where you'd find Toby."

"Any idea when he started using drugs?" I ask. "Did you see a radical change in his personality or behavior?"

She frowns, looking thoughtful. "Not really, but then I'm not sure I would have. I didn't interact with him that often. You should talk to Heath Monroe. He was his roommate."

"There are some other boys we think he might have been close to," Bob says. He takes out his phone and reads off the names of the boys who responded to Toby's emails, both the one he sent himself and the one I inadvertently sent.

"Ah, yes, our gaming team," Carol says with a wry shake of her head.

"Gaming team?" I say.

"Yes. Some of our boys belong to a club that meets every week to strategize and organize new tournaments centered around some online games. They play against other frat house groups, other campus groups, and even some outside groups that have nothing to do with the university. Toby was a member."

"And these other three boys are as well?" I ask. Carol nods. "Are they here now? We'd really like to talk to them."

"I think Alex Parnell is at swim practice, but the other two are here. Let me get them for you." She gets up and walks out of the room, leaving us to ourselves.

The boys in the center of the room are still debating their various political strategies, but I see a curious look cast our way every so often. There is an odd air of superiority I sense in them that puzzles me at first. But as I study them longer, I begin to think it's more affluent arrogance. I recognize money behind their clothing and shoe choices, their precise haircuts, and even in the arguments they are making for political strategies that protect big business and reduce taxing on the wealthy.

After a few minutes, a tall, thin, gangly boy with a pock-marked face enters the room. He pauses just inside the door, stares at us, and swallows hard, his Adam's apple bobbing wildly. Then he makes his way over to us looking like a death row inmate walking to the electric chair. I can tell right away that this boy doesn't come from money. His clothes and shoes look old and well-worn, and while this could be a fashion choice, I don't think it is. My opinion is only strengthened as he passes the group of boys and I see a couple of them look at him with a hint of disdain.

"I'm Mitch Sawyer," he says, stopping in front of us. He offers no hand to shake; in fact, his hands are clasped behind his back. "Carol said you wanted to talk to me about Toby Cochran?"

"Yes, we do," I say, before Bob can speak and scare the kid away. Mitch looks like he would explode up through the ceiling if we said a gentle *boo* to him. "Please have a seat." I gesture toward the chair Carol occupied earlier. The kid looks at it, back at me, and then at Bob. Then he casts a wary look over his shoulder toward the group of boys. "Is it okay if I stand?" he says.

"If it makes you more comfortable," I say.

"It does." He swallows hard again, making the Adam's apple bounce.

"We're trying to help Toby's mother," I say, craning my neck to look up at him. Given his height, my lack thereof, and his desire to stand, it's a strain. "We were hoping to chat with some of the people who knew him best, who spent time with him before he died, to see if we can get any insight into what led up to his drug problem."

"How would I know?" Mitch says. "I didn't do drugs. I *don't* do drugs," he emphasizes. "I'd lose my scholarship if I did, and then I'd have to drop out."

This confirms my guess about his financial status.

"We're not implying anything," I assure him. "We're just trying to understand what went wrong with Toby at the end. His mom, she's been a single mom all of Toby's life, and she's convinced that she failed him somewhere, somehow. She needs some answers. You can understand that, can't you?"

"She didn't do anything wrong," Mitch says without hesitation. "Toby talked about her a lot, about what a rock she was for him, about how hard she worked. He loved her, and it sounded like she loved him."

"Were you aware of anything that was troubling Toby toward the end?" Bob asks. His tone surprises me a little. It is tender, conciliatory, kind. No hint of cop in it.

Mitch turns his head to the side, and his eyes dart toward the other boys, who are still in their group but suddenly quiet.

"You know what?" I say, pushing up from the couch. "It's a beautiful day outside. Why don't we go walk?"

Mitch appears to consider this, glancing first out the window, then over his shoulder toward the front entrance. "I'd like to, but I'm afraid I need to be somewhere. I'm late already. And I don't think I have anything to offer you. I'm sorry."

With that, he whirls around with amazing grace, given his gangly build, and strides from the room, not giving the group of boys a second look. They, however, watch him, I note. And as soon as Mitch is out of sight, they turn in unison, as if they are one multiheaded creature, and look at us. Bob and I stare back at them for an interminable amount of time until the boys finally break our visual standoff, turning away in unison. As they take up their debate again, with several of them speaking at the same time, I suppress a shiver and give Bob a wide-eyed, wary look.

"Are we supposed to wait for the second boy, do you suppose?" I ask in a low voice.

He answers me with a nod of his head toward the living room entrance. Another boy is coming into the room, this one short, bespectacled, and pudgy. I guess that this one is Liam Michaelson since Mrs. Barlow told us Alex isn't here. He has a hint of a smile on his face, and I get a sense that this is his default expression, that he's an inherently happy, fun-loving kind of person who always has a joke at the ready. The social worker part of my brain immediately questions my assumption, wondering if I'm stereotyping the boy because of his build and an oft-held belief that overweight people are jolly and love to joke. I suspect this typecasting exists because a lot of kids use humor to deflect hurt feelings when they're picked on or made fun of, and overweight kids almost always fall into the picked-on category. I too, fell into the picked-on category a lot, not because of weight—I was thin as a child—but because I was noticeably different due to my foster child status and a wardrobe that often consisted of used clothing and ill-fitting hand-me-downs.

I watch Liam cross the room, noting that he acknowl-edges the group of boys with a smile and a brief "Hey, guys" as he passes them. None of them smile back at him but they also don't look at him with the same level of con-tempt they afforded Mitch.

When Liam's attention turns back to us his smile broadens.

"Hi there," he says, extending a hand to Bob. "I'm Liam Michaelson." They exchange a vigorous shake and Liam then extends his hand to me. His grip is solid and warm, not limp or wimpy, but also not bone-crushing. I wonder if his approach to Bob was the same, or if he displayed a little more strength in the man-to-man exchange. After releasing my hand, he takes the seat we had tried to give to Mitch, sitting forward eagerly on its front edge, forearms resting on his legs, hands clasped by his knees.

My instincts tell me to let Bob take this one, and I'm trying to figure out a subtle way to communicate that to him when he does so.

"I'm Bob, and this is Hildy," he says. "Thanks for taking the time to talk with us."

"No problem. Carol said this is about Toby?"

"Yes," Bob says, nodding solemnly. "Toby's mother is my sister and she's having a really difficult time dealing with Toby's death. We're trying to help her out. She's shouldering a lot of guilt, guilt we don't think she deserves. A counselor suggested that we try to convince her of that, so we're hoping to get a better read on Toby's life in the months before he died. We understand you were a close friend of his."

I'm impressed with how easily and glibly Bob has adopted and regurgitated our lie. Then again, I imagine cops lie all the time when questioning people, enough so that they probably get to be good at it.

"Don't know if I'd say we were close," Liam says. "We knew each other and played on the same game teams. I mean, we hung out from time to time, but it was always in a group. He didn't confide in me or anything like that."

Based on the emails we read, this would seem to be a lie, and I wonder why Liam is trying to distance himself from Toby.

"Do you know why he dropped out of school?" I ask.

Liam grimaces and shrugs. "Not really, though there was a rumor going around that he was really devastated over his breakup with Lori."

"Lori?" Bob says.

"His girlfriend, or at least the girl he was seeing around the time he dropped out."

"What is Lori's last name?" Bob asks.

"Davenport," Liam says. "She lives in a house downtown on West Wash," he explains, using the shortened vernacular for Washington Avenue I've heard other Madisonians use. "Shares it with four other girls. I don't know the exact address, but I went to a party there once and I remember that it's the only yellow house on the block."

"Were Toby and Lori dating for long?" I ask.

"Since the start of the second semester," Liam offers. "They seemed like one of those couples that's destined to be, you know? They really liked each other and had a lot in common. They were both kind of shy, very academic, not sports inclined, and from single-parent homes. I was surprised when I heard that Toby had broken things off with her."

"Toby broke up with Lori?" I ask to clarify.

"That's the rumor," Liam says with a shrug. "Though I didn't talk to either of them about it, so I don't know for sure."

"And you've never heard anyone speculate as to why?" I ask.

Liam shakes his head. "Not really. One of her roommates was dating my roommate at the time, so I got some insider info for a while. I know Lori was upset over it, but I never heard any details about why it happened. I don't think Lori knew."

"Did you ever see Toby using drugs, or hanging out with people who were using drugs?" Bob asks.

Liam rolls his lips inward and arches his brows, looking like the proverbial cat that swallowed the canary. "Well, it depends on your definition of drugs," he says in a low voice. "Anyone who's been to any kind of campus shindig has been around people who smoke pot, even if they don't do it themselves." He pauses, looking thoughtful for a moment. "I don't think I ever saw Toby smoke any pot, though. And he never bought anything on his own that I know of. That kind of stuff is for the rich kids. People like me and Toby, we don't have money for drugs. We barely have enough to buy a cup of coffee from the student union." He looks from Bob to me and then back to Bob again. "I heard Toby died of a drug overdose. Is that true?"

I jump in to answer this because I'm afraid Bob might not want to. "He was found with heroin in his system and a syringe in his arm," I say. I feel, rather than see, Bob give me a look.

"Heroin?" Liam says, making a face. "How the heck did he get into that? It's about as far from the Toby I knew as you can get."

"No idea who might have provided him with the drugs?" Bob asks.

Liam glances over at the other boys and leans in closer to us, dropping his voice down several decibels. "Like I said, the kids from the wealthier families do that stuff a lot. But there are class divisions here in this house just like there are out in society." He shrugs and gives us a sad smile. "The rich kids don't socialize with us poorer kids much."

"Did you stay in contact with Toby after he dropped out of school?" I ask.

Liam starts to shake his head but hesitates. I suspect he is recalling the email from the dead that he received yesterday. "Not really," he says finally. "Though I did get an email from him yesterday. Kind of freaked me out because I heard about his death two weeks ago. Eventually I realized someone else had to have sent it using his email address, but I confess it freaked me out at first."

"Sorry about that," Bob says with a smile. "That was my sister's doing. She was looking through Toby's laptop and I think when she opened up his email program it sent an email out that had been sitting in his outbox."

"That makes sense," Liam says with a nervous laugh

and a look of relief. "I let my imagination get the better of me there for a while. I think I need to back off on the horror flicks."

"It looks like Toby wrote that email right before he died, but it got hung up in his outbox because the power went out," Bob says, pinning Liam with his laser blue eyes. "It said 'I need to tell someone.' What was he referring to?"

Liam's smile fades. "I have no idea," he says. "I figured it was someone who was spoofing Toby's email address, playing a practical joke."

I recall that Liam's response to the email had been to ask if it was really Toby sending it, and then questioning if his death had been a hoax.

"That email went to two other people besides you," Bob says, looking at his phone. "Mitch Sawyer and Alex Parnell. How do you know them?"

Liam fidgets and shifts in his seat while casting a brief sidelong glance at the group of boys. "Well, they live here," he says.

"As do a lot of other people," Bob fires back. He's reverting to cop mode, and I try to figure out a way to get him to back off.

"Why did you three get Toby's email?" Bob pushes, leaning closer to the boy. "What else did you have in common?"

Liam licks his lips and looks at Bob's hands, then mine. He shifts his gaze to Bob's face and narrows his eyes. "You two aren't married, are you?" He doesn't wait for an answer. "And you're not Toby's uncle, either, are you?" Again, he doesn't wait for an answer. He slaps himself on the side of the head and says, "How stupid am I? Toby was always going on about how he and his mom were all alone in the world, how it was just the two of them, and how much he admired her for working so hard and providing him with a good home." His expression changes to one of cynical disbelief. "Now he suddenly has an uncle who is worried about how well his mom is coping? I don't think so."

There's a long silence while Liam and Bob stare at each other. Suddenly the boys in the other group rise from their seats, moving with uncanny coordination, and file out of the room.

When they're gone, Liam says, "You're a cop, aren't you?"

Bob, knowing the jig is up, nods but says nothing.

"Why are you here? Is there something suspect about Toby's death?"

"What do you think?" Bob asks. "Is there?"

Liam pales, and shoots a nervous glance at me. He wipes his hands on his pant legs and licks his lips again. "I need to go," he says. And then, with no additional explanation, he hoists himself up and leaves the room.

Bob sighs and looks at me questioningly. "Do you get a sense that there's something strange going on here?"

"Most definitely. That group of boys that was in here, even they were acting strange."

Bob gets up from the couch and stares out the window, hands in his pockets.

"What about Toby's roommate, Heath Monroe?" I say. "Should we try to talk to him next?"

"Yeah, I suppose," Bob says to the window. "But now that they know who we are, I doubt we'll get much out of anyone."

"We won't know unless we try, right?"

Bob glances at me over his shoulder, giving me a wan smile. "Are you always this upbeat and positive? Because that can get downright annoying at times."

I don't hear any irritation in his voice and sense he is only teasing me. "I assure you I can be as much of a Debbie Downer as the next guy," I tell him.

"Good to know." He turns and looks across the empty room toward the door. "I guess we should go find someone."

As if she was waiting just around the corner—and I wonder if she had perhaps stationed herself there during our talks with the boys—Carol sweeps into the room with a smile painted on her face. "How's it going?" she asks, and something about her forced congeniality and overdone effort to appear casual convinces me she's been eavesdropping.

"We'd like to talk to Toby's roommate, Heath Monroe," Bob says.

"Oh, dear," Carol says with a frown. "You just missed him. And I'm not sure when he'll be back. If you'd like to leave a number where he can reach you, I'll see to it that he gets it. I'm sure you have a business card, given that you're a cop, right?"

She and Bob engage in a staring contest that lasts an impressive thirty seconds or more without either of them blinking or altering their expressions in any way. I mentally place my money on Bob as the winning holdout, but no sooner does this thought cross my mind than Bob looks away, lips pursed.

"I see," he says.

"Of course you do," Carol says with frigid politeness, her smile never wavering.

Bob looks at me and nods toward the door. "Looks like we're done here."

I push myself up from the couch, and grit my teeth against the pain I feel in my muscles. I follow Bob as Carol shows us to the main entrance, determined not to grunt, groan, or show my agony in any way. By the time we reach the door my muscles are easing their way back into movement.

The expression on Carol's face as she opens the door is smug. It's a look I saw a lot on people's faces when I was growing up, usually other kids, but sometimes the grown-ups as well. That look always meant they felt they had scored a point somehow, emerged victorious in some battle of wits, strength, or power. The fact that Carol's face now bears that same expression tells me that she has more of an investment in our inquiries than she let on at first, and that she feels she has somehow beat us at our own game. Her smugness irritates me, striking a nerve that has been plucked in me once too often.

As I walk past her and step over the threshold, I pause and turn to look back at her, stretching myself as far as I can to make the most of my barely five-foot height, which puts me a little above eye level with her boobs. I'm forced to look up at her, but I long ago mastered the art of looking fierce despite being in what seems like the weaker position. I'm a rat terrier, about to take down a rottweiler.

"You may have won this battle," I say to Carol, "but the universe has a funny way of evening things up." I flash her my best predatory smile. "The secrets always come out no matter how hard you try to keep them buried."

She says nothing, but I have the satisfaction of seeing her smile falter ever so slightly. And when I turn away and step down from the porch, she slams the door hard behind us, letting me know I got to her.

Score one for us little people.

Chapter Twenty-Two

Bob arches his eyebrows at me, looking impressed as we walk the block and a half back to his car. When we're safely out of earshot of the frat house, he says, "You continue to surprise me, Hildy. What was that all about?"

"I think our housemother knows a lot more than she's letting on," I say, a little out of breath with my efforts to keep up with him. "Over the years, between my time bouncing around the foster system and my career in social work, I've gotten to be good at reading people. And my read of Carol Barlow says she's hiding something."

"I agree," Bob says. "But it could be that she's simply trying to protect her boys."

I shake my head. "Nope, it's more than that. I'd stake my reputation on it."

Bob gives me a ponderous expression that, ironically, after bragging about how good I am at reading people, I can't read at all. We say nothing more until we're back inside his car.

"So, what's next?" I say. "Should we visit the person who owns the property where the footbridge is located?"

Bob starts the car but doesn't pull out right away. Instead, he looks at his phone while answering me. "Not yet."

"Why not? And who is it, anyway?"

Bob chuckles and shakes his head. "Too many questions. As for who it is, it's a gentleman by the name of Warren Sheffield. Perhaps you've heard of him?"

I have indeed. Pretty much anyone who lives in this part of Wisconsin has heard of Warren Sheffield, owner of Sheffield Inns, a nationwide chain of highly successful motels.

"No wonder you want to take things slow," I say. "He's not the kind of guy you want to piss off."

"Precisely," Bob says. "I called early this morning and left a vague message, asking that he call me back. So, we wait for now."

"What about Toby's girlfriend, Lori Davenport? It sounds like whatever was bothering him when he dropped out of school might have had something to do with her. We should talk to her."

"Should we, now?" Bob says in a slightly mocking tone.

"Well, don't you think so?"

"I do. That's why I sent a text message to the station to get an address for the girl. That's where we're headed now." He flips his turn indicator, glances over his shoulder, and pulls out of the parking space.

"Well, you might have told me," I say sourly.

"Where's the fun in that?"

I shoot him a look, hoping he's teasing me. I'm not sure, though, and it's a little unnerving.

"Hildy, do you like what you do?" he asks, throwing me for a loop since it seems arbitrary, sudden, unrelated to what we were discussing, and as potentially dangerous as an active minefield. I hesitate before answering him, trying to gauge where he's going.

"I do," I say after a moment. "I enjoy helping people, particularly people who get caught up in the holes in our systems. Having spent some time down those holes myself,

I like trying to help others out of them. Or better yet, help them to avoid them."

"What about the counseling parts of your job? Do you enjoy doing that?"

"It's my favorite part of the job, to be honest. I mean, directing people toward available resources that can help them is great, and it's a big part of counseling services much of the time, but the part of it I really love is digging into people's psyches, trying to figure out what makes them tick, and determining if that ticking might be the count-down for a time bomb. I like it when people open up to me and let me get a glimpse of what goes on in their minds. I like peering into the darkest, dankest recesses of their brains. If I can then let a little light into those black abysses, I feel like I've made a difference, left my mark on the world, you know?"

"I've got a stun gun that will leave a mark, and a more visible one at that," Bob says in a joking tone.

I chuckle, and then say, "Think about it, Bob. Why are we here? You and I were born, we've lived lives that played out while walking different paths, we've encountered people along the way, and what does it all mean? When we die, what is there to show that we were ever here? Do we make a difference? Or are we simply one more cog in some mys-terious entity's wheel?"

Bob looks over at me, brows drawn together in wary contemplation. "That sounds deep and existential," he says. "Too deep for me."

"Really? You don't ever contemplate the meaning of life? The meaning of *your* life?"

"I catch bad guys," he says with a shrug. "Isn't that enough?"

"I don't know, is it? I think each person must answer that

question for themselves. Do you feel like your existence is meaningful? Are you leaving something behind?"

Bob runs a hand through his hair and widens his eyes. "Wow. You're waxing very philosophical," he says. "But to answer your question in simple terms, yes, I feel like I make a difference. What I do helps to shape society, and that helps to shape both the present and the future. As for leaving anything behind, I don't suppose I will, other than a rotting corpse. I don't have any kids, and I'm not someone who will be written about in recorded history. Though I suppose everyone who ventures onto the Internet leaves a footprint behind these days."

"That's something we have in common, then," I say. "That is, a job that helps us shape our current society, and a lack of anything to leave behind other than the influences we may have had on the lives of others. But eventually our influence will fade, as will anyone's memory of us. With each subsequent generation, our existence becomes less relevant and meaningful until no one alive remembers us anymore."

"This discussion is getting depressing," Bob says, frowning.

"It *is* kind of depressing, but I think it's that knowledge of our eventual and inevitable demise and loss of meaning to the world that prompts some people to do great things. And it prompts others to do horrible things, all in the name of being remembered, of being a part of history. It's what makes great leaders, and serial killers."

"Now I'm getting a headache," Bob says.

"You started it when you asked me if I like what I do."

"I just wanted to know if you're happy in your current job. And I had an important reason for asking, but that discussion will have to wait, because we have arrived at our destination."

As Bob pulls into an open parking spot on the wide expanse of West Wash, as it's called, I eye the old houses lining the street. Dating back to the early nineteen hundreds, most of them show their age in some way, whether it be a slight sag in the roof, or the weathering of the boards beneath peeling paint, or the Victorian styling of the architecture. While most of these homes were at one time owned by wealthy families, these days many of them are student housing, though there are still some single-family homes mixed in.

Straight ahead of us, atop the hill four blocks away, sits Madison's capitol building, its 187-foot-tall, gleaming white dome visible from miles away. Capitol Hill isn't all that high, but there's legislation that prevents any structures taller than the capitol building from being built anywhere around it, ensuring the awe-inspiring view.

The block Lori Davenport lives on is crammed with houses that sit close to one another, each one with a small front yard, a tree-lined park row, and sidewalks that connect them all. As Liam told us, Lori's house is the only yellow one on this block, an old prairie-style home located two from the end.

"What if she isn't home?" I ask Bob. "Should we have tried to call her first?"

"I prefer not to warn people that I'm coming. Unless they have the kind of power Warren Sheffield has. I like it when people's responses are more spontaneous and they haven't had time to prepare. If Lori Davenport isn't home, we'll wait until she is."

"Wait? You mean in the car?"

"Yep. A surprising amount of police work involves waiting, Hildy. If you want to do ride-alongs, you have to expect that."

"Okay," I say, resigned. Other than concerns for my

bladder capacity, I have nowhere I need to be today. The bladder thing is a serious concern, however, and as we walk up to Lori's house, I scope out the surrounding area, looking for any place that might have a bathroom. I'm relieved when I see a sign for a health clinic two blocks up.

The floorboards on the porch of Lori's house creak ominously beneath our feet. Bob spins a small handle fixed to the axis of a round doorbell located in the middle of the door, and from inside I hear a sound emanate that sounds like the ring of an old-fashioned telephone.

I have no idea what Lori Davenport looks like, so I also have no idea if it is she who answers the door. It's a girl with short-cropped black hair, heavy kohl eyeliner, bright red lipstick, and foundation that makes her face look very pale, particularly beneath that dark hair.

"Can I help you?" she says, looking puzzled and impatient.

"We're looking for Lori Davenport," Bob says.

"Are you?" She cocks a hip to one side and her expression turns defiant. She holds the door close to her body, clearly not inclined to invite us inside. "Why are you looking for Lori?"

"We want to talk to her about her old boyfriend, Toby."

The girl's expression alters in an instant. Gone is the defiance, replaced with curious suspicion. "Who are you?" she asks, her eyes darting back and forth between the two of us.

I look at Bob, letting him decide which tack to take. "We're friends of Toby's mother. She's really struggling with his death and we're trying to help her find some answers. It would really help if we could talk to Lori."

The girl considers our request, her mouth skewed as she chews at the inside of one cheek. Finally, she says, "Wait here," and shuts the door in our faces.

Bob and I exchange looks. Neither of us says a word. Time ticks by and behind us is the sound of steady traffic. Inside the house I hear the murmur of voices, but I can't make out any of the words. Just when I start to think we need to ring the bell again because there was an obvious misunderstanding, the door opens.

Chapter Twenty-Three

Standing on the other side this time is a tall, slender girl with huge blue eyes, a waterfall of straight brunette hair, and a heart-shaped face. She is wearing yoga pants that outline long, perfectly shaped legs, and a fitted tank top that shows off perky, ample breasts. There isn't an ounce of fat on her. Her face is devoid of makeup; she doesn't need it. She is beautiful, her porcelain skin unblemished, her eyes rimmed with dark, long lashes, her lips full and shaped into a perfect Cupid's bow. Standing in front of her I feel old and dowdy.

"I'm Lori Davenport," she says, and even her voice is beautiful. "You wanted to talk to me about Toby?"

"If we could, yes," Bob says. I steal a glance at him and see that his expression reflects a level of enchantment similar to my own. What on earth could have made Toby break up with this gorgeous creature? What flaw might she be hiding? Had she done something so horrific that Toby couldn't see past it?

"Come on in," Lori says, and she steps aside to allow us through.

We enter a small foyer area and wait for her to close the door. There is a stairwell to the second floor on our right, its polished wood banister ending in a beautifully carved newel post, and there is a doorway to the left that leads into a family room. The walls and windows I can see are all framed with wide wood trim typical of the era for this house, and I notice a quaint push-button light switch by the door. Along the wall beneath the stairs is a small table with a dish that contains several sets of keys. Next to that is another dish holding what appears to be leftover Easter candy: jellybeans, foil-wrapped chocolate eggs, and some small, individually wrapped marshmallow and chocolate bunnies.

Once Lori closes the front door, she has us follow her through the living area into a dining room, and from there into a large, eat-in kitchen. I'm thinking she's going to have us sit at the kitchen table, but instead she heads for a laundry room that was probably a back porch at one time, and from there outside to the backyard. There is a small concrete pad off the back door with a table and four chairs, and Lori directs us to take one of these seats while she grabs a sweater from the laundry room. Bob and I sit across from each other, and Lori settles into one of the empty chairs between us, folding her hands in her lap. Her figure is so lithe, and her movements all so graceful and flowing that it makes me wonder if she's a dancer.

The day is cool, with the current temperature in the low fifties, but with our jackets on and the sun shining down on us, it's comfortable.

"How is Sharon doing?" Lori asks. The concern I hear in her voice and see on her face seems genuine.

"Not well," I say, making a quick decision to drop any pretense. "She's having a difficult time understanding how Toby got to where he was when he died. I'm a social worker and I run a grief support group. I've been counseling her, but I think she needs to have a better understanding of what happened in Toby's life in the weeks before his death before she can come to any level of acceptance. Can you shed any light on that for us?"

Lori eyes me with critical appraisal, then does the same to Bob. "You aren't a counselor," she says to him.

"No, I'm not." He shoots me a look and then follows my lead. "I'm a police detective. I'm looking into Toby's death because we have reason to believe that it wasn't an accident."

"Really?" Lori says, her perfectly manicured brows drawing down into a V over her dainty nose. "You think he did it on purpose? Committed suicide?"

Bob doesn't answer right away. Lori isn't one to jump in and fill the silence, however, so I give her a prompt. "What do you think?"

She looks at me for a few seconds, then she tips her head back and looks at the sky, letting the sunlight dance over her skin. We wait, letting the silence work, and when she lowers her gaze, I see tears welling in her eyes.

"Toby wouldn't have killed himself." There is a strong note of conviction behind the words, and while I can't know if she's right or not, I have no doubt that she believes what she's said.

"Were you aware of his drug use?" Bob asks.

Lori shakes her head. "I don't believe he was into any of that stuff. Toby was as straight as they come. I couldn't even get him to try pot."

"When was the last time you saw or heard from him?" I ask.

Lori grimaces, as if the memory is causing her physical pain. "He broke things off with me a little over a month ago. Did it over the phone. On a Friday . . . the Ides of March, in fact." She lets out a humorless laugh, her expression laced with irony. "I was looking forward to the two of us spending the weekend together." She pauses and swallows hard, looking away for a second as if she's seeing something else.

"His decision caught me by surprise, to say the least," she says, tears welling again. "I thought things between us were great. And then out of the blue, he says we can't be together anymore. I asked him why, if something had happened, or if he'd met someone else, but all he would say was that he was ruined, and he wasn't the right guy for me." She lets out a ragged breath and shakes her head. "It made me angry, and I said some things to him that I probably shouldn't have. Later I tried to apologize, to take it all back, but he wouldn't answer my calls or my emails. And when I tried to go see him at the frat house, I found out he'd dropped out of school and left."

"And up until the day he broke things off, everything seemed okay with him?" I ask.

She starts to nod but stops, looking hesitant.

"Any idea what he meant when he said he was ruined?" Bob asks.

She shakes her head in dismay. "I think something happened that week, but I have no idea what it was. I didn't see him at all, because he was engaged in this gaming competition that he did from time to time with some of the other guys in his house. It's a crazy twenty-four-hour-a-day thing that lasts for a week, so they all take shifts of play time and try to work that around their class and sleep time." She squeezes her eyes closed and swipes at a tear that escapes down one cheek. "The next time I talked to him was when he called me to break things off. I don't even know if they won their stupid competition. I never talked to him again after that."

She reaches into the pocket of her pants and pulls out a cell phone. She taps the screen a couple of times and then starts swiping. After a moment she shows us the screen. It's a picture of a group of people, one of whom I see is Toby. There are four other guys and two girls who look to be

Toby's age, and one middle-aged man. Two of the four guys I recognize as Liam Michaelson and Mitch Sawyer. I gather one of the remaining two is Alex Parnell, and based on the knowledge that he's a swimmer, I guess it's the taller, leaner fellow with the broad shoulders standing behind Toby.

"That's Toby's gaming group," Lori explains. "He sent that to me two days before he broke up with me. Why would he do that?" She looks at us with red-rimmed, tear-stained eyes, searching our faces for answers because we have no verbal reply.

"Can you forward that picture to me?" I ask Lori.

"Sure." She hands me her phone. "Just do it."

"Send it to me, too," Bob says to me, and I nod. "You have my number, right? Mattie gave it to you?"

I nod and go about forwarding the photo to both of our phones.

"Did you know any of Toby's close friends?" Bob asks Lori.

"Some of them," she says. "Mostly guys from the house, though he did have a couple of other acquaintances on campus, more classmates than friends, though, I think. You know, study buddies . . . that sort of thing. He hung with that gaming group more than anyone." She lets out a humorless chuckle and shakes her head. "I never got their interest in the gaming thing. The degree of it, that is. They practiced all . . . the . . . time." She widens her eyes and adds an impatient emphasis to the last three words. "Toby told me that the competitions offered money prizes, so if they won they'd get cash. Yet despite all that practice, his team almost never won the official competitions. I sometimes wondered if he was really practicing, or . . ."

"Or what?" I urge.

"Do you think he was seeing one of those girls from the

gaming group? Do you think that's why he broke things off?" she asked.

All we have to offer are shrugs of ignorance and sympathetic looks.

"Did you ever see any of his friends do drugs?" Bob asks, steering Lori away from the topic of the girls. "Or did he talk about any of them doing drugs?"

Lori makes an equivocal face. "It's college," she says, sounding apologetic. "So, yeah, some of the kids use weed, there's often some pill popping going on to get revved up for long study sessions or to wind down after a test. And I know some people who do coke now and again. But no one in my circle does any hard stuff or even uses regularly. And as far as I could tell, no one in Toby's circle did, either. But I didn't spend a lot of time around his frat brothers or his gaming buddies, so . . ." She shrugs, looking sad. "I certainly didn't get the sense that Toby was into that. If I had, I never would have gone out with him. It's not my thing."

Bob takes out his cell phone and taps at the screen a few times. At first, I think he's checking to see if I sent the picture to him as promised, and I feel a glimmer of annoyance at his doubt. But then he shows his phone to Lori and asks, "Does this look familiar to you?"

I catch a brief glimpse of the screen as he turns it toward her and see that he's showing her a picture of Toby's bridge drawing. I'm surprised he has it. When did he take it?

Lori stares at the picture, a thin smile forming on her lips. "Toby drew this, didn't he?" she says, looking at Bob. He nods, and she looks admiringly at the drawing. "I'd know his work anywhere. He's very talented." Her eyes dart back to Bob then and the smile drops off her lips like a lead weight. "Was . . ." she says, her voice hitching on the word. "He *was* very talented." She hands the phone back to Bob and I slide her phone back across the table to her.

"What about the bridge in the drawing, the setting? Does any of it look familiar to you?" Bob asks.

Lori shakes her head slowly, staring at Bob. "No, sorry," she says. Then her eyes grow wide. "Oh my God," she says. "You're a cop."

Bob, looking a bit puzzled by this outburst, says, "Yes, I told you that."

"I can't believe I didn't see it sooner," Lori says, staring at Bob with an expression of pain dawning. "Toby loved life, he had his future all planned out, and he told me once that he was afraid of death. I know he didn't kill himself. And Toby didn't use drugs, so how could he have overdosed, and on something as hard-core as heroin?" She shakes her head vigorously. "Nope, it makes no sense. If you're look-ing into his death this hard, it's because you don't think it was an accident or a suicide, do you?" Bob opens his mouth to answer but Lori doesn't give him a chance. "That only leaves one other possibility. You think someone killed him, don't you?"

A strained silence builds between us. Then Bob answers Lori's question with one of his own. "Do you know of anyone who would want to kill him? Or any reason some-one would want him dead?"

"God, no," she says, looking horrified. "But it makes sense." She lets out an ironic chuckle. "I can't believe I didn't figure it out before."

"What makes sense?" Bob asks, leaning toward her eagerly, his eyes narrowing.

"When Toby broke up with me, he kept saying it was for my own good. And when I wouldn't stop pleading with him to give us another chance, he got mean." She looks from Bob to me, and then back to Bob again, a big smile on her face. "Don't you see? Toby was never mean, not to anyone, and particularly not to me. I didn't understand it at the time, but now it makes sense. He was trying to protect me. He wanted to make sure I stayed away."

As far as jumped-to conclusions go, this one ranks right up there. To say it is far-fetched would be reasonable. Plus, it wouldn't be unusual for a confused, heartbroken, jilted lover to try to rationalize or sugarcoat being dumped by coming up with an explanation like Lori's. Yet I'm inclined to agree with her.

Lori then surprises me, and judging from the way he jumps, Bob, too, by shoving her chair back, standing, and reaching across the table to grab Bob's wrist. She does it all in one rapid, fluid motion, demonstrating that gracefulness even now.

"Someone killed Toby," she says, her voice suddenly steely. "I don't know why, but I'll do whatever I can to help you figure it out. You catch whoever did this. Promise me you'll catch whatever scumbag did this."

The vehemence in her voice is frightening and makes me look at her in a new light. But it also reaffirms my sense regarding her feelings for Toby. Lori Davenport might look like a delicate flower and have a voice as soft and sweet as a baby's coo and a face that would give Helen of Troy a run for her money, but beneath it all is a steely edge and a take-no-prisoners resolve if she, or someone she cares about, is done wrong. Toby Cochran managed to find himself one hell of a woman.

It makes the whole situation all that much sadder knowing that the two of them will never get a chance to be a couple.

Chapter Twenty-Four

Bob's phone starts dinging like crazy on the way back to his car. This makes him walk even faster for some reason, and I struggle to keep up, my pace an awkward mix of running, power walking, and a speed I've nicknamed please-cut-my-legs-off-because-they-hurt-so-bad. I start to think that if I hang out with Bob long enough, I won't need to go to any gym for exercise. Just keeping up with him will be exercise enough. Once we're settled in the front seat, I breathe a sigh of relief, and then look over at him, brows raised in question.

"What?" he says, swiping and tapping at the screen of his phone.

"What's next? Where do we go from here?" He reads something on his phone and starts swiping some more. I wait as patiently as I can, though I'm itching to get moving. "What are you doing?" I ask finally, leaning over and trying to peek at the screen. "Are you reading emails? Is there more info about the case?"

The corner of Bob's mouth twitches up ever so slightly, not quite a smile, but bordering on one. "Yes," he says finally, though I'm not sure which of my questions he's answering. "I got a text from Jonas. He and Arnie analyzed the trace amounts of heroin and other substances that were left in the syringe we found in Toby's arm and they figured out the percentage of each one present in the sample. They put it out for a search."

"Put it out for a search?" I say, not sure what he means.

"To see if it matches other samples collected by other jurisdictions. And we just got a hit. It seems the ingredients and their concentrations exactly match a heroin sample taken from a dealer in Pardeeville who the sheriffs there have arrested."

"Does that mean we're going to jail?" I say, sounding much more chipper than those words would generally imply.

Bob glances at his watch. "We can. It's an hour's drive to Portage from here. But I'm thinking it might be time to grab some lunch first. I don't know about you, but I haven't eaten since early this morning, and I'm getting hungry."

"Let me settle something right now," I tell him. "Stopping to eat is always fine by me. I can eat anytime, and pretty much anywhere. I don't do organ meats, and I'm not big on raw fish, but other than that, I'm good to go."

"Got it," Bob says with a smile.

"I thought you said the death occurred in Pardeeville. Why are we going to Portage?"

"Because that's where the jail is. Are you up for Chinese? I know a place not far from here in Madison."

"Yum," I say, licking my lips. "Shrimp lo mein, here I come."

Twenty minutes later we are seated in a booth in a typical Chinese restaurant, our orders placed, waiting on our food. It's quite warm inside, and as I slip out of my jacket, I hear and feel something crinkle in one of the pockets. Puzzled, I look inside and see one of the individually wrapped marshmallow and chocolate bunnies that was in the dish on the foyer table in Lori's house. I have no memory of taking anything from that dish, and I know no one offered me anything. Feeling a flush of shame and embarrassment, I shove the candy deeper into the pocket, sneaking a glance at Bob to see if he's noticed what I'm doing. He hasn't; his attention is focused on his phone, where he's slowly but methodically texting away. He has broad, stubby fingers, I note, and judging from the muttered curses and the frustrated frown on his face, texting isn't one of his strong suits.

My phone dings then, letting me know I have a text message, so I check to see who it's from and what it is. I don't get a lot of texts that aren't either work-related or from P.J., and as expected, this one is from P.J. There is a picture of Roscoe attached, holding a big stick in his mouth.

See what Roscoe caught! reads the text message. I smile at it, and then another text follows. **Should I walk him for you this afternoon again?**

I text P.J. back saying yes, and thanks.

When I'm done, I set the phone on the table and realize that Bob is watching me. I smile awkwardly at him, wondering if he knows about the candy in my pocket after all and is using some silent staring technique to get me to confess.

"There's something you should know," he says just as I'm about to seize the candy from my pocket and toss it to him while throwing myself at his mercy. "I have an ulterior motive for letting you come along with me today."

"Do you?" I say, breathing a sigh of relief even though my heart is still clipping along at a fast rate. That's because I think Bob is about to confess his undying love for me. Or at least his mild interest in me, though truth be told, I'd settle for a smidge of curiosity.

"I do," he says. "Chief Hanson loves to apply for grant funding. The last one he applied for got us our video cameras and eventually a full-time videographer. It's a very state-of-the-art, advanced practice for any police department, much less a small one like ours. It comes in very handy when we're processing crime scenes."

I feel my hopes sink like the *Titanic*. Unless he's using the videography thing as a lead-in to a kinky sex suggestion, I don't think his "confession" will have anything to do with his romantic interest in me. Since I have no idea where he's going with this, I sit back and listen, trying not to look too disappointed, and wishing the food would arrive so I would at least have something else to look at, something else to do besides twiddle my thumbs. I shove my hands down between my thighs to stop the twiddling.

"Anyway," Bob goes on, "the chief has applied for several more grants, one of which recently got approved. And that's why I invited you to come along with me today."

"Invited?" I scoff. "I had to practically beg and then blackmail you into letting me come along."

"Well, no, you didn't have to do that," he says with a sheepish smile. "But I let you, because I wanted to see how interested you really were."

Fortunately, our food arrives . . . fortunate because I have a sudden urge to rip Bob's head off his shoulders. A few choice comments bubble up in my throat, but I manage to both quell my urge and squelch my words, smiling as our waiter places the dishes on the table. I see Bob's expression when he looks at me once the waiter is gone and I know my eyes aren't reflecting the calm I'm trying to display with my body language and general absence of speech. Bob looks like he wants to get up and run, or maybe pull a gun on me.

"Let me get this right," I say in a low but seething voice. "You made me beg and barter to ride along with you even though you'd already decided I could?"

"You make it sound meaner than it was," Bob says with a frown. He ignores the chopsticks and takes up his fork, making me wonder if it's his preference for eating, or if he thinks that the fork is a better weapon for self-defense. His eyes follow my hand as I pick up my own fork, his expression wary. "It was something of a job interview," he says.

I don't know what I was expecting him to say, but it wasn't this. I'm momentarily stymied as I feel my balloon of anger deflate. "What do you mean, job interview?"

"The chief got funding for a trial program involving the use of a ride-along social worker for patrols. There are any number of situations cops encounter where a social worker would come in handy for things like on-the-spot counseling, child placement, community resource referrals, that sort of thing. Even counseling for the cops themselves at times. The chief put together a proposal for what he's calling the Helping Hands Program. He just informed us of the approval and funding at our staff meeting two days ago, and he plans to start looking for someone to fill the social worker role right away."

I gape at Bob, wondering if I'm being punked. "Are you serious, or are you playing some kind of joke on me?"

"I'm very serious," he says. "In fact, I spoke to Chief Hanson about you last night."

"You did?"

He nods, having just forked a mound of rice, beef, and broccoli into his mouth.

Still reeling, I take a stab at my own plate, embarrassed to find myself slurping a lo mein noodle seconds later. I chew contemplatively, staring at my plate because I'm afraid to look at Bob.

"It's only on a trial basis to start with," he says once he's swallowed, and I risk a look at him. "You wouldn't necessarily have to quit your job at the hospital, because the chief wants to try out the program on the night shift in the beginning, maybe some weekends, times when other resources tend to not be available."

I nod my understanding, trying to swallow. My mouth is

dry suddenly. I grab the teapot that our waiter placed on the table when we first sat down and pour myself a cup. Even though the tea has been sitting out for a while, it's still boiling hot, and I manage to scald my tongue and the inside of my mouth. It does help me swallow, though it's more of a half gasp that nearly chokes me, and I set my fork down to grab my water as a chaser. My eyes start to water, and I blink rapidly to try to quell the flow.

"You work a Monday through Friday day schedule at the hospital, don't you?" Bob says, seemingly oblivious to my current suffering. Apparently, the question is a rhetorical one, because he continues without waiting for me to answer. "I'm not sure it will work given your hospital schedule. You wouldn't want to ride around all night long with a police officer and then have to work all day at the hospital. But I'm also sure you wouldn't want to quit your job at the hospital for one that might only be part-time and temporary."

"Of course," I manage to say after a swallow of water cools down the inferno that is my mouth. The response is an automatic one, but in my mind, I'm thinking I can do it. I can sleep in the evenings, ride with the cops at night, and work at the hospital during the day. I kept a similar schedule when I was going to school, and it isn't like I have a life I need to worry about. I'm single, childless, and dateless, and my social life consists of coffee and cookies with my grief support group one evening a week and a movie and popcorn night with P.J. on the occasional Saturday night because I have cable and her parents don't.

"I could make it work," I tell Bob. "And I'd be very interested in doing something like that."

"You wouldn't be doing a lot of investigative stuff like you and I are doing now," Bob cautions. "I mean, you'd likely be present at crime scenes, probably one of the first people on site, in fact. But your job would be to help the police deal with the people who are involved, not investigate the crime."

"Of course," I say again with a smile, making a face that suggests I can't imagine it any other way. Though I can. He's not fooling me. Helping or dealing with the people at a crime scene could easily end up being a part of the investigation. They'd go hand in hand.

The mere thought of it triggers a montage of possible scenarios in my mind: me counseling possible suspects, me watching the police conduct their investigations, and maybe, just maybe, me having access to some of the investigative aids and resources the cops use all the time. That might help me finally make some progress on my mother's case.

Best not to seem too eager, though, I caution myself, and I focus on keeping my expression professional and neutral.

"I don't want to get your hopes up too much," Bob says.

Too late for that.

"We haven't officially begun the search process to fill the spot, and the chief was thinking we might try out several people in the beginning. You know, get three or four people who are interested and rotate them through to see how they work and who might be the best fit."

I try not to frown at this, even though I know I'm the best fit. My mind has already imagined me in the position. For a few seconds I start pondering ways to sabotage the other candidates, but then realize what I'm doing.

"Anyway, I thought I should be up front with you about things," Bob concludes. "Give you something to think about."

He has certainly succeeded in doing that. For the next few minutes we eat in silence, Bob looking at his phone, me trying to sort through the thoughts racing through my mind as I try to figure out how I can secure this new position and keep anyone else from being a part of it. I want this job. I want it bad.

One thing I think might play in my favor is that I know there aren't a lot of social workers in Sorenson, but that doesn't mean someone outside of town might not be interested. *How wide a net will they cast for the job?* I wonder. Perhaps I could get a leg up by interviewing with the chief before anyone else, an interview that would have to be perfect, so the man wouldn't feel the need to look for anyone else. What could I do or say to convince him that I'm the perfect person for the spot? My résumé is decent enough. I spent several years working for the city of Milwaukee and was involved in counseling for addiction issues, mental health problems, and crisis situations. I spent a year working with a hospice program and two years as a counselor at a high school in Milwaukee. I also worked with child and family services for a few years in Milwaukee and one year in Green Bay, when I moved there for the love of a man who turned out to be a two-timing scumbag. Best not to mention my poor judgment in that situation, however, I think, stealing a glance at Bob as if he might be trying to read or see my thoughts.

I'm starting to feel positive about my chances. My work experience is varied and good. My references are impeccable. And since moving to Sorenson, my hospital job has allowed me to provide a multitude of services at one time or another and given me a good knowledge base of community resources in the area.

Of course, I realize there might be other social workers out there with better résumés than mine, or at least as good as mine. I need something to make me stand out from all the rest, to give me an edge. And I think I know what I can use.

"Any chance I can get an interview with your chief soon?"

"Hunh?" Bob says, looking up from whatever it is on his phone that has him engrossed.

"I'd like a chance to talk to your chief about this position.

I think I'm qualified and have the attributes and experiences that would make me a highly suitable candidate."

"Such as?"

"Well, for one, I have a varied background when it comes to my experience. I've done all kinds of counseling to a variety of age groups. I've dealt with addiction problems, domestic abuse, grief and loss, sexual abuse, and a host of mental health issues, including PTSD in military personnel and first responders. I've provided child and family welfare management, community outreach, and resource management for people with illness and disability. I've worked for municipal and government entities, health care facilities, and a school system."

Bob listens, occasionally taking bites of his food, his expression telling me nothing about his reaction to my verbal résumé. I had hoped he'd look a little more impressed.

"I suppose there may be other social workers out there with a comparable work history," I say, "but I have a personal history that sets me apart."

This gets me an arch of Bob's brows, but no comment. Probably because his mouth is full.

"I'm the child of a murder victim," I say. "And I spent my life growing up in the foster system. I am well versed in the types of issues that most of the people the police are likely to encounter will be facing, because I've faced them myself, not just professionally, but personally."

Bob swallows and eyes me with smiling approval. "Sounds good," he says. "I'm sure Chief Hanson will want to interview you, though it might not be until next week sometime."

"Anything you can do to facilitate that would be much appreciated," I say. "Thank you."

"Don't thank me yet," he cautions. "I can't promise you anything. There are no guarantees. But if our time together this weekend goes well, I think it will give you a leg up."

Right. No pressure there. I'm filled with self-doubt suddenly, whereas before this day and this experience were little more than a lark, a bit of fun in what would have been an otherwise boring day. Now it's become important to me, critical to my future, or at least my desired future. I start playing back all the things I've said and done so far, trying to evaluate my performance as objectively as I can. Have I been too aggressive? Too forward? Professional enough?

Damn Bob for not telling me about this sooner! What should I do going forward? Should I let Bob handle all the questioning and sit by as a dutiful observer? Or should I step up and participate? What is he looking for? What will make me look better in his eyes?

I finish my meal and slip my jacket back on. Then I excuse myself to go to the bathroom. While I'm in there, I eat the stolen chocolate bunny.

Bob is already at the counter paying for our meal when I come out. "Let me buy my own," I say.

"I have this one; you get the next one."

That seems reasonable, and it implies that there will be a next meal. I let it go, and minutes later we are back in his car, heading for Portage.

Chapter Twenty-Five

The village of Pardeeville, which has a population of a thousand souls or so, has no jail. Anyone arrested there and needing confinement is taken to the Columbia County Jail in Portage, much like anyone needing overnight jailing in Sorenson has to go to one of the larger cities. The county jail in Portage consists of two buildings, and Bob explains to me that one of them houses inmates who qualify to be in something called the Huber program, a work-release program. I log this info in my brain, knowing that if I get the job with the police department, it might prove useful.

The prisoner we want to talk to is not in the Huber program, however, and we have to go through a series of check-in spots in the second building before we get taken to a small, private interview room.

A guard brings in our drug dealer, whose feet and hands are cuffed. All I know from Bob is that the fellow's name is Stewart Thomas—one of those people who has what seems like two first names instead of an obvious first and last name. These names tend to throw me off for some reason, and I find them annoying. Stewart—and in my mind I think of him as Stewie to help me remember which of his names is the first one—appears to be twenty-something, and he's a skinny dude with hair that looks like it hasn't been washed, cut, or even combed in weeks. He is also sporting several days' worth of sketchy beard growth, and he has a pale, pasty color to his skin that suggests he rarely sees the sun. There are dark circles under his eyes and a sickly, glazed look to his face that makes me think he samples too much of his own product. I glance at his arms to look for track marks, but he is wearing a long-sleeved T-shirt beneath what I assume are jail-issue scrubs in an unflattering shade of orange.

A guard pushes Stewie into the room and tells him to sit. Stewie shuffles two steps and drops into the indicated chair.

Bob says, "Hello, Mr. Thomas. I'm Detective Bob Richmond, and this is Ms. Schneider."

Stewie sneers, "Whatever," and lets out a breath of mocking antipathy that flows across the table like a toxic miasma. His breath is foul-smelling, and I see that his dentition is no healthier than the rest of him. The few teeth he has left are broken and rotten-looking, and his gums are puffy, red, and inflamed. All of this adds to my suspicion that Stewie is a regular user of his product—likely multiple products.

His fidgety behavior tells me he's starting to feel the effects of withdrawal. He raises his cuffed hands to his face every few seconds, swiping at his mouth and nose, or rubbing a hand over his cheek, creating a raspy sandpaper sound. One eye keeps twitching uncontrollably. His body is in constant motion, rocking slightly back and forth and side to side. The guard standing behind him keeps a wary eye on him.

Bob explains to Stewie that we just want to talk, that our conversation is not being recorded and isn't official. "We aren't interested in prosecuting you for anything," Bob says, trying to sound reassuring, though I suspect the nuances are lost on Stewie. "We're more interested in knowing who your customers have been recently. I want to know if you sold any of your heroin product to the man in this picture."

Bob shows Stewie a picture of Toby Cochran on his phone, and Stewie spares it a glancing look before shaking his head.

"Are you sure?" Bob asks. "Look close."

Stewie lets out an exasperated sigh, thrusts his face forward toward the photo on Bob's phone, and widens his eyes dramatically, staring for several seconds. "There. Happy now?" he says when he sits back and looks at Bob again, an insolent cock to his head. "I still don't recognize him."

Bob pulls the phone back and swipes at the screen while asking, "Have you sold to any college students from Madison recently?"

Stewie gives him a look of incredulity and laughs. "Geez, let me check my files," he mocks. "Or you could call my secretary and have her check on it." He shakes his head and chuckles in amusement, taking another swipe at his nose. Bob's expression doesn't change. He stares at Stewie, waiting, and it doesn't take Stewie long to cave. "Dude," he says with a shrug, "if they got the cash, I got the goods. I don't ask a lot of questions or check their résumés."

Bob turns the phone toward Stewie again, showing him a different picture. "How about this guy?"

I'm able to glimpse the screen briefly and realize it's a picture of Liam Michaelson, probably a DMV photo. Stewie looks and shakes his head. Bob takes the phone, swipes and types and then shows Stewie another picture. This goes on until Bob has shown Stewie a picture of all the boys involved in the email exchange we read on Toby's computer. Stewie claims not to recognize any of them, but I figure his word is about as reliable as a roll of the dice would be in predicting the weather. Of course, if he suspects we're here investigating the death of someone who used his "product" he'd be crazy to admit to selling to anyone lest he be brought up on homicide charges. Wisconsin has gotten quite serious about prosecuting the dealers as well as the users. And Stewie has no reason to believe Bob's claim that our discussion today is informal and off-the-record. Criminals and cops aren't known for the trust they have in one another.

I sense Bob's frustration, which mirrors my own. I knew this chat with Stewie was a long shot, but I did hope it might help us make a little progress. I get an idea then and take my phone out. A moment later I have the picture of Toby and the gaming team that came from Lori's phone, and on a whim, I show the picture to Stewie and ask him if he recognizes anyone as someone who has bought product from him.

He gives the screen a cursory glance much the way he did with Bob's phone and starts to shake his head. Or maybe it's a spasm. His whole body is twitching and jerking like water drops on a hot skillet. Then he squints and looks closer. "Maybe," he says, swiping at his nose for the hundredth time. Bob perks up, leaning forward eagerly. Stewie jabs at the screen, his shaking finger coming down squarely on Toby's face. "That guy, I think."

Bob visibly deflates, and I feel my own hopes flag.

"That's the guy we showed you in the beginning," Bob says irritably. "Are you recognizing him now because you sold stuff to him, or because we showed him to you back at the start of this charade?"

Stewie tips his head to one side and gives Bob a pained, pitiful look. "Not that kid," he says with disdain. "The guy standing right behind him."

I grab my phone and turn it around, looking at the picture. Bob leans over and stares at it with me. Standing behind Toby, his head seeming to float above him, is the middle-aged man. I turn the phone back toward Stewie and carefully position my finger on the screen beside the man's face. "This guy?" I say.

Stewie rubs his raspy cheek and gives one exaggerated nod that looks hard enough to make his head fall off his scrawny neck. "Yep, that guy," he says, enunciating with great care. "Pretty sure that guy bought some heroin off me about three weeks ago."

"Do you know his name?" Bob asks.

"Hell, no," Stewie says dismissively. "Couldn't care less about names. Don't want to know 'em. Tell the truth, I don't much remember faces, either, but this guy sticks."

"Why is that?" Bob asks.

"Two reasons," Stewie says, holding up two fingers on his right hand while his left dangles in the cuffs below it. "One, he asked for the strongest stuff I had, and he didn't look like no tweaker, you know? Pretty sure that guy wasn't using anything stronger than aspirin. And two, he offered to pay me twice what the stuff was worth, so he clearly wasn't very up on things, get my drift?"

Stewie's drift has gone precariously to the right, and he catches himself just before he's about to lose his balance and topple from his chair. I notice that the guard makes no move to stop this; in fact, he watches the kid tip with a hint of a grin on his face, and then looks disappointed when Stewie manages to straighten himself.

"How did he find you?" Bob asks. "How did he contact you?"

Stewie's face forms into an exaggerated expression of thoughtfulness for a few seconds before he resumes his usual clueless look and shrugs. He raises his right hand, the left one dangling again, and points a finger at Bob. "Now, that's a good question," he says, withdrawing his right hand to take another swipe at his nose. "He just found me."

"What do you mean, he just found you?" Bob asks impatiently.

Stewie, again drifting precariously to one side, rights himself at the last second and narrows his eyes at Bob. "I have a spot. I can't say where because . . . well . . . him." He flashes Bob a conspiratorial smile and tries to point a thumb over his shoulder at the guard standing behind him. Unfortunately, the weight of his other, cuffed arm interferes with the gesture, and all Stewie manages to do is to jab himself in his own shoulder with his thumb. Still, the inference is clear. "It's a spot some of my regulars know. You know, my best repeat customers."

"And you only saw this man and sold to him one time?" Bob asks.

"Yeah, I'd remember him."

Bob's brow wrinkles in thought for a moment and then he says, "Thank you. That's all." He pushes back his chair and gets up. I do the same. Stewie stays seated and watches us leave, and I swear he looks disappointed. I suspect the guard will be yanking on him any second.

"Who is this guy?" Bob says once we're back in the car. His face is screwed up into a frown. "And what's he got to do with these college kids?"

"I'll bet our frat boys know."

Bob looks over at me, his eyes narrowed. He looks ticked, and I'm hoping that ire isn't directed my way. Without another word, he starts the car and takes off. We ride in silence for half an hour, long enough for me to figure out that we're headed back to Madison and, I'm guessing, the frat house. I'm about to ask if this is the case when Bob's phone rings.

"Detective Richmond," he says into the phone, after a quick thumb swipe and subsequent frown at the screen. He pulls off onto the shoulder of the road and shifts the car into park. I lean a little closer to him, hoping I might overhear some part of the conversation on the other end, but I can't make out any words.

"I'd like to come out and talk with you regarding a case I'm working," he says. "And I'd like to take a look at your property."

My heart leaps when I realize the call is likely from Warren Sheffield.

"I see," Bob says in a tone of voice that suggests otherwise. "May I ask why not?" He listens, the angles of his face growing harder with each passing second. I can tell he doesn't like what he's hearing.

"Yes, sir, I do know him," Bob says, his jaw tight. "And I'll be sure to let him know that you have no interest in seeing justice done." With that, Bob takes the phone from his ear, jabs angrily at the screen to disconnect the call, and then throws the phone up on the dashboard.

"I take it that was Warren Sheffield," I say after a few seconds of electric silence goes by.

"The guy's an ass," Bob mumbles. "He claims people of his stature," Bob puffs himself up mockingly when saying this, "are constantly bothered by us lowlifes who are always looking for any reason to take them down a peg."

"He called you a lowlife?" I say, surprised.

"No," Bob admits irritably. Then he puffs his cheeks out in a prolonged sigh. "But the inference was there. He told me if I wanted anything to contact his lawyer. And at the end he asked me if I knew who Gerhart Albrecht is."

"Albrecht the state senator?"

Bob nods, shooting me a *can you believe it?* side glance. "Sheffield suggested that if I have any issues with his refusal that I run them past Albrecht." Bob shifts the car back into drive, and after checking for traffic, he pulls back onto the highway. He doesn't say anything for the first few miles and I can tell from the look on his face that he's mulling things over in his mind.

"You think he's hiding something, don't you?" I say.

Bob looks at me and nods. "Why else would he be such a hardhead about a visit from the police? Though to be honest, he didn't really say no until I mentioned that we wanted to look at some areas on his property." He lets out another sigh. "You were right, Hildy. I think that footbridge is significant somehow. We just have to figure out how and then find a way to get to it."

"How do you propose we do that?" I ask, secretly thrilled that he's using a plural pronoun when discussing future endeavors, and hoping he means me when he does so.

"We have a couple more boys we need to talk to from that frat house," Bob says. "But I think this time we need to take a different approach."

I assume he's driving us back to Madison but then he exits the highway we're on and heads for Sorenson.

"Where are we going?" I ask.

"Back to the station. We're done for today."

I frown at him, wondering if he's being honest or simply trying to dump me. "I thought we were going to go back to the frat house," I say. "Hit up the boys we didn't catch earlier."

"Oh, we will," he says. "But not today. We're done for today. Let's let the folks at the frat house think they're rid of us, give them some time to relax and get back to normal."

"And then?"

"And then we pull off a sneak attack. But we've got a bit of homework to do first."

Chapter Twenty-Six

When we arrive back at the station, Bob parks in the secured lot, gets out, and walks toward the rear entrance without a word to me. Since he hasn't told me goodbye, get lost, or go away, I follow along, assuming I'm invited. My assumption is confirmed when he holds the back door for me, letting me pass beneath his arm into the station break room.

I glance around the room, enjoying the fruits of my labor as I take in the clean table and countertops. The linoleum-covered floor, however, is still scuffed and covered with crumbs and other debris, enough of a distraction to kill my brief buzz. If Bob wasn't in such a determined go-mode, I'd seriously consider trying to clean the floor.

Instead, I follow Bob down the hall to the front of the station, through the doors to the evidence garage and processing area, and down the stairs to the floor below, each step a tiny bit of leg muscle torture. He makes a call on his cell as we enter the second area. There is no one here, a disappointment for me, as I was hoping I might get to see Jonas again.

"Hi, Jonas," Bob says, pausing in the middle of the room. "I need to look at the cell phone we found on Toby Cochran. And I'd like to peruse his social media activity.

Can you help me out?" He listens for a moment, then says, "Thanks," and hangs up. "He's going to come down and help us," he tells me. "In the meantime, we can look through the cell phone. It's in the storage locker. Jonas is going to access the database from his home computer, look up the location number, and text it to me. That way we can get the phone and start looking through it while we're waiting."

"Okay, sounds good," I say, though I'm not sure why we're doing all of this. "What are you hoping to find on the phone? Haven't the calls and text messages already been gone through?"

"They have," Bob says, walking toward the far end of the room, where there is a locked door with a keypad next to it. "But when the team looked through it, they didn't know what we know. I think a new perspective might reveal something useful."

I don't know if he's being deliberately vague or not, but I can't figure out what it is he's hoping to find. I don't want to look too stupid and clueless by continuing to ask, and I figure I'll find out soon enough anyway.

Bob punches a four-digit number into the lockbox, standing in a way that hides it from me. He opens the door to reveal a dark cave, though the moment he steps over the threshold, there is a flicker of light from above. Seconds later there is a blinding brightness as long rows of fluorescent lamps come to life.

"Holy cow," I say, staring at the sight before me. "How big is this area?"

"Sixty feet wide and one hundred feet long," Bob says. He glances toward the ceiling. "And I believe it's twenty feet high. All of this front area is filled with shelving, but in the back, there's room for storing larger items that won't fit on a shelf or in a box. There's also a cargo door there that opens onto the street." His phone dings, and he takes it out and looks at the screen. "That's Jonas's text," he says. After taking a moment to access and read the text, he then points to the first shelf area, which is filled with boxes of various shapes and sizes, each one carefully labeled with names and numbers to identify their contents. Each portion of shelving is also labeled with a letter and a number. This first area is marked as A-1.

"Every piece of evidence that is stored in here is labeled and marked," Bob explains. "And it's assigned a specific shelving area, which is recorded both in our computer database and in a catalogue book. The books are kept over there." He points to the far-right corner, where I see a desk area backed by a wall of metal filing cabinets. "I could have located the cell phone using the catalogues, but I knew Jonas could find it a lot faster."

"Impressive," I say, feeling an odd sense of satisfaction as I view this orderliness.

Bob looks again at his phone and says, "We need to go to area G-thirty-eight." He heads off down the rows, which are labeled A through M. When we reach the one marked G, he turns into the row and heads for the back of the building. It takes us a good thirty feet into the row before we reach the number we are looking for. There I see a box bearing Toby Cochran's name, a string of digits that I assume is some type of case number, and a date—the date of his death.

Bob takes the box down from the shelf, sets it on the floor, and opens it. He doesn't have to look far; there is a surprising and depressingly small amount of stuff in the box, a sad summation of Toby's cruel and untimely death. I see sealed and labeled bags that contain clothing, a watch, a pair of running shoes, and several small, paper envelopes that I can't see through, though the label on one tells me it contains a syringe. The cell phone is there, contained inside a clear evidence bag, neatly taped closed and labeled. Bob removes it from the box and is about to put the lid back on when I see another small envelope whose label I can read.

"Hold it," I say. "There are keys in there?" I point to the envelope in question.

Bob looks at the packet, shrugs, and nods.

"It just hit me," I say. "How did Toby get around? Did he have a car?"

"He did."

"Where is it? Did you guys look at it?"

"It's at an impound lot in Madison. It's a junker, an old car with over 160,000 miles on it. We looked through it but there wasn't anything of interest in it."

"Where did you find it?"

"It was parked on the street by his house. His mother wasn't interested in keeping it, and there wasn't anything in it she wanted."

"Any chance anyone tested the inside of it for drug residue?"

Bob makes a face. "Doubt it. It wouldn't serve any purpose."

"Any drug paraphernalia in it?"

"No."

"Seems odd, doesn't it?"

"Perhaps," Bob says a bit irritably. "In retrospect." He replaces the lid and returns the box to its spot on the shelf. I follow him out of the evidence room and back into the main processing area. Bob sets the phone down on a side table, takes out a pocketknife, and slices the outer seal open. The phone doesn't have a cord to go with it, and when Bob tries to turn the device on, nothing happens. He moves a little farther down the table toward an outlet strip mounted on the wall. Above the strip is a pegboard, and several different types of charge wires are coiled around pegs. Bob examines the ends of a couple of them, comparing them to the port on Toby's phone, and selects one. He uncoils the wire and plugs one end into the outlet strip and the other end into the phone.

"That's better," he says, as he turns the phone on and it scrolls through its startup screens. I wonder if this will be password protected the way the laptop was, but as soon as the main screen is showing, Bob is able to start tapping and swiping. He opens the photo gallery and starts sorting through the pictures.

"What are you looking for?" I ask.

"The picture he sent to Lori. It came from his phone, and that means it might have been taken on his phone. If we can find it, we should be able to tell when it was taken, and maybe, with a bit of luck, where."

"I see," I say. "You're hoping we might be able to connect that picture to Sheffield's house."

"Exactly."

"And the reason you want to peruse Toby's social media is to see if he might have posted that picture, or others, and perhaps tagged the people in it, thus giving us the mystery man's name."

Bob shoots me an approving look. "You catch on fast, Hildy."

The door to the room opens then and Jonas comes in. He's not alone. Walking just ahead of him is a little girl who looks to be around seven. She's dressed in green and blue pants with a floral design and a pale yellow top. She has her father's dark brown eyes and dirty blond hair, though hers falls over her shoulders in a wavy curtain of curls, whereas Jonas's is straight. Her overall features don't resemble Jonas's, however, and I gather she takes after her mother. "I hope you don't mind me bringing Sofie along," he says. "My mother couldn't take her on such short notice."

"No skin off my nose," Bob says.

"Sofie, this is Detective Richmond," Jonas says, kneeling beside the girl. "I work with him a lot."

"Hello," she says with an adorable smile.

"And this," Jonas goes on, gesturing toward me, "is Hildy Schneider. I've not worked with her before today, but she's going to have dinner with me tomorrow night."

"Hello, Sofie." I say. "How nice it is to get to meet you."

"Are you a cop, too?" Sofie asks, checking out my clothing with a skeptical expression.

"No, I'm a social worker."

"What's that?"

"Well, social workers wear a lot of different hats. We can be counselors, planners—"

"How come you're not wearing a hat right now?" Sofie says staring at my head.

"Not real hats," I say with a smile. "I meant pretend hats, like the kind that tell you what job someone has." Sofie frowns and I look to the two men for help, but they seem to be enjoying my unsuccessful attempts to explain things. "I help people figure out ways to solve their problems," I say finally.

Sofie considers this, her head cocked to one side. Her feet are adorned in a pair of bright red sneakers, and I see one of her feet start drawing circles on the floor as she contemplates me and my answer. I wonder if she picked out her own outfit or if Jonas did it.

"If you help people with problems, can you help me with my homework?" Sofie asks. "My teacher gave me math homework. I don't like math."

"I could," I tell her with a smile. "But I'm betting you're smart and you can do it yourself. I don't think you need any help."

She lets forth with a coy smile, shrugs, and skips over to the desk. She opens one of the drawers, removes a coloring book and a box of crayons, and climbs into the chair. Clearly this isn't the first time Jonas has brought her along to work.

"How far have you gotten?" Jonas asks Bob.

"Not very. The kid had a lot of pictures on here."

"Maybe if you look at them by date," I suggest. "Lori said Toby sent her the picture just days before breaking up with her. And according to his mother, that was around spring break. Look for pictures taken around the middle of March."

Jonas nods agreeably, but Bob just frowns. "How do I find a date on here?" he says, staring at the phone screen. I look, realize he has the photos expanded, and do a *gimme* gesture with my hand. Surprisingly, he hands it over. Then he positions himself over my shoulder and watches as I exit out of the expanded view to the main gallery with its thumbnails and dates. I don't have to scroll far to find the date in question, and soon I see the picture. I tap it, making it larger.

"Here it is," I say, showing it to both men.

"Yep, that's the one," Bob says. He takes the phone from me and hands it to Jonas. "Can you see if there's any GPS data embedded in this picture?"

Jonas takes the phone from Bob, messes with it for a few seconds, and then hands it back. He walks over to a table with a computer on it, wakes it up, logs in to his email, and downloads the photo to the computer's desktop. Then he hovers over the picture with his cursor and right clicks his mouse.

"There's your GPS info," he says, pointing to a series of numbers.

"Latitude and longitude?" Bob says, clearly disappointed. "I thought it would be more specific."

"Oh, that's very specific," Jonas says. "I think what you meant is that you were hoping it would list out an address for you."

"Something like that," Bob admits with a grumble.

"Hang on, ye of little faith," Jonas says. His fingers fly

over the keyboard and I watch the monitor screen, enthralled. I see a satellite picture of the earth appear and then Jonas quickly zooms in to North America, then Wisconsin, and then the area surrounding Sorenson to the north and west. As he zooms, I recognize Viking Park, which includes a large fenced-in dog park located on a river that provides several beaches where dogs can swim. I've taken Roscoe there many times, as he loves the water and socializes well with other dogs.

Jonas taps again and before I can say *abracadabra*, the screen shows an aerial view of the footbridge. I realize then that it's only about three miles beyond the Viking Park perimeter, not far from one of the trails outside of the doggy area that I've hiked with Roscoe. It's just the other side of the woods that border the trail.

"Is that Warren Sheffield's property?"

"It is," Bob says.

"Is it enough to get a search warrant?" I ask hopefully.

Bob shakes his head. "Probably not, but we're getting warm. And we're not done yet." He looks at Jonas. "Can you pull up Toby's social media for me?"

"Sure can. There's some of it here on his phone, but it will be easier to see and access on his laptop. Let me go get it."

Jonas disappears into the huge evidence room, leaving Bob and me with Sofie, who seems oblivious to our presence as she colors a picture of a unicorn. Then she surprises me by revealing just how tuned in she really is.

"So you want to date my father?" she says, not looking up from what she's doing.

I open my mouth but have no answer at the ready as I'm searching my brain for the best response. No spontaneity here. Apparently seeing my hesitancy, and perhaps my discomfort as well, Bob jumps in and answers the child.

"Nah, he's cute and all, but he's really not my type."

Sofie spins around in the desk chair and looks up at us,

giggling at Bob's answer. "I wasn't talking to you, silly," she says to Bob. She shifts her gaze to me. "I was talking to her." She points at me in a disturbingly accusing manner, eyes narrowed, arm thrust out straight, and with a very serious expression on her face.

"To be honest, Sofie, I don't know if I want to date your father. I don't know him. We just met for the first time today. But I like him, and he asked me if I'd have dinner with him, so I said yes. After the dinner I might get a better idea of whether or not I want to actually date him."

Bob shifts uncomfortably where he's standing, clearing his throat. Sofie has dropped the accusing hand back into her lap, but she's still staring at me, gauging me.

"How do you feel about your father dating?" I ask Sofie. "Does it bother you?" I have no idea what the family situation is with Jonas and Sofie. Does he share custody of the child with her mother? Are he and the mother divorced? Or did they have a child together outside of wedlock? Is there animosity between them, or do they get along? And perhaps more important than Sofie's feelings about her father dating other women is how Sofie's mother feels about it. Was I about to step into the middle of a soul- and life-sucking emotional quagmire?

"My dad doesn't go on dates much," Sofie says with a shrug. "He says he doesn't have time and that some girls don't like that he's a package deal."

"A 'package deal'?" I repeat.

Sofie gives me an exasperated look. "Yes," she says emphatically. "A package deal. A family. We're a family."

Just who she is including in this description is uncertain. "You and your father, you mean?"

"Of course, silly," she says, looking at me like I have less intelligence than her box of crayons. "Who else?"

I hesitate a split second before deciding to dive into the deep end of this pool. "What about your mother?"

Sofie's forehead wrinkles slightly and she looks away for a moment. Then she straightens herself, takes on a very grown-up looking expression, and says, "She ran away."

"I don't have a mother anymore, either," I say. "She died when I was about your age. That was a long time ago, but I still miss her a lot."

I'm hoping this line of conversation might get Sofie to reveal something more about her mother without me coming right out and asking. But it leads her in a slightly different direction instead.

"Did your dad go on dates, too?"

I smile at her. "I didn't have a dad," I say. "At least not one I know of."

Sofie looks stricken. "No mom or dad?"

Bob is standing off to one side, looking at some papers on one of the countertops. Though he is trying to look like he's engaged in reading, I know he's listening in on our conversation. I know I need to tread carefully here because I'm getting into some awkward territory with any explanations I give Sofie. How do you explain to a seven-year-old that your mother was a prostitute and you don't know who your father is? *You don't,* my voice of reason tells me.

Fortunately, I'm saved from having to explain any more because Jonas returns with Toby's laptop. He sets it on the counter where the charge cords are hanging, plugs it into a power strip, and boots it up. I watch, seeing that the computer no longer prompts for a password. As Jonas starts typing on it, I look over at Sofie, who is back at her picture, studiously coloring in the unicorn's horn in a bright shade of purple.

"I'm sure Laura has already been through his social media sites," Jonas says. "According to her notes, Toby was active on Facebook, Instagram, and Twitter. Laura was probably looking for mention of any hookups that might have been disguised drug deals. She didn't report anything, so I'm guessing she didn't find any."

"I'm not interested in drug deals," Bob says, taking out his phone and showing Jonas the picture that Lori let us have from her phone. "I want to see if he put up photos of the people in this gaming club he belonged to, and if he did, if he tagged any of them. I need a name for this guy." He points to the middle-aged man standing behind Toby in the picture, the one that our drug dealer pointed out.

"Okay," Jonas says. "Let's start with Facebook and see what we can find there. If this guy is on any social media, he's more likely to be there than on Instagram. The Instagram crowd tends to be younger. And frankly, there's enough overlap between these two apps that we can cover a lot of ground in both by cruising through one of them."

I figure it could take hours to wade through this online stuff, but Jonas proves himself quite adept at hunting down what we need. In a matter of minutes, he has found the same photo Lori had on her phone in one of Toby's Facebook albums. And I can't resist letting out a little whoop of joy when I see that Toby did, indeed, tag everyone in the picture.

"Gotcha!" Jonas says with a satisfied grin. "Your mystery man is one Vadim Belov. Let's see what he has in his Facebook account."

Chapter Twenty-Seven

Vadim Belov doesn't have much of a Facebook presence, and what little he does have seems geared toward picking up women. He has forty-six friends, all but ten of them women. Of the ten men, eight of them are college-age boys—including our fraternity friends—and I wouldn't be surprised if most of them turn out to be gamers.

Jonas starts clicking around and comes up with a couple of other names we don't have. While he's doing that, Bob walks off to a distant corner and talks on his phone with someone. I'm tempted to drift closer so I can eavesdrop, but think better of it and continue to watch Jonas's efforts over his shoulder instead.

After a couple of minutes on his phone, Bob says, "I need to go upstairs to my office and check on a few things. I'll be right back."

I consider chasing after him, not wanting to be left behind, but he's gone so fast that I don't have a chance. The idea of simply heading back upstairs occurs to me, but I'm afraid I might get stuck in a hallway, unable to escape without an ID badge or key fob to swipe.

Resigned to waiting, I continue watching Jonas's mining efforts on Facebook. He goes back to Toby's posts and scrolls through them. Nothing jumps out at me as significant, other than the fact that Toby quit posting anything not long after that group photo went up.

"I'm not seeing much here that looks helpful," Jonas says finally. "You?" I shake my head. "I'll check out Instagram next, and then Twitter." He switches websites and has barely gotten started when Bob returns.

"I have some information on Mr. Belov," he says. "I didn't find anything about him in our usual databases, so I hit up a friend of mine at the FBI and had him check some federal databases for me. Lo and behold, our Mr. Belov is here from Russia on a work visa. Want to guess who his employer is?"

I don't need to guess, because I'm certain of the answer, but it doesn't matter, because Bob doesn't give me a chance to respond.

"He works for a company called WIS Productions. One might assume that the WIS is an abbreviation for Wisconsin, and maybe it is, but it also happens to be the initials of the person who owns the company."

I make the connection instantly. "Warren Sheffield?"

"Yes," Bob says, looking surprised, and maybe a tad annoyed that I guessed so quickly, thus stealing some of his thunder. "And Mr. Belov lists Mr. Sheffield's house as his home address."

"What does this company produce?" I ask.

"They supposedly make videos, self-help stuff. But my friend at the FBI said that they've been trying to infiltrate Sheffield's business because they think he's really producing . . ." He pauses, glances over at Sofie, and frowns. "Adult movies," he says finally.

"Do we have enough to get a search warrant yet?" I ask.

"Perhaps," Bob says, looking thoughtful. "We have a victim who we're certain was murdered, and we have evidence that he was at Sheffield's estate. We also have a witness who says Mr. Belov bought some of the, um . . ."

He glances toward Sofie. "He bought the substance that was found in our victim, and he lists Sheffield's place as his home address. Now that we have connected Mr. Belov to Mr. Sheffield, I think I can convince a judge to at least let us have a look at the house and grounds."

"Are you planning to question both Mr. Sheffield and this Mr. Belov?" I ask, determined to be involved if this is the case.

"I'll try," he says. "But someone with Sheffield's kind of money and pull is bound to have a lawyer at the ready who will advise him to keep his mouth shut." Bob shrugs. "Guess we'll have to see how it goes."

"How soon can you get the warrant?" I ask.

"Depends on what judge is on call," Bob says glancing at this watch. "Weekends are always tough, and there isn't any crucial time element involved here. My guess is it probably won't be until Monday."

I curse to myself. Monday I will have to be back at work at the hospital, and if Bob goes out to the Sheffield place then, I won't be able to go along. I seriously consider calling in sick, but then dismiss the idea. Sorenson is too small a town to tell a lie like that and hope to get away with it. Odds are I'd bump into someone from the hospital who would mention seeing me to my boss, Crystal, and then I'd get in trouble. I could call Crystal and ask to take a personal day. I've got enough hours built up to cover it. But doing so on such short notice feels wrong. And what if Bob doesn't get the warrant until Tuesday? Then I will have wasted a day off and I'll be facing the same dilemma all over again.

"You don't think we could go to Sheffield's place now and try to talk to him or this Belov character?" I ask, trying one last time.

Bob shakes his head, his expression firm. "I don't want to tip them off before we get a warrant. It's too easy to hide things or have people disappear if you know the cops are going to be nosing around."

Okay, I tell myself. *Better to play it straight and take whatever comes.* Skipping work at the hospital won't look good to the police chief, and I don't want to do anything that would make me look less than professional for this new job. If I can't go along with Bob to the Sheffield place, then so be it. Surely Bob will fill me in on whatever he finds later. At least I hope he will.

"I'm not seeing anything else in Toby's social media that's going to help," Jonas says. He logs off of Toby's computer and shuts it down, closing the machine and unplugging it. He then tucks it under one arm, grabs Toby's cell phone, and starts to carry both items into the evidence room.

"Hold on a second," I say to Jonas. "I just remembered that Sharon Cochran told me Toby got a message on his phone right before he went out on the night he died. Who was that from?"

"Some burner phone that was bought in Michigan," Jonas says. "Toby had sent a message to it saying that he needed to meet and talk. All the reply said was 'Meet in the usual place,' and there was no name attached to it other than Mr. Moneybags."

"'Mr. Moneybags'?" I repeat, scowling.

"It's probably a drug dealer," Jonas says. "That's how a lot of them operate. Code names, code words." He shrugs.

"I think I'm going to call it a day," Bob says. "I'll work on getting the warrant paperwork done tonight and see if I can get it in tomorrow, though I doubt we'll get an answer then."

I nod, and Jonas once again heads for the evidence locker to return the laptop and phone. I watch as Sofie boxes up her crayons and returns them and the coloring book to the drawer they came from. Then she turns to me. "When are you having dinner with my dad?"

"Tomorrow," I say, trying not to look at Bob as he starts the awkward fidgeting again.

"Can I come with you?" Sofie asks.

Bob tries to stifle a chuckle.

"Are you asking if you can come with us to dinner?" I ask Sofie.

She nods once emphatically, her chin sticking out in a gesture of what looks like defiance. "You know what, I think that's a great idea," I tell her. "As long as your dad says it's okay."

She looks startled by my answer.

"Of course, it will be a school night, so I don't know if your father will let you stay out very late," I add.

"Stay out late for what?" Jonas says, returning from the evidence room.

"Sofie wants to know if she can go to dinner with us tomorrow night." Before Jonas can utter the automatic refusal I see on his face, I add, "I told her it was fine with me if it was okay with you."

Sofie manages to recover her composure and appeals to her father, her big brown eyes growing even bigger. "Please, Dad? Can I?" she wheedles.

"Sofie," he says, frowning. "We've talked about this."

The little girl pouts adorably, and Jonas sighs.

"I think it will be fun," I say. "I'd like to get to know Sofie better." Jonas gives me a skeptical look. I nod slightly and smile at him. "It will be fine."

"Okay," Jonas says. "But it's straight home after that, and I don't want you to give me any fuss about bedtime," he lectures. "Monday is a school day."

"I promise," Sofie says, her face alight with delight. She hops off the chair and runs over to her father, wrapping her arms around his legs and hugging him. The whole thing is utterly adorable on the surface, though I'm starting to realize that Sofie is quite the manipulator. I may have my work cut out for me.

"Why don't we try for an earlier time?" I say to Jonas. "I don't mind at all, if that helps."

"It might be better," he says. He looks thoughtful for a moment and then says, "Would you be okay with having dinner at my place? I'll cook, and while I'm no chef, I have a few old reliables I can make."

"That would be fine," I say. "What time?"

"Can we get together around four, plan to eat around five, and then play it by ear after that?"

"Sounds wonderful. Text me your address, and I'll be there at four." I like this plan, as it's much more informal and leaves me with my own wheels should I need to escape.

"See you then," Jonas says. He takes Sofie by the hand.

"See you then," she echoes.

"See you then," I agree with a smile. I watch them go and then turn my attention back to Bob. "She's a cute kid."

He makes some sort of grunting noise that might or might not be agreement.

"Will you call me tomorrow if anything happens?"

"I will, but it won't. Sundays are dead around here. No pun intended."

"I have to work seven to three at the hospital on Monday," I tell him. "I can be available after that."

"We can figure things out at the gym on Monday morning," he says. "No gym tomorrow, remember. I don't go on Sundays typically. It's my one day a week of rest, and I suspect you'll be a bit sore tomorrow anyway. I know I was at first."

Right, the stupid gym thing. I smile, trying not to show the mix of horror and relief I feel—horror at being reminded of my commitment to Bob, and relief that tomorrow morning will bring a reprieve.

"Meet me there at five on Monday?" Bob says cheerfully.

I wonder if my face has a deer-in-the-headlights expression on it, because that's how I feel. His reminder of the gym thing makes me feel like I'm standing on a train rail wearing heavy, magnetic boots and there is a very big, very fast locomotive hurtling toward me.

"Sure," I hear myself say. I groan inwardly, and if it wouldn't hurt so much just to move my arms the way I'd need to, I'd give myself a slap upside the head. "See you there at five."

"Great!" Bob walks over to the entry door, opens it, and holds it, looking at me. We head back upstairs, and as if the reminder has somehow enhanced my pain, my thigh muscles scream with every step. Once we are back on the first floor behind the dispatcher's desk, Bob says, "See you Monday," and starts to turn away. He might as well have said, "You're dismissed."

I'm nothing if not tenacious, however, so I wrap a hand over his wrist, halting his escape. "Thanks for letting me go with you today," I say with a smile. "I really like this work, and I'm very excited about this new job. You will keep me in mind for it, yes?"

"Absolutely. You're at the top of our list."

I beam at this, then remember our earlier discussion. "Wait, you haven't officially listed the position, so I'm the only one on the list at the moment, right?"

Bob smiles, looking guilty. "Busted," he says. "But look at it this way. At least you have a head start over the others." With that he wriggles loose of my grip, turns, and disappears down the hallway.

I glance over at the dispatcher, who is someone new I haven't seen before—clearly a shift change has occurred. Her name tag says Miranda, but she is about as far from my mental image of a Miranda as she can get. The name makes me envision a dark-haired, curvaceous, flirty woman dressed in bright colors, like Carmen Miranda, someone I remember one of my foster mothers watching on TV. But the dispatcher has a slight build with a boyish figure, big blue eyes, and a short blond pixie haircut.

"I don't think I've met you before," I say, extending a hand. "I'm Hildy Schneider. I'm a social worker over at the hospital. I'm working with Detective Richmond on a case."

Miranda takes my hand with a surprisingly firm grip and shakes it. "Miranda Knopf," she says, and her voice, like her grip, is surprisingly strong. I try not to wince, as even my hands hurt from this morning's workout. "I'm new here. Just took the weekend evening dispatcher's job. And I also volunteer with EMS, so you might see me at the hospital if you're ever in the ER."

"I'm there all the time." I'm sure I haven't seen this girl before, so I ask, "Are you new here in town?"

"I am. Moved here a month ago from Seattle."

"Seattle to Sorenson, Wisconsin?" I say with surprise. "How did that happen?"

"I met a guy," she says with a shrug. Then, letting me know she isn't inclined to provide any more details, she buzzes me through the door to the main lobby.

I take the hint, say, "Nice to meet you," and step through. As I walk toward the entrance, I reach into my pocket to get my keys and feel something odd in there, something wrapped in plastic. Several somethings, in fact. I pull them out and look at them: it's two packets of Chinese mustard and one packet of soy sauce.

As I settle into my car I toss the offending packets on the seat beside me and stare at them accusingly for a few seconds, as if hoping to convince myself that they are somehow at fault. But I know better. This is too many pilfers in too little time, and I know what it means.

I need an appointment with my shrink ASAP.

Chapter Twenty-Eight

I've been seeing some sort of counselor for most of my life. Thanks to my propensity for acting out in reckless and violent ways when I was younger, a psychiatrist was assigned to evaluate me for any mental health issues and to determine the need for medications. I didn't take to shrinks well, and during the first five years of being in the system I went through eight of them. Most of them made recommendations for transfer to a different psychiatrist based on a "failure to establish trust and bond professionally with the client." Later I learned that this was shrink-ese for "I don't like this kid, so dump her on someone else."

When I was twelve, and at my fifteenth foster home, I was sent to Dr. Desmond Hyde. Like most of his predecessors, he began our sessions with some tests designed to identify my personality type and, apparently, my psychological shortcomings. He was older than most of my previous counselors—I guessed in his fifties—and his name sounded stuffy. This impression was enhanced by the fact that he always dressed in suits with bowties and had a hint of a British accent. I pegged him from the get-go as a rich, spoiled type who would never be able to relate to a gutter rat like me.

I couldn't have been more wrong. Not that I made it easy

for him. I stubbornly refused to refer to him as Dr. Hyde and called him Mr. Jekyll instead, telling him he had his names ass-backward. He laughed at this, told me I was better read than most of his other child clients, and seemed unbothered by it. To be honest, I was flattered by his observation. It was true that I was well read. From the time I first learned how, my mother would ply me with books from the local library, most likely as a means of keeping me occupied and distracted in my room while she did things in her room. But I didn't mind. I loved books and the stories I read. They provided me with an escape, with adventures I might not otherwise have, and with characters whose lives I could step into and borrow for a time to replace my own.

Unlike the other counselors I had, Mr. Jekyll didn't try to force topics on me, or even address issues that might have recently occurred, such as the time I called my then–foster mother a fat-assed pig and oinked every time she entered a room. In my defense, I only started doing this after the woman sat in front of me several times eating luscious-looking desserts—cheesecakes, baklava, tiramisu, ice cream sundaes—and refused to let me have so much as a lick, bite, or crumb. Rather than addressing transgressions such as this one directly, Mr. Jekyll simply let me talk at my own pace and on my own topics. Our sessions always felt more conversational than therapeutic, and yet they were the most therapeutic ones I had with anyone. I never felt judged, I felt surprisingly understood, and I came to enjoy my time with Dr. Hyde.

I stayed with him for six years and would probably still be with him today if he hadn't upped and died on me. By then I was old enough to be on my own and couldn't imagine finding another counselor I liked as much as Mr. Jekyll. Convinced I no longer needed psychiatric help, I quit seeing anyone.

The stresses of college cured me of that way of thinking,

and when one of my roommates threatened to turn me in if I didn't quit stealing her food—acts I had no memory or awareness of—I decided it was time to find another counselor. Of course, now that I was no longer part of "the system," I had to pay for it myself. I did poorly enough in my life's circumstances and well enough in school to earn several scholarships that fully paid for my education, but I didn't have much in the way of spending money, so my counseling choices were limited to what I could get through the university. For the most part I saw psych grad students who were supposedly supervised by psychiatric advisors, none of whom I ever saw, talked to, or even met. The grad students treated me like a study project and/or a guinea pig, but they were at least sincere in their desire to help me, and they got me through six years of school.

Once I finished school and walked away with my brand-new shiny MSW degree, I entered the working world and prepared to become an adult member of regular society. I decided to go without counseling again and did okay for a few years. But over time, stressors like boyfriends who dumped me and jobs I got laid off from led to unrealized pocketing of lots of items, and it made me realize that a counselor was likely going to be a lifetime thing for me.

Finding a counselor you feel comfortable with, someone who understands you and fits your style, is a challenge. Sometimes it can take a few tries. It took me five this time, and except for the woman who told me she was working on a new version of scream therapy, I gave them all six sessions to make sure we had time to work out the kinks. But the kinks stayed until I moved to Sorenson and met Dr. Maggie Baldwin.

Maggie, as she insists on being called, reminds me a lot of Mr. Jekyll. She is an attractive woman who dresses nice, wears a lot of perfectly applied makeup, and looks both hoity-toity and professional. I'm not sure how old she is.

My best guess is mid-forties, and that's based mostly on events and topics she seems familiar with, but I could be off by a decade or more in either direction. My first impression of her was that we'd never click. And yet click we did.

Maggie has always treated me more like a colleague than a patient, in part because I've consulted with her on some of my cases. In fact, that was how I found her. Our professional relationship came before the one of doctor and patient. I've been seeing her for a little over two years now, and I continue to consult with her and refer patients to her. It would be easy to blur the lines, given our multifaceted relationship, and yet I always know where I stand with Maggie and what level we're on. She makes it easy.

Feeling a strong need to talk to Maggie, I give her a call from my car. When she doesn't answer, I leave a message stating that I'd love to be able to talk with her about a couple of things sometime this weekend if possible and let her know it's a personal need.

When I arrive home, I find P.J. in the kitchen with Roscoe. P.J. is sitting at my island counter drinking a bottle of water, her face flushed, the edges of her hair sweaty. Roscoe is lapping away madly at his water bowl, slurping puddles all over the floor.

"Looks like you two had a nice walk," I say.

"More of a run," P.J. says. "Roscoe looks a little pudgy to me lately, so I'm backing off on the treats and ramping up the exercise. Plus, I'm in track at school now, so I need the practice."

"Just be careful as the weather gets warmer. Golden retrievers are known for being so eager to please that they keep going and going until they drop. Plus, they overheat easily."

P.J. reaches down toward her feet and comes up with a backpack. "I have it covered," she says, zipping open the pack. She pulls out a collapsible plastic dish, four full bottles of water, and something that looks like a short, narrow condom that has a plastic spray head attached to one end of it.

"I have water for him to drink and I can squirt him down if it gets too hot," she explains. She then takes the condom-looking thing, rolls the open end of it over the water bottle she's drinking from, picks the bottle up, aims the spray head at me, and gives the bottle a squeeze.

I manage to back up in the nick of time, though a few drops hit my top. "Very funny," I say as she laughs. The sudden movement reminds me that my muscles are currently engaged in a major uprising, but P.J. interprets my wince as being from the water rather than pain.

"Hey, Roscoe likes it," she says with a shrug. "And it does the work of keeping him cooled down. Though I'm thinking I'll start running along the river path and letting him go in for a swim from time to time, if that's okay."

"That's fine. He loves to swim. Thanks for taking such good care of him, P.J.. What do I owe you for this week?"

"Just the usual twenty," she says.

I dig out my wallet, sort through the bills I have, and slide two tens across the counter to her. I consider it a heck of a deal. On occasion, I offer her extra money for helping me with odd jobs around the house, like raking leaves, shoveling snow, pulling weeds . . . that sort of thing.

"How was today's date?" P.J. asks me, stripping her spray top off her bottle and grabbing a paper towel to dry it and clean up the water mess. To my delight, she also goes about cleaning up the slurp puddles Roscoe has left on the floor. One of the reasons P.J. and I get on so well is that we both like things neat and orderly.

"It wasn't a date," I tell her. "I did a ride-along with Detective Richmond. We went around and talked to some people in a case he's investigating."

P.J. frowns at this, returning her squirt attachment, the

water bowl, and the extra water bottles to the backpack. "But weren't you with the same cop you went to dinner with last night?"

"Yes."

"But it wasn't a date?"

"Not really."

"But your dinner last night was a date?"

I shrug. "I suppose. Sort of."

"You're not very good at this dating stuff, are you?" she says with her usual bluntness.

"I'm a little rusty," I admit. "But I must be doing something right because I have a date tomorrow with someone else."

"Really? Do tell." P.J. waggles her eyebrows at me.

"He's an evidence technician for the police department. His name is Jonas Kriedeman."

"What kind of date will it be? Are you going somewhere to eat again like you did with the cop?"

"Yes, we'll be eating, but at his place. His daughter, Sofie, who I think is around seven, will be with us."

P.J. scoffs a laugh. "He's not looking for a romantic partner, he's looking for a babysitter."

"No, he isn't," I say. "And for your information, it was me who suggested that Sofie join us." This isn't exactly how it happened, but I don't want P.J. thinking I was outmaneuvered by a seven-year-old.

P.J. gapes at me. "Why?"

"She asked," I say with a shrug. "I thought it would be fun to let her."

"You thought it would be fun to have a seven-year-old kid along with you on a first date?" P.J. says, her voice rife with disappointment and skepticism. She shakes her head sadly. "Man, you do suck at this dating stuff."

"And you're some kind of expert?" I toss back. "How many dates have you been on?"

"None," she says matter-of-factly. "I may not have personal experience, but I read a lot and I remember everything I read. Those women's magazines my mother gets are full of advice for this kind of stuff. And I've read some of those romance novels she has, too. Maybe we should try to put together a plan for you."

I look at P.J., a smile on my face. This discussion would be ridiculous under most circumstances, but P.J. has a near photographic memory and is much older mentally than she is physically. She is also practical and, for the most part, unemotional. Despite her age and lack of experience, her suggestion is not without some merit.

"Thanks, but I'll manage," I tell her.

P.J. doesn't respond to this, but she cocks her head to one side and regards me with narrowed eyes for a moment. Then she hops off her stool and heads for the front door. "I'm going home. Should I come and walk Roscoe later?"

"Anytime," I tell her. "He always welcomes your visits, as do I."

She exits with no further response, shutting the door behind her.

Roscoe watches her leave, his head resting on his front paws, his huge, dark eyes staring at her with unmitigated adoration. As soon as the door closes, he sighs, lifts his head, and looks over his shoulder at me.

"I know," I tell him with a smile. "She's a sweetheart." He gets up and walks over to me, nudging my hand with his nose. I stroke his soft head, letting my palm settle between his shoulders. His touch is instantly relaxing and calming to me. Roscoe is a sweet-tempered, affectionate, and intuitive dog who always seems to sense what any human in his sphere of existence needs or wants. It makes him the perfect therapy dog. Though his size could be intimidating—he weighs just under ninety pounds—his dark eyes, soft fur, and sweet nature make him come across like a big, cuddly teddy bear. Then it dawns on me that there might be a therapy use for him with the police social worker job, as well.

"You might be my secret weapon," I tell him, and he thumps his tail eagerly, his tongue lolling out one side of his mouth. With this thought, I realize I should buff up my résumé and have it ready in case—*No, when,* I tell myself, trying to think positively—I get my interview with Chief Hanson.

I settle in with my laptop and get to work. It's a simple matter to update my résumé, since I did it just before getting my job at Mercy Hospital here in town. I add my current position to it, along with a list of the duties I think would be most relevant to the police job, and then I print it out on some thick vellum paper. After reading it over and trying to judge it, and myself, as objectively as possible, I decide it needs something more. When I talk to Chief Hanson, I want him to know that I've given this position a lot of thought, pondering exactly how social work services might be of benefit to both the police department and the community it serves.

I start a new document on my laptop, type SERVICES, centering it at the top of the page, and then start a bullet list. I include all of the typical social service duties, but cast them in terms related to police business and possible scenarios I might encounter. Included in my list is the potential for using Roscoe and canine therapy to comfort people in distressing situations, particularly children.

When I've accumulated a list of a little over twenty services, I sit back and start playing back episodes from the various Law & Order franchises in my head to try to think of other situations I might encounter and what I could potentially do with them. My concentration is broken when my phone rings. It is facedown on the table and my first impulse is to ignore it. But I realize it might be Bob or Dr. Baldwin calling, so I give in and pick it up to look.

It is Dr. Baldwin. "Hi, Maggie," I say. "Thanks for calling me back so quick."

"No problem," she says. "I would have called sooner but I was in session with someone. Do we need to get together?"

"That would be great, if you can manage it. I have some personal issues I need to talk about. It's not emergent, but there is a time constraint of sorts for part of it, so if we could talk sooner rather than later, that would be better for me."

"I've got plans for this evening," she says. "But I'm totally open tomorrow. Why don't we meet at my office around eleven in the morning? Will that work?"

"That's fine. Thank you. Should I pick up some croissants and coffee on the way?"

"Will the sun rise tomorrow?" she replies with a hint of laughter in her voice.

I brought lattes and croissants from a new coffee shop in town for my first visit with her, and somehow it became something of a ritual. I don't bring them every time, but often enough to make it a special treat and to provide me with a way of saying thank you to Maggie for her willingness to be so readily available to me whenever I need her. I know that her handling of me is outside of the norm for her profession, but my relationship with her has never been your typical psychiatrist and patient association.

"See you at eleven," I say, and then I disconnect the call.

When I try to get out of my chair to head for bed, I discover rigor mortis has set in. My back feels tighter than an overtuned guitar, and every time I try to move it seizes up even more. I realize I should have taken some ibuprofen when I first got home. It's in the medicine cabinet, some thirty feet away, and right now that might as well be thirty miles.

I try several stretches and movements, experimenting with combinations of leg, arm, and back muscles until I find the one that hurts the least. It still makes me grunt and groan in agony, causing Roscoe to eye me worriedly.

Eventually I manage to hobble my way to my bedroom, and from there into the bathroom, walking like I'm fifty years older than I am. The bottle of ibuprofen has a child-proof cap on it, and my hands hurt enough that it's a struggle to get the darned thing open. After several tries I finally manage to get it off, but also manage to drop the bottle. Little round pills fly out and scatter over the bathroom floor.

I curse to myself, make a half-hearted attempt to bend over and pick up the bottle, which has landed close to my foot, and quickly abandon the idea as my back muscles seize up. Roscoe, who is lying in the doorway, picks his head up and looks at the pills, then at me.

"No," I say. "Leave it." This command is one of the first ones I taught him, one of the requirements for a therapy dog who might be exposed to any number of dropped pills or food items in a hospital patient's room. He sighs, drops his head back onto his front legs, and watches me.

Plan B, I decide, and I scan the medicine cabinet shelves. I find a bottle of aspirin, manage to get it open without dropping it, and take two of them.

I'm not a very religious person, and none of my foster families were church-going people. But when I finally get settled in bed for the night, I say a prayer to whoever or whatever might be listening, hoping that I'll be able to walk come morning.

Chapter Twenty-Nine

I hate being late. I hate it so much that I often arrive for appointments ridiculously early. That's why I got out of bed at six this morning even though my appointment with Maggie isn't until eleven. Okay, truth be told, pain might have played a small role in my early rising, as my body made it crystal clear somewhere around five that it was still rebelling against all the things I did to it at the gym yesterday.

The aspirin I took last night helped some, but my back, thigh, and upper arm muscles are about as loose as an oak plank and feel like they've been beaten with one. I took a dose of acetaminophen first thing this morning, and when P.J. showed up at eight to walk Roscoe, I asked her if she would do me an extra favor for an extra buck and pick up the ibuprofen pills scattered all over the bathroom floor.

She did so without asking any questions and handed me the bottle with the pills and a small amount of dog hair inside it when she was done. I handed her a dollar in return, which she stuffed into a pocket. Then she leashed up Roscoe and took off. I downed four of the ibuprofen tablets and made myself a piece of toast to go with them. My body still feels achy and sore, but the medication is helping some, and the more I move, the better I feel. Getting dressed is a slight challenge—let's face it, it takes a contortionist to put on a bra on a good day—but I manage.

Fortunately, the coffee shop/bakery has a drive-through window, so it doesn't slow me down much. I arrive at Maggie Baldwin's office at ten minutes before eleven. Good thing, because getting out of my car and into the building takes twice as long as usual. I feel like I'm a hundred years old, but my aversion to tardiness is greater than my physical agony, so I push myself on.

If I'm ever late for anything it's because of circumstances beyond my control. I'll do everything humanly possible to mitigate these situations, but sometimes it can't be helped. When that happens, I know I'm likely to find myself straightening things an extra time or two, counting footsteps as I cross a room, or discovering odd food items stashed inside one of my pockets. Lateness is a trigger for me and my obsessive compulsions, and the step counting, organizing, and stealing are my coping mechanisms, my way of handling these situations and maintaining some level of control over my environment.

I was diagnosed with OCD—obsessive compulsive disorder—when I was nine. Over the years, my shrinks agreed that my case was milder than some and likely brought on by being thrust into the foster system. I was warned that it could worsen at any time, particularly in the event of certain stress triggers. I've worked hard as an adult to find ways to mitigate my symptoms that don't involve medications, as the ones they tried on me as a kid left me feeling stuporous and weird. I quit the meds as soon as I was old enough to do so, though truth be told I became adept at not taking them when I was a kid. I can cheek pills like a squirrel collecting acorns for winter. So far, I've managed my symptoms well on my own, and I hope to keep it that way. I've seen too many people drugged into a

near zombie state by modern medicine's attempts to help
people like me.

Maggie is never late, either, one of the traits I like best
about her, and she is waiting for me. She is dressed casually
today, or at least what passes as casual for her, as opposed
to her usual professional dress. Most days she wears
suits—skirt or pants—and sturdy but fashionable pumps
with just the right accessories in terms of jewelry, belts, and
such. But when we get together on an off day, she dresses
down, which for her is close to my version of dressing up.

Today she is wearing jeans, which sounds laid-back,
but hers are a shade of indigo that suggests they are
brand-spanking-new and might lend her thighs a blue
tint by the end of the day. There is a crease ironed down
the front of each pant leg. Her top is a long-sleeved, cream-
colored blouse that she wears neatly tucked in, and she has
a pale blue cardigan sweater tied loosely around her neck
by the sleeves . . . *Her superhero cape,* I think with a smile.
Her footwear is a pair of sensible navy blue slip-ons.
Contrary to her workaday wear, today she has no accessories: no belt, no jewelry, no hair adornments. Her hair,
makeup, and nails are all done to perfection, however, and
I've never seen them otherwise. Maggie Baldwin is a
single, successful professional with no children and plenty
of time and money to indulge herself. It shows.

I can't help but feel a bit dowdy beside her. I'm also
wearing jeans and a blouse, but my jeans are well-worn and
partially hemmed with duct tape, and my blouse, while
clean and relatively new, is untucked, the shirt tails hanging
down to help hide my tummy and butt. My feet may be en-
cased in a ragged old pair of running shoes I've owned for
at least ten years, but my socks are brand-spanking-new.

While I, too, am single and have no children, I don't
have the sort of money I imagine Maggie does. Still, I'm
well enough off, thanks to frugal spending habits and a

solid savings plan. I have a decent amount of disposable income, but I find it hard to spend it on things like clothes. Maggie has a long, lean build that I'm sure makes dressing up a fun and rewarding experience. I, on the other hand, have a pear-shaped body, and a stunted pear at that. I used to have to buy most of my clothes in the kids' aisles because of my height, but these days I'm forced to hit up the women's section to accommodate my more mature stature. Almost nothing I buy off the rack fits properly, and rather than spending a lot on trendy, fashionable new clothes, my money goes to paying for alterations. Tamela does a great job of this for me, and for a reasonable price, but the end results will never be mistaken for haute couture. Plus, because of the work I need to do to make my clothes fit, I tend to hang on to them longer than I probably should. I still have stuff I wore in college hanging in my closet.

Maggie eyes the white paper bag I'm holding, its sides turning almost transparent due to the fat content of the croissants inside. She licks her lips and I proffer the cardboard cup holder first, letting her take her latte. Then I set the drink tray down and hand Maggie the bag. She digs in with a childlike delight that makes me smile.

"I only get these when you bring them to me," she says, removing one of the pastries from the bag and eyeing it greedily.

The croissants have either chocolate or cream cheese filling, and they are dusted with powdered sugar. I see Maggie has chosen a chocolate one and watch as she takes a bite, closes her eyes, and spends a moment relishing the flavor. I watch her with some amusement as I take a seat and pull my own coffee from the cup holder. There is a tiny chocolate-rimmed flake of croissant stuck to her lower lip and a faint dusting of powdered sugar spattered over her blouse. After a few seconds, Maggie opens her eyes, smiles happily, and hands me the bag.

"Thank you," she says, settling into the chair across from mine. She licks her lip, snagging the tiny croissant crumb, and then brushes the front of her blouse with her hand.

"My pleasure," I say, reaching into the bag and pulling out a cream-cheese-filled treat.

For the next couple of minutes, the two of us sit comfortably inside a cloud of gustatory silence, the only sounds the ticking of the clock on Maggie's wall and the chewing and slurping noises the two of us make as we indulge in our morning treats.

When I see Maggie lick her fingers, I know we are about to get down to business.

"What brings you in today?" she asks.

"Several things. For one, I have someone in my grief support group who has issued something of a challenge, one that I find myself liking and wanting to meet."

Maggie looks intrigued. "What sort of challenge?"

"She lost her son two weeks ago from a heroin overdose that may have been accidental or a suicide. But she came to our group insisting that the kid wasn't a drug user and that something about his death didn't ring true. She thinks someone might have killed him, and she begged us to help her investigate."

"Ah," Maggie says, a knowing look on her face. "A possible homicide investigation. That's hitting you where you live, isn't it?"

"It is," I admit, "but I do think there's something to it. I'm not jumping on it just because of, well, you know why." She nods. "It turns out there are some irregularities in the kid's death, and even though the case was closed with accidental death listed as the cause, the homicide detective in charge of the case has now decided to reopen it based on some things I pointed out to him."

"You've always been a keen observer," Maggie says.

I smile, basking in her praise for a moment before I say,

"Well, to be honest, I had some help. Mattie Winston worked the case at the ME's office, and she told me she felt there was something off about it. I think I just figured out what some of that offness might be. And it was enough that Detective Bob Richmond decided to reopen the case."

Maggie tilts her head to one side, eyeing me narrowly. "And you handed your information over to him?" she says in a tone that suggests she doesn't believe this for a minute.

"No," I say with a sheepish smile. "I kind of black-mailed him into letting me help. He's allowing me to ride along with him while he looks into things."

"Ride along?" Maggie says, looking a little concerned. "What exactly does that mean?"

"It means I have to sign a form that says the police can't be held responsible for my maiming, crippling, or death from any cause ranging from a routine car accident to a zombie apocalypse. In exchange for agreeing to that, I get to ride with Detective Richmond and watch what he does. He's even letting me participate in the investigatory process."

"You've done this already?"

"I have, for one day. Yesterday, in fact."

"How did it go?"

"I think it went very well. I really enjoyed Detective Richmond and the work we did together. And we made some progress into the investigation of this kid's death."

Maggie nods, leans forward, picks up the grease-stained croissant bag, and peers inside it. "You said you black-mailed this policeman into letting you participate?"

"Detective," I correct her. "And yes. The kid's mother let me take his laptop to see if I could find a way to get into it. And I did. It had a fingerprint scanner on it, and I was able to collect a usable print from the kid's bedroom and use it to gain access. Once I got in, I changed the password on the computer and disabled the fingerprint scanner. When Detective Richmond was debating reopening the case, he wanted me to hand over the laptop. I refused, and he threatened to simply seize it. That's when I told him about the password and said that if he wanted it, he was going to have to let me in on the investigation."

"Clever girl," Maggie says. She has removed another croissant from the bag and she utters these words around a mouthful of pastry. She swallows, licks her lips, and then adds, "Though I'm fairly certain the cops have ways to get around things like passwords."

"Yeah," I say with a sigh and a smile. "It turns out the detective had an ulterior motive. He basically allowed me to blackmail him, or rather let me think I was doing so."

"How very convoluted," Maggie says, amused.

"I know. And there's more to it. A lot more."

"Of course, there is," Maggie says arching a brow. She consumes the last of her second croissant, leans back with latte in hand, and makes herself comfortable for the long story ahead. "Go ahead. Tell me everything."

I bow my head slightly and give her a guilty smile. "For one thing, I kind of like this detective," I tell her. "I like him a lot, as in I see him as potential dating material. In fact, we had dinner the night before the ride-along, and then he invited me to come with him to his gym yesterday morning."

Maggie's eyebrows shoot up at this. "You were with him the next morning?" she asks.

"Oh, not that way," I say, realizing what she's thinking. "I didn't sleep with him or spend the night with him. I just met him at the gym early the next morning. *Very* early." I roll my eyes at the memory.

"For exercise?" Maggie asks in a disbelieving tone.

"Yes." I try not to sound too insulted. "Why is that so hard to believe?"

Maggie stalls her answer by taking a sip of her latte. I can tell she's weighing her next words to me.

"Exercise is a very big part of his life," I tell her before she can jump to too many wrong conclusions. "He's lost a lot of weight over the past few years, like two hundred pounds or more. And he said he really wanted to have an exercise partner. Granted, that's not something that's been high on my to-do list, but it certainly could be, and it wouldn't hurt me to get into better shape and shed a few pounds. I agreed to try it for two weeks."

"Okay," Maggie says slowly, drawing the word out and sounding a little skeptical. She takes another drink of her coffee.

I lurch onward, eager to get everything out, wanting to purge myself. "And get this," I say. "Detective Richmond told me the Sorenson police chief applied for a grant that will allow them to have a social worker ride around with the cops. That means going with them on calls and responding to situations where counseling or referral services might be helpful. And it got approved. They're getting ready to start interviews."

"Ah," Maggie says, her eyes bright and knowing. "Now we're getting to the meat in this sandwich. I take it you're interested in applying for this position?"

"Heck, yeah. I think I'd be good at it. I really enjoyed what we did yesterday. We not only got to interview people about the case—Detective Richmond took me to the police lab and let me watch and participate in the analysis of some evidence. And we visited a jail and talked to a prisoner there." I realize the excited tone in my voice isn't the best match for the subject matter. "It was productive, interesting, and educational," I add, trying to put a more professional spin on it.

"Yes, I can see how the day fed into your need to investigate things. But I'm not sure that's what this job is about. It sounds like it's going to be more frontline stuff."

"I know," I admit. "But I'm sure there will be some of that involved. Simply being at the scene of a crime will require some basic investigatory processes, right? I mean, if I'm talking to, or counseling, people at a crime site, isn't that tantamount to interviewing a witness or even a potential suspect?"

"I suppose it could be," Maggie says. "Are you thinking this job might somehow help you with your investigation into your mother's death?"

"No."

Maggie narrows her eyes at me.

"Okay, maybe a little," I admit. "But it would be a secondary motivation, maybe even tertiary, not the primary reason why I'm interested in the work." I pause, hesitant to tell her the next part. Maggie knows me well enough to sense this, and she sips her drink, waiting. "I met the evidence tech who works at the police station. He asked me out. I'm seeing him later today."

Maggie's eyebrows arch. "You're dating two men? Two men who know each other? How interesting."

"I know, it's a potential quagmire, but I like them both. And I'm due. It's a chance to make up for the utter lack of a social life I've had for the past few years. I swear I'm starting to see the word *spinster* in little thought bubbles floating above the heads of people who talk to me. And then there's my biological clock. It's moving forward faster than the national debt clock. Not that I expect to have kids of my own, though I suppose that's still possible. I'd be happy either way. And Jonas, he's the evidence technician, has a daughter who's seven-ish and adorable." I realize I'm babbling and sound a lot like Laura, the lab tech.

"You met Jonas's daughter already?" Maggie says when I pause for breath.

"He brought her with him to the lab," I explain. "She's joining us for an early dinner tonight."

Maggie frowns at this. She sits forward, setting her cup on the table between us. "That worries me a little," she says. "Having this man involve you with his child this soon and to this degree seems fraught with potential problems."

I sigh. "I know, but technically it wasn't Jonas who made that happen. The kid, Sofie, did. She's one of those precocious types, you know the kind, the ones who are much older than their physical age? She basically invited herself along."

"And her father didn't put a stop to it?"

"He didn't have a chance. I'd already agreed to it."

"I see," Maggie says. She smiles at me, shifts in her seat, and says, "Let's go back to this job situation. Would it mean quitting your current job at the hospital?"

"Not necessarily. It will involve night and weekend shifts in the beginning. I could do that and still work at the hospital. I'd just have to sleep in the evenings."

"That seems like a lot," Maggie says, though there is no real judgment in her voice. Just a statement of fact. "Do you think you're up for it?"

"I do." I don't hesitate with this answer, and I'm pleased with the level of conviction I hear in my voice. Then Maggie shatters my confidence with one simple question.

"Then why are you here today?"

One hand moves toward my jeans pocket in an automatic, subconscious gesture that I only realize I've made when I find myself fingering the stitched trim of the outer edge.

"It doesn't sound like you're seeking my approval," Maggie goes on. "From what you're telling me, I gather that you've made your decision already. And yet you're here. Why?" She waits for me to answer, letting the silence build between us.

I frown at her. "I've found things in my pockets over the past two days. Several times."

"So, more than usual." I nod. Maggie is familiar with my history and my tendencies. "Why do you think that is?" she asks. One of the reasons I like Maggie is because she often lets me help myself. She doesn't condescend, or dictate, or diagnose, and she knows I have a good base of knowledge and a decent sense of self-awareness when it comes to the psychological issues I have. Together we puzzle things out in a systematic, skilled way that helps me keep my ego intact and lets me exercise my work muscles.

"Stress?" I say with a shrug. "That's what usually triggers it."

"And you have ways of coping with that, things you've used successfully in the past. Have you tried any of those?"

"Not yet."

"Why not? Why did you come straight to me first?" She's forcing me to self-analyze my behavior and actions, to understand the reasons behind them.

"For one, I haven't had the time. Everything happened so fast." I pause, suck in a breath, and let it out in a sigh. "And for another, I can't tell if this is good stress or bad stress. Is my subconscious trying to steer me away from all this new stuff, warning me that I'm biting off more than I can chew? Or am I simply excited at the prospect of so many opportunities on both a professional and a personal front?"

"Those are excellent questions," Maggie says. "And I don't have any definitive answers for you. I can't tell you what to do, but I can help you sort through your feelings and make an informed decision . . . several informed decisions, from the sound of things. But ultimately the decisions have to come from you."

"I know," I say with another sigh. "I think the dating thing is an easy decision. I mean, how often does a woman like me have two men interested in her at the same time?" Even as I say this, I realize I might be jumping to conclusions. I'm interested in Bob as a dating companion, but his motivation for going to dinner with me is mixed up in this case we're investigating. How much of his interest is in me as a person versus in my knowledge and possession of the relevant bits of Toby's life? Still, nothing ventured and all that.

"I'd be nervous about dating anyone, much less two guys at the same time," I tell Maggie. "But I want to stay on this ride for as long as I can. I realize it might lead to some stressful situations, but I think I'm mature enough to handle them."

"I think you are, too," Maggie says. "But are the men involved mature enough?"

I chuckle at that. "I guess we're going to find out," I say.

"Do they know about each other?"

I think about this for a moment and realize they don't. "Bob knows about Jonas asking me out because he was there when it happened. But I don't think Jonas knows that I went out to dinner with Bob. And to be honest, I'm not totally sure that dinner qualified as a date anyway. Things are a little gray there."

"You should be up front with Jonas," Maggie says. "Particularly since he has a child. I'm all for letting adults do what they want and stumble about and get hurt in the process. But when kids are involved it gets more sensitive."

"I know," I say, sharing her concern. "I realize I need to handle the situation with kid gloves, pun intended." Maggie smiles. "Though I confess, I'm no expert at this. In fact, I seriously considered giving up on dating when I moved here to Sorenson. My past experiences haven't gone very well."

This is an understatement of astounding proportions. My last three attempts at dating or developing a relationship with someone were utter disasters. The most recent one involved a fellow named Greg I met in Milwaukee through a coworker. Greg was a nice-looking guy who had his own handyman business. Our first date was a blind one that included the coworker who fixed us up and her husband. Greg and I hit it off well over dinner and he asked for my number. He called a few nights later and asked me to his place for dinner. I was a little wary of this but figured he couldn't be a serial killer since my friend had professed to know him for years. This is the kind of logic you see on an episode of *Dateline* or *Snapped* that makes you yell at the screen, amazed that anyone could be so stupid, but I'm only human.

Greg offered to pick me up, but I insisted on driving so I'd have my own wheels, my own means of escape. He gave me an address, and I arrived, of course, several minutes early. I staked out the neighborhood, which was a nice one filled with single-family homes. I arrived at his door exactly on time, and it was answered by a woman in her fifties or sixties wearing an apron. I thought I had the wrong house, but when I mentioned Greg's name she said, "You're at the right place. Come on in." My initial impression was that the woman was some sort of housekeeper and cook for Greg, and while I was mildly disappointed at the thought that Greg wouldn't be the one cooking, I was fine with the idea. Unfortunately, the woman turned out to be Greg's mother, and when she proceeded to tuck his napkin in around his shirt collar for him once he was seated at the table, I knew this would be our first and last date.

The guy before that seemed personable enough. I met Jeff in line at a coffee shop I visited every morning on my way to work, and we struck up a conversation. Two weeks' worth of morning encounters and he asked me out. We went to the movies twice and had dinner out several times, all of them enjoyable. Things were going along swimmingly, and I was prepared to take the next step when he invited me to his apartment after dinner on our fifth date. That's when I discovered he was one box shy of being a hoarder. His apartment was the filthiest and most cluttered living space I've ever seen, and when I saw a cockroach skittle across the kitchen counter, I feigned an illness, called a cab, and left.

The guy before that, Nick, was super nice. He was, and still is, a social worker like me, so we hit it off very well and became fast friends. Unfortunately, that's all we ever became. We enjoy each other's company and are able to converse easily, but there is no spark between us at all. He's still a friend, and while I don't see him much anymore since he lives in Milwaukee, we still chat via texts and emails on occasion, even sharing some of our dating horror stories.

"What is your gut telling you?" Maggie asks me, interrupting my embarrassing trip down memory lane.

"With regard to the dating thing, it's a little on edge," I admit. "And I suppose I should have found out more about Jonas before agreeing to have dinner with him. Like where the kid's mother is. I don't need another date like that guy Tom Henry, the one who kept talking to his dead wife all night long."

And one more reason not to like people who seem to have two first names instead of an obvious last name, I think.

"But as far as the job thing goes, I feel good about it," I go on. "I want to do it. In fact, I'm so hopped up about it that I'm starting to worry about how I'll deal with it if I don't get it."

"Would it help if I offered myself up as a reference?" Maggie says. I think I must be looking horrified at the suggestion, because she quickly clarifies. "As a colleague only, of course, not as your therapist. You and I have discussed cases together enough times that I feel comfortable recommending you."

"And given what you know about me as my therapist, you don't have any reservations?"

Maggie takes a few seconds to give the question serious

consideration. "I do not," she says with a smile. "In fact, I think your background gives you an edge."

"Thank you," I say, feeling both excited and a little emotional. "I accept your offer."

"As for your recent pocketing of the food items, I'm not overly concerned," she says. "I think the stress of all you have going on, both in your personal and your professional life, explains it. And to answer your earlier question, I think this stress, all of it, is good stress, at least for the moment. I do worry that you'll spread yourself a little too thin trying to work two jobs, though. So my only caution with the professional stuff is to get plenty of rest and stay healthy. As for the personal stuff, more power to you, Hildy. Aside from the precautions I mentioned regarding the involvement of a child, I think you have enough sense to sort things out. And though I know you can hear your biological clock ticking, don't rush into things. Enjoy this dating scenario for as long as you can."

Why not? I think. What could possibly go wrong?

Chapter Thirty

After leaving Maggie's office I head home, checking my phone to make sure I haven't missed a call from Bob. It saddens me that I likely won't be able to go with him when he gets his warrant for the Sheffield place, but I'm excited enough about the potential job and my pending date with Jonas that it doesn't get me down too much.

I give my résumé one last buff, adding Maggie as a reference, and print it out again so that I have it ready to go. I slip it into my briefcase and then get an idea. I get on my computer and do a little searching. It doesn't take me long to find what I want, and after debating what I'm about to do for a few minutes, I decide to go bold or go home. I spend an hour crafting a short, concise, and hopefully intriguing cover letter, and then I email it with my résumé attached to Chief Hanson. I wonder if Bob will be upset with me for taking this step without telling him, but figure he'll get over it.

With that done, I leash Roscoe up and take him for a short walk. My muscles are still sore, but I'm pleased to note that the stiffness is less than it was. With each step I take, things get a little better, and by the time we return to the house, my muscles are feeling almost normal.

Worried that things might stiffen up again if I don't

keep moving, I go off on a cleaning frenzy in the house, starting with the kitchen and bathrooms.

P.J. comes by as I'm finishing up my dusting chores in the living room, but she doesn't go for Roscoe right away. Instead, she plops down on the couch and watches me for a few minutes. I ignore her, letting her sit for a while, figuring she'll talk when she's ready, but my curiosity is apparently less patient than her reluctance to speak up.

"What's on your mind, P.J.?" I ask, giving the coffee table in front of her one last swipe.

She is picking at a cuticle and looks up at me briefly with a fleeting smile before focusing on her finger again. "I was wondering how you can tell when a boy likes you," she says. Her cheeks flush red with the words, and she continues to maintain a laser focus on her finger.

"Well, it depends," I say, settling into a chair off to one side of the couch. "The signs tend to change with age. When you get to be my age, the men generally just tell you they're interested by asking you out on a date."

"What about boys my age?" she asks, still not looking at me.

"Why do you ask? Is there a particular boy you're curious about?"

She looks away toward the kitchen. "Maybe. Sometimes he acts like he likes me, but sometimes he acts like he doesn't."

"Boys that age are too young to really know what they want," I say, and this earns me a pout. "They often don't know how to handle what they're attracted to. When they like a girl, they sometimes show it by teasing her, or picking on her, or even being mean to her, all bad behaviors that shouldn't be tolerated. They don't really know how to approach girls but they don't want to be teased by their friends, so they may pretend not to like a specific girl when they actually like her more than the others."

P.J. considers this, shrugs, and then hops up from the couch, walks over to the coat tree, and grabs Roscoe's leash. Seconds later, the two of them are gone.

I spend half an hour trying to decide what to wear to dinner at Jonas's. I finally settle on an old standby: black slacks with a straight-hemmed blouse I can wear untucked. The blouse has vertical stripes in blue, white and beige, which, according to the advice I've read in fashion and women's magazines, will help to make me look taller. Jonas isn't very tall himself, so in that regard I feel we share a kinship of sorts. Being short can be difficult for either sex, but I think men feel more self-conscious about it than we women do.

P.J. returns and eyes my outfit but makes no comment on it. "How late will you be?" she asks.

I shrug. "Not very, I wouldn't think. It's a school night for Jonas's daughter."

She considers this, looks like she's about to ask a question, but then simply hangs up the leash and says, "Have fun. I'll walk Roscoe again later." With that, she's gone.

At three thirty I drive to the address Jonas gave me. I arrive fifteen minutes early and scope out the neighborhood. It's a typical one for Sorenson, located in an older section of town and comprised of an eclectic mix of home styles. Jonas's house is a standard Colonial saltbox, kind of square and plain on the outside. He has offset this ordinariness with a spectacular landscape in the front yard. There is a stone walkway leading to the front stoop, and several mulched flower beds filled with blooms in a multitude of colors line the front of the house and the walkway. Matching ornamental Japanese maple trees sit on either side of the front stoop, and the lawn is green, lush, and hasn't a weed anywhere in sight. Clearly Jonas has a green thumb. Either that, or he hires someone to tend to his lawn. I'm curious to see what the backyard looks like.

I climb the three steps to the front door and ring the bell. Sofie answers a moment later.

"Hi, Hildy," she says with a big smile, holding the door. "Oops, is it okay if I call you Hildy? Dad said I had to ask you if it is okay."

"Yes, that's fine," I say. "Is it okay if I call you Sofie?"

Her brow wrinkles with surprise and her smile goes quirky for a second. "Yes, it is," she says with great solemnity, though she can't keep the pleasure from her face.

"Hildy, please come in." Jonas has appeared behind his daughter, and he opens the door wide and waves an arm toward the inside.

I enter an immaculate foyer with a wooden stairway to the left and a coat tree to the right. I'm not wearing a coat of any sort as the temperature today is hanging comfortably in the high sixties and low seventies. There is a small table along the wall beside the stairs, and at the far end of the hallway I can see part of a kitchen. To my right is a living room furnished with a matching sofa and chairs in a rich plum color. The walls are painted a pale yellow, and the throw pillows on the couch capture both the wall color and the plum.

Everything is neat as a pin, and the wood floors look polished and shiny. So far, so good.

"I'm in the middle of cooking," Jonas says as he closes the front door. "Do you mind sitting in the kitchen for now?"

"Not at all. Can I help?"

"I don't need it, but thanks." He leads the way into the kitchen, which is small but well organized. There is a bistro-style table with two stools positioned in the middle of the room, and Jonas directs me to take one of the seats. I hang my purse on the back of the stool and settle in as Sofie climbs up onto the other one.

"What would you like to drink?" Jonas asks me. "I have

white wine, red wine, a few microbrew beers, generic cola and un-cola, and a big pitcher of cherry Kool-Aid."

Sofie is staring at me from across the table, her little face screwed up in what looks like a very serious assessment. I look at her, smile, and say, "Ooh, cherry Kool-Aid sounds wonderful." Once again, her brow wrinkles in surprise, and her expression softens into a smile. "Will you drink some with me?" I ask her.

She nods once and says, "Cherry Kool-Aid sounds wonderful."

Jonas shakes his head and smiles, and then takes down two glasses from a cupboard. He sets them on the table in front of us and then removes a plastic pitcher from the fridge. Once he has filled both glasses, he returns the pitcher to the fridge and removes a bottle of beer. "The chef is going to indulge a little," he says.

I eye a frying pan on the stove filled with some sort of ground meat. The scents of onion, garlic, and oregano fill the air. "What are you cooking?" I ask. "It smells delicious."

"It's his cheater's lasagna," Sofie informs me. "It's really good."

I arch a brow at Jonas, who shrugs and nods. "She's right. That's what it's called, and it is really good."

"What part of it is cheating?" I ask, amused.

"It's made with layers of sausage, cheese ravioli, and spinach," he says. "It comes out like lasagna, but it's a lot easier to make."

Over the next ten minutes I watch as Jonas layers the bottom of a glass cake pan with thawed but uncooked ravioli, adds a layer of cooked ground sausage on top of it, pours some spaghetti sauce from a jar over the top, and then sprinkles it liberally with grated mozzarella. He then does a second layer, this time substituting a box of thawed frozen spinach for the sausage. He tops the whole thing off with a final layer of the ravioli, floods it with more spaghetti sauce, and adds more mozzarella. After topping the pan with some foil, he puts the whole thing into the oven.

The entire time he is doing this, Sofie is regaling us with a tale about her day in school last week when the teacher had to make Joey Barber stand in the corner for ten minutes. "Miss Wigand calls it the think-about-it corner," Sofie explains. "If we do something we aren't s'posed to, we have to go stand there and think about it."

"Sounds like a good idea," I say, liking the teacher's logic.

"I think it's stupid," Sofie announces. "And Joey's mother was really mad when she heard about it."

"Mad at who?" Jonas asks, beating me to the question by a nanosecond.

"Mad at Miss Wigand. She came to the room and talked to all of us about it, and then told Miss Wigand she thought the corner was almost as bad as coral punish."

Both Jonas and I give Sofie a quizzical look, and a few seconds later I suss out what I think Sofie heard. "You mean corporal punishment," I say, and I see Jonas give me an approving nod.

Sofie shrugs. "Whatever," she says with great impatience and a roll of her eyes. It's an amusing imitation of a clichéd valley girl, and I wonder what show or movie she stole it from.

"Do you know what corporal punishment is?" I ask Sofie.

Her brow furrows, and I can almost see the wheels turning inside that little head of hers. I can tell she doesn't want to admit to not knowing but I sense she's also curious.

I save her from making a choice by offering up the definition. "Corporal punishment is physical punishment, like spanking."

Sofie makes a face of disbelief. "The corner is nothing like that," she says.

"Good thing," I say. "Have you ever had to stand in the think-about-it corner?"

Sofie looks surprised, then wary of this question. Jonas, who at this point is chopping up lettuce for a salad, pauses and turns to look at his daughter. Sofie, clearly on the spot, blushes and fidgets.

I start to think it might not have been a good idea to ask her something this sensitive this early in our relationship, so I try to ease the tension. "I had to stand in a lot of corners. And in school, I got sent to the principal's office quite often."

"Why?" Sofie asks, and her father asks the same thing by casting a questioning look my way.

"Lots of reasons," I say. "Sometimes it was because I talked too much or said stuff I shouldn't. Sometimes it was because I hit someone."

"You hit people in school?" Sofie says, wide-eyed.

"Only if they hit me first," I explain.

"You mean like cor-prill punishment?" Sofie says, pronouncing the word with great care.

I smile at her. "Something like that. One time a boy who sat behind me was jabbing a pencil into my back. I kept whispering at him to stop, but he didn't. So finally, I just turned around and smacked his hand, knocking the pencil out of it."

"Why was he doing that to you?" Sofie asks.

"I think it was because he asked me if I would let him copy my answers on a test the day before by leaning to the side so he could see my paper. I told him no and then I kept my paper covered the whole time. I got an A and he got an F. It made him mad."

"Boys are stupid," Sofie says.

"Sometimes, yes," I say with a smile and a glance toward Jonas.

"Dinner in twenty," he says, suddenly focusing on his

task again. "Sofie, can you set the table while I get the salad ready?"

There is a dining room off the kitchen to the left, a long narrow room that has a small wooden table with four chairs around it. I offer to help with the table setting, and soon Sofie has shown me where the dishes and silverware are kept. I take care of the place settings while Sofie retrieves paper napkins from a cupboard in the kitchen.

"No, no, Sofie," Jonas says from the sink when he sees the napkins. "We do the cloth napkins when we have company, remember?"

Sofie shoots a glance at me to see if I've overheard. When she sees that I have, she looks wounded.

"You know what?" I say. "If it's okay with you, I prefer paper napkins. The cloth ones sometimes make me get a rash on my face, some sort of allergy I think." This isn't true, but the crushed look on Sofie's face prompts me to tell the little white lie.

She looks over at her father, awaiting his verdict.

Jonas acquiesces with a smile. "Okay, that's fine. Paper it is."

Sofie's face beams and she proudly and carefully folds the napkins, placing each one beside the plates just so.

I hear my phone ding with a text message notification while this is going on, and at one point when Jonas and Sofie are conferring about something in the dining room, I slide it out of my purse and sneak a peek. My first thought was that it might be P.J. texting me about Roscoe, but my heart skips a beat when I see the message is from Bob Richmond.

"Meet me at the gym tomorrow morning at five?" it says.

I roll my eyes and sigh. Did he forget about the date I arranged with Jonas or is he purposely messaging me at a time when he knows I'll be in the middle of it? I text back a quick "Yes" and pocket the phone.

By the time we have the table set, Jonas is done with the salad and places it on the table along with two bottles of salad dressing, one ranch and one Italian. I guess that the two kinds are because Jonas likes one and Sofie another, and I try to guess who likes what. After a moment of contemplation, I finger Sofie for the ranch dressing, and I'm happy to see I'm right once we are settled in at the table.

Our meal passes by pleasantly enough, with Sofie talking more about school and some of her friends, and me talking about some of my childhood moments. When I mention that I grew up in the foster system and briefly summarize my experience there in somewhat banal terms, Sofie is clearly intrigued.

"How come you didn't have a dad?" she asks.

I consider my answer carefully, and finally decide on one that isn't the whole truth but that I hope is safe enough. "He went away before I was born and never came back."

"My mom did that," Sofie offers. She says it nonchalantly and with no emotion, as if explaining that the color of salt is white. She stabs a piece of ravioli and stuffs it in her mouth. I look at Jonas, who gives me a subtle nod and a *go figure* look.

"You had pretend moms and dads?" Sofie says after she swallows.

"I guess you could call them that. Though the proper titles are foster mom and foster dad."

Sofie looks over at her father. "Maybe we could get a pretend mom," she says. Then she shoots me a conciliatory look. "I mean a foster mom," she corrects. "That way you'd have someone to help with the laundry and cooking and maybe clean the house once in a while."

The way Sofie says this last part makes me certain she's

mimicking something her father has said in the past. I look at Jonas, see him blush from chin to forehead, and smile. "I think those people are called housekeepers," I say to Sofie. "Or slaves," I add with a sly look toward Jonas.

"That's not what . . . I mean, it's not how I think about . . . I just grumble sometimes." Jonas says, looking utterly humiliated.

"He grumbles a lot," Sofie says to me in a loud aside, her eyes wide.

I can't help but laugh. I love the relationship these two have and find that I'm quite enjoying their company. But Maggie's warnings sober me up. I need to be careful before getting too close or attached to the child. If things between her father and me go wrong in a bad way, it could be hurtful to the kid, and I wouldn't want that. Jonas and I might not end up as romantic partners, but judging from what I've seen of him and his daughter so far, I would hope we could be friends. In the meantime, best to tread carefully.

I make sure to keep the conversation light and friendly through the rest of supper and dessert, which turns out to be a Sara Lee cheesecake that hasn't fully defrosted yet. Still, I give credit to Jonas for making the effort on such short notice. I'm sure he had a dinner out somewhere in mind before his daughter took control and forced him to cook, and first dates are stressful enough.

After dessert, I help clear the table and load the dishwasher. It's a comfortably domestic scene that makes me uncomfortable for some reason. Once the cleanup is done, I thank Jonas and Sofie for everything and tell them I need to get home because I have a very early morning the next day, and I need to let my dog out. Yet another white lie with regard to the dog, but I suddenly feel an overwhelming need to escape this tableau of domesticity and grasp at any halfway plausible excuse I can think of.

"You have a dog?" Sofie says, clearly intrigued.

· "I do. His name is Roscoe. He's very smart and very sweet. Maybe you can meet him one of these days."

Looking pleased with this tentative plan, Sofie dashes off into the living room, where she grabs a remote control and turns on the TV.

I make my way to the door with Jonas on my heels.

"I have enjoyed this very much," I tell him when I reach the door.

"You don't have to leave yet," he says. Judging from the disappointed look on his face, my departure is not what he was expecting. "We could watch a movie or something."

"Another time, perhaps. I really do have an early day tomorrow. Your daughter is a charmer and I'd love to get to know her better at some point. I'd like to get to know you better, too. Let's you and I do something else soon, okay? Just the two of us?"

Jonas looks mildly relieved. "Yes," he says. "Sorry about . . . this." He nods toward the living room and his daughter.

"Don't be. I truly enjoyed both of you. But I do think it best to keep things low-key with Sofie until we know how things will or won't work out between us, don't you think?"

He runs a hand through his hair and smiles. "It *is* complicated when you're a single parent."

"I'm sure it is. But you seem to be doing a great job. Thanks for letting me be a part of your family tonight. I had a great time."

"I'm glad."

I take in a deep breath and brace myself for what I have to say next. "There is something I need to tell you. I've been on a dinner date with someone else recently, and it's someone I'll be seeing again."

Jonas looks crestfallen. "Who?"

"Bob Richmond."

Jonas looks askance. "Really? Isn't he kind of . . . old?"

"Perhaps. We'll see."

"I'll call you," Jonas blurts out with sudden determination. Then he backpedals and says, "If that's okay."

"It is. I look forward to it." With that I lean forward, kiss him on his cheek, and leave.

I reflect on the date during my drive home, and overall I'm feeling pretty good about things. Still, I try not to get too excited about it all. Life has taught me that the pendulum inevitably swings the other way. For now, I just want to bide my time and enjoy my chance to play the field, as they say.

Chapter Thirty-One

Five in the morning is an ungodly hour to be up, much less trying to exercise. As I stumble my way into the gym on Monday morning feeling like I'm sleepwalking, I consider asking Bob if he'll change his workout time.

He is there when I arrive, looking bright-eyed and eager. It's almost enough to make me hate him. I'm not much of a morning person. I don't mind getting out of bed early, but I need some time to sip my coffee and shake off the cobwebs in my head before I'm ready to face the day. I'm still nursing my coffee when I arrive at the gym.

"Are you ready to go?" Bob asks, greeting me just inside the door.

"I don't know. I'm barely awake."

"The warm-up routines will help with that," he says. "Where's your program?"

I fish a crumpled piece of paper out of my pocket, my copy of the routine that Sherri figured out for me on Saturday morning. I hand it to Bob and take another sip of coffee. He looks at me with a frown.

"What?" I say. "Do I have boogers hanging out of my nose?"

"The coffee," Bob says. "I've found it's better to wait until after you work out to drink it."

I stare at him for a moment, stunned into silence. "How can you expect me to do any exercises without coffee? Hell, how do you expect me to be awake enough to get dressed and drive here without coffee?"

"I struggled with it, too," Bob says. "I'm not a morning person by nature."

I don't believe him for a minute, and my skeptical expression must make this clear.

"I swear," he says, holding one hand up like he's about to be sworn in to give testimony. "But here's the thing about coffee. If you drink it and then work out, odds are you'll end up with terrible heartburn. Not to mention the fact that some of these exercises will work your abs hard enough that you might find a full coffee bladder a bit, um, awkward. If you get my drift."

I do. An image of wetting myself on the machine that resembles a gynecologist's exam table pops into my head. I look longingly and forlornly at my coffee cup and say, "Do you ever work out at times other than this?"

"I do evening workouts, but I find the early morning ones work the best, and it's also when this place is less crowded. That's how I got into it in the beginning. I was so flabby and out of shape and worked up such a sweat that I was embarrassed to be seen by anyone, so I started coming when there were fewer people here."

This confession softens my disappointment and endears me some to Bob. Looking at him now it's hard to imagine what he looked like some two hundred pounds of flab ago.

"Okay, where do I start?" I say, resigned.

"Let's do the upper body stuff first," Bob says. "We'll save the really sweaty stuff for last."

Yippee.

At least I have Bob helping me out this time. And surprisingly, I find the exercises a little easier to do with him coaching me along. He makes me laugh a few times, and as much as my body, and at times my mind, protests at the agony I'm experiencing, I find myself enjoying it.

When we are done, Bob says, "Are you showering here?"

I shake my head. "I'm going home. Public showers aren't my thing. I never had enough privacy growing up, so I kind of protect it fiercely now."

"Makes sense," Bob says. "Same time tomorrow?"

I sigh and roll my eyes. "I suppose."

"Good." He turns to head for the showers, but I stop him with a hand on his arm.

"Any news on the Cochran case?"

"Still waiting to hear on the request for the search warrant." He makes a face. "The judge who was on call this weekend isn't one of my favorites. He's typically overly strict about these things."

I nod, briefly debating if I should confess my most recent transgression. Might as well put it out there, I decide, because he'll likely find out soon anyway. "I emailed your chief about the social work position and sent him a copy of my résumé." I wait, watching Bob's face closely for a reaction.

"That's great," he says. "I was planning on talking to him about you this morning anyway."

I let out a sigh of relief. "You were?"

"I am. Best of luck. I hope you get it." With that, he heads for the men's locker room, leaving me standing there sweaty, exhilarated, and a bit surprised.

Once I get home and take my shower, I decide to wear something dressier to work today, just in case I get a call for an interview. I opt for a gray skirt suit with a hunter green silk blouse and a pair of pumps with a mostly green, multicolor floral pattern on them.

I'm feeling quite chipper when P.J. shows up to take Roscoe for his pre-school morning walk just before seven.

"Did you go to the gym again today?" she asks.

"I did. It wasn't quite as bad this time."

"Was that policeman there with you?"

"He was."

"And how did your date with Jonas go?"

"It went very well."

"Did you kiss him?" I give her raised eyebrows for an answer. "Well, did you?" she insists, not phased in the least by my look.

"Just a quick one on the cheek," I say.

"Hmph." She bends down and clips the leash onto Roscoe's collar.

"What does that mean?" I say, frowning at her.

"I didn't say anything," she says, feigning innocence. Then, in a brilliant effort to change the subject, she quickly adds, "You look very nice today. Is there something special going on at work?"

"No. I just felt like getting a little fancy today."

P.J. tilts her head and stares at me. I can tell she doesn't believe me and suspects I'm holding out on her. But she decides to let it go.

"I have a big math test today," she says. "Wish me luck."

"Good luck, though you don't really need it. You have smarts, and that's much more reliable."

She smiles at me, nudges the leash, and goes out the door with Roscoe. I head for my car in the garage and drive to work.

The hospital is quiet for a Monday morning, with nothing of interest in the ER and only a few patients on the floors. I head for my office and start in on paperwork, but my mind won't stay focused. I keep thinking about Toby Cochran and the case, wondering if Bob will get the search warrant for the Sheffield place.

I go down to the cafeteria to grab a breakfast sandwich

around eight thirty, and as I'm standing in line behind a couple of lab techs to pay, I overhear their whispered conversation.

"I hear they're going to cut back twenty percent of the staff in all departments," says one of them.

"That's one-fifth of the staff. We should be safe," the other says. "There are only three of us on days, and they can't lay off part of a person."

"It might not be layoffs. Andy thinks they're going to cut hours. And that might affect benefits."

I frown as I listen, but their conversation stops there because they have reached the cash register. Their topic concerns me because I've learned that hospital gossip, while overblown and exaggerated at times, often bears a kernel of truth. But if there are staffing cutbacks coming down the pike, Crystal hasn't informed me of them.

When I get back to my office, I know the overheard gossip is true. Crystal is waiting for me, sitting in my chair, chatting on her phone. She waves me into the room and then holds up a finger to let me know she's almost done.

I sit in the chair meant for visitors and unwrap my sandwich, taking the first bite as Crystal concludes her call. She looks over at me and smiles, but it's clearly forced. "I have some unexpected news," she says.

"Am I losing my job?"

"What? How? Who?" The shock on her face is real. Clearly, she didn't think I had a clue. Of course, I didn't until just a few minutes ago.

"The grapevine," I say. "You know how gossip is in this place."

"Yes, I should have known," Crystal says, running an anxious hand through her hair. "You haven't lost your job. Frankly, I didn't think our department would be affected by the coming cutbacks, given that there's only three of us and one of those is a PRN employee."

A PRN employee is someone who picks up shifts when they can but isn't scheduled for any regular time. It's a position that comes without guarantees of time and with no benefits. We have one PRN employee, a semiretired social worker named Jane Lawson who lives in a neighboring town about twenty miles away. Jane comes in and helps to cover things whenever Crystal or I take a vacation. Otherwise, Crystal and I are the entire social work show. It's a small hospital, so we manage well enough, though the nursing staff is always griping about the lack of social services on the weekends and night shifts.

"But our department didn't escape unscathed," she says. "I have to cut your hours."

"How much?"

"One day a week. You'll still be salaried because of the off hours you put in for support groups and such. And your benefits won't change. Basically, it's a money cut."

It could be worse. Losing some of my pay isn't great news, but I'll survive it. I've always been thrifty with my money, and I have a healthy savings account, a good start on my retirement plan, and few bills. And, I realize, if by some miracle I get the job at the police department, this might prove to be a good thing.

"How do you want me to schedule it?" I ask Crystal.

"I was thinking you could take Fridays off. You have the grief support group on Thursday nights, so you're typically here late. That way you'll get a three-day weekend most of the time. You will still get comp time, but that comp time will be based on a thirty-two-hour workweek, not forty. There will be times when I might need you to change it up, but for the most part I think we can live with that sort of schedule. What do you think?"

"Sounds fine to me." In fact, it sounds fabulous.

"I'm relieved you're taking this so well," Crystal says. "I thought you might get upset."

This seems like the perfect segue, so I say, "Actually, it may fit in well with something I'm working on."

I then tell her about the police department job and that I've applied for the position. Crystal asks me several questions about the position, expresses some concern over my ability to balance the two jobs should I get it, and then wishes me luck.

The remainder of my day goes by without any excitement, and that includes any word from either Chief Hanson or Bob Richmond. At three o'clock I start preparing to leave for the day, and my cell phone rings. I feel a little kick of adrenaline when I see that it's Bob and wonder if the feeling is triggered by the prospect of more police work or Bob himself.

Maybe both, I decide, and I answer the call with, "Got any news for me?"

Bob chuckles in response. "Indeed, I do," he says. "I've had chats today with Alex Parnell and Heath Monroe, Toby's roommate. Neither of them had much to offer me, and they both made excuses for why they had to leave in a hurry."

"Figures," I say. "And it sucks."

"It does, and it doesn't get any better."

"Uh-oh."

"Yeah, the judge won't grant the search warrant. Says Sheffield is too connected and well-known in this area. He is a man of power and we've got squat in the way of any real evidence that ties him to the kid's death."

"Rats. What do we do now?"

"I had Jonas bring Toby's car in to have another look at it. He found traces of that coconut oil on the floorboard."

"Not surprising," I say.

"It is when you consider he found it on the passenger side."

It takes me a moment to digest this. "You think someone else drove his car with him on the passenger side," I say.

"Could be. Jonas is inspecting the driver's side of the car more closely, looking for trace. It's a long shot, but who knows? In the meantime, I'm doing some more digging into our friend Mr. Belov and the boys at the frat house. I'll let you know if anything turns up."

"Okay." I can't hide the disappointment in my voice. I worry that I may have gotten Sharon Cochran's hopes up for nothing.

"Jonas said he really enjoyed the time he spent with you last night," Bob tosses out.

This sudden change in direction throws me. "Um, yes, so did I."

"Does that mean you aren't interested in another dinner with me?"

"No . . . I mean, yes." I roll my eyes and let out a nervous chuckle. "What I meant to say is no, it doesn't mean that, and yes, I'd like to have dinner with you again."

"Good. I'll be in touch."

Before I can utter another word, the call is disconnected. I hold the phone in my hand and stare at it a moment before shaking my head and dropping it into my purse.

I head out, but I don't get far. Crystal practically runs into me in the hallway outside my office.

"Oh, Hildy, good. I was hoping I'd catch you. I want you to know that I applied for that position you mentioned at the police station."

"You did?" I say, momentarily stunned.

"What with all the cuts here it's hard to feel very secure in one's job, and I think I'm due for a change. I hope you won't be upset over it."

I am more than upset. I'm freaking furious! I can't believe she has done this to me, but then I realize that it's my own damned fault for telling her about the job in the first place.

She gives me an apologetic smile. "If I take the police job, you'll likely get my job and be back to full-time hours. And with a pay raise!"

I want to rip her lips off her face. Instead, I force a smile to my own lips and say, "May the best woman win." I start to leave when I realize what she said to me in that last sentence: "If I take the police job . . ."

"Did they offer you the position?" I ask, not wanting to hear the answer but knowing I have to.

"Not yet," she says in a tone that implies she considers it a done deal. "But my interview is today at four thirty."

"You have an interview set up already?"

"Yes, they called me a couple of hours ago. When is yours?"

I don't answer her. I'm afraid if I try to speak right now, all that will come out is a string of curses and other bad language that would make the saltiest sailor blush. Instead I point to my watch, indicating the time, and push past her. When I reach the parking lot, I let loose with a string of expletives that could make a Bible spontaneously combust.

Chapter Thirty-Two

I arrive home in a maelstrom of emotion. I feel angry, betrayed, stupid, and naive. Roscoe, sensing my mood, greets me in a subdued manner, licking my hand tentatively. After tossing my purse and briefcase onto the couch, I head for the fridge, grab an open bottle of chardonnay, and pour myself a glass. Then, I settle in at the kitchen counter and try to think.

I'm crestfallen. Clearly, I've overplayed my hand with the police job. *Or maybe I've underplayed it,* I think. Maybe I need to do something more, something to grab the attention of Chief Hanson and make it clear that I'm the better woman for the job.

Roscoe sits at my feet staring up at me with those soulful eyes of his. It's then that I see the note on the counter. It's from P.J., informing me that she has an out-of-town track meet after school today and she won't be able to take Roscoe for his evening walk.

I realize that a walk might do both me and Roscoe some good. Some fresh air and exercise will help me think. I hop off my stool, grab Roscoe's leash, and hook him up. There are some minor aches and pains as we take off at a fast clip, a reminder of my morning workout. But as we go, my muscles loosen up and we get into a steady, dynamic rhythm that feels good.

A few blocks into our excursion, we run into Milly Ames, a widow in her fifties who lives in the neighborhood and owns a yellow Labrador retriever named Moe.

"Hi, Hildy," she greets me with a wave and a smile. As we close the gap between us, the two dogs start wagging their tales excitedly, their version of a greeting. "Haven't seen you and Roscoe out at the dog park lately," Milly says. "How are you doing?"

Forcing a smile onto my face, I greet her back, and the two of us exchange some brief pleasantries while the dogs sniff at each other. By the time we part company, Moe and Roscoe have thoroughly nosed each other from head to tail and my face feels stiff from forced smiling.

It's a few minutes before four thirty when we return home, and I let Roscoe inside and head for the garage. A few minutes later I'm parked on the street that runs by the police station with a view of the front parking lot. Crystal's car is there, and I sit and wait.

She emerges from the station just before five, and as I watch her walk across the lot to her car, I feel my hopes sink even deeper. There is an energy to her step and a satisfied smile on her face that makes me think her interview must have gone well. I slump down in my seat as she pulls out and drives off. Once she's gone, I sit up and stare at the police building, tempted to go inside and demand a meeting with the chief. I know that's not the best approach, however, and eventually I start my car and drive home in a funk. My now-warm glass of wine is still sitting on the counter. I grab it and down it in one swallow. Then I start cleaning.

My mind is racing the entire time, thinking over different aspects of the case, the job situation, and creative ways I could kill off Crystal and get away with it. After I've cleaned the house into a state of near sterility, I prepare to do a load of laundry. As I'm standing in front of the washing machine holding my dirty workout clothes, I get an idea. I call Roscoe into the room and hold my sweatpants in front of him. He sniffs them, and then I toss them across the room.

"Fetch, Roscoe!" I say.

The dog dutifully crosses the room, picks up the pants, and brings them to me. No surprise. Fetch is a game Roscoe learned long ago.

"Good boy!" I go into the kitchen and get him a treat, which he inhales. We play this game awhile, with me letting him sniff the pants first each time. After several more retrievals, I walk Roscoe out to the living room and tell him to sit. I let him sniff the pants and then tell him to stay. I head for my bedroom and, after looking around, I toss the pants on my closet floor. This messes with my cleanliness sensibilities, but I tamp my anxiety down, close the door, and return to the living room, where Roscoe is waiting patiently.

"Fetch!" I tell Roscoe.

He tilts his head to one side and thumps his tail on the floor a few times.

"Fetch," I say again.

With this, Roscoe gets up, trots into the bedroom, and starts sniffing around. I follow him and watch as he zeroes in on the closet door, sniffs beneath it, scratches at the door once, and then sits, looking back at me. I walk over and open the door, and Roscoe immediately darts inside, grabs the pants, and brings them to me.

"Good boy!" I say with great enthusiasm, scrubbing him behind his ears and then giving him another treat. After stashing the sweatpants in several other hiding places around the house, including a few on the second floor, I deem us ready.

Next, I log on to my computer and launch one of the

satellite mapping programs, zooming in on the dog park I sometimes take Roscoe to, the one where we used to see Milly and Moe. It takes some shifting of the map to the east, but eventually I find what I'm looking for: the wooden footbridge. Looking at the legend on the map, I gauge the distance from the park to the footbridge to be around three miles. An easy walk on most days, but at night, and with muscles that are still not happy about my new workout agenda, it's daunting. Not to mention that there is a heavily wooded area I will need to cross.

Still, how impressed would Bob and Chief Hanson be if I were to discover something? I arm myself with a flashlight, make sure my phone has a good charge, and grab Roscoe's night collar, which has a small lamp on it that lights up the ground in front of him.

Next, I place a call to Sharon and tell her I need a piece of clothing that belonged to Toby, something he wore recently. I know she wants to ask questions of me as to why and what I have planned, but she refrains when I tell her I'll explain it all later.

I don a jacket as protection from the cool night air and grab the longer, retractable leash, and then Roscoe and I head out to the car. A few minutes later we arrive at the Cochran house, and I leave Roscoe in the car while I walk up to the front door. Sharon meets me there, hands me a plastic shopping bag containing a T-shirt that's seen better days and smells musky even to me, and says simply, "Good luck with whatever you're doing."

It's a four-mile drive to the dog park, and I expect to be the only one out there, given the hour. But to my surprise there are a half dozen other dog owners there with dogs wearing colorful light collars. For the sake of my planned cover story, I take Roscoe toward the group and let him play with the other dogs while I chat with the owners. During this time, I let it slip that I've been having issues with Roscoe wanting to run off lately, something he never used to do. I get all sorts of suggestions as to why this might be: a nearby female in heat, a middle-age dog crisis, a wild hair, and one depressing downer who suggests Roscoe might have a brain tumor.

Over the next hour, the other owners gradually drift off, and finally Roscoe and I are the only ones left inside the fenced park area. Outside of this enclosed area are more park grounds, including trails that wind through the surrounding wooded areas and along the river that runs next to the park. Roscoe and I have walked parts of these trails in the past. Someone once told me about the abundance of raspberry bushes that could be found along them, and when the berries have been in season I've meandered along the trails picking for hours at a time. On other occasions, I've walked the trails simply because the wooded area is peaceful and quiet, and I enjoy the solitude and a chance to commune with nature. Roscoe and I have seen lots of wildlife during these walks: beaver, rabbits, deer, muskrats, groundhogs, chipmunks, turtles, birds of all kinds, and Roscoe's favorite critters to try and catch—frogs.

I walk Roscoe to the gated entrance to the park, leash him up, and turn on my flashlight. I return to the parking lot and my car, and there I take out my cell phone and launch the GPS-enabled app I've used in the past to measure my walking distance. Once I've verified that it is accurately displaying the park area and our position on the screen, I start the app's counter. Next, I remove the plastic shopping bag containing Toby's T-shirt from my car and loop the handles over my arm, letting the bag hang from my elbow. Then Roscoe and I head for the park path that I think will take us closest to the footbridge.

The first couple of miles are easy going. The path is well traveled and often used, so it's clearly marked and easy to navigate. It takes us just over thirty minutes to get to a spot where the main path continues straight ahead but there is a second path that veers off to the right. I know that if I stay on the main path, it will eventually emerge on the backside of an industrial park that sits just outside of Sorenson. The path to the right is a large circle that will bring me back here, its circumference about a mile. After studying the aerial map earlier, I determined that the woods on the far end of this circular trail are where I need to veer off to reach the footbridge.

The moon has risen and it's a bright, fat, gibbous phase that helps to light our way well enough that I turn off the flashlight and shove it into my jacket pocket. I mark the half-mile spot using my phone app, and after studying the woods and trying to find the path of least resistance, Roscoe and I plunge in.

It is very slow going, the ground wildly overgrown and marked by treacherous tree roots and branches that try to trip me up and snag at the bag hanging from my arm. Early on I roll the bagged shirt up and stuff it in my pocket. It doesn't take long after that to realize I need to let Roscoe run free. Twice his leash becomes tangled around shrubbery badly enough that I'm forced to unhook him, and the third time it happens I don't bother to reconnect it. Freed of his restraint, Roscoe charges ahead of me, nose to the ground, though every few feet or so he glances back to make sure I'm still with him.

As I stumble along, I occasionally see the glow of eyes off to the sides, making me think I should have brought along something I could use to defend myself. At one point I trip over a fallen tree branch that I realize would make both a decent walking stick and a weapon should I need one, so I pick it up. After about fifteen minutes of wending my way through the trees, I take out my cell phone and see that I no longer have service. Cussing to myself, I stop and look around. Second thoughts about this venture begin to creep in. These woods cover a huge chunk of land, and if I get too turned around, I could get lost and wander around all night long.

Roscoe, seeing that I've stopped, comes back to me. There is a rustling in the branches overhead, and when I look toward the sound I see the white, heart-shaped face of a barn owl staring down at us. For a moment I'm enthralled and transfixed; then the bird spreads its wings and takes off, making me flinch. It lets forth with a bloodcurdling shriek that makes a chill race down my spine, and even Roscoe is momentarily intimidated, startled as the bird takes flight and emits its eerie call. Roscoe looks to me for reassurance, and I give it, telling him it's okay and patting him on the head.

But I'm not sure it is okay. I know that barn owls are considered a bad omen in some cultures because of their ghostly appearance and the fact that they shriek rather than hoot. While I don't normally ascribe to such legends and rumors, the current setting and situation does little to reassure me. Not sure if I should continue onward or abandon what is starting to seem like a dumb idea, I stand there surveying the woods around me, chewing on my lip. Then Roscoe makes the decision for me when he spots a rabbit in the underbrush and takes off after it. I scramble after him, following the sound of thrashing branches.

A moment later the trees break, and I emerge into a clearing. And there, just ahead of me, is the footbridge.

Chapter Thirty-Three

Feeling exposed and vulnerable suddenly, I quickly step back into the shelter of the tree border. At first, I don't see Roscoe anywhere, but then he comes bounding across the grass to my right, clearly excited after his bunny chase. He gives a vigorous shake—he's been in the creek that's babbling forth some fifty feet in front of us—and I'm splattered with cold water drops that make me wince. I need Roscoe focused, so I stroke his head and speak softly to him, hoping to calm him down for the job ahead.

I'm keenly aware that I am now on Warren Sheffield's property, and I see no less than three no-trespassing signs that also announce this is private property. Technically, I'm trespassing, and despite the cover story I have planned, I could get into some serious trouble. My next moves must seem convincing, particularly if . . .

I scan the open area, looking for manmade structures other than the bridge, but I don't see any. Carefully I scrutinize the border of the woods, looking at the trunks and lower branches. Next, I inspect the bridge the best I can, searching for any odd protrusions or additions that seem out of place. But it's impossible to tell, because the bridge arches just high enough over the creek bed that I can't see the other side of it. I'm looking for security cameras, and while nothing obvious jumps out at me, it doesn't mean they aren't there. They could be cleverly disguised or located in one of the spots I can't see well.

I drop the stick I've been carrying and take out the bag that has Toby's T-shirt in it. So much hinges on what comes next. This is the moment I've waited for, the reason I trekked through those god-awful woods, the reason I spent time playing fetch with Roscoe, and the thing my hopes for a different career path hinge upon. Will Roscoe understand how to play the game if I don't hide the shirt? If he doesn't find anything, does it mean there's nothing here, or simply that he doesn't get the game? Will the scents of wildlife confuse him? Am I a complete idiot for even considering this?

I've come too far to go back now, so I squat down and offer the shirt to Roscoe. He dutifully sniffs at it, then looks at me. I push it toward him again and he smells it some more. Then I stick the shirt back in the plastic bag, roll it all up tightly, and shove it into my jacket pocket next to the flashlight.

"Fetch, Roscoe!" I say. He thumps his tail, grins at me like he's thinking, *This is way too easy*, and nudges my jacket pocket.

I point toward the bridge and again say, "Fetch!"

Roscoe cocks his head and thumps his tail but doesn't move. My hopes begin to flag. I try again, aiming toward the bridge and mimicking a toss with my arm, though I don't throw anything. "Fetch, Roscoe!"

This time he turns and runs out into the clearing, nose to the ground, trotting a serpentine path toward the bridge. When he reaches the edge of the bridge, I expect him to cross it, but he doesn't. Instead he moves to his left and does another serpentine search along the grassy area there. After some thirty feet of this, he returns and does the same thing to the right. Looking downtrodden by his lack of success, he comes back to me in the trees, sits at my feet, and whines.

Okay, then, crossing the bridge it is. There is no escaping it. I pick up my walking stick and step out of the trees. Then I cross the grassy area to the start of the bridge and pause, Roscoe at my side. I'm surprised to see how high and steep the banks are alongside the creek. From the aerial photos we looked at online, it was difficult to discern, but now I can see that the creek runs through a steep-sided gully that is easily six feet deep, maybe more.

The footbridge has railings on either side, though they are very basic wooden posts placed every couple of feet with a simple top rail attached that matches the arch of the bridge floor. At the end of each railing is a newel post with a simple block finial on top. The whole structure is about three feet wide with a span of what looks like ten to twelve feet. When I peer underneath the bridge, I see a large wooden support beam that sits in the middle of the creek and runs up to the center of the bridge. Despite the railings, extra support, and generous width, it still makes for a daunting crossing when you consider the drop to the creek bed below, which at the apex of the bridge is probably close to eight feet.

I take a closer look at the wooden floor and see that there is an odd gap between two of the boards a few feet in front of me. Most of the boards have an eighth to a quarter of an inch of space between them, but these two have a much wider gap of more than an inch.

I tell Roscoe to stay and take a couple of tentative steps onto the structure, testing each board beneath my foot before shifting my full weight onto it. Despite the odd gap in that one spot, everything seems solid enough, and I make my way to the apex of the bridge's arch.

As I start down the other side, moving faster due to both

the incline and my increased level of confidence in the sturdiness of the bridge, I call to Roscoe. He trots up and over the bridge, a little tentative about this unfamiliar ground as he peers over the sides. Just as I'm about to step off the bridge, Roscoe comes barreling down the last stretch of it, sideswiping me in his eagerness to get to solid land again. My arms windmill as I try to keep my balance, and I end up dropping my walking stick. With my left hand I grab the finial on the newel post to keep from falling, but the piece rotates beneath my palm and I feel my balance edge over into *timber!* territory.

I hit the ground on my side, and quickly turn to a sitting position. Roscoe is beside me in a flash, licking my face.

"I'm fine," I tell him, pushing him back and laughing. I become aware of an odd whirring sound that I assume at first is coming from Roscoe, but then I see something in front of me that makes me think I'm losing my mind.

The entire bridge appears to be rising into the sky. No, not the entire bridge, I realize, just this end of it. Except there is something attached to the closest end—hanging from it—as it rises into the air, something long and solid, and nearly as wide as the bridge itself. The structure continues its rise until the bottom edge of the thing hanging off the end of it, which seems to have come straight out of the earth, clears the level I'm sitting on by about two feet. The end of the bridge I just stepped off is towering more than eight feet above me. Out in the middle of the creek, I see that the support beam I spied earlier houses some type of metal piston that has risen from the wood and pushed the bridge into the air.

After gaping at the scene before me, I'm brought back to my senses by Roscoe's whine. He nudges the pocket with the flashlight in it, then looks at the cliff edge just in front of us. His tail thumps several times and he whines some more.

"Right, a flashlight would be helpful," I tell him. I take it out, wiggling it past the bag with Toby's shirt in it, and turn it on. Then I shine it toward the other side of the bridge. That's why there was that unusual gap, I realize. There is a hinge there that allows the rest of the bridge to be raised.

Unsure what any of this means but sensing that it's all important, I set the flashlight down, dig my cell phone out of my other pocket, open the camera app, and snap a picture of the raised bridge. The moonlight and the flash from the phone make for a decent enough picture, and I see that I have one weak bar of service available. I tap the option to share the picture and send it to Bob Richmond's phone. It doesn't go through, a little whirling circle my only indication that it's trying. I set it on the ground next to me, hoping it will get as much signal as possible, and pick up the flashlight.

Roscoe nudges my pocket again and whines some more. He moves over to stand at the very edge of the cliff that has appeared in front of us, looking down to the creek bed. I get on my hands and knees, and crawl over to the edge beside him. Below us, built into the side wall of the gully, is an opening framed in timber. Roscoe is crouching down, wanting to jump into the crevasse but frightened by the height. That's when I realize that he wasn't nudging my pocket to tell me to use the flashlight—he's smart but not that smart—he was nudging the bag with the shirt. He has picked up Toby's scent. Had Toby been here? Had he been in that opening?

There is only one way to find out, and Roscoe seems to have the same thought. He starts digging at the ground in front of him, as if he can somehow lower our cliff height by removing some of the muddy dirt. I see a faint glow of light emanating from the opening below, and I crawl back and then stand to get a better view of my surroundings.

I know there must be an easier way to get down to the

creek bed, because Roscoe came back wet from his bunny chase. Bordering the creek on either side I see a narrow, rocky shoreline large enough to navigate on foot if I'm able to get down there. I look to my left and then to my right, shining the flashlight in both directions. Then, I shine it on the large object hanging from the bottom end of the bridge, which I now realize is a type of door that covered the opening below. I hadn't noticed it before, but near the bottom of this door there is a lever.

I get back down on my hands and knees, crawl up to the edge, and pull the lever. There is a mechanical whirring sound, and then a ladder miraculously begins to slide out from the bottom of the door, stopping half a foot from the ground. I look over at Roscoe, who is looking from the ladder to me and back again, a nonverbal question.

"You can't climb ladders, and the cliff is too high for you to jump down," I tell him. "I need you to stay, Roscoe." I give him a scratch behind the ears, kiss the side of his nose, repeat the stay command a bit more sternly, and then descend the ladder.

When I reach the bottom, I step off to one side of the ladder. The aperture isn't large: it's the same width as the footbridge and is barely six feet tall, if that. I take a few steps toward the water and glance at the backside of the hanging door. The surface, which looks like it's made of boards, is cleverly disguised with what looks like dirt, roots, and foliage. I run my hand over the surface and realize it isn't real, but rather a brilliantly rendered façade. When down and in place, it would look like a long-standing retaining wall built into the cliff side.

I step closer to the opening and peer inside. It's a hallway, its walls, floor, and ceiling made of poured concrete. It winds around to the right hard enough that I can't see the end of it, just a faint light emanating from that direction. I recall seeing a hillock off to the right about fifty yards away and suspect it, too, is a clever disguise for whatever is beneath it. I step through the narrow doorway, its low height no problem for me. My heart is hammering in my chest, I hear my breath coming hard and fast, and I think I also hear the faint hum of machinery off in the distance.

As I follow the curve of the hallway, I realize it's descending slightly. There is a damp smell to the air, and I see drains built into the floor near the walls. About forty feet in I come to a stop. There is a large, windowless door in front of me, and alongside it is a lock requiring a key card. Stumped, I stand there a minute, thinking, and then I reach into my pocket to take out my cell phone so I can take pictures of the door and the hallway. But my pockets are empty of anything except the flashlight and Toby's bagged shirt. That's when I remember that I set my phone on the ground outside.

I hear Roscoe start barking, a frantic, excited bark that makes me wonder if he's seen another rabbit. I'm about to turn and head back outside when the door in front of me opens. Standing on the other side of it, looking as surprised as I feel, is Carol Barlow, the frat boys' housemother.

"What the . . ." she mutters.

"What the heck?" I mutter at the same time.

We engage in a brief stare-off that ends abruptly when I feel a blinding pain on the back of my head and my brain explodes into darkness.

Chapter Thirty-Four

Bright white pain provides a stark contrast to the darkness around me. Then I realize my eyes are closed, and I open them. I look around, blinking to clear my vision, and see that I am lying on a bed. I hear voices from somewhere above my head, but when I try to rise so I can look, the pain in my head makes me stay still.

"How did she find the place?" I hear a woman say just above a whisper. I think it's Carol Barlow.

"You said she and that cop talked to the other boys. Did one of them say something?" This is a male voice, one I don't recognize at all. But there is a distinct accent to it, Russian I think, and my brain struggles to make some connection I know is in there hiding behind the pain. Then it comes to me: *Vadim Belov*, Sheffield's work visa employee who is somehow involved with the frat boys' gaming competitions.

"No, absolutely not. I'm sure of it. I was listening in the whole time." This time the voice is louder, and I'm certain it's Carol. "Father said he got a call from the cop. He wanted to come out and talk to him as well as look over the grounds, but Father told him no."

"Then why is she here snooping around?" the man asks.

"I don't know," Carol says. "Good thing you came back

when you did though. She startled me when I opened the door. If you hadn't hit her on the head with your flashlight, who knows what would have happened."

"They must know something," the man says in a worried voice.

"Relax," Carol says. "They may suspect something is up, but I don't think they know anything."

"They will now," the man says. "Thanks to her."

"Unless we make her disappear," Carol suggests in an ominous tone.

It doesn't take my battered brain long to figure out that the *her* they are referring to is me. And I harbor no illusions about what is meant with the talk about me disappearing. I've really done it this time. I'm about to join the ranks of my mother by becoming a victim of murder. And likely one that will go unsolved. The irony.

The cylinders in the engine that is my brain are starting to fire regularly now rather than sputter, and I zero in on what Carol said just before she decided I was a problem to be disposed of. "Father said . . ."

I'm at the footbridge. And that footbridge is located on property belonging to Warren Sheffield. And Bob Richmond spoke with Sheffield about looking around his grounds. Is Carol Barlow Warren Sheffield's daughter? Her last name is different, but that doesn't mean anything. She could have taken the name of her husband. Or maybe she's the illegitimate daughter of some woman Sheffield had an affair with. I recall Carol telling Bob and me the story of how she had to raise her son on her own after her husband died. She made some comment about moving in with her family and that they were well off. Warren Sheffield certainly fits that bill.

"If the woman was with a cop, we cannot just dispose of her," I hear the man say, bringing me back to the shocking present. "Then they will start digging around for sure."

"Not if it doesn't seem to be related to us. It needs to look like an accident and look like it happened far away from here."

I knew all along there was something about Carol that didn't sit right with me. But I had no idea the woman was so cold-blooded.

"What about the other boys?" the man asks. "They are bundles of nerves already after Toby's death. Can we trust them?"

"They won't talk," Carol says. "They need the money too much."

I hear a heavy sigh but I'm not sure who it comes from.

"Leave her to me," Carol says. "I'll take care of it."

I hear nothing for a few seconds, then I hear footsteps, some moving away from me, some coming toward me. There is the sound of a glass clinking near my head, and then I hear running water. I keep my eyes closed and continue to feign unconsciousness. Suddenly a hand grabs my shoulder and shakes me hard.

"Come on, Hildy," Carol says close to my ear. "Wake up now."

I debate my next move for a second or two and decide to wake up. I let my eyes flutter, and I moan for good measure, though the pain in my brain lends it a level of realism. "Oh, my head," I say, putting a hand on the back of it. I feel a good-sized goose egg there and wince.

Carol snakes an arm around my shoulders and forces me to sit up. My head swims nauseatingly, and for a moment I think I might pass out again. I shake it off, blink several times, and stare at Carol as if just now realizing she's here. "Mrs. Barlow," I mumble, squeezing my eyes closed. "Where am I?"

"That's not important," she says. "Take a drink of water. It will make you feel better."

She shoves a glass toward my lips and I take a small sip,

swallowing it. Carol sets the glass of water on a table beside the bed and then reaches into the pocket of her slacks. A moment later she thrusts her open hand in front of me. On her palm is a white pill. "Take this. It will help with the headache."

I have no idea what the pill is. It might be a headache pill. Or it might be something worse. My money's on the latter.

"Come on, take it," Carol cajoles. She sticks her palm in front of my mouth and I know that if I don't take the pill, she'll force it between my lips. So I open my mouth and let her drop it in. She turns to pick up the glass of water from the table next to the bed. "Take another drink," she says, and she pushes the edge of the glass against my mouth hard enough that it clinks against my teeth.

I take another drink, a small one, and swallow hard.

"Good girl," Carol says. "Now let's take a little walk." She gets up and extends a hand to me.

I take it, even though touching her right now is repulsive. I stand, my legs shaking, and then I let my knees give way and collapse into a sitting heap. My head lolls forward and I catch my chin in one hand and push my head upright.

Carol emits an exasperated sigh. "Oh, for Pete's sake," she says. "Get a grip." She uses her not inconsiderable bulk and strength to hoist me to my feet. "Let's move. One foot in front of the other. Atta girl."

I shuffle my feet forward, letting her steer me with one arm firmly beneath my own. As we move forward slowly, I get my first good look at the room I'm in. It's a concrete bunker, but the bed I've just left is part of a tableau that doesn't fit the rest of the room. If not for the standing industrial lights and bare concrete walls elsewhere in the room, one would think they were in the bedroom of some-one's house.

Carol urges me toward a door, opens it, and pushes me into another room. In an instant I am transferred from the surreality of the makeshift bedroom into what looks like a high-tech military or police surveillance room. There are computers and screens lining both walls on either side of me, and seated in front of them are some faces I recognize: the boys from the frat house.

Liam Michaelson, Mitchell Sawyer, and Alex Parnell—who I never met but recognize from his pictures—are typing away on keyboards, focused on the computer screens in front of them, speaking in low voices into their headsets. Also sitting in front of computers, similarly outfitted and occupied, are two girls who I recognize from the picture Lori showed us on her phone, the one Toby sent her of his gaming team.

I glance at the screens, expecting to see a game tableau, but the displays appear to be filled with text. I try to read some of it, but Carol is urging me along at a fast clip, and my vision is still foggy from the blow to my head. We cross the room quickly, and just before we reach the door on the opposite side, I see Liam Michaelson turn and glance my way. There is a brief look of shocked recognition on his face, but it's gone in a flash as he quickly shifts his focus back to his computer screen and resumes talking.

The murmur of all the voices in the room blends together into an incomprehensible din. I fake a stumble and teeter to my right, close to where one of the girls is sitting. She's by the end wall, and this allows me to catch myself with a hand on that wall. Then I lower myself to the floor just beside her seat. The girl glances over at me with a worried expression, then she looks at Carol.

"Ignore us," Carol tells her.

The girl looks back at her screen and starts talking again. I'm close enough to her that I can discern her words from the room's overall racket.

"Yes, sir, you did agree to the charge. It was in the fine print that flashed on your screen when you paid for the video. Of course, if you want to dispute the charge, I'm sure we can run it by your wife to see what she says. Does she know you like kiddie porn?"

Carol tugs painfully on my arm. "Get up," she says crossly. She is pulling hard enough that she's dragging me across the floor. It's quite painful, so I give in and rise to my feet, though slowly and with a noted lack of coordination.

Carol shoves me through the door into a third area that looks like some type of main computer room. There are towers of blinking lights and hardware, and bundles of thick cables snaking around the perimeter of the room, disappearing through conduits in the walls.

I can't make sense of any of it, but I do sense the danger I'm in. I need to find a way to stall, to give myself time to think. Then I remember the pill Carol gave me, or at least the pill she thinks she gave me. All those years I spent in my childhood cheeking the psych pills various doctors and foster parents tried to foist on me have come in handy. I never swallowed the pill Carol gave me, and I spit it out when I faked my collapse onto the floor. At this moment it's in my pocket. I don't know what it is, but I have a good idea.

I let my knees go again and crumple to the floor. Carol isn't expecting it, and she loses her grip on me. "Ach!" she spits out, giving me an irritated look.

I make my face go flat and expressionless and let my head loll slightly on my neck. While my face may look zombified, which is what I want Carol to think I am, my mind is racing like a bipolar patient in the throes of a major manic episode. I look around the room at all the flashing and blinking lights. "What the heck is this place?" I ask, slurring my words ever so slightly. Then I assume a blissful smile. "It's like magic."

Carol frowns down at me, hands on her hips. "It's a business," she says. She steps behind me, bends down, and wraps me in a bear hug. Then she tries to hoist me to my feet. I let my body go utterly limp. Carol grunts with her efforts to make me stand, but it's hopeless. Despite her size, she can't get my dead weight up from the floor. For the moment, I'm glad for the pounds I've let creep on over the past few years.

"What kind of bid-ness?" I say, all sloth-eyed.

Carol rolls her eyes. "Criminy, woman, am I going to have to drag you out of here?"

"You're helping the boys, aren't you?" I say slowly, managing a half smile. I blink with exquisite slowness. "They need money and you help them make it." I smile broadly at her now. "You're so nice."

I'm hoping this appeal to her ego, coupled with my apparently drugged state of my mind, will allow Carol to let her guard down. But no such luck.

"I've had just about enough of you," she says, grabbing both of my wrists and dragging me across the floor.

I'm determined not to make it easy for her, so I don't try to get up or help her. But I don't resist her, either. She drags me across the room, grunting with each pull. When she reaches yet another door, she opens it and drags me over the threshold into a hallway. Here the floor is concrete and rough, not the smoother finish I encountered in the other rooms.

"Ouch!" I yell, pouting.

"Well then, get up and walk," Carol snaps. She stops, panting, hands on her hips. There is sweat dripping from her forehead and a look of major irritation on her face.

I do as she says and stand. Then I start walking in the direction she was dragging me, passing her by in the process. She lets me take the lead and falls into step behind me. For a crazy half second I consider trying to run. But I quickly dismiss the idea for two reasons. One, Carol's legs are easily twice the length of mine, so it wouldn't be hard for her to catch me, even if she's slow. And two, I have no idea what's up ahead. If there is a door that requires a badge or card to open, I'll be trapped, and Carol will be very angry. And she's not someone I want to make mad just now. Better to continue with the drugged façade for the time being and look for another opportunity.

As it turns out, there are no other doors. This hallway is the same one I first entered from outside. As I round a curve I see a dark maw appear up ahead and think I might as well try to run. It's probably my only chance.

I kick it into high gear, feeling my abused muscles protest loudly. Running as fast as I can, I close in on the opening, wondering if the ladder will still be there or if I'll have to run along the creek. Behind me I hear Carol cuss under her breath as her footfalls quicken and grow heavier. I've only gone about ten feet, and I can tell she's rapidly closing in on me. By the time I reach the opening, I can feel the heat of her breath on the back of my neck.

I give it every bit of energy I have left, thankful that adrenaline is starting to mask the pain. I dart through the opening just as Carol's heavy hand clamps down on my shoulder, her grip fierce and relentless. I try to break free, but she doesn't let go, and I find myself spinning around to face her.

But this time, instead of the world going dark, it explodes with light.

Chapter Thirty-Five

"Hold it!" commands a voice from somewhere behind the blinding light. I recognize it as Bob Richmond's voice. Roscoe's barking is replaced with a whine, and behind me I hear Carol utter a cuss word. I feel a hand in the middle of my back and I'm thrust forward, falling onto the stone shoreline of the creek. I hear the hard thud of running footsteps behind me moving away, and when I look over my shoulder I see that the entrance to the underground bunker is empty.

Bob's voice is suddenly by my ear. "Are you okay?" he says, shining his flashlight over my body.

"Yes," I say, though both my knees and the palms of my hands where I hit the stones are burning and stinging.

"Can you get up the ladder?" Bob asks.

"I think so."

"Brenda Joiner is up there with your dog. She can help you some, but that dog of yours is champing at the bit to get to you."

"Roscoe, be still!" I say in a commanding voice. The whining stops.

"Impressive," Bob says. "What's inside that door? Was that Carol Barlow I saw behind you?"

"Last question first. Yes, it's Carol Barlow. And down that

hallway you'll find a doorway that you won't be able to get past without a key card. But if you do get in, there are lots of people inside. All of Toby's gaming team comrades . . . and I choose the word *comrade* on purpose, because our Mr. Belov is also in there."

"It's a gaming place?" Bob says, confused.

"No. I'm not sure exactly what they're doing or how they're doing it, but I believe they're extorting people."

"What?" Bob snaps.

"Something to do with porn, I think," I say. His eyebrows shoot up at that. "I bet the kids who are on that gaming team are all from poorer homes. And they aren't practicing whatever computer game it is they play, they're extorting people. That's why they never win the gaming competitions, because they never really practice. My guess is they're earning money doing whatever it is, enough to keep them from talking. Maybe they get other perks, too. I don't know. Whatever it is, they're serious enough about keeping it a secret that the Barlow woman was going to 'make me disappear.'" I do air quotes around the last three words.

"She tried to drug me," I say, reaching into my pocket and pulling out the pill Carol tried to make me take. "I'm betting it's GHB, the same stuff they used on Toby. I think he had a crisis of conscience and wanted out, but they didn't want to let him. He tried to get the other guys to side with him, but they were too afraid, and maybe too greedy, to do it. They couldn't get Toby in line, though, so, they had to make him disappear, too."

Bob looks around with a frown. "I need an evidence team out here. And more officers." He nods at the pill in my hand. "Hang on to that for now. Did you see any weapons in there?" He gestures toward the entrance to the bunker.

"No, but I wasn't looking for them, and I don't know if there were areas I didn't see."

Bob undoes the clip on his holster and then yells up to

Brenda, "Hey, Joiner. Get on the horn and get us some help. We need all the officers we can get. Hit up county and state if you need to. And get forensics out here, too."

"On it," she yells back.

I stuff the pill back into my pocket and smile at Bob. "I'm glad you showed up when you did."

"I confess, you had me intrigued with that photo you sent."

"It finally went through?" I say with surprise and relief.

"It came through, but to be honest, I couldn't tell what it was at first. And then you didn't answer me when I messaged back and tried to call. I checked the location of your phone and it came up here, and that's when I realized what the picture was. I didn't have a way to get here without Sheffield's permission, but I realized you didn't, either. I've seen Sheffield's property, at least the area around his house. It's got more cameras than a group of Japanese tourists."

"Inappropriate and racist," I say, gently chastising.

"Whatever. Anyway, I knew you couldn't easily sneak onto Sheffield's property from the road because it's gated and fenced, and there are all the cameras. And I was pretty sure Sheffield wasn't going to let you just go roaming around if you asked. So I started thinking about how you might have gotten out here. That got me to looking at the areas surrounding the property, and that's when I saw the dog park."

"That's where we were," I say, trying to look and sound innocent. "P.J. couldn't walk Roscoe tonight, so I brought him to the park. And after his playtime, I decided to walk the trails in the main park area to get my muscles loosened up better. They're really stiff from the gym, you know."

I smile at Bob, but he's stony-faced. I'm glad I have P.J.'s note to back up my story—that and the false stories I told the other dog owners about Roscoe's recent desire to run off.

"Anyway, while we were walking the back trails Roscoe took off after a rabbit, and his leash got all tangled up in some shrubbery. I had to unhook him to get it untangled, and when I did, he just took off. He doesn't usually do things like that, but, he is a dog." I shrug and smile some more.

"I went after him and ended up wandering in the woods. Eventually I came out here and found him running around the property. I couldn't believe it when I saw the footbridge."

I'm looking at Bob with what I hope is wide-eyed innocence. He's looking at me with an expression that says he isn't buying a word of it. "And how is it you discovered the hidden entrance?" he asks.

His cheek pouches out as his tongue patrols the inside of it, and I get a strong sense from that and the look of skepticism on his face that he isn't going to believe anything I tell him. Technically I haven't lied to him yet. I just haven't shared the whole truth. And I don't intend to.

"It was purely accidental," I say—still the truth. "I'd crossed the bridge to this side and was about to step off it when Roscoe came running over it. I think he was spooked, because he slammed into my legs and knocked me off balance. I grabbed the top of one of the newel posts to try to catch myself, and the finial turned. And then the bridge just started going up."

Bob sighs and looks up at the raised bridge. "Quite the setup. No wonder Warren Sheffield didn't want us out here looking at his property." An oddly satisfied smile creeps over his face. "I bet he's going to be real mad."

Chapter Thirty-Six

Not surprisingly, I've had a sleepless night, in part because I didn't get home until five in the morning, and in part because of all the excitement. It's now just before seven on Tuesday morning and I feel wide awake. I called Crystal when I first got home and left her a voice mail telling her I wouldn't be in. I was relieved that I didn't have to speak to her. If she's been offered the job at the police station, I don't think I could bear to hear her gloating about it.

Bob kindly excused me from my gym time this morning, given that I walked the extra miles last night and all. Plus, he missed gym time, too, because he's still out at the footbridge processing the scene.

And what a scene it is. I had a front-row seat to the whole thing. Warren Sheffield's money and influence protect him from a lot, but now that the bunker has been discovered and Bob has the state and county police involved, it was a simple matter to find a judge to authorize the necessary search warrants.

There was a bit of a standoff at the bunker, with all of those inside refusing to come out and those outside unable to get in. I thought there might have been a back entrance, an escape route that the bunker inhabitants could have used, but it turns out there isn't. One had been planned, but

Sheffield apparently decided to put it on hold, impressed with what he had in place already, arrogant enough to think it would never be discovered, and tightfisted enough not to want to spend the money on it. Thus, it seems only fitting that Sheffield was the one who had to access the locked door to the bunker and let the police inside. Later, when both Sheffield and Belov were standing around outside in cuffs, they got into an argument about the escape route, or rather the lack thereof. Apparently, Belov had tried hard to convince Sheffield to put one in, and now he was in full-blown, ticked-off I-told-you-so mode.

When Carol was brought out, a few questions verified my earlier suspicion about her relationship to Sheffield. She is his daughter, though an illegitimate one, and she was also the overseer and supervisor for the blackmail operations that have been going on.

It was the frat boys who gave away most of those details, despite the malicious stares and glowers they got from both Sheffield and Carol. The boys, and their female counterparts, had been approached by Belov, who scouted them out when they were in high school. He was looking for kids who were IT savvy and poor. He offered them full-ride scholarships, the sourcing and true nature of which were well masked—the funding came from Sheffield—and in exchange they had to work for Belov, though technically everyone involved was working for Sheffield.

The work, as it turns out, was blackmailing customers who stayed in one of Sheffield's many hotels and who accessed certain pornography videos from their rooms. These are not your run-of-the-mill pornos, but rather socially unacceptable ones that feature kiddie porn, bestiality, and some hard-core S&M stuff.

When the videos loaded, a brief screen with what looked like a copyright infringement warning appeared, but it also contained language that gave WIS Productions the right to bill the customer for several thousand dollars' worth of additional pornographic videos, a subscription of sorts, the charge for which would appear on the credit card used to book the hotel room and access the original porn video.

When the customers called WIS Productions to question the charge, it was explained to them that if they didn't approve the charge, it would be made public to their employers or family members what they had paid to watch at the hotel. Then similar types of videos would start to arrive via the mail at home and at work without any plain brown wrappers. And to make matters worse, the customers then learned that while they were watching their porn, WIS Productions was watching them. All the TVs in Sheffield's hotel rooms have hidden cameras in them that were activated whenever one of the target porn videos was purchased. If the humiliation of having employers and loved ones learn of your perverted sexual proclivities wasn't deterrent enough, the threat of having a video released that showed what you were doing during the video was enough to convince the resisters.

In exchange for manning the phones, relaying the blackmail terms to customers, and handling the necessary computer programming and networking, the college kids were offered their school scholarships and a little spending money on the side. If all went well and the students kept their mouths shut, they would graduate with a degree and free of debt.

At one point during these revelations, Bob took me aside and told me he suspects Sheffield has been doing this for years, but they might not be able to prove it. For one thing, WIS Productions is a valid business engaged in the creation and distribution of all kinds of legitimate videos, from popular movies to self-help titles. Secondly, getting people who would be willing to come forth and admit to the extortion, much less testify to it, would be hard, given the nature of the blackmail.

I learned that there were security cameras hidden in

the bridge part of the property, so I was glad I hadn't lied outright to Bob. In fact, by the time I was given a ride home this morning, he told me he had obtained and viewed the footage of my escapades and that the video supported my version of events . . . for the most part. Technically I am still guilty of trespassing, but given the fact that Sheffield has bigger problems to deal with, it is unlikely that it will come to anything.

By the time Roscoe and I got home, I was feeling quite good about myself and what I did. But now, after two hours of insomnia and restlessness, my spirits have taken a dive. They get a brief boost when my phone rings a little after seven and I see it's Bob.

I answer without any greeting. "Anything new?"

"You weren't asleep, were you?" he says.

"Heck, no. How could I sleep with all that's happened?"

"Are you at work?"

"Nope. I'm taking a personal day. I have a lot of comp time built up, so I might as well use it. Besides, I understand my boss applied for the position at the police station and has had an interview already. Might as well get as much out of her as I can while she's still at the hospital."

Bob says nothing to this, and my spirits start tanking again. I was hoping for some encouragement at the least, or an outright denial of Crystal's chances at the most. "Have you learned anything new?" I ask Bob, eager to change the subject.

"I have. It turns out that little bedroom setup they have in the bunker is where they sometimes shoot their own videos. There are some college kids who are willing to do porn for money. And when Toby started balking at the blackmailing scheme, Carol tried flipping it back on him by drugging him with GHB and having him involved in a porno of his own, with him as the star. And guess what they use for lube during these sessions?"

It's an unexpected question, and I have no answer.

"Coconut oil," Bob says with obvious satisfaction.

I make the connection. "That's how it ended up on Toby's shoes, and the other footprints where his body was found."

"Yep."

"Poor Toby," I say.

"Yeah. The day he broke up with Lori, Carol had shown him the porn video and told him she would release it to his mother and girlfriend if he didn't shut up about the blackmail."

"That explains why he broke up with Lori. And why he quit school and came home."

"Yeah," Bob says again. "I think the kid tried to live with it but couldn't. Carol's son couldn't, either. He did himself in to escape it."

"That's why he killed himself?" I say, shocked. "They were doing this back then?"

"Apparently so. And other than Carol's son, Toby is the first participant to go rogue, or at least the first one we know about. Who knows what we might dig up in the past? Anyway, when Toby emailed the other guys with his doubts, one or maybe all of them told Carol and Belov what was going on. That text message Toby got on the night he died was to get him out to the bunker so they could silence him once and for all."

"So Sharon Cochran was right all along," I say. Somehow, I don't think the knowledge will help her much. Her son is still dead. But at least his reputation will be exonerated. "Does this mean our ride-along is over with?"

"It does," he says. "But there will be more to come."

"How so?"

"When you start the new job."

"Do you think I stand a chance?" I say with little hope.

"Nope," Bob says, and despite my own pessimism, I'm

devastated by his blunt reply. Then he adds, "You don't need a chance. The job is yours."

My fuzzy, sleep-deprived brain struggles to figure out what Bob really said, because I know it wasn't what I think I heard. "What did you say?" I ask.

"I said, the job is yours. I've been talking to the chief regularly since you and I had dinner the other night, telling him you'd be perfect for the job. And then the résumé and letter you sent him convinced him I was right."

"But Crystal . . ."

"Yeah, the chief wasn't planning on advertising the position or interviewing anyone else. But when Crystal applied, he had to give her an interview. So he did it fast, to get it out of the way."

"Are you kidding me about this?" I ask Bob. "Because I'm too tired right now to appreciate being the butt of someone's joke."

"Hildy, I swear to you, the job is yours. The chief is going to call you to set up an interview with him later today, but it's just a formality. It's a done deal. He's already started the paperwork. If you don't pull any more stupid moves like the one you did last night, you'll need to be ready to start in two weeks. Are you up for it?"

"Heck, yeah."

"The chief wants Roscoe, too."

"Of course. We're a team."

"You should probably try to get some sleep. You'll want to be fresh for your interview with the chief."

"Right. Okay. I'll do that, and I'll check back with you later."

"Congratulations, Hildy."

"Thank you, Bob. And thanks for all you've done for me."

"You're welcome."

I disconnect the call and then do a crazy happy dance, hollering, jumping, and writhing in place. It hurts me in odd places on my body, but I don't care. I feel delirious. Roscoe watches me with a curious eye, his tail thumping. Movement catches my eye in the middle of a jerk and Watusi move, and I realize P.J. has come in. She is standing in the living room watching me.

"Do you have bedbugs or something?" she says once I've stopped my gyrations.

"No, that's my happy dance. Sit down for a minute and let me tell you how my life is about to get a whole lot more interesting."

She makes a face. "I should probably walk Roscoe," she says.

"I'll make you toaster waffles."

"Okay," she says with a shrug, and then she slides onto one of the kitchen bar stools.

Annelise Ryan has another bestselling mystery series, the Mattie Winston Mysteries.

Watch for

DEAD OF WINTER,

coming to readers in paperback format in February 2020.

Turn the page for a sneak peek!

I awaken and peer out of one eye at the clock on my bedside stand, hoping for another hour or two of sleep. Sadly, it is not to be. The clock reads 7:28—two minutes before the alarm is going to sound. I want desperately to close my eyes and go back to sleep, to snuggle down in the warmth of the covers and hide from the morning cold, to cuddle up next to my sleeping husband, bathing in the feelings of love and sanctuary he instills in me. Instead, I reach over and turn off the alarm before it starts clamoring. Bleary-eyed, I ease out from under the covers and sit on the edge of the bed, giving my senses a minute or so to more fully wake up. I listen to the sounds of the house and the gentle snores of Hurley behind me, feeling the coolness in the air, and letting my eyes adjust better to the dark.

Eventually I grab my cell phone and unplug it from the charge cord; then I slip off the last of the covers and tiptoe my way to the bathroom, hoping not to disturb my husband. He's a homicide detective here in the Wisconsin town of Sorenson, where we live, and he works long hours a lot of the time. Plus, we are working parents of a teenager and a toddler, so sleep is a precious commodity for us both.

In the bathroom, I brush my teeth, don a robe against the morning chill, and tame my blond locks as best I can, though a cowlick on one side refuses to stay down, sticking out near my right temple like a broken, wayward horn. I eventually give up on the hair and tiptoe back the way I came, through the walk-in closet, and across the bedroom to the hallway. Our dog, Hoover, is asleep on the floor in front of the fireplace—a fireplace whose warmth I could use right now, though at the moment it's dark and empty— and the dog gets up and falls into step behind me. I shut the door as quietly as I can, and then Hoover and I pad down the hall toward the bedroom of my two-and-a-half-year-old son, Matthew. I'm surprised he isn't awake because he's proven himself to be an annoyingly early riser who is typically anything but quiet. But when I reach his room, I realize he has stayed true to form and is, indeed, awake; he just hasn't bothered anyone yet. His silence doesn't bode well, and sure enough I find him standing stark naked, busily becoming the next Vincent van Gogh by drawing on his bedroom wall with an assortment of crayons.

"Matthew!" I say in an irritable tone that loses much of its effect because I don't raise my voice. "Why are you drawing on the wall?"

Matthew looks guilty, but not enough so that he stops the scribble he's currently making, something that looks like a giant purple cookie. He doesn't answer me. I shake my head, walk over to him, and take the crayon from his hand, dropping it in a box at his feet that contains an assortment of crayons in all colors and sizes. When I pick up the box and place it on top of his dresser, Matthew lets out a bloodcurdling scream loud enough that a passerby might think he was being physically tortured. Some dark corner of my mind briefly entertains the possibility, before I take a deep breath and slowly release it, coming to my senses.

"I want crayons!" Matthew screams, pounding his fists on the wall.

"Hush before you wake up your father!" I rummage

through his dresser drawers and grab some clothing for the day, and then take Matthew by the hand and head for the bathroom down the hall. As soon as we reach the hallway, he pulls free of my grip, runs back into his room, and resumes his crayon mantra, growing louder and more infuriated with each rant. I'm about to pick him up and haul him bodily to the bathroom when my cell phone rings.

"Damn it," I mutter, taking the phone out of my robe pocket. I swipe the answer icon and back out into the hallway so I can hear above my son's screeches. "Mattie Winston."

"Hey, Mattic, it's Heidi." Heidi is a day dispatcher at the local police station.

"What's up?" I plug a finger in my free ear to try to block out the sound of my son's meltdown. I hear the bedroom door open down the hall and see our two cats, Tux and Rubbish, come flying out of the room as if the hounds of hell are on their heels. Behind them, Hurley, or "the hound of hell in our house," shuffles and rubs his eyes. Hurley hates cats.

"The ER has a death to report," Heidi tells me.

"Okay," I say, stifling a yawn. "I'll call them." I disconnect and give Hurley an apologetic look. "Sorry about the noise." I walk over and kiss him on his cheek. His morning stubble feels scratchy on my lips, and I note that he, too, has a cowlick on one side of his head. His, however, looks adorable. But then with that dark hair of his and those morning-glory blue eyes, how could he look anything but?

Hurley looks in at Matthew, who has decided to halt his screams now that his father is here. For some reason, Matthew saves most of his meltdowns for me. "I have to call the hospital," I tell Hurley. "And your son over there has decided he's Michelangelo and his bedroom wall is the Sistine Chapel."

"I got it covered," Hurley says, midyawn. He ventures

into the room barefoot, clad only in his pajama pants, and I take a moment to admire his physique.

"I pulled some clothes out for him," I say, setting them on top of the dresser.

Hurley scoops Matthew up in one arm, props him on his hip, and grabs the clothing with his free hand. The socks that are in the pile drop to the floor.

"Damn it," Matthew says, looking down at the socks.

Hurley shoots Matthew a chastising look. "Hey, buddy, we don't talk like that."

"Mammy does," Matthew says, using his unique combination of "Mattie" and "Mommy," fingering me with no hint of guile or guilt.

Hurley looks over at me, eyebrows raised.

I flash him a guilty but remorseful smile, and make a quick escape back to the bedroom, where I shut the door and dial the number for the hospital. A minute later, I'm on the phone with a nurse named Krista.

"Sorry for the call," she says, "but I have a young girl here in the ER who came in badly banged up. Shortly after arriving, she coded, and we weren't able to bring her back. She was dropped off by this guy who was acting really weird. He disappeared sometime during the code and hasn't come back."

I close my eyes and sigh. I had hoped the death would be something straightforward, like an older person with a history of heart disease who came in with a myocardial infarction and died. Something like that I could have cleared over the phone after a quick consult with my boss, Izzy, the medical examiner here in Sorenson. But this death sounds like it won't be a simple one.

"Okay," I say. "I'll be there in fifteen minutes. In the meantime, don't let anyone into the room. If the guy comes back, see if security can get him to stay."

"Got it." She disconnects the call without any further niceties. All business, this dead stuff.

I strip off my robe and pajamas, and don some slacks and a heavy sweater. The February weather has been harsh of late, and I can hear wind howling through the trees beyond the bedroom window. I head into the bathroom, wishing I had enough time to take a shower and wash my hair. Instead, I wet a comb and attempt once again to make my cowlick lie flat. It refuses until I saturate that section of hair thoroughly, plastering it down to my head with my palm. But a few seconds later, it begins a slow rise again, the Lazarus of cowlicks.

I shrug it off, knowing I've gone out looking far worse. My job as a medico-legal death investigator often requires me to go out on calls in the middle of the night, and there have been times when my sleep-addled brain lacked the ability to accomplish basic tasks during those first few minutes of wakefulness. I've gone out on calls with my shirt inside out, wearing mismatched shoes, boasting Medusa hair, and displaying the remnants of makeup smeared beneath my eyes that I was too tired to remove the night before. I'm always fully awake and alert by the time I get into my car and head out, but by then the damage is done.

I find my boys in the kitchen, Matthew standing next to his father, who is tending to something in the toaster. I have a good guess about what's in there, since there is a box of toaster waffles on the counter next to him. The smell of freshly brewed coffee hits me, and I take a moment to relish the smell. Then I indulge in what has become a morning ritual for me of late—I look around me.

Hurley and I have only been in this house for two months, and the newness of it is still a treat for me. We had it built after spending almost two years crammed into his small house in town. As a family of four—Emily, Hurley's teen-age daughter from a previous relationship, also lives with us—his house was crowded and uncomfortable. And for whatever reason, it never felt like my home. The entire time we lived there, I felt like a guest who had overstayed her welcome. Almost nothing in the house was mine, or even anything I'd had a say in picking out. I'm not sure why I felt this way, because when I left my first husband, a local surgeon, I abandoned, with nary a regret, all of the furnishings I had purchased and the décor I had chosen. I moved into the small mother-in-law cottage behind the house of our neighbor and my best friend, Izzy, and paid Izzy rent. The place was already furnished, so nothing there was mine, either. But I didn't share it with anyone and it felt like mine, making it different somehow.

After bumping around together with Hurley in his house for a year or so, we bought a five-acre parcel of land just outside the city limits and built a house on a bluff that overlooks the countryside. We were able to move in right before Christmas, and while we didn't have much time to decorate—not to mention an inability to find all the right boxes—I still reveled in our first Christmas here and knew I'd remember it forever. I love our new home; it is a place uniquely ours, a perfect blend of our ideas, tastes, and needs. Despite the fact that it is a large house with an open floor plan, it feels warm, cozy, and comfortable. Part of that comes from the design and décor, but another part of it is the sense of safety and family that it provides for me. Our house is my sanctuary, the place I go to when I need to escape the sadness and the sometimes-hectic pace of my job.

I step around Hurley so I can pour myself a cup of coffee to go. The hospital has coffee, but it's rotgut stuff. I know this because I used to work there. I spent six years working in the emergency room and another seven in the OR. I loved working in the emergency room and had it not been for meeting David Winston, the surgeon who would eventually become my first husband, I probably would've stayed in the ER. But I made the change to the OR so that David and I could spend more time together. Unfortunately, David eventually decided to spend some very intimate time with one of my coworkers instead, and I caught the two of them one night in a darkened, empty OR. As shocking as this was—and it shocked my life into a state of major chaos for quite a while—the fallout from it led to both my current job and, via a rocky, roundabout trail, to my marriage to Hurley.

There are times when I regret making the change from the ER to the OR, though I have to admit that the slicing and dicing I learned how to do in the OR was good preparation for the job Izzy offered me when I fled both my marriage and my hospital job. David's dalliance was well timed in one respect, because Izzy's prior assistant had just quit. And since Izzy was offering me his cottage to stay in, it benefited both of us for him to offer me a job as well. It's hard to pay rent when you're unemployed.

I will be forever grateful to Izzy for taking a chance on me. I wasn't trained in the intricacies of the investigative and forensic aspects of my new job, but I'm a quick study. It didn't hurt that I'm also nosy, and fell into the investigative portion of things quite easily. Now, three years and a number of educational conferences and classes later, I have graduated from my original job as a diener—a term used to describe folks who assist with autopsies—to a full-fledged, medico-legal death investigator, trained in scene processing, evidence collection, and a host of investigative techniques.

As I reach for the coffeepot to fill my cup, I notice something on the door of the cupboard below. It is yet another of Matthew's artistic creations, this time in Magic Marker.

"Matthew!" I say, pointing to the scribbled lines. "Did you do this?"

Matthew looks at the cupboard door, then at me. Without so much as a blink, or a hint of hesitation, he says, "No."

"I think you did, Matthew," I say. "Who else could have done it?"

"Hoovah," he says.

"Really? Well, I guess I better punish Hoover then. What should I do to him?"

Matthew's eyes roll heavenward for a moment, and he sticks his tongue out, a sign that he is thinking. Then he looks over at Hoover, who is lying beneath the table in hopes of a dropped morsel. "Bad dog!" Matthew says, apparently willing to throw Hoover under the bus if it will get him out of trouble. He wags a finger in the dog's direction and repeats his admonition. "Hoovah bad dog!"

Hoover looks over at me and sighs, as if he knows the kid has just fingered him for a crime he didn't commit. I look at my son, trying hard not to laugh. His antics and quick-on-his-feet lies amuse me, but I don't want him to know it, lest it encourage more such behavior.

The toaster pops, revealing four waffles, and Matthew's attention is instantly diverted, his crime forgotten. The kid inherited his father's dark hair and good looks, but his food fixation is all from me.

"Awful," he says, reaching up with one hand and doing a *gimme* gesture with his fingers.

Hurley takes one of the waffles out, puts it on a plate, and says, "It's hot. Go sit at the table and I'll bring it to you when it's cool enough to eat."

Matthew pouts, mutters, "Damn it," and walks to the table with a scowl on his face.

Hurley shoots me a look. I smile and shrug, and then I give him a kiss on the cheek. "Can I beg one of those from you?" Taking a cue from my son's clever diversionary tactics, I don't wait for an answer. I snatch a waffle from the toaster, plug it into my mouth, and then head for the coat closet.

"Tell Richmond I'll be in around nine if he picks up this, or any other case," Hurley says to me.

"I'm sure he'll be involved with this one," I say, donning my coat. "Sounds like it may be a case of domestic abuse."

I put on boots, gloves, and a hat, tearing off bites of the waffle as I go. It's not much of a breakfast, but it will do for now. As soon as I'm fully armored against the elements, I walk over and grab my coffee cup from the counter, kiss my husband on his lips, kiss my son on top of his head, and head for the garage.

I start up my car—an older-model, midnight-blue hearse with low mileage—and hit the garage door opener. Outside, the sky has a heavy, leaden look to it, a harbinger of what is to come. I flip on the radio and listen as the morning-show host tells everyone that a huge winter storm is headed our way, due to hit our area tomorrow afternoon. "This one is going to be a doozy," he says with a classic Wisconsin accent. "Expect heavy winds, freezing rain followed by snow, with up to a foot or more of accumulation." Then, after issuing this forecast of gloom and doom, he says in a chipper voice, "Get those snowmobiles tuned up, people. And make sure you stock up on brats and beer."

Despite his cheery tone, he's promising this will be an impressive storm, even by Wisconsin standards. And that's saying something.

I hope it's not an omen for the day ahead of me.

Connect with

Us

Visit us online at
KensingtonBooks.com
to read more from your favorite authors, see books
by series, view reading group guides, and more.

for sneak peeks, chances to win books and prize packs,
and to share your thoughts with other readers.

**facebook.com/kensingtonpublishing
twitter.com/kensingtonbooks**

Tell us what you think!

To share your thoughts, submit a review,
or sign up for our eNewsletters, please visit:
KensingtonBooks.com/TellUs.

Grab These Cozy Mysteries
from
Kensington Books

Forget Me Knot Mary Marks	978-0-7582-9205-6	$7.99US/$8.99CAN
Death of a Chocoholic Lee Hollis	978-0-7582-9449-4	$7.99US/$8.99CAN
Green Living Can Be Deadly Staci McLaughlin	978-0-7582-7502-8	$7.99US/$8.99CAN
Death of an Irish Diva Mollie Cox Bryan	978-0-7582-6633-0	$7.99US/$8.99CAN
Board Stiff Annelise Ryan	978-0-7582-7276-8	$7.99US/$8.99CAN
A Biscuit, A Casket Liz Mugavero	978-0-7582-8480-8	$7.99US/$8.99CAN
Boiled Over Barbara Ross	978-0-7582-8687-1	$7.99US/$8.99CAN
Scene of the Climb Kate Dyer-Seeley	978-0-7582-9531-6	$7.99US/$8.99CAN
Deadly Decor Karen Rose Smith	978-0-7582-8486-0	$7.99US/$8.99CAN
To Kill a Matzo Ball Delia Rosen	978-0-7582-8201-9	$7.99US/$8.99CAN

Available Wherever Books Are Sold!

All available as e-books, too!

Visit our website at **www.kensingtonbooks.com**

Follow P.I. Savannah Reid
with
G.A. McKevett